D1372192

GODS OF RIVERWORLD

PHILIP JOSÉ FARMER

TOR®

A TOM DOHERTY ASSOCIATES BOOK

New York

GODS OF RIVERWORLD

Copyright © 1983 by the Estate of Philip José Farmer

A Tor Book
Published by Tom Doherty Associates, LLC
175 Fifth Avenue
New York, NY 10010

www.tor-forge.com

Tor® is a registered trademark of Tom Doherty Associates, LLC.

Library of Congress Cataloging-in-Publication Data

Farmer, Philip José.
    Gods of riverworld / Philip José Farmer.—1st Tor trade paperback ed.
        p.   cm.—(Riverworld series)
    ISBN 978-0-7653-2656-0 (pbk.)
    I. Title.
PS3556.A72G6 2011
813' .54—dc22

2010036531

First Tor Trade Paperback Edition: February 2011

Printed in the United States of America

0 9 8 7 6 5 4 3 2 1

To those who won't knuckle under

PREFACE

Those who have not read the previous volumes of the Riverworld series, *To Your Scattered Bodies Go, The Fabulous Riverboat, The Dark Design,* and *The Magic Labyrinth,* should go to the outline at the back of this book. There the reader can acquaint himself or herself with some events and items only referred to *en passant* in the book at hand. I have written the outline to avoid lengthy recapitulation. Those familiar with the series so far might also want to read the outline to refresh their memories about certain matters.

I stated in the fourth volume, *The Magic Labyrinth,* that it would be the final book in the series. I had intended it to be so, but I did leave myself a tiny escape hatch in the final paragraph. My unconscious knew better than my conscious, and it made me (the devil!) install that little door. Some time after the fourth volume appeared, I got to thinking about the vast powers possessed by the people who had entered the tower and how tempting the powers would be.

Also, as I knew and some readers pointed out, the truths revealed in the fourth volume might not be the final truths after all.

The opinions and conclusions about economics, ideology, politics, sexuality, and other matters re *Homo sapiens* vary according to the characters' knowledge or biases. They are not necessarily my own. I am convinced that all races have an equal mental potential and that the same spectrum of stupidity, mediocre intelligence, and genius runs through every race. All races, I'm convinced, have an equal potential for good or evil, love or hate, and saintliness or sin. I'm also convinced from sixty years of wide reading and close observation that human life has always been savage and comically absurd but that we are not a totally unredeemable species.

DRAMATIS PERSONAE

Thirty-five billion people from every country and every age of Earth's history were resurrected along the great and winding River of Riverworld. The reader will be relieved to hear that only a few of them will play a part in this story.

Loga: A grandson of King Priam of ancient Troy, born in the twelfth century B.C., slain at the age of four by a Greek soldier during the fall of that city. Resurrected on the Gardenworld by nonhuman extra-Terrestrials and raised there. He became a member of the Ethical Council of Twelve, which was charged with creating Riverworld and resurrecting there all human beings who had died between 99,000 B.C. and A.D. 1983. He became a renegade and involved various Terrestrial resurrectees in his plot to overthrow the other Ethicals and their Agents and to subvert the original plan for the destiny of those reborn in Riverworld.

Richard Francis Burton: An Englishman, born in 1821, died in 1890. During his lifetime a *cause célèbre* and *bête noire*. A famous explorer, linguist, anthropologist, translator, poet, author, and swordsman. He discovered Lake Tanganyika; entered the Muslim sacred city of Mecca in disguise (and from the experience wrote the best book ever written about Mecca); did the most famous translation of *A Thousand and One Nights (The Arabian Nights)*, full of footnotes and essays derived from his vast knowledge of the esoterics of African and Oriental life; was noted as one of the greatest swordsmen of his day; and was the first European to enter the forbidden city of Harar, Ethiopia—and leave alive.

Alice Pleasance Liddell Hargreaves: Born in England in 1852, died there in 1934. Daughter of Henry George Liddell, domestic chaplain to the Prince Consort, vice-chancellor of Oxford University, dean of Christ Church, Oxford, and coeditor of the famous Scott-Liddell *A Greek-English Lexicon*, which is still today the standard Classical Greek-English dictionary. When ten years old, Alice inspired Lewis Carroll to write his *Alice in Wonderland* and to base his fictional Alice on her.

Peter Jairus Frigate: An American science fiction writer, born 1918, died 1983.

Aphra Behn: An Englishwoman, born 1640, died 1689. She was a spy for Charles II in the Netherlands, and later a famous—or infamous—novelist, poetess, and playwright. The first English-woman to support herself solely by writing.

Nur ed-Din el-Musafir: Born in Moorish Spain in 1164, died in Baghdad 1258. A Muslim, though not orthodox, and a Sufi, a member of that mystical yet realistic discipline to which Omar Khayyám belonged.

Jean Baptiste Antoine Marcelin, Baron de Marbot: Born 1782 in France, died there in 1854. Like Nur, small in stature but very strong and swift. He served very bravely under Napoleon and was wounded many times. His *Memoirs of His Life and Campaigns* so fascinated A. Conan Doyle that he modeled his stories of Brigadier Gerard, the dashing French soldier, on de Marbot's exploits.

Tom Million Turpin: Black American born in 1871 in Savannah, Georgia; died in 1922 in St. Louis. Turpin was a piano player and composer of considerable talent; his *Harlem Rag*, published in 1897, was the first published ragtime piece by a black composer. He was also the boss of the Tenderloin red-light district in St. Louis.

Li Po: Born in 710 of Turkish-Chinese lineage in an outlying district of ancient China; died in 762 in China. Considered by many to be China's greatest poet, he was also a famous swords-man, drunkard, lover, and wanderer. In *The Magic Labyrinth*, his pseudonym was Tai-Peng.

Star Spoon: A female contemporary of Li Po, who suffered much both in China and on the Riverworld.

The Earthbred and their fates are Yours
    In all their stations,
Their multitudinous languages and many colors
    Are Yours, and we whom from the many
You made different, O Master of the Choice.
                            —*Ancient Egyptian hymn*

And hell is more than half of paradise.
                            —*Edwin Arlington Robinson,*
                                "Luke Havergal"

When Moses struck the rock, he forgot to
stand out of the way of the water and so barely
escaped drowning.

                            —The Book of Jasher

Gods of Riverworld

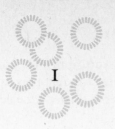

I

Loga had cracked like an egg.

At 10:02, his image had appeared on the wall-screens of the apartments of his eight fellow tenants. Their view was somewhat above him, and they could see him only from his naked navel to a point a few inches above his head. The sides of the desk almost met the edges of their field of vision, and some of the wall and floor behind him showed.

Loga looked like a red-haired, green-eyed Buddha who had lived for years in an ice-cream factory and had been unable to resist its product. Though he had lost twenty pounds in the last three weeks, he was still very fat.

He was, however, a very happy Buddha. Smiling, his pumpkin face seeming to glow, he spoke in Esperanto. "I've made quite a discovery! It'll solve the problem of . . ."

He glanced to his right.

"Sorry. Thought I heard something."

"You and Frigate," Burton said. "You're getting paranoid. We've searched every one of the thirty-five thousand, seven hundred and ninety-three rooms in the tower, and . . ."

The screens flickered. Loga's body and face shimmered, elongated, then dwarfed. The interruption lasted for perhaps five seconds. Burton was surprised. This was the first time that any screen had displayed interference or malfunction.

The image steadied and became clear.

"Yaas?" Burton drawled. "What's so exciting?"

The electronic vision blinked into enigma.

Burton started, and he clamped his hands on the arms of his chair. They were a hold on reality. What he was seeing certainly seemed to be unreal.

Zigzag cracks had run from the corners of Loga's lips and curved up over his cheeks and into his hair. They were deep and seemed to go through his skin and the flesh to the mouth cavity and the bone.

Burton shot up from his chair.

"Loga! What is it?"

Cracks had now spread down across the Ethical's face, chest, bulging belly, arms and hands.

Blood spurted onto his crazing skin and the desk.

Still smiling, he fell apart like a shattered egg, and he toppled sideways to the right from the armless chair. Burton heard a sound as of glass breaking. Now all he could see of Loga was the upper part of an arm, the fragments stained as if they were pieces of a broken bottle of wine.

The flesh and the blood melted. Only bright pools were left.

Burton had become rigid, but, when he heard Loga cry out, he jumped.

"*I tsab u!*"

The cry was followed by a thump, as if a heavy body had struck the floor.

Burton voice-activated other viewers in Loga's room. There was no one there, unless the red puddles on the floor were Loga's remains.

Burton sucked in his breath.

Seven screens sprang into light on Burton's wall. Each held the image of a tenant. Alice's big dark eyes were larger than normal, and her face was pale.

"Dick? That couldn't have been Loga! But it sounded like him!"

"You saw him!" Burton said. "How could he have cried out? He was dead!"

The others spoke at once, so shaken that each had reverted to his or her native tongue. Even the unflappable Nur was speaking in Arabic.

"Quiet!" Burton shouted, raising his hands. Immediately thereafter, he realized that he had spoken in English. That did not matter; they understood him.

"I don't know what happened any more than you do. Some of

it couldn't have happened, and so it didn't. I'll meet you all outside Loga's apartment. At once. Bring your arms!"

He removed from a cabinet two weapons that he had thought he would never need again. Each had a butt like a pistol's, a barrel three inches in diameter and a foot long, and at the firing end, a sphere the size of a large apple.

Alice's voice came from her screen.

"Will the horrors never stop?"

"They never do for long," he said. "In this life or that."

Alice's triangular face and large dark eyes were set in that withdrawn expression he disliked so much.

He said harshly, "Snap out of it, Alice!"

"I'll be all right," Alice said. "You know that."

"Nobody is ever *all* right."

He walked swiftly toward the door. Its sensory device would recognize him but would not open until he had spoken the code phrase, "*Open, O sesame!*" in the classical Arabic. Alice, in her apartment, would be saying in English, "'Who are *you*?' said the Caterpillar."

The door closed behind him. In the corridor was a large chair made of gray metal and a soft scarlet-dyed material. Burton sat down on it. The seat and back flowed to fit the contour of his body. He pressed a finger on the black center of a white disc on the massive left arm of the chair. A long thin metal rod slid up out of the white disc on the right arm. Burton pulled the rod back, a white light spread out from under the chair, and it rose, stopping two feet above the floor when he eased the rod into the dead center position. He turned the rod; the chair rotated to face the opposite direction. Using the rod to control vertical movement, and pressing on the central black spot of the left disc to control speed, he moved the chair down the corridor.

Presently, floating swiftly past walls displaying animated murals, he joined the others. They hovered in their chairs until Burton had taken the lead, then followed him. Burton slowed the chair slightly when he entered a huge vertical shaft at the end of the corridor. With the ease of much practice, he curved the path of the chair up the shaft to the next level and out into another corridor. A hundred feet beyond the shaft, he halted the chair at the door to Loga's apartment. The chair sank down onto the floor, and Burton got out. The others were only a few seconds behind him. Babbling, though they were not easily upset, they got out of their chair-vehicles.

The wall extended for three hundred feet from the shaft to an intersecting corridor. Its entire surface displayed a moving picture in what seemed to be three dimensions. The sky was clear. Far away was a dark mountain range. In the foreground was a jungle clearing in which was a village of dried-mud huts. Dark Caucasians in the garments worn by Hindus circa 500 B.C. moved among the huts. A slim, dark young man clad only in a loincloth sat under a bo tree. Around him squatted a dozen men and women, all intently listening to him. He was the historical Buddha, and the scene was not a reconstruction. It had been filmed by a man or woman, an Ethical agent who had passed for one of them, and whose camera and sound equipment were concealed in a ring on a finger. At the moment, their conversation was a slight murmur, but a codeword from a viewer could make it audible. If the viewer did not understand Hindustani, he could use another codeword to switch the language to Ethical.

Another codeword would make the picture emit the odors abounding near the photographer, though the viewer was usually better off without these.

Directly in front of Burton was a treestump on which someone had painted a symbol, a green eye inside a pale yellow pyramid. This had not been in the original film; it marked the entrance to Loga's apartment.

"If he's got the door set for his codeword only, we're screwed," Frigate said. "We'll never get in."

"Somebody got in," Burton said.

"Perhaps," Nur said.

Burton spoke loudly, too loudly, as if he could activate the opening mechanism by force of voice.

"Loga!"

A circular crack ten feet in diameter appeared in the wall. The section moved inward a trifle, then the section became a wheel and rolled into the wall recess. The scene on it did not fade out but turned with the surface.

"It was set for anyone who wanted to enter!" Alice said.

"Which was not the right thing to do," Burton said.

Nur, the little, dark, and big-nosed Moor, said, "The intruder may have overridden the codeword and then reset the mechanism."

"How could he have done that?" Burton said. "And why?"

"How and why was any of this done?"

They went cautiously through the opening, Burton leading. The room was a forty-foot cube. The wall behind the desk was a pale green, but the others displayed moving scenes, one from that planet called the Gardenworld, one of a tropical island as seen from a great distance, and one, which Loga must have been facing, of a daytime thunderstorm at a high altitude. Dark angry clouds roiled, and lightning spat brightly but silently from cloud to cloud.

Incongruous in the clouds, the active screens hung glowing, still displaying the rooms of the tenants.

Red pools glistened on the desk and the hardwood floor.

"Get a sample of the liquid," Burton said to Frigate. "The computer over there can analyze it."

Frigate grunted and went to a cabinet to look for something with which to take a specimen. Burton walked around the room but saw nothing that looked like a clue. It was too bad that the other viewers had not been on. However, whoever had done this must have made sure that they were not active.

Nur, Behn, and Turpin went to search nearby rooms. Burton activated the screens that would display these rooms. Doubtless, none but the three would be in them, but he wanted to keep an eye on them. If one person could be turned into a liquid, why not others?

He stooped and passed a finger through the wetness on the floor. When he straightened up, he held the tip of the finger a few inches from his eyes.

"You aren't going to taste it?" Alice said.

"I shouldn't. In some respects, Loga was rather poisonous. It'd be a strange form of cannibalism. Or of Christian communion."

He licked the finger, made a face, and said, "The mass of the Mass is inversely proportional to the faith of the square."

Alice should not have been shocked, not after what she had gone through on this world. She did look repulsed, though whether it was by his act or his words he did not know.

"Tastes like blood, vintage human," he said.

Nur, Behn, and Li Po came into the living room. "There is no one there," the Chinese said. "Not even his ghost."

Aphra Behn said, "Dick, what did Loga say?"

"I don't think he could have said anything. You saw him crack and melt. How could he have spoken after that?"

"It was his voice," Behn said. "*Whoever* said it, what did it mean?"

"*I tsab u.* That's Ethical for 'Who are you?'"

"That's what the Caterpillar said," Alice murmured.

"And Alice in Wonderland couldn't tell him," Burton said. "The whole event is crazy."

Frigate called them to the console in the corner.

"I put the specimen in the slot and asked for identification. There you are. You couldn't identify an individual by his blood in A.D. 1983, but now . . ."

The console screen displayed, in English, as Frigate had requested: INDIVIDUAL IDENTIFIED: LOGA.

Beneath that was the analysis. The liquid was composed of those elements which made up the human body, and they were in the proper proportions. Flesh had indeed turned into liquid.

"Unless the Computer is lying," Nur said.

Burton swung around to face him. "What do you mean by that?"

"The Computer may have an override command. It could have been told to give this report."

"By whom? Only Loga could do that!"

Nur shrugged thin, brown, and bony shoulders.

"Perhaps. An unknown could be in the tower. Remember what Pete thought he heard when we were celebrating our victory."

"Footsteps in the corridor outside the room!" Burton said. "Frigate said he thought it was his imagination!"

"Ah, but was it?"

It was not necessary to use the console. Burton asked the

Computer—as distinguished from the small auxiliary computers—a few questions. A circular section of the wall glowed, and words on it indicated that no unauthorized person had entered Loga's room. It denied that Loga's commands had been overridden.

"Which it would, I must admit, if this mysterious stranger had told it to do so," Burton said. "If that's happened . . . well, by God, we *are* in trouble!"

He asked for a rerun of the scene they had witnessed through their viewers. There was none. Loga had not directed the Computer to record it.

"I thought everything was going to be clear, unmysterious, straightforward from now on," Frigate said. "I should have known better. It never is."

He paused, then said softly, "He cracked open like Humpty Dumpty, except that Humpty Dumpty broke after he fell, not before. And then he turned to water like the Wicked Witch of the West."

Burton, who had died in 1890, did not understand the last reference. He made a mental note to ask the American about it when there was time.

Burton was going to ask the Computer to send in a robot to clean up the liquid. He decided, after some thought, to leave the room as it had been found. He would lock the door to the apartment with a codeword that only he knew. And then, if someone unlocked it . . .

What could he do?

Nothing. But he would at least know that there *was* an intruder.

Nur said, "We've been assuming that what we thought we saw take place here actually did take place."

"You think that what we saw was computer-simulation?" Frigate said.

"It's possible."

"But what about the liquid?" Burton said. "That's not simulated."

"It could be synthetic, a false clue. Loga's voice could have been reproduced to deceive and confuse us."

Alice said, "Wouldn't it be more logical just to abduct Loga?

We might have thought that Loga had just gone away for some reason or another."

"Why in the world would he do that, Alice?" Burton said.

"We were to return to The Valley day after tomorrow," Li Po said. "If Loga wanted to get rid of us, he'd have it done in two days. No, that liquid . . . the whole thing . . . there's someone else in the tower."

"That makes ten in the tower then," Nur said.

"Ten?" Burton said.

"The eight of us. Plus the unknown who did away with Loga, though more than one might have done that. Plus Fear. That makes at least ten."

2

I n a sense, we're gods," Frigate said.

"Gods in a jail," Burton said.

If they felt godlike, their faces did not show the vast assurance and happiness that must distinguish gods from humanity. The first area they had gone to from Loga's apartment was the highest story in the tower. Here, in a huge chamber, was the hangar of the Ethicals. There were two hundred aerial and spacecraft of various kinds there, in any of which they could have flown to any place in The Valley. However, the hangar hatches had to be opened, and that the Computer refused to do. Nor could they operate the hatch mechanisms manually.

The unknown who had liquefied Loga had inserted an override command in the Computer. Only he—or she—or they—had the power to raise the hangar hatches.

They stood close together in a corner of the immense room. The floor, walls, and ceilings were a monotonous, overpowering gray, the color of prison cells. Their means of escape, the saucer-shaped, sausage-shaped, and insect-shaped machines, seemed to brood in the silence. They were waiting to be used. But by whom?

At the opposite wall, a thousand feet away, was a fat cigar-shaped vessel, the largest of the spaceships. It was five hundred feet long and had a maximum diameter of two hundred feet. This could be used to travel to the Gardenworld, wherever that planet was. Loga had said it would take a hundred years, Earth-time, to arrive at its destination. Loga had also said that the ship was so computerized-automatic that a person of average intelligence and little knowledge of science could operate it.

Burton's voice broke the silence.

"We have some immediate pressing problems. We must find out who did that horrible thing to Loga. And we must find a way to cancel the override inhibits in the Computer."

"True," Nur said. "But before we can do that, we must determine just how much control of the Computer we have. What our limits are. When you fight, you must know your strengths and your weaknesses as well as you know your face in the mirror. Only thus can we determine how to overcome the strengths and weaknesses of our enemy."

"If he is our enemy," Frigate said.

The others looked at him with surprise.

"That's very good," Nur said. "Don't think in old categories. You're learning."

"What else could he be?" Aphra Behn said.

"I don't know," Frigate said. "We've been so manipulated by Loga that I'm not one hundred percent convinced that he is on our side or that he is right in what he's done. This unknown . . . he may be doing this for the right reason. Still . . ."

"If Loga was his only obstacle, the unknown's removed it," Burton said. "Why doesn't he come forward now? What could we do to oppose him? We're like children, really. We don't know how to use all the powers available. We don't even know what they are."

"Not yet," Nur said. "Pete has proposed another way of looking at events. But, for the time being, it's not useful. We have to assume that the unknown is our enemy until we find out otherwise. Does anyone disagree?"

It was evident that no one did.

Tom Turpin said, "What you say is OK. But I think that the very first thing we got to do is protect ourselves. We got to set up some kind of defense so what happened to Loga don't happen to us."

"I agree," Burton said. "But if this unknown can override any of our commands . . ."

"We should stick together!" Alice said. "Keep together, don't let anyone out of our sight!"

Burton said, "You may be right, and we should confer about

that. First, though, I propose that we get out of this gloomy, oppressive place. Let's go back to my apartment."

The interior door to the hangar opened, and they rode their chairs down the corridor to the nearest vertical shaft. The next level was five hundred feet down, which caused Burton to wonder what was between the hangar level and the second one. He would ask the Computer what it contained.

Inside his quarters, with the entrance door shut by his codeword, he began to act as host. A wall section slid back, revealing a very large table standing on end. This moved out from the recess, turned until the tabletop was horizontal, floated to the center of the room, extended its legs, which had been folded against the underside, and settled on the floor. The eight arranged chairs around it and sat down. By then they had gotten their drinks from the energy-matter converter cabinets along one wall. The table was round, and Burton sat in what would have been King Arthur's chair if the room had been Camelot.

He took a sip of black coffee and said, "Alice has a good idea. It means, however, that we must all live in one apartment. This one isn't quite large enough. I propose we move into one down the hall near the elevator shaft. It has ten bedrooms, a laboratory, a control room, and a large dining-sitting room. We can work together and keep an eye on each other."

"And get on each other's nerves," Frigate said.

"I need a woman," Li Po said.

"So do all of us, except Marcelin, and maybe Nur," Turpin said. "Man, it's been a long, hard time!"

"What about Alice?" Aphra Behn said. "She needs a man."

"Don't speak for me," Alice said sharply.

Burton slammed the tabletop with a fist. "First things first!" he bellowed. Then, more softly, "We must have a common front, band together, no matter what the inconvenience. We can work out the other matters, trifling, if I may say so, at this moment. We've been through a lot together, and we can cooperate. We make a good team, despite some differences that have caused some abrasion recently. We must work together, be together, or we may be cut down one at a time. Is there anyone who won't cooperate?"

Nur said, "If anyone insists on living apart, that one is under suspicion."

There was an uproar then, stilled when Burton hit the table again.

"This bottling-up will be scratchsome, no doubt of that. But we've been ridden gallsore by worse things, and the better we work together, the sooner we'll be free to pursue our own interests."

Alice was frowning, and he knew what she was thinking. Since their final breakup, she had avoided him as much as possible. Now . . .

"If we're in jail, we're in the best one in two worlds," Frigate said.

"No jail's any good," Turpin said. "You ever been in the slammer, Pete?"

"Only the one that I made for myself all my life," Frigate said. "But it was portable."

That was not true, Burton thought. Frigate has been a prisoner several times on the Riverworld, including being one of Hermann Göring's slaves. But he spoke metaphorically. A most metaphorical man, Frigate. Shifty, a verbal trickster, ambiguous, which he would cheerfully admit, quoting Emily Dickinson to justify himself.

"Success in circuit lies."

Quoting himself, he would say, "The literal man litters reality."

"Well, Captain, what do we do next?" Frigate said.

The first priority was to go to their individual apartments and bring their few possessions to the large apartment down the hall. They went in a body, since it would not do to go alone, and then they picked out their bedrooms. Alice took one as far from Burton's as possible. Peter Frigate chose the apartment next to hers. Burton smiled ferociously on noting this. It was an acknowledged but mostly unspoken fact that the American was "in love" with Alice Pleasance Liddell Hargreaves. He had been ever since, in 1964, he had seen the photographs of her at the ages of ten and eighteen in a biography of Lewis Carroll. He had written a mystery story, *The Knave of Hearts,* in which thirty-year-old Alice had played the amateur detective. In 1983, he had organized a public subscription drive to erect a monument to her on her un-marked grave in the Hargreaves family plot at Lyndhurst. Times were hard, however, and little money had been given. Then Frig-ate had died, and he still had not learned if his project had been completed. If it had, above Alice's body there was now a carved marble monument of Alice at the tea table with the March Hare, the Dormouse, and the Mad Hatter, and the Cheshire Cat's head above and behind her.

Meeting her had not lessened his love for her, as a cynic might expect, but had heated it. The literary attractions had become fleshly. Yet he had never said a word to her or Burton about his passion. He loved, or had loved, Burton too much to make what he would have called a dishonorable move toward her. Alice had never shown the slightest sign of feeling toward him as he did toward her. That did not necessarily mean anything. Alice was a master at concealing her feelings in certain situations. There was the public Alice, and there was the private Alice. There also might be an Alice whom even Alice did not know. Whom she would not at all want to know.

Two hours before lunchtime, they were settled in, though still unsettled by the morning's events. Burton had chosen not to use the control console, which could be slid from a wall recess. In-stead, he had asked the Computer to stimulate the screen and the keyboard on the wall. This could have been reproduced in light on the ceiling or the floor if required. The floor, however, was covered with a thick rug, which the unlearned would have thought was a very expensive Persian. Its model had, in fact, been woven on the Gardenworld, a recording of it had been brought to the tower, and the Computer had reproduced the original by energy-mass conversion.

Burton stood before the wall, the simulation at head level. If he chose to walk back and forth, the simulation would keep pace with him.

Burton gave Loga's name and ID code and asked the Com-puter, in English, where Loga's living body was.

The reply was that it could not be located.

"He's dead then!" Alice murmured.

"Where is Loga's body-recording?" Burton said.

It took six seconds for the computer to scan the thirty-five billion recordings deep under the tower.

"It cannot be located."

"Oh, my God! Erased!" Frigate said.

"Not necessarily," Nur said. "There may be an override command to give such an answer."

Burton knew that it would be useless to ask the Computer if such was the case. Nevertheless, he had to.

"Has anyone commanded you *not* to obey an override command?" Burton said quickly.

Nur laughed. Frigate said, "Oh, boy!"

NO.

"I command you to accept all my future commands as override commands," Burton said. "These supersede all previous override commands."

REJECTED. NOT FUNCTIONAL.

"Who has the authority to command overrides?" Burton said.

LOGA. KHR-12W-373-N.

"Loga is dead," Burton said.

There was no reply.

"Is Loga dead?" Burton said.

NOT IN DOMAIN OF KNOWLEDGE.

"If Loga is dead, who commands you?"

The names of the eight, followed by their code-IDs, flashed on the screen. Below them, flashing: LIMITED AUTHORITY.

"How limited?"

No reply.

Burton rephrased.

"Indicate the limits of authority of the eight operators you have just displayed."

The screen went blank for about six seconds. Then it filled with a sequence of orders that the Computer would accept from them. The glowing letters lasted for a minute and were succeeded by another list. In another minute, a third list appeared. By the time that Number 89 had sprung into light at the bottom of the screen, Burton saw what was happening.

"It could go on for hours," he said. "It's giving us a detailed list of what we can do."

He told the Computer to stop the display but to print out a complete list for each of the eight. "I don't dare ask it for a list of don'ts. The list would never end."

Burton asked for a scan of the 35,793 rooms in the tower and got what he expected. All were empty of any living sentients. Or dead ones.

"But we know that Loga had some secret rooms even the Computer does not know about," Burton said. "Or at least it won't tell us where they are. We know where one is. Where are the others?"

"You think that the unknown might be in one of those?" Nur said.

"I don't know. It's possible. We must try to find them."

"We could compare the tower dimensions with the circuitry," Frigate said. "But, my God, that would take us many months! And the rooms might still be so cleverly concealed that we would not find them."

"That sounds as interesting as cleaning spittoons," Turpin said. He went to a grand piano, sat down, and began playing "Ragtime Nightmare."

Burton followed him and stood by him.

"We'd all love to hear you play," he said—he wouldn't, he had no liking for music of any kind—"but we're in conference, a very important one, vital, you know, in the full sense of the word, and this is no time to divert or distract us. We need everyone's wits in this. Otherwise, we may all die because one didn't do his share."

Smiling, his fingers running spiderlike on the keys, Turpin looked up at Burton. The long, exhausting and dangerous trip to the tower had thinned him to one hundred and seventy-five pounds. But since he had been in the tower, he had stuffed himself with food and liquor, and his face was waxing into full moonness. His large teeth were very white against his dark skin—not as dark as Burton's—and his dark brown hair was wavy, not kinky. He could have passed for white, but he had chosen to stay in the black world on Earth.

"Nigger is how you was raised, how you think," he would sometimes say. "As the Good Book says, it don't do no good to kick against the pricks." He would laugh softly then, not caring whether or not his hearer understood that by "pricks" he meant "whites."

"I thought I'd give you thinkers some background music. I'm no good at this kind of thing."

"You've a good mind," Burton said, "and we need it. Besides, we have to act as a team, as soldiers in a small army. If everybody does what he wants, ignores this crisis, we become just a disorganized mob."

"And you's the captain, the man," Turpin said. "OK."

He brought his hands down, the chords crashed, and he stood up.

"Lead on, MacDuff."

Though he was furious, Burton showed no sign of it. He strode back to the table, Turpin following him too closely, and he stood by his chair. Turpin, still smiling, took his seat.

"I suggest that we wait until we have mastered the contents of those," Burton said, waving a hand at the mechanism that was piling, sorting, and collating the papers flying from a slot in the wall. "Once we thoroughly understand what we can and cannot do, we may make our plans."

"That'll take some time," de Marbot said. "It'll be like reading a library, not one book."

"It must be done."

"You talk of limits," Nur said, "and that is necessary and good. But within what we call limits we have such power as the greatest kings on Earth never dreamed of. That power will be our strength, but it will also be our weakness. Rather, I should say, the power will tempt us to misuse it. I pray to God that we will be strong enough to overcome our weaknesses—if we have them."

"We are, in a sense, gods," Burton said. "But humans with god-like powers. Half-gods."

"Half-assed gods," Frigate said.

Burton smiled and said, "We've been through much on The

River. It's scourged us, winnowed out the chaff. I hope. We shall see."

"The greatest enemy is not the unknown," Nur said.

He did not need to explain what he meant.

3

A n ancient Greek philosopher, Herakleitos, once said, "Character determines destiny."

Burton was thinking of this as he paced back and forth in his bedroom. What Herakleitos said was only partly true. Everyone had a unique character. However, that character was influenced by environment. And every environment was unique. Every place was not exactly like every other place. In addition, a person's character was part of the environment he traveled in. How a person acted depended not only upon his character but also on the peculiar opportunities and constraints of the environment, which included the person's self. The self carried about in it all the environments that the person had lived in. These were, in a sense, ghosts, some of thicker ectoplasm than the others, and thus powerful haunters of the mobile home, the person.

Another ancient sage, Hebrew, not Greek, had said, "There is nothing new under the sun."

The old Preacher had never heard of evolution and so did not know that new species, unfamiliar to the sun, emerged now and then. Moreover, he overlooked that every newborn baby was unique, therefore new, whether under the sun or under the moon. Like all sages, the Preacher spoke half-truths.

When he said that there was a time to act and a time not to act, he spoke the whole truth. That is, unless you were a Greek philosopher and pointed out that not acting is an act in itself. The difference in philosophy between the Greek and the Hebrew was in their attitudes toward the world. Herakleitos was interested in abstract ethics; the Preacher, in practical ethics. The former stressed the why, the latter, the how.

It was possible, Burton thought, to live in this world and only

wonder about the how. But a complete human, one trying to realize all his potential, would also probe the why. This situation
demanded the why and the how. Lacking the first, he could not
function properly with the second.

Here he was with seven other Earthborns, in a tower set in the
center of a sea at the north pole of this world. The sea had a diameter of sixty miles and was ringed by an unbroken range of
mountains over twenty thousand feet high. In this sea The River
gave up almost all of its warmth before it plunged from the other
end and began picking up heat again. Thick mists like those
from the gates of Hell hid a tower that rose ten miles from the
sea surface. Below the waters and deep into the earth, the tower
extended five miles or perhaps even deeper.

There was a shaft in the center of the tower that housed some
billion of *wathans* at this moment. *Wathans*. The Ethical name
for the artificial souls created by a species extinct for millions
of years. Somewhere near the tower, deep under the earth, were
immense chambers in which were kept records of the bodies of
each of the thirty-five billion plus who had once lived on Earth
from circa 100,000 B.C. through A.D. 1983.

When a person died on the Riverworld, the resurrector, using
a mass-energy converter and the record, reproduced that body
on a bank of The River. The *wathan*, the synthetic soul, the invisible entity that held all of what made that person sentient, flew at
once to the body, attracted as iron by a magnet. And the man or
woman, dead twenty-four hours before, was alive.

Of the thirty-five billion plus, Burton had experienced more
of death than any. A man who had died 777 times could claim a
record. Though he had been dead more often than anyone else,
there were few who had lived as intensely on Earth and the Riverworld as he. His triumphs and sweet times had been few; his
defeats and frustrations, many. Though he had once written that
the bad and the good things of life tended to balance out, his
own ledger had far more red ink than black. The Book of Burton
showed a deficit, a heavy imbalance. Despite which, he had refused to take bankruptcy. Why he continued fighting, why he
wanted so desperately to keep living, he did not know. Perhaps it
was because he hoped to balance the books someday.

And then what?

He did not know about that, but it was the then-what? that fed his flame.

Here he was, trailing a horde of ghosts and placed by forces, which he had not understood and still did not understand, in this vast building at the top of the world. It had been erected for one purpose, to allow Terrestrials a chance for immortality. Not physical foreverness but a return, perhaps an absorption into, the Creator.

The Creator, if there was one, had not given Earthpeople, or indeed any sentients, souls. That entity which figured so largely in religions had been imaginary, a nonexistent desideratum. But that which sentients could imagine they might bring into actuality, and the *might-be* had become the *is*. What Burton and others objected to was the implied *should-be*. The Ethicals had not asked each resurrectee if he or she wished to be raised from the dead. They had been given no choice. Like it or not, they became *lazari*. And they had not been told how or why.

Loga had said that there just was not enough time to do that. Even if a thousand Agents were assigned to asking a thousand people per hour whether or not they wished to be endowed with synthetic souls, the project would take thirty-five million hours. If fifty thousand Agents conducted the interviews, it would take half a million hours. If the interviews could be conducted on a twenty-four-hour basis, and they couldn't, it would take somewhat over fifty-seven years to question every person.

What would have been accomplished at the end of that time? Very little. Perhaps ten or twelve million might decide not to keep on living. Even a man like Sam Clemens, who insisted that he wanted the eternal peace and quiet of death, would opt for life if he was given a chance for it. He would at least want to try the life offered, one with conditions different from those on Earth. A hundred considerations would make him change his mind. The same would apply to those others who felt, for various reasons, that life on Earth had been miserable, wretched, painful, and altogether not worthwhile.

"The resurrectees have to be dealt with en masse," Loga had

said. "There is no other way to handle them. We have, however, made a few exceptions. You were one, because I secretly arranged to have you awaken in the resurrection area so many years ago. You became a special case. The Canadian, La Viro, was visited by one of us, and certain ideas were given him so that he would found the Church of the Second Chance. Their missionaries spread teachings that contained some of the truths about this situation. They stressed the ethical reasons for the *lazari* being here; they stressed that each person must advance himself ethically."

"Why couldn't everybody have been told the truth at the outset?" Burton had said. And then, before Loga could reply, Burton had answered himself.

"I see. For the same reason that every person could not be asked if he wished to have another life and another chance at it."

"Yes. And even if we Ethicals had appeared in The Valley and told the truth to all, only a certain percentage would have believed us. And our teachings would have been perverted, changed, and denied by many.

"Believe me, our way is the best, even if it has its disadvantages and limits. We know because of what our predecessors told us about their projects in resurrecting other sentients. Besides, when Earthpeople were all raised on that day, there were one hundred thousand languages spoken by them. We would not have been understood by many. All the people could not hear the message until the Church of the Second Chance had spread a common language, Esperanto, throughout the Riverworld."

Burton had then said, "In the previous projects, uh, I'm almost afraid to ask, how many, what percentage, Passed On?"

"Three-quarters of those raised on the Gardenworlds did," Loga had said. "The remaining one-fourth . . . their recordings were dissolved when they died after their grace period was up."

"Died or were killed?" Burton had said.

"Most of them killed each other or committed suicide."

"Most?"

Loga had ignored this.

"One-sixteenth of the people resurrected as adults or juveniles in previous projects passed the test, Went On. Each of these projects had at least two phases. Here, after the phase with those who died before or during A.D. 1983 is done, then those who died after that will be raised for the second stage. The final one."

"But the first stage is going to take longer than planned because of your interference," Burton had said.

"Yes. I believe . . . I know . . . that the percentage of those Going On could have been higher, much higher, if the *lazari* had been given more time. I could not endure the thought of so many being doomed, so I became a renegade. I betrayed my fellow Ethicals. I . . . I may have condemned myself to . . . not Going On. But I don't believe that. I did it for my love of humanity."

The Christians and the Muslims on Earth had believed in a physical resurrection. And so it had been. But the ultimate goal of the Ethicals was Buddhistic, absorption of the soul into the All-Being.

As if reading his mind, Loga had said, "Tell me, Dick, do you really believe, believe in the innermost and deepest part of your mind, where it counts, that you will Go On?"

Burton had stared at Loga for a moment. Then, slowly, he had said, "No. Not in the sense you mean. I just cannot believe it. There is no evidence that such a thing as Going On occurs."

"Yes, there is! Our instruments cannot perceive the *wathan*, what you call the soul, when its owner has died after attaining a certain stage of . . . let's call it goodness instead of ethical advancement."

"Which only means that the instruments can't detect it," Burton had said. "You have no knowledge of what really happens to the *wathan* at that point."

Loga had smiled and said, "In the end, we have to fall back on faith, don't we?"

"From what I've seen of its manifestations on Earth, I have no faith in faith," Burton had said. "How do you know but what the *wathan*, as you call it, has simply worn out? It's an artificial thing, but its life may end naturally, just as all synthetic things . . . and natural, too . . . end. The *wathan* is not a material entity, as we know material things, but that's the point. We don't really know if it's material or not. It may be a form of matter unknown to us.

Or a thing of pure energy. If so, a form of energy unknown to us. But how do you know that it may not change into another form, which your instruments cannot detect?"

"It does! It does!" Loga had said. "Into the Undetectible! How else could you explain that the *wathan* only passes beyond the instrument range when the owner has reached a certain stage of ethical advancement? Those who don't reach this stage may die again and again, but always, always, the *wathans* return to their resurrected bodies!"

"There may be an explanation you haven't thought of."

"Hundreds of thousands of minds greater than yours have tried to find another explanation, and they have failed."

"But one may yet come along who won't fail."

"You're depending upon faith now," Loga had said.

"No. Upon history, logic, and probability."

Loga had been upset, not because he was beginning to doubt his beliefs but because he feared that Burton would not Go On.

As it had turned out, *Loga* was not going to Go On. His body-record had been destroyed, and he would no longer have the opportunity to attain that final goal. Yet . . . it was Loga's own fault that he did not have that chance now. If he had not set the project on a different course, he would still be alive, and his body-record would insure that he could keep striving for that mysterious event known as Going On.

Was the unknown who had committed Loga to oblivion an Ethical who had somehow survived Loga's mass slaughter of his fellows? If he was, why didn't he show himself? Was he afraid of the eight *lazari*? Was he biding his time until he could kill them and raise them in The Valley where they could no longer inter-fere with the original design?

Anyone who knew how to input override commands in the computer should not be afraid of the eight. But then perhaps the unknown knew something that the eight did not know yet but might find out. If that were so, the unknown would try to get rid of them as quickly as possible.

However, it was possible that one—or more—of the eight might have made Loga vanish.

Burton was thinking of this when Nur's head appeared on a wall-screen. "I'd like to speak to you."

Burton gave the codeword that allowed Nur to see him.

"What is it?"

Nur was wearing a green turban, indicating that he had made the pilgrimage to Mecca. The choice of color was probably accidental, though, since the little Moor was not one to set store by such things. His long, straight black hair fell from under the cloth onto skinny brown shoulders. His narrow face was intense.

"The inhibit input against resurrecting Monat and all the Ethicals and their agents still holds. I expected that. But something even more momentous has occurred!"

He paused.

Burton said, "Well?"

"You know that Loga told us three weeks ago that he'd told the Computer to start resurrecting the eighteen billion in the records. We all assumed that it had been done. But it's not so! Apparently, Loga changed his mind for some reason. Perhaps he intended to wait until we were out of the tower. Anyway, not a single person has been resurrected since then."

The shock silenced Burton for a moment.

When he recovered, he said, "How many bodies are on hold now?"

"As of now, eighteen billion, one million, three hundred and thirty-seven thousand, one hundred and ninety-nine. No. Now . . . two hundred and seven."

"I suppose you . . . ?" Burton said.

Nur, anticipating him, which he did with annoying frequency, said, "Yes. I ascertained that the Computer now has a reinforcing override from the unknown. The hold is still on."

"Just think," Burton said, "only three weeks ago we thought that our long hard struggle was over. That all the big issues were dissolved and our only problems from then on would be personal."

Nur did not reply.

"Very well. What we must do first is to subject each of us to a truth test. We can't proceed on the assumption that there is an unknown until we've eliminated all of our group."

"They won't like it," Nur said.

"But it's logical that we do it."

"Humans don't like logic when it's inconvenient or dangerous for them," Nur said. "However, they'll submit to the test. They have to to avoid suspicion."

4

If not telling a lie was the same as telling the truth, the results of the test were positive. If telling a lie could result in an indication that the truth was being told, the results were negative.

Whether the indications were true or not, the eight seemed to be innocent.

Each sat in turn inside a closed transparent cubicle and answered questions from Burton or Nur. The field generated inside the cubicle showed the *wathan* floating just above the head of the questionee and attached to it by a thread of bright scarlet light. The *wathan* was a sphere that swelled and shrank, whirled or seemed to whirl, and flashed a spectrum of glowing colors. This was the invisible thing that accompanied every person from the moment of conception and did not leave him or her until that person was dead. It contained all that was a person, duplicating the contents of the mind and nervous system and also giving him or her self-consciousness.

Burton had taken the first test, and Nur had asked him several questions to which he had to give an answer he believed to be true.

"Were you born in Torquay, England, on March 19, 1821?"

"Yes," Burton said, and the Computer photographed his *wathan* at that second.

"When and where did you die the first time?"

"On Sunday, October 19, 1890, in my house in Trieste, that part of Italy then belonging to the Austro-Hungarian Empire."

The Computer took another photograph and compared the two. It then compared these two to others that had been taken many years ago when Burton had been questioned by the Council of Twelve.

Nur looked at the flashing display on a screen and said, "The truth. As you know it."

That was one of the deficiencies of the test. If a person believed that he was telling the truth, the *wathan* indicated that he was.

"That is the truth," Frigate said. "I read those dates many times when I was on Earth."

"Have you ever lied?" Nur said.

Burton, grinning, said, "No."

A narrow black zigzag shot over the surface of the *wathan*.

"The subject lies," Nur told the Computer.

On the screen appeared: PREVIOUSLY VERIFIED.

"Have you ever lied?" Nur said again.

"Yes."

The black lightning streak disappeared.

"Did you make Loga vanish?"

"No."

"Were you implicated with anyone in Loga's destruction?"

"Not that I know of."

"That's the truth, as far as you know it," Nur said after glancing at the screen. "Do you have any knowledge about anyone who might have made Loga vanish?"

"No."

"Are you glad that Loga did vanish?"

Burton said, "What the hell?"

He could see the image of his *wathan* on a screen. It was glowing with orange overlaying the other shifting colors.

"You shouldn't have asked that!" Aphra Behn said.

"Yes, you devil, you had no right!" Burton said. "Nur, you're a scoundrel, like all Sufis!"

"You were glad," Nur said calmly. "I suspected so. I also suspect that most of us were. I was not, but I will allow the same question to be put to me. It may be that I, too, was glad, though deep in my animal mind."

"The subconscious," Frigate murmured.

"Whatever it is called, it is the same. The animal mind."

"Why should anyone be glad?" Alice said.

"Don't you really know?" Burton shouted.

Alice recoiled at the violence.

Having been cleared, for the moment, anyway, Burton left the cubicle and interrogated Nur. When the Moor appeared to be innocent, Alice seated herself. Burton forbore asking her if Loga's death had given her any joy. He doubted that it had. But when she had time to consider what she might do with the powers here, she might understand why some of the others had felt, to their shame, elated.

One by one, the others showed their innocence.

"But Loga could have passed the test while lying like a diplomat," Nur said. "It is possible that one of us has had access to his *wathan* distorter."

"I don't think so," Turpin said. "Ain't none of us got the smarts to operate one of those. We ain't smart enough to override Loga's commands either. I think we're wasting time, besides insulting all of us."

"If I interpret you correctly," Nur said, "you're saying that we're not intelligent enough. That's not true. We are. But we don't have the knowledge we need."

"Yeah, that's what I meant. We just don't know enough."

"Three weeks is long enough for a diligent person to get the knowledge from the Computer," Burton said.

"No. The Computer ain't going to tell anyone how to override Loga," Turpin said. "I just don't believe that that could be done."

"We could do a memory-strip of the past three weeks," Frigate said. "It'll take time, but it might be worth it."

"No!" Alice said vehemently. "No! I'd feel violated! It would be worse than rape! I won't do it!"

"I understand your feelings," Nur said. "But . . ."

The Computer could unreel their memories back to conception and display them on a screen. The process had its limits, since it could not reproduce nonvisual and nonauditory thoughts except as electronic displays, the interpretation of which was still uncertain. It was capable of transmitting tactile, olfactory and pressure memories. But, memory was selective and apparently erased many events that the individual considered unimportant. However, it did show clearly what the subject had seen, heard and spoken. On demand, emotion-pain fields could be projected.

"I won't want you seeing me when I went to the toilet," Alice said.

"None of us want that, for you or for ourselves," Burton said, and he laughed. It sounded like a stone skipping across water. "All of us fart and belch and most have probably masturbated and picked our noses, and Marcelin and Aphra, I'm sure, would not care to have us see them in bed. But it's not necessary to show everything. The Computer can be ordered to be selective, to display only the events we're interested in. Everything else will be irrelevant and so will not be shown."

"It's a waste of time," Frigate said. "Anyone clever enough to do what the unknown did wouldn't overlook the possibility of a memory-strip."

"I agree with you," Burton said, "though I seldom do. But it is one of those routine things that have to be done. What if the guilty person—if there is one—had anticipated that we would think a memory-search was useless?"

"He wouldn't take such a chance," Li Po said.

"Nevertheless, I insist that we do it," Burton said. "If we don't, we'll all be wondering about one another."

"We'll still be wondering when it's all done," Frigate said sourly. "But if it must be."

The search could have been run simultaneously with each one in a separate cubicle, but who then would supervise each subject to make sure that he or she did not order the Computer to cancel the relevant events? Burton went first, and, after three hours, the time it took the Computer to strip three weeks of memory, he emerged. The screen had been blank during the entire strip.

It was, as expected, empty while the others underwent the search.

Twenty-five hours passed before the last one, Li Po, stepped out of the cubicle. Long before then, others had drifted off to bed one by one. Burton and Nur saw the work through from beginning to end. Some were getting up when the two decided they should sleep. First, though, Burton wanted to make sure that no one could enter the suite.

"The unknown could override the codeword locking the door."

"How do you suggest that we block the door?" Frigate said, and he yawned. "Do we shove a bed against it? Pile more furniture on top of that?"

"The door swings inward, so that's not a bad idea. What I'm going to do, however, is to order the Computer to make a burglar alarm."

Burton did just that. Five minutes later, he pulled out from an energy-matter converter cabinet a dozen pieces of equipment. He taped two boxes to the wall on each side of the door and secured several other boxes to these. Then he adjusted a dial on one of the large boxes.

"There," he said, stepping back to admire the set. "No one can enter without setting off a hell of a loud siren. I think. We'd best test it. Pete, will you go outside, close the door, then come back in?"

"Sure, but I hope I don't disappear while I'm standing in the hall."

Burton turned a knob on the box. Frigate spoke the code-word, the door swung open, and he walked out. He turned, spoke the word, and the door shut. Burton reset the dial on the box. A few seconds later, the door began opening. A bright orange light flashed from the box, and an ear-pummeling whooping filled the room. Aphra Behn and de Marbot came running through the doorway. Turpin, who had been eating breakfast and not paying Burton much attention, leaped up from the table, his mouth spewing food. "Go-o-o-d damn!"

Burton turned the alarm off.

"The unknown could learn what the combination for the alarm is from the Computer. So I asked for one that I could set myself. There's no way the Computer can know which I chose, not as long as I blocked the line of sight from its screen with my body when I set the alarm."

"Admirable," Frigate said. "But our bedrooms are sound-proofed. How are we going to hear the alarm from there?"

The walls, floor, and ceilings were several inches thick and packed with circuits and power lines, most of them unused. Burton could have ordered the Computer to set up a circuit that would set off alarms in all rooms when the door alarm went off. But the unknown could override these circuits.

Burton was thinking about what to do when Frigate spoke.

"We could have the Computer make mass detectors. These could be set inside the bedroom doors so that, even if we didn't hear the apartment door alarm, we'd hear anybody trying to get into our bedrooms. These should be activated and deactivated by some sort of hand signals. The unknown *can* eavesdrop on us through the Computer. He's probably doing it now. But, as far as I know, he can't see us unless he turns on a screen. And we can see that."

"You say, as far as we know," Burton said. "Isn't it possible that he could turn on a screen but make it invisible to us?"

"I suppose so. I don't really know enough about Ethical science to be sure of what can or can't be done."

"Then the unknown may be also watching us."

"Yes. What we should do is erect some sort of tent in this room and write communications to one another inside it. Or the Computer could make us a soundproof cubicle. Even the floor would be soundproof. The trouble with that is that its walls might contain detectors put in by the order of the unknown. We'd have no way of checking that. Come to think of it, a tent made of cloth could contain detectors, too."

Burton became angry. "Is there nothing we can do?"

"We can do the best we can and hope that it'll be enough."

"We'll keep the door alarm," Burton said. "I'll write the combination on paper. You'll memorize it, and I'll make sure that the papers are destroyed."

"Destroy the papers with a beamer," Frigate said. "If you just burned them and crumbled the ashes before dropping them in a disposal hole, the Computer might be able to reconstruct the combination."

Burton said that they would have to make hoods to put over them when they reset the combination. They could make sure that the hoods did not contain detectors by using their bedsheets.

"We can't trust the mass detectors," he added. "The Computer will make them for us, but the unknown might hide turn-off devices in them."

"True," Frigate said. "He may have installed a turn-off in your burglar alarm, too."

"Then anything the Computer makes for us could betray us?"

"Sure. Including the food. The unknown could order poison put in it."

"By God! There must be something we can do to fight this devil!"

Nur, who had been standing near them and smiling slightly, spoke.

"If the unknown had planned to kill us, he would have done it before now. I suggest that if the unknown can override even Loga's commands, then he or she must be an Ethical. If so, why hasn't he resurrected Monat and the others? That would be his first thought and his first duty, after he's immobilized us, of course. Which, I don't have to point out, he's accomplished. The only thing is . . ."

He hesitated so long that Burton said, "Yes? What is it?"

"Would any Ethical erase Loga's body-recording? I think not. So . . . the unknown can't be an Ethical. Unless . . ."

"Unless what?"

"Patience, my friend. We are not on a schedule. Unless . . . it is Loga who's behind all this."

Burton exploded. "We've been through that line of reasoning! Why would he do this?"

Nur shrugged skinny shoulders and raised the palms of his long hands.

"I don't know. I doubt that it is Loga. Would Loga erase his own body-recording? Of course not."

"But he could have a secret resurrection chamber some place in the tower," Frigate said.

"Just what I was going to say," Nur said. "We still don't have an explanation for such irrational conduct. But I keep thinking of the footfalls Frigate heard, or thought he heard, in the corridor outside the room where we were celebrating our victory over the malfunctioning Computer. Loga was disturbed when Pete told him about it. He ran out into the corridor and down to the intersecting hall, and he looked up and down the lift shaft. Then he asked the Computer some questions, but these were in his language, and he talked so fast we did not understand them."

"I asked him what he was so upset about," Burton said. "He

replied that he wasn't anymore and that Pete's experiences had made Pete so paranoiac that he was hearing sounds that did not exist. Pete's suspicions were infectious. So Loga said."

"That's like throwing a stone through your own window!" Frigate said. "There was nobody more paranoiac than Loga!"

"If he was, then we've been on the wrong side," Nur said calmly. "Those who follow a crazy man are as crazy as he. However, talking about that is useless. What do we do *now?*"

Frigate's sarcastic suggestion that they pile furniture by the door was, realistically, the best offered. It was an inconvenient arrangement if they were to use the door much, but, at the moment, they planned to stay within the suite.

Moreover, there now seemed little chance that the unknown could poison their food and water. Frigate and Nur got simplified schematics of the e-m converters and studied them. The unknown could cut off the power to the converters and so starve them. But the food was produced by e-m conversion via preprogrammed circuits that the unknown could not change. He had no way of introducing poison into them. But their drinking and bathwater came through pipes, and the unknown could put toxic substances into them.

Frigate and Nur made arrangements whereby the water would be produced from the converters in the rooms. The Computer did not balk at producing the necessary plumbing for them to connect the water outlets to the converters. The eight had a plumbing job to do, but their inexperience was overcome by instruction books and tools furnished by the Computer. Meanwhile, the eight would get their water in bowls and pails from the converters.

"This seems useless and stupid," Li Po said. "There are so many other ways the unknown could get at us."

"Nevertheless, we must do what we can to avoid his tricks," Nur said. "That is, if he has any up his sleeve. And if he does indeed exist."

5

I 'm going to bed," Burton said.

"I'll eat first," Nur said.

The little Moor looked as fresh as if he had just had eight hours of very good sleep. By then, everybody but de Marbot and Behn was in the big room. Burton left it to Nur to explain the door blockade, and he walked down the hall a few steps and entered his apartment within an apartment. It consisted of three rooms: a living room twenty-four feet square, luxuriously furnished yet usable as a workroom, a bedroom, and a bath. Burton unbuckled the belt holding the holster, which encased the beamer, and he shed his single garment, a scarlet kilt decorated by bright yellow male lion-shapes. The floor was covered with a thick carpet like that in the big community entrance room. The inwoven figures were different, each consisting of three interlocking circles. The walls were pale cream, but a word from Burton to the Computer could change the color to whatever he wished. He could also order any shape or symbol, anything, imposed on the basic color. Here and there were paintings that looked like oil originals but had been reproduced by the Computer. No art specialist could have distinguished the original from the copy, since the two were exactly alike down to the molecular level.

Burton crawled into bed and was asleep at once. He awoke feeling drugged and with a vague memory of a nightmare. A hyena twice as tall as he had threatened him with fangs that were curving steel swords. He remembered parrying the scimitarlike teeth with a fencing foil and the hyena laughing at him. The cachinnations had been remarkably like his.

"I've been called, quite unjustifiably, a human hyena," he

murmured, and he rolled out of bed. He would have to make the bed himself, though androids—protein robots—were available to do it. For the time being, no androids would be admitted into the suite. They were a potential danger because the unknown might have ordered them to attack the eight.

Burton exercised vigorously for an hour, then ordered breakfast from the Computer. The coffee was the best that had ever been produced on Earth; the shirred eggs, the best; the brown bread toast, exquisitely heated and covered with the best butter Earth had ever known. There was also a jam to send the palate into ecstasy, and a fruit unknown to Earth but tasting somewhat of muskmelon.

He brushed his teeth and took a medium-warm shower despite the possibility that the water could be poisoned. As Frigate had said, if the unknown had intended to kill them off, he could have done it by now.

He selected a dark green kilt and a long flowing robe of green decorated with a design of yellow birds of an unknown species. Then he activated a wall-screen to see what was going on in the main room. Li Po, Nur, Behn, and Turpin were sitting in chairs and reading the lists of control limits. The furniture was still stacked in front of the door.

Burton went into the main room, greeted them, and said, "Have the others reported in?"

Nur said that they had. Burton went to an auxiliary computer and activated the screens in the bedrooms of those absent. He could not see them, but he could hear their voices as they said that they would be right out. A few minutes later, Alice, Frigate, and de Marbot appeared. Alice was wearing a loose Chinese-looking robe, scarlet with green dragons, and brocade slippers with turned-up toes. Her short dark straight hair shone as if it had been brushed many times. Her only makeup was a light red lipstick. She could have used some powder to cover the dark smudges under her eyes.

"I didn't sleep well at all," she said as she sat down in a chair. "I couldn't get it out of my mind that someone might be watching me."

"If we could trust the androids, we could have them put paper over the bedrooms," Frigate said. "That'd block out the screens."

"If . . . if," Burton growled. "I'm getting sick of these almighty ifs. I'm fed up with being in a cage. As soon as we find out what we can and can't do, we'll conduct a manhunt. It'll be dangerous, but I, for one, will not keep on hiding like a rabbit in its burrow. We're not rabbits. We're human. And human beings are not meant to be cooped up like pigeons."

"Rabbits and pigeons," Frigate muttered.

Burton swung around to face him. "What the devil do you mean by that?"

"The rabbits and the pigeons don't have the slightest idea why they're caged. They don't know they're being fattened up to be eaten. But we, we don't know why Loga was done away with or what's planned for us. We're worse off than the rabbits and pigeons. They, at least, are dumb but happy. We're dumb but unhappy."

"Speak for yourself," Nur said. "I would like to point out to those who may not have thought of it that this list may be incomplete. The unknown may have kept certain powers from the list. Even if he has not done so, he can eliminate almost any of those he wishes to eliminate."

There was a long silence. The Chinese rose, went to a converter, and ordered a huge goblet of rye whiskey. Burton grimaced but said nothing to him. It would have been useless, and Li Po's defiance would lessen Burton's authority.

Li Po sipped the rye, belched to indicate his appreciation, and went back to his chair. He said, "I need a woman!"

Burton had thought that Alice was past blushing, but the Victorian in her was a long time dying.

"You'll just have to keep jacking off," Burton said. "We have enough problems without resurrecting a woman just so she can drain off your lust."

Alice's face became redder. Aphra Behn laughed.

"It's unnatural," Li Po said. "My yang needs its yin."

Burton laughed because "yang" meant "human excrement" in a West African language. Po asked him why he was laughing. When Burton explained, the Chinese laughed uproariously.

"Well, if I can't have a woman, I'll work out my desire with exercise. What say we fence for an hour or so, rapiers or sabers?"

"I need it, too," Burton said, "but you're drunk. You'd be no match."

Li Po protested loudly and shrilly that he could have drunk twice as much and still beat Burton with any weapon Burton cared to choose. Burton turned away from him, and the Chinese staggered to his chair, fell into it, and began snoring. Frigate and Turpin carried him to the bedroom door. This, however, was locked with Po's codeword, which his bearers did not know. They placed him on the hall floor and returned to the big room.

"We'll all be behaving like Po if we have to stay here," Turpin said. He went to a converter and ordered a tall glass of gin with a lemon twist. Aphra, who had a glass of the same, raised it and said, "A toast to craziness! This may be a jail, but it beats Newgate."

She knew what she was talking about; she had twice been in debtors' prison.

She could also afford her cavalier attitude, though it was not realistic. She had a lover, de Marbot, with whom she was happy, and she had every luxury she'd ever had on Earth and many more. Except freedom. That, however, did not bother this adaptable and cheery woman just now.

What was keeping some of them from studying their peril was the vast potentialities of the list. Where they should have been examining what limited them, they were considering what gratifications it offered. Though Burton could understand their excitement over this, he was disturbed by their lack of concern for the dangers that were—as it were—just around the corner.

Judging from their facial expressions, Nur was the only one thinking of the unknown enemy. Burton felt like kicking the others. Instead, he slapped his hands together sharply, jolting them from their dreams.

"That's enough nonsense," Burton said. "The situation is serious. Deadly. There's no time to think of anything but how we're going to fight the enemy. If we defeat him, you may play all you want. Till then . . . The unknown has a great advantage over us in that he can use the Computer better than we. But if we can learn how to use it against him, it becomes our ally. Let me remind you that the Computer is not just that huge protein electroneural mass at the bottom of the central shaft. The Computer is also the tower, this vast building in which we reside. The *brain* is the central protein organ, the clearinghouse. But the majority of circuits are in the floors, the walls, and the ceilings of the tower. We're in the heart, the nerves of the enemy. And we can find ways to strike at that heart, those nerves. Or perhaps I should say, ways to seize them and use them as weapons."

"If you're thinking of belling the cat," Alice said, "we don't even know where the cat is."

"It may be another mouse who's buffaloed us into thinking it's a cat," Nur said.

"If . . . if . . . may be," Burton said. "No more speculations on ifs. We abandon speculation; we act."

"Fine. But how?" Nur said. "Everything we're saying now or will say may be, probably is, overheard. And perhaps seen."

"I said, 'No more ifs and may bes!'" Burton thundered.

Frigate laughed and said, "We can't help that, we're all mad here. I'm mad. You're mad. We must be, or we wouldn't have come here."

"What are you talking about?" Burton said.

"He's paraphrasing the conversation between the Cheshire Cat and Alice in Wonderland," Alice said.

"The mention of the cat reminded me of the Cheshire Cat," Frigate said. "In a way, the unknown is the grin without a cat."

Burton threw his hands up.

"I wish I had all of you in the army!" he cried.

There was silence, but Burton knew that it would not last long. Not in this group.

"That," Frigate said, "may be just what we need."

"What?"

"An army. We can have the Computer make us an army of robots and androids. We'll set it up so that the unknown, the Snark, let's call him, can't override our commands to the robots. We can set them to looking for the Snark and guarding us. We'll also order them to seize or kill anyone who is not us. Non-us is the enemy. The robots and androids can do in a short time what would take us years."

Burton stared at the American, then said, "You wrote that—what do you call it?—science fiction too long. It's rotted your brain."

"It's within the capabilities of the tower," Frigate said. "If we're going to win, we have to think big. I know it sounds crazy, but we need an army, and we can get it. I'd say, oh, a force of about one hundred thousand."

Some burst out laughing. Frigate grinned, but he said, "I'm serious." He went to a console and punched out some numbers and an operation. Simple multiplication. The screen showed: 107,379.

"Three automaton soldiers to a room makes one hundred seven thousand, three hundred and seventy-nine. We could have a whole army in several days. The soldiers could watch every known room and keep an eye out for a stranger and also probe for hidden rooms."

Nur, smiling, said, "I admire your creativity but not your lack of restraint or your contempt for realities."

"What do you mean?" Frigate said. "Restraint is good only in situations that call for it. This doesn't. As for realities, the army could be easily realized."

Nur admitted that twice the number proposed could easily be raised. However, androids were not self-conscious and were not at all intelligent. Their actions had to be programmed. The army would have to be separated into small groups acting on their own. This required command levels of noncoms and officers, androids who could act on their own initiative when situations not in their programming arose. The leaders simply would not know what to do. For that matter, they would not even know that they had to do anything.

"Moreover," Burton said, "there's still that nagging worry. Can the unknown install in the robots and androids some sort of channel whereby he can override our commands?"

"He's probably thinking about that right now," Alice said. "If he's watching us, he can anticipate anything we do."

She shuddered.

"My answer to your objection," Frigate said to Burton, "is that we could make some modifications in the neural systems of the androids. We could make them partly mechanical. By that, I mean that we could install mechanical devices in them. Say, something like a locker or safe combination that would set our commands mechanically but that would then transmit them electrically.

"We would set the combinations after we'd received the basic device from the Computer. That way, neither the Computer nor the Snark could control what we did. And . . . oh, hell! The Snark could still put a neuron complex in the android that would tell it to override the combination command by radio or whatever."

"The hard facts," Nur said, "are that we are in the power of this Snark. He does not have to attack us. All he has to do is shut off our power, and we'll starve to death. If he intended to do that, he could have done so. He has not done so, therefore, we can assume that he isn't going to. He has set certain limits to our use of the Computer but allowed us considerable powers. There are certain things he doesn't want us to have. Otherwise, he just doesn't care. He's ignoring us."

"The question, one of the questions, is why?"

"We can't answer that. He'll have to, if he ever does," Frigate said.

"Right," Nur said. "Now, while you were all sleeping, I had the Computer locate the secret entrance that Loga arranged long ago. The entrance we used to get into the tower after we'd crossed the mountains and taken that boat to the base of the tower. I tried to get the Computer to open that. It seemed to me that perhaps the unknown might be wanting us to leave the tower and return to The Valley. He did not wish us to use the aircraft for obvious reasons.

"But the secret door would not open when I asked the Computer to do it for me.

"Therefore, the unknown does not wish us to leave the tower.

"There may come a time when he'll wish us to go, and, if so, he'll open an exit for us. Until then, we're prisoners. But this prison is vast and has, in a sense, more treasures to offer than the Earth we lived on or the Rivervalley. The treasures are physical and mental, moral and spiritual. I suggest that we find out what these are and use them. We might as well. We can't stay caged in this suite.

"Meanwhile, of course, we'll be trying to think of ways to override the unknown's overrides. What one person sets up, another may knock down. The unknown is not a god."

"What you're suggesting is that we move back into our apartments and live as if there were no unknown?" Burton said.

"I say that we should leave this particular area, which is a small prison, and go out into the larger prison. After all, Earth was a prison. So was the Rivervalley. But if you're in a large enough space to give you the illusion of freedom, then you don't think of yourself as a prisoner. The half-free man is one who thinks he is free. The really free man is one who fully knows what he can do in prison and does it."

"A Sufi's wisdom," Burton said, smiling but with a sneer in his voice. "We do look rather ridiculous, don't we? We run into a hole and then ask ourselves why we ran and decide that we didn't have to."

"We were following instinct," Nur said. "It was wrong to do so. We had to find a place where we could be safe. At least, think we were. Then we had the relative peace of mind to evaluate our situation."

"Which turned out to be no peace of mind. Well, I do feel better, I won't feel as much a prisoner. And that pile of furniture irks me. Let's tear it down."

Frigate said, "Before we do, I have something to tell you."

Burton, who had started for the door, stopped and turned around.

"Nur wasn't the only one who did a little independent investigating," Frigate said. "As you know, Monat can't be resurrected because of Loga's command, which the Snark reaffirmed. Monat's body-record is still on file. But I asked the Computer to locate his *wathan* in the shaft, and the Computer said that it had been there but was now gone. You know what that means. Monat has Gone On."

Tears welled from Burton, and with the grief was mixed surprise that he should feel such grief. He had not known until that moment how he really felt about Monat. One of the first people he had encountered during his first resurrection had been the strange-looking, obviously non-Terrestrial Monat. Monat had accompanied him for a long time in The Valley and had impressed Burton with his compassion and wisdom. He had seemed *warm*. Thoroughly human despite his appearance, that is, what humans ideally should be.

Somehow, Burton had come to regard Monat as a father, a being stronger and wiser than he, a teacher, a pointer-out of right paths. And now Monat was gone forever.

Why should he shed tears and be choked up? He should be happy, gloriously happy because Monat had arrived at the stage where he no longer had to suffer the encumbering flesh.

Was it because he suffered a sense of loss? Had he thought, deep in the dark unconscious, that Monat wold somehow free himself from Loga's lock on him and be, in short, a savior? Had he felt that Monat would come up out of the records like Jesus from the tomb or Arthur from the lake or Charlemagne from his cave and rescue the defeated and the besieged?

It was strange to be thinking such thoughts. They must have been circulating somewhere in him, waiting for the right moment to break out.

His own father had not been a real father, not what a son wanted as a father. So, in some manner, Burton had taken Monat as one, perhaps because he could never accept another Earthman as one. Monat was from another world, therefore not, what was the word . . . *tainted*? That was a curious word to leap to his mind.

In any event, Monat was forever out of reach of anybody in this world, Gone On. To what?

To conceal the tears, Burton strode to the furniture and began dragging it away from the door. By the time the others had joined him, his eyes were dry.

He opened the door and breathed deeply. The air was no fresher than that in the suite. But it offered liberation.

6

Near their apartments was a room containing a swimming pool sixty meters long and thirty meters wide. When no one was in the room it was dark, but the heat detectors would turn the light on if a single person entered it. The light was a simulated sun at zenith in a cloudless blue sky. The walls displayed a forest surrounding the pool and snow-capped mountains far in the distance. Even if a person stood within an inch of the wall, the trees seemed to be real. As real-looking as the trees, birds flew among the branches or lit on them, and their songs cried out pleasantly. Occasionally, the swimmers could see a rabbit or fox among the trees and, rarely, a pantherlike beast or bear moving silently in the twilight under the branches.

The water was fresh and about 68°F and had a depth of twelve meters at the deep end. Here the eight tenants usually gathered for an hour or so of swimming in midmorning.

Burton had been studying the list of operational limits until 11:00 A.M. He entered the huge echoing chamber noisy with cries and splashes and stood for a moment. All were there except Nur. The men were in scanty trunks and the women in bikinis. They did not seem to have a care nor had they posted a guard. Beamers, however, lay along the edge of the pool, and he saw several at the bottom outlined against the red, black, and green mural.

Burton dived in and swam the length of the pool seven times. Then he hauled himself out and waited until de Marbot swam by. He called out to him; the Frenchman turned, came to the edge, and looked up. Burton considered his merry blue eyes, slick black hair, round face, and snub nose.

Burton squatted down and said, "I'm going to make a flying

trip, an exploratory one, through the tower. Do you want to come along?"

"That sounds like fun," de Marbot said. He narrowed his eyes and grinned. "Do you hope to surprise the Snark?"

"There's little chance of that," Burton said. "But . . . well . . . we might entice him to take some action. We'll be human decoys."

"I'm your man," the Frenchman said, and he pulled himself out. He was only five feet five inches tall and shared with Nur the distinction of being the smallest man in the group. Burton had chosen him as his companion, however, because he was utterly courageous and had more experience in martial action than any of them. Serving under Napoleon, he had been in most of the conqueror's great battles, had been wounded seventeen times, had fought in hundreds of small engagements, and had led so adventurous a life that A. Conan Doyle had written a series of stories based on his exploits. He was an excellent swordsman and a deadly shot and had an unsurpassed coolness under fire.

They dried themselves off in an anteroom, changed into dry clothes, sleeveless shirts and shorts, put their beamers in holsters, and walked along the pool. Burton paused for a minute to tell Turpin that they were going exploring.

"What time you coming back?" Turpin said through a mouthful of baked Montana grouse fed on huckleberries.

"About six P.M.," Burton said, glancing at his wristwatch.

"Maybe you should report in every hour on the hour."

"I don't think so," Burton said in a low voice, looking at the wall as if it had ears. Which it did. "I'm not going to make it easy for the unknown to find us."

Turpin smiled. "Yeah, that's right. Hope I see you again." He laughed, spewing out bits of meat and bread.

Burton was worried about Turpin. The man had lost much weight during the trying and dangerous passage over the mountains to the north polar sea. Now he seemed to be intent on becoming as fat as he had been on Earth, close to three hundred pounds. He was always eating, and he was not far behind Li Po in drinking.

Burton said, "We'll be flying around at random. I don't have the slightest idea where we'll be."

"Good luck," Turpin said.

Burton started to walk away but became aware that the Frenchman was not with him. Looking around, he saw him talking to Aphra. Evidently, he was explaining to her why he would be absent for a while. De Marbot was envied because he had a bedmate, but there were disadvantages to that. He had to account for his time to her, and, judging by their expressions and gestures, they were probably arguing over why she could not come along. Burton had no strong objections to taking her along at another time; she was tough and cool and skilled. Just now, he did not want more than one companion.

De Marbot, looking a little angry, returned to Burton.

"I have never heard that English expression, 'Take a flying fuck at a galloping goose,'" he said. Then, with that mercurial swiftness distinguishing him, he laughed, and he said, "How droll! How indeed could one do that?"

"It's a matter of synchronization," Burton said, grinning.

They left the pool and the door closed behind them. The noise was cut off; the corridor was huge and silent. It was easy to imagine someone—something—waiting around the corner for them, crouching, ready to spring.

Burton pointed out to de Marbot that he had filled the pockets on the sides of both chairs with power boxes for the beamers. They got into their chairs and caused them to rise into the air. Burton in front, de Marbot about twelve feet behind him, they sped toward the vertical shaft at the end of the hall. With a skill learned during the past three weeks, Burton curved the flight path so that he entered the shaft with only a slight decrease in speed, and he shot upwards.

He came out of the shaft at the next level at such velocity that his head was a few inches from the ceiling. He sent the chair down until his feet were twelve inches from the floor, and he hurtled along the muraled walls until he reached the end of the corridor. Then he stopped, pivoted the chair, and said, "You lead for a while."

The Frenchman led him through every passageway on that floor. The doors of every room were closed. For all Burton knew, their enemy was behind one. He did not believe this, however. Surely the Snark would have been notified by the Computer of the detection of heat from the two men. He would have told the Computer to warn him if the two were on an approach that would take them anywhere near him. He also might have activated the wall-screens, so that he could be watching them.

When they had passed through every corridor, de Marbot stopped his chair by a shaft. "This is fun," he said, "the wind on your face, your hair blowing, the scenery, such as it is, whistling by. It is not as good as riding a horse, but it will do. And, certainly, no horse would jump off into the shaft."

Burton took the lead now and rose up the shaft until he came to the top level. Down the corridor would be the entrance to the hangar, visited several days before. They entered the very wide entrance into the vast area with its brooding craft. Burton counted them and found that there were the same number as before. The unknown was still in the tower. That is, unless he had a ship secreted somewhere else. There was always an *unless*.

"I suppose we could remove the navigational tapes," he said, "and that would keep the Snark from using the spacecraft. But I'm sure that they'll be recorded. All he'd have to do would be to have the Computer run off new ones."

"Why would he want to use a spaceship?"

"I don't know. But I'd like to throw a monkey wrench in his plans, upset him somehow."

"The bite of the mosquito."

"That, I'm afraid, is all it would be. However, a mosquito may kill a man if it gives him malaria."

He was not expressing pure bravado. He believed that there must be a weakness, a hole, however small, somewhere in the Snark's defenses.

They sped on their chairs to the centrally located shaft and dropped to the level just below the top one. They entered a circular area with a 150-foot diameter and 500-foot-high walls. Twelve square metal doors were set equidistantly in the walls. Each, according to the Computer diagrams, gave entrance to a triangular chamber, pie-slice-shaped, which was 5.4 miles long and 401 feet high. The tip of each was blunted somewhat, ending in the walls of the central circle.

When Burton had viewed the diagrams, he had meant to ask the Computer about the contents of the vast chambers. An urgent matter had interrupted him before he could do so, and he had forgotten to return to his question. Now, while here, he would see for himself what they held.

Each door bore on its center a gold symbol indicating the identity of the member of the Ethical Council of Twelve whose property was beyond the door. The symbol directly in front of Burton was two horizontal bars crossed by two longer vertical bars. This was Loga's symbol. It could, Burton thought, be called a doublecross.

Burton gave the codeword that identified him, and a glowing screen formed above the bars.

"I wish to enter the room behind this door," Burton said. "Do I need a codeword to open the door?"

The screen displayed: YES.

"What is the codeword needed to activate the door?" Burton said.

He had expected that the Computer would reply that that information was unavailable to him. It flashed, however, in Ethical characters: LOGA SAYS.

"That, it is simple enough," de Marbot murmured.

Burton, hoping that the words were not keyed to Loga's voiceprint, pronounced perfectly the Ethical phrase.

The door opened outward, revealing a small, bare, well-lit room. At the farther wall was a staircase to a small platform. The two went up it, and Burton pushed in on the conventional oblong door. The area beyond was bright, the light having come on just as the door was opened. They stood blinking for a while before they grasped what they were seeing.

Though they must be standing next to the outcurving walls, they were under the illusion that the walls stretched for miles to right and left. The horizon seemed very far away.

The distance ahead of them was no illusion, however. This vast room was 5.4 miles long.

"It's a little world," de Marbot said softly.

"Not so little."

Most of it seemed to be a great well-kept park with many trees and clipped grass. Ahead, seemingly about two and a half miles away, was a sloping hill on top of which was a building gleaming in the noon sun. The villa was probably real; the sun was undoubtedly simulated.

"It looks rather Roman," Burton said. "I'd wager, though, that if we got close, we'd see a difference in the details."

Their chairs would have gone through the doors, but Burton decided not to explore. They returned to the central area and asked the Computer for the codeword to the chamber next to Loga's. This had been the property of Loga's wife and had the same kind of anteroom. But it opened to a vista that bewildered them. The entire Brobdingnagian area was a labyrinth of small and large mirrors in a complex arrangement that they could not figure out. Their images were caught by near mirrors and reflected inward for as far as they could see. The source of the light was not apparent; it seemed to come from everywhere. Far off, dimly seen, was a circle of pillars. These, too, were reflected, but the arrangement was such that they saw their own tiny figures standing inside the pillars.

"What is the purpose of this?" de Marbot said.

Burton shrugged and said, "We'll have to find out. Not just now, though."

The next chamber admitted them into what seemed to be an Arabian desert. Under a hot sun was an expanse of sand and rock, mostly a plain but with hills here and there. The air was much drier than that in the first two places. About three miles distant was what looked like a large oasis. Tall palm trees grew from grass, and the moving waters of a lake in the midst of the trees gleamed in the midmorning sunlight.

Near them were the skeletons of three animals. Burton picked up a skull and said, "Lion."

"*C'est remarquable,*" de Marbot muttered, reverting in his wonder to his native tongue. Then, in English, "Three different worlds. Lilliputian, yes. Yet large enough for all practical purposes, though I do not know about the practicality."

"I'd venture that these are . . . were . . . retreats for the Council," Burton said. "Sort of, ah, vacation areas. Each made his world according to his wishes, his own temperamental inclinations, and retired here now and then for spiritual and, of course, physical satisfaction."

De Marbot wished to look into all of the vast rooms, but Burton said that they had plenty of time for that later. They should continue their patrol.

The Frenchman opened his mouth to say something. Burton said, "Yes, I know. But what I'd like to do is see all that we can as swiftly as we can. It's better than having the Computer show us everything while we're lolling about in our rooms. Besides, how do we know that the Computer *is* showing us everything? It can delete as the Snark wishes it to, and we can't be sure that it's not doing so. We have to make a be-there visit. We'll make a flying patrol, be birds, get an overall view of everything. Then we can take our time and get the details."

"You mistake me," de Marbot said. "I was merely going to comment on the state of my stomach. It is complaining of its emptiness."

They took their chairs through the tube in the center of the floor to the next level, went down a corridor to the nearest door, opened it, and walked inside. It was a suite unfurnished except for a converter against a wall. De Marbot selected for lunch *escargots bourguignonne* with French bread and a glass of white wine. Thirty seconds later, he removed the dishes and silverware and glass and napkin. His blue eyes were big with admiration as he sniffed the delicate aroma. "*Sacrée merde!* Never on Earth could I get such perfection, such ecstasy! Yet surely the Ethicals must have gotten the original from some Parisian chef and copied it! What could be that genius' name? I would like to resurrect him, if only to thank him!"

"Someday, I'll order a deliberately badly cooked meal just for the sake of variety," Burton said. "Don't you find all this exquisiteness, this perfection, tiring? Every meal is a gustatory triumph."

"Never!" de Marbot said. He rolled his eyes on seeing Burton's eclectic choice, buttermilk biscuits and squabs marinated in cream and a schooner of dark beer.

"Barbaric! And I thought that you did not like beer?"

"I do when I eat ham or squabs."

"*De gustibus non disputandum.* Whoever said that was an idiot."

A section of wall folded out to make a table, and they ate.

"*Délicieux!*" De Marbot cried, and he smacked his lips loudly.

Until three weeks ago, he had been whip-thin. Now his face was becoming moonlike, and a slight roll was entrenching itself around his waist.

"There is a *glacé de viande* I must try," de Marbot said.

"Now?"

"No. I am no pig. Later. Tonight."

For dessert the Frenchman had a fig soufflé and a glass of red wine.

"Superb!"

They washed up in the bathroom and returned to the chairs. "We should be walking this off," Burton said.

"We'll work it off with saberplay before supper."

7

The illuminated halls they passed through had been dark a few seconds before they got to them. Heat detectors in the walls reacted to their bodies and activated switches that turned the lighting on ahead of them and off behind them. Because of this, the unknown probably knew exactly where they were. All he had to do was to command the Computer to give him images of every lit area. However, he could not spend all his time just watching the screens; he would have to sleep. If, however, by some means the tenants managed to get on his track, he could be awakened by the Computer.

The two came down a vertical shaft and came out into a hall. Halfway down this, they stopped their chairs and got out of them. A transparent outward-leaning wall enclosed a vast well glowing brightly from a source below them. The upper part of the enclosure was empty, but a few hundred feet below them was the illumination: a shifting dancing whirling mass of what seemed to be tiny suns. De Marbot got two pairs of dark spectacles from a box on a ledge and handed one pair to Burton. Burton put them on and looked for the twelfth time at the most gorgeous display he had ever seen, more than eighteen billion souls collected and made visible in one place. The Ethicals called them *wathans*, a word more precise than the English *soul*. These were the entities of artificial origin, each of which had been attached to an Earth-person the moment that the sperm and the egg united to form the zygote of that person. These remained attached to the head of each individual until he or she died, and it was these that gave *Homo sapiens* its self-consciousness and held its immortal part.

Each was invisible unless seen with a special device, in this situation the polarized material of the wellwall. They were glowing spheres of many colors and hues, with tentacles that shot out and contracted as the spheres whirled. Seemed to whirl, rather. Burton and de Marbot were not seeing the reality, the whole; they were seeing what their brains could grasp, a reshaping formed by their nervous systems.

The *wathans,* the souls, danced or seemed to dance, whirling, glowing, changing colors, passing through one another, occasionally seeming to coalesce and form a super*wathan,* which broke up into the original spheres after a few seconds.

Were they, when free of the human bodies, their hosts, conscious? Did they think when in this free state? No one knew. None of those who had been dead remembered anything of their existence when they were resurrected and the *wathan* was united again with the physical body.

The two stood rapt for a while before the awesome wonder surely unsurpassed in the universe.

"To think," Burton murmured, "that I have been part of that spectacle, that glory, many times."

"And to think," de Marbot said, "that if the Ethicals had not made these, our bodies would have been dust for thousands of years and would have stayed dust until even dust had died."

Far below, seen dimly through the coruscating nebula, was a great gray mass. It seemed to be shapeless, but Loga had assured them that it was not.

"That is the top of the titanic mass of organized protein that is the central part of the Computer," he had said. "It is the living but unselfconscious brain, the body of which is the tower and the grailstones and the resurrection chamber."

The "brain" was not, however, shaped like the human brain when within the skull.

"It resembles, more than anything, one of your great Gothic cathedrals with its flying buttresses and spires and gargoyle-decorated exterior and doors and windows. It is enveloped in water holding sugar in suspension. The brain would collapse and become a gray ooze if the liquid were removed. It is a lovely thing to see, and you must do so sometime."

It must be vast indeed to be visible from where they stood,

and through the glowing *wathans*. It was three miles below them, and they could see only a part of the top as a gray cloud. The rest of it occupied an expanded part of the well, a dome.

So far, the tenants had not ventured to the level where they could view the brain in its entirety. Nor did Burton plan on going there now. Instead, he returned to his chair and led his companion to the other side of the tower and down a shaft. Burton counted the levels passed—he had counted them during his first ascent from the level that was his destination—until he came to the one containing Loga's hidden room.

Before reaching the room, Burton stopped his chair. The Frenchman pulled up alongside him and said, "What is it?"

Burton shook his head and put a finger to his lips. He could see no mobile wall-screen, but the unknown might have other ways to monitor them. Even if he was not watching them now, it was probable that the Computer was recording their actions for later viewing.

They entered a big laboratory containing equipment whose functions Burton did not know—except for four huge gray metal cabinets. These were energy-matter converters. Their walls held all the needed circuits. In fact, the walls were the circuitry. Their power came through orange circles on the floor, which were matched to the orange circles in the center of the cabinet bottoms. Two cabinets were permanently attached to the floor, but the others could be taken from the room. Not, however, by the muscle power of two men alone.

Burton turned his chair, and, followed by de Marbot, flew out of the room and through the corridor past the wall behind which was Loga's hidden room. De Marbot must have wondered why Burton did not stop there, but he refrained from comment. By the time that they had returned to their suite level, after speeding up and down shafts and along corridors chosen at random, he no longer looked puzzled. He looked bored. But when they were in the hall, he pulled a notebook from the pocket on the outside of the chair and wrote on a sheet.

Burton took the note and held it close to his chest, his left hand partly covering it. He read: *How long must I wait before you tell me your plans?*

Burton wrote with a pen taken from the container on the side of his chair.

Sometime this evening.

De Marbot read it and smiled. "I will have something to look forward to," he murmured.

He tore the note into tiny pieces, placed them on the floor, and ignited them with his beamer ray. He ground the ashes with the toe of his sandal and blew them away.

They waited, and presently a recess in the wall opened and a wheeled, jointed, cylindrical machine rolled out. It headed for the ashes, a scooplike extension sliding out from its front. It sprayed the dirty area with a liquid that quickly dried into many tiny balls and then sucked the spheres onto the scoop and into an opening. A minute later, it had retreated into the cavity from which it had come, and the recess closed.

De Marbot spat on the floor just to see the robot in action again. As it rolled back to its lair after its cleanup job, the Frenchman kicked it. Unperturbed, the machine disappeared into the cavity.

"Really, I prefer the protein-and-bone robots, the androids," de Marbot said. "These mechanical things, they give me the shivers."

"It's the flesh-and-blood ones that disturb me," Burton said.

"Ah, yes, if one kicks them, not out of a desire to hurt, you comprehend, but a desire to evoke an emotion, one knows that, since they're of flesh and blood, they do hurt. But they do not resent the insult or the injury, and that makes them nonhuman. Still, one does not have to pay them wages, and one knows that they will not go on strike."

"It's their eyes I don't like," Burton said.

De Marbot laughed.

"They look no deader than the eyes of my Hussars at the end of a long campaign. You are reading into them a lack of life that does not exist. The lack, I mean. You know that they are brainless, rather, to be exact, use only a tiny portion of their brains. But one can say that of certain humans we have met."

"One could say a lot," Burton said. "Shall we join the others?"

De Marbot glanced at his wristwatch. "An hour until supper.

Perhaps I may be able to make Aphra jolly again. There is nothing that upsets one's digestion like a sullen companion at the table."

"Tell her that she'll be in on the next phase of the project," Burton said. "She'll brighten up then. But don't tell her what we did unless you use this."

He indicated the notebook.

De Marbot grimaced and said, "That one, the watcher, must be wondering what we're up to. How can we hide anything from him? One can't fart without his knowing about it."

Burton grinned and said, "Perhaps we'll make him fill his pants. In a manner of speaking."

The eight had agreed that each would take turns hosting the others. Tonight was Alice's, and she greeted them wearing a long, very lowcut, Lincoln-green evening gown of the style of 1890. Burton doubted that she was also wearing the numerous undergarments of that period. She was too accustomed to the comfortable cool clothes of the Rivervalley, a towel serving as a short skirt and a thin, light cloth serving as a bra. She did have elegant green high-heeled shoes on, and silk stockings, though the latter probably did not reach to her knees. Her jewelry, provided by an e-m converter, was an emerald set in a gold ring, small gold earrings, each with a single large emerald, and a string of pearls.

"You look lovely," he said as he bowed and kissed her hand. "Eighteen-ninety, heh? The year of my death. Are you trying to tell me in a subtle manner that you are celebrating that occasion?"

"If I am, I am doing so unconsciously," she said. "Let's not have any wisecracks, right?"

"Wisecrack. Nineteen thirty-four word," Frigate said to Alice. "The year of your first death."

"The only one, thank God," she said. "Must we speak of the Grim Reaper?"

Frigate bowed and kissed her extended hand.

"You are absolutely devastating. Say the word, and I'm all yours. No, you don't have to say it. I'm yours anyway."

"You're very gallant," she said. "Also, very pushy."

Burton snorted and said, "That's one thing he's not. Except when he's been drinking. Dutch courage."

"*In bourbono veritas*," the American said. "But you're wrong. Not even then. Am I, Alice?"

"Alice is a well-garrisoned castle on a steep hill surrounded by a wide moat," Burton said. "Don't try to mine her. Take her by storm."

The American flushed. Alice did not lose her smile, but she said, "Please, Dick. Let's not be unpleasant."

"I promise," Burton said. He turned, and started. "My God! Who're . . . ?"

Two men in servant's livery were standing near the dinner table. Not men. They were androids. One had the face of Gladstone; the other, of Disraeli.

"No one else has ever had two prime ministers of Great Britain wait on them," Alice said.

Burton spun toward her, his face red and scowling.

"Alice! We talked about the danger! The Snark could program them to attack us!"

She met his fury calmly.

"Yes, we did. But you, or somebody, also said that the Snark has a thousand ways of getting at us. He hasn't done anything yet, and if he were going to, he'd have done it. Two androids, a thousand, won't make any difference."

"Agreed!" Li Po said in his loud shrill voice. "Bravo, Alice, for taking the first step! I myself have some plans for androids! I may put them into effect tonight! Ah, tonight! You will suffer no more, Li Po!"

Burton had to admit, to himself, anyway, that she was right. She should not, however, have done this without getting the consent of the others. At the very least, she should have consulted him about it.

Perhaps, if the leader of this group had been someone other than him, she would have. It seemed to him that she took every opportunity to defy him now. Under that quiet soft demeanor, behind those large soft dark eyes, was a stubborn woman.

De Marbot and Behn arrived somewhat flushed and perspiring, as if they had just gotten out of bed or were in the midst of a quarrel. If the latter was the case, they were covering it up well. They smiled and joked and seemed perfectly at ease.

Burton greeted them and strode to a side table loaded with bottles and goblets and a huge bucket of ice. He waved away the android with Gladstone's face, which had approached him and asked if he could pour him a drink. Alice had done a very good job if she had reconstructed the prime minister's features from memory. She could have done so, since the man had dined a number of times at her house when her parents had been alive. More probably, though, she had asked the Computer to locate Gladstone's photograph in the files and it had done so. Then she had given the Computer her specifications, and it had reproduced this living but mindless being.

"By the Lord," he murmured, "it even has his voice!"

He sipped on the rye whiskey, smoother than any he had tasted on Earth, though it must be reproduced from some Terrestrial brand, and he went to talk with Nur. The little Iberian Moor was holding a glass of some pale yellow wine, which would last him for the evening.

"The Prophet did not forbid any alcoholic beverage except wine made from dates," he had once told Burton, who already knew it. "His excessively zealous disciples later extended the ban to all liquor. Though I felt that I did not have to obey the dictates of those ignoramus fundamentalists, I just did not care for strong waters. However, I have acquired a taste for this Chinese wine. Besides, even if I were a drunkard, what would Allah do to me that I had not done to myself? As for Mahomet, where is he?"

Burton and Nur talked of Mecca for a while, and then the android who looked like Disraeli announced that dinner was served. Since each guest had told Alice in the morning what he or she would like, the menus were in the Computer's memory. It took one microsecond for the food to appear inside a giant e-m converter; the servants took longer putting the appetizers on the table. Burton had ordered a salad with devil's-rain dressing followed by *sturgeon fumé a la muscovite* and for dessert two tarts with rhubarb filling. The appropriate wine was served with each course.

Burton, Behn, Frigate, and Li Po had cigars of the finest Cuban tobacco. Nur smoked his after-dinner cigarette, the only nicotine he allowed himself.

Burton approached the Frenchman, who backed away. "Spare my precious lungs that vile poison!" he cried.

"A man could die happy breathing this," Burton said. "However, as you said, *non disputandum de gustibus*. Did you inform Aphra that she might join us in our next venture if she wished?"

"That, yes, I did," de Marbot said. "Unfortunately, I could not tell her just what that venture was."

Burton handed him a note. De Marbot read it and looked up. "What . . . ?"

He came close to the Englishman and stood on his tiptoes to talk into Burton's ear. Burton still had to lean over.

"We will, I will, anyway, be ready. But . . . you can give me no indication, no clue, as to what you have in mind?"

"It's best not to."

"Ah, how intriguing," de Marbot said. "May the realization come up to my expectation. Danger, romance, skullduggery, an open charge upon the enemy or a silent stealth, apprehension, uncertainty, a task demanding all of one's courage and a straining of one's steel nerves."

"All of those," Burton said. "Perhaps."

8

A few minutes after one in the morning, Burton parked his chair outside de Marbot's and Behn's apartment. The door, as he had required, was open. He went into the big living room, the shadowless illumination coming on just as he passed through the doorway. He went down the hall and knocked on the bedroom door. Sleepily, de Marbot called, *"Quelle?"*

"C'est moi, naturellement," Burton said.

A moment later, the Englishwoman and the Frenchman stumbled through the doorway, rubbing their eyes.

"You owe me six hours of sleep," the Frenchman said. "How does one repay such a debt?"

"With six hours' loss on my part," Burton said. "But this is for your benefit, also, so I owe you nothing."

De Marbot had put on a towel-kilt, and Aphra was wearing a delicate black lace bra and black panties.

De Marbot said, "Hey, my cabbage, is that all you care to don?"

"It's what I always wear for midnight assignations," she said.

De Marbot laughed, hugged her, and kissed her cheek.

"My wild English rose. Always the unexpected, the delightful."

She was, however, deceiving him. She went back into the bedroom and reappeared clad in a thin blouse, a short skirt, and ankle-length boots. By then Burton had ordered three large mugs of Brazilian coffee from the converter. They sipped while he told them that he would explain just what they would do when they got to their destination.

"Sealed orders," de Marbot said. "But the enemy, he is watching and listening to us. We are like the cat with a bell around his neck."

"By the time we get through, he won't be able to see or hear us," Burton said.

De Marbot's eyebrows rose, and he smiled.

"Ah! I anticipate, I quiver, I revolve inside myself with excitement."

"There's a lot of work involved," Burton said. "You'll be tired before we're done."

"Not I. I am a man of iron, and Aphra, she is hard as platinum and twice the worth of that worthy metal in her weight."

"Which is increasing," she said, patting her hip.

Burton gestured impatiently, and they followed him to the corridor. They were armed with two beamers and knives, though they had no reason to expect to use them. They got into their chairs, and Burton flew in the lead. He steered the chair down the shaft to the level even with the surface of the cold dark sea surrounding the tower.

When Burton stopped the chair, de Marbot said, "This is not far from Loga's secret room."

Burton nodded and indicated that they should go into the nearest room, the laboratory that he had visited the day before. Aphra looked around it and said, softly, "He must be wondering what we're up to. He's no more puzzled than I."

"Richard is the general," de Marbot said, "and he tells us common soldiers as little as possible. It is an ancient tradition."

Burton ignored their remarks. He went to the largest converter and ordered parts of stepladders, five hundred spray cans filled with black paint, a dozen powerful lamps, and a small nuclear-powered air generator.

"*Mon Dieu!*" de Marbot said. "We are to be house painters! And what else?"

Burton began removing the equipment, emptying the converter when the first consignment appeared, closing the door of the converter, waiting a few seconds until the second consignment had filled the cabinet, and then removing this. When this was done, he told the two to take out the spray cans while he put the sections of the stepladders together.

De Marbot looked at Aphra with raised eyebrows as if to say, "What next?" She shrugged and, sweating, bent to her work. De Marbot, now sweating also, said, "Hey, my little cabbage. We must pay for all that divine food and exquisite wine, isn't it?"

"You pay for everything," she said.

Breathing hard, Aphra straightened up and looked at the wall in front of her. "The watcher is like God," she said. "He knows everything we are doing. I only hope that, like God, he is indifferent to what we do."

"Unlike God, the Snark sleeps," Burton said. "And he is limited by his body, like all us mortals. And his intelligence, though it may be great, is also limited."

"Perhaps, like God, he does not exist," de Marbot said.

"That's a possibility," Burton said. "There! The stepladders are done."

"Could we not have some androids to help us?" de Marbot said. "Perhaps to do all the labor? We shall be the supervisors who loll around, taking our ease while the helots sweat for us."

"I don't want to risk using them," Burton said. "To the task. Each of you start at a corner at the far end."

He had asked the Computer for an estimate of the number of cans needed to spray the area. Now he asked for two wheelbarrows, took them from the converter, and piled one high with cans. While the others stood near the tops of the stepladders and covered the ceiling corners with the paint, he wheeled the cans not needed in the room into the corridor. After four trips, he told the Computer to furnish him with twelve cans of quick-drying spray cement. Having gotten these, he took them out into the corridor. Then he ordered the number of bricks he needed, also estimated by the Computer.

De Marbot, watching him, said, "There is nothing like using the enemy to fight him."

There was one thing that Burton had to make sure of before he continued, though whether or not the door to Loga's room still opened he would complete the first part of his project. He knocked on the wall, said, "Ah Qaaq!" and watched as the entrance wheel rolled into the recess. He had not been sure that the Snark had not inhibited the operation since Burton's first visit. Now he stuck a chair in the opening to assure that the door could not close if the Snark changed his mind and decided to shut it permanently.

Burton had done many things on Earth. Bricklaying was not

one of them, but he had often observed Arab workmen building adobe brick walls. In any event, the erection was simple. He laid a row from one wall to another a few feet from the doorway to Loga's room. He sprayed the top of the row and set another layer on top of that. By the time he had laid the last brick of that row, the cement—it was really a glue—had dried.

Pausing only to drink water twice, he sealed in that area of corridor from side to side, top to bottom.

He went to the other side of the entrance to the laboratory and began laying bricks there. Aphra stuck her head out of the door and said, "We're almost finished with the walls." Sweat ran from down her face and soaked her garments.

He went into the room and looked around. "Inspect what you've done," he said. "Make sure that every square inch is covered. Then spray the floor. When you're done, tell me."

Groaning in mock-agony, de Marbot moved his stepladder to where he had begun spraying and climbed up it. Burton returned to his bricklaying. Working quickly and efficiently, he blocked off that part of the corridor. By the time he was done, de Marbot came to him.

"It's finished. Not a bit of wall, ceiling or floor is uncovered. The Snark may put all the screens he wishes on them. He'll be as blind as I am ignorant of your ultimate intentions."

Burton went to the laboratory and said, "Now spray the windows in the doors of the converters. And move any furniture that can be moved, and spray the bare spots where they were."

De Marbot gestured at the two mobile coverters. "Under them, too?"

"Yes."

"How do you move them? We have been working like Samson at Gaza, but we are not as strong as he."

"Use your flying chairs to slide them from the bare spots."

De Marbot struck his forehead with the heel of his palm. "Of course! How stupid of me! It is that I am not used to menial labor! It has dredged my intelligence from me!"

"Don't carry on so," Burton said. "You would have thought of it!"

"It is not military work," the Frenchman said, as if that explained it.

Aphra went into the corridor with Burton. "How do we get out now?"

"The bricks are ordinary ones, made of clay."

Behn pointed at his beamer and looked at him. Burton nodded.

"Then how will that keep him . . . the Snark . . . out?"

"It won't."

He looked at his wristwatch. "We've much to do yet."

Aphra shook her head and said, "I just don't know what you have in mind."

"You'll see. In time."

He took a stepladder, set it up by the corner of the brick wall and began spraying. When he had worked down to the door of the laboratory, having painted ceiling, walls, and floor of the corridor, he looked inside. The power cables connected to the bases of the two mobile converters had been disconnected, and the cabinets had been shoved onto the painted floor. The bare areas beneath were sprayed, and his coworkers were leaning against a wall and drinking water. Aphra Behn was also smoking a cigar.

"As soon as you're rested," Burton said, "come help me paint the corridor."

When de Marbot came out, he stopped, his eyes widening.

"Sacred blue! You have painted the brick wall!"

"Yes," Burton said. "The bricks *seem* to be just clay. I broke one open to examine it. But it's possible that the Snark inserted some conductive material in it. I want to make sure that he can't see us through it."

"Not very likely," de Marbot said.

"We take no chances."

"Ah, you bloody British! No wonder we lost the war."

De Marbot was not sincere. He maintained, furiously and with great conviction and many facts, that it was the mistakes and errors of Napoleon's marshals—and a few by the Corsican—that had caused the downfall of the empire. If his brave countrymen had been led by men who always made the right decisions, they would have been unbeatable.

Burton, so far, had refrained from pointing out that the same might be said for any army.

By the time that they had spray painted the corridor and Loga's room, it was 5:00 A.M.

The light and air from the wall material and vents had been cut off, but the lamps and air generator replaced these.

De Marbot said, "*Voilà! C'est fini!* I think."

"You think incorrectly," Burton said. "Now we move the largest converter into the secret room."

This was done by shoving the cabinet with a flying chair, Burton standing by the chair and operating the controls. The task took ten minutes, and the top and sides of the converter scraped against the round entrance. Having, the day before, measured the dimensions of the cabinet and of the doorway, Burton knew that it would be a tight but workable fit. When he had maneuvered the cabinet from the laboratory and into the secret room, he connected the cable to the power inlet of the cabinet.

Aphra Behn said, "You've covered the area that detects the entrance codeword. What do you plan to do if you want to get in again? Or will you leave the door open?"

"The paint can be easily scraped away over the area if it's necessary," Burton said.

The Frenchman gestured at the walls. "Everything is impenetrable. The Snark can no longer see or hear us. May we be permitted to know what you intend to do now?"

The light from the lamps on the floor drew heavy shadows on their faces and made them look like masks. The masks of tired and desperate people. The blue eyes of de Marbot and Behn, however, seemed to shine with an unflagging light. Their wills were not weary.

"The power line to the converter is tapped in to the main power line," Burton said. "But it is not in the Computer's schematic files, and any power through it is not recorded by the Computer. Not, that is, unless the Snark has changed things. We can make whatever we wish, and the Snark won't have the slightest idea of what we're doing. He'll know we're up to something, and he'll be concerned about it. But he can't find out what it is unless he comes down here. He'll have to investigate personally."

"That ain't so," Aphra said. "He could send androids."

"If he's sentient, that is, human, he'll be as curious as a monkey. He'll want to look into this himself."

"Perhaps."

"Did you tell the others anything?" de Marbot said.

"No. I didn't feel it was necessary."

The Frenchman looked at his wristwatch.

"In about two and a half hours, some of our companions will be meeting for breakfast. You're always there. Won't they look for you?"

"Probably. And they won't find me. Eventually, they'll know that you two have disappeared, too."

"They'll think the Snark took us!" Aphra said. "They'll be very worried."

"It'll shake them from their lethargy," Burton said. "They won't be bored, at least."

"That's a little cruel," Aphra said.

"And they'll come looking for us," de Marbot said.

"There's not much chance they'll find us," Burton said. "Not when they have thirty-five thousand, seven hundred and ninety-three rooms to search."

"But they can use the Computer, it'll scan for them. And when it reports . . ."

He stopped, smiled, and said, "Ah, I see. The Snark may, probably will, prevent the Computer from telling them where we are."

"They'll be searching for us, and the Snark will have to keep tabs on them," Burton said. "I hope they'll provide some distraction for him."

"Yes, but," Aphra said, "they could have done the same thing if you told them to do so, and they wouldn't be upset about our being missing."

"The fewer know about us, the better. If they truly believe we're missing, they won't be acting. I'm not sure that the Snark wouldn't detect their insincerity. After all, he can read their voices for emotion and scan their *wathans*. He could tell if they're pretending."

"It's like fighting God," Aphra said.

"You said that," Burton said. "And I told you that the Snark is not God. Even if he was, I'd give him a run for his money."

"*Morbleu*," de Marbot said. "What if he doesn't come? What if he just lets us sit here like rats in a self-made trap? What then?"

"You can see a rat in a trap. He can't see us."

They were silent for a while. They had painted themselves into a dark corner, but they had all they needed to wait there for as long as they could endure it. There was a toilet in Loga's room and several in the laboratory. They could use the converter in Loga's hideaway to make food or whatever they wished. The converter was now tied in with a small auxiliary computer unconnected to the main one.

Seven o'clock came. Their conversation was infrequent and uninspired. The silence, the lighting, which seemed strange and unnatural after the shadowless illumination, and the waiting for something to happen wore on them. At seven-thirty, Burton suggested to the other two that they eat breakfast. They could sleep on the big bed while he stood guard.

At eight o'clock, the two decided that they would eat and then rest. Breakfast was provided by the converter in Loga's room. Burton ate lightly; he did not want to be sluggish if quick action was required. De Marbot and Behn got into the bed, but the Frenchman said, "I do not feel right sleeping. You might need me."

"It's all right," Burton said. "You're a light sleeper. Besides, I don't really expect the Snark to do anything for a long while."

"But you do not know."

"Right."

Burton went back to his station by the entrance to the secret room. Sleepy, afraid that he might nod off, he began pacing back and forth close to the doorway. He did not know if anything would happen but, if it did, it would be to his advantage. Whatever did come, it would probably be unexpected.

Perhaps he was acting senselessly, stupidly. Still, it was better than doing nothing at all. If he were the unknown, would he be able to just let the unobserved three stay behind the walls? Would he not wonder what they were doing? Would he not try to think of everything they could possibly do? Wouldn't he even ask the Computer to run off a list of everything that could be done?

No. He wouldn't do that. The Computer was not sentient; it had no imagination. Its output never exceeded its input. In that, it was unlike and inferior to human beings. Some human beings.

You're too cynical, he told himself. But am I? Aren't millions, billions of people protein robots? They differ only in that they can feel sorrow, grief, disappointment, love, ambition, despair, frustration, irritation, amusement, rage, sympathy, empathy . . . well, not many could feel that . . . imagination . . . some of them . . . *Vive la différence!*

Frigate had once said that most people were persons and a minority were human beings. "What the Ethicals are trying to do is to turn the many persons into human beings. I wish them success, but I don't have high expectations. And I'll be the first to admit that I'm not as yet a human being."

Frigate talked much about proper philosophical principles but did little to act them out. Nur was also a philosopher, but he acted out his philosophy. And you, Burton? What about you?

He had explored continents and minds, those of the legion of devils known as Burtonia excepted.

"There is only one great adventure," Frigate had said, "and that is the descent into oneself." He was quoting or paraphrasing some twentieth-century writer, Henry Miller, whom the American greatly admired at the same time that he despised some of his attitudes.

"The darkest Africa, the highest Everest, the deepest Pacific Abyss is your own mind. So why do so few set out to conquer it?"

"Because it's like a fish trying to find out the nature of water," Burton had said.

Talk, talk, talk. Parrots. Language was the plumage of human beings.

How did one burst through the self-erected barriers?

At that moment, something did break through. There was a crash and a roar. Burton leaped into the air and whirled toward the noise, his heart beating almost loud enough to drown out the uproar.

When he looked around the doorway, he saw that the corridor

was dark except for the lamplight coming from inside Loga's room and through the half-opened door of the laboratory. No. There was also light shining through a huge hole in the brick wall. It dimly revealed a monstrous thing, a horizontal cylinder with a conical nose, a dark mass that rolled on wheels toward him.

9

Burton jumped inside the doorway, turned, and stuck his head out far enough to see the thing. It was moving slowly, though it must have been traveling very swiftly to breach the wall, the bricks of which were held together by cement far stronger than anything on Earth in his time. The light from the corridor walls beyond the big hole showed that the monster was traveling on ten wheels.

Burton pointed his beamer at a spot behind the nose. The end of the scarlet rod-shaped ray struck, but though it could burn through twelve inches of nickel-steel in five seconds, it made no visible impression on the gray metallic-looking surface. He pulled back into the doorway and hurled himself backward and to one side as a violet-colored ray from the side of the machine leaped over his shoulder. Other rays followed; then the conical end of the monster was passing him. Daring to look around the doorway again, he saw that its large beamers were projecting the rays at various angles from both sides and many places.

When it was within a few feet of the other wall blocking the corridor, it stopped and began moving back. The beams were still going off and on at intervals of a few seconds. Moreover, the angles of fire were changing. Where they had struck were bare spots. The paint had been burned off.

Burton backed up behind the wall. A ray streaked through the doorway and burned off the paint on the far wall. Another, at a higher angle, destroyed more paint.

De Marbot called, "Dick, are you all right?"

"I'm not hurt!" Burton yelled. "Don't expose yourself!"

"I am not stupid!" the Frenchman screamed back.

But he was stupid; at least, from Burton's viewpoint, he was.

De Marbot ran past him and out into the corridor toward the machine. Burton cried out after him to stop. The Frenchman did not hesitate but leaped upon the back of the juggernaut and grabbed a rung near the top. Burton had expected him to be cut through by a ray, but the beams had stopped the moment de Marbot had run into the corridor. Later, Burton wondered if the rays that had been shot at him had only been to discourage him from getting close to it or following it when it left.

Now the machine rolled backward and past the opening to Loga's room. De Marbot, clinging with one hand and smiling, waved at Burton.

"Get off it!" Burton shouted. "You can't do anything to it! Get off before it kills you!"

"Where it goes, I go!" de Marbot yelled.

He lost his bravado then, because the machine, having halted, suddenly sped forward, its tires screaming as they burned on the floor. All the beams had been turned off, but now one sprang from the nose. The violet lance struck the brick wall and pierced it, and then the beam widened into a cone, the base of which melted the bricks within its area and made an opening just large enough for the machine to pass through.

De Marbot, screaming, had, however, loosed his grip before he was hit by the bricks at the edge of the breach. He lay face-down, silent.

"That crazy frog!" Burton said. The machine was whipping around a distant corner, revealing that it was not solid but had articulations that permitted it to turn corners, though just barely. De Marbot was sitting up by then and was holding his head.

Burton ran to him, beating Aphra by a few steps.

"Are you hurt?"

De Marbot sat up, grimaced, then smiled.

"Only my pride. I became frightened. I screamed with fear."

Assisted by Burton, he got to his feet. "I do have a few scratches, bruises, and contusions. I have taken worse spills many times from a horse while fighting for my glorious emperor. But never, never, have I had such a short ride!"

Aphra wrapped her arms around him and snuggled her face into his chest. "You stupid son of a bitch! You scared me to death!"

"You are most lively and reproachful for a corpse," he said, hugging her. "Oh, my poor arm and shoulder! I cannot embrace you, little cabbage, with all my huge and accustomed strength and love!"

She freed herself and wiped her tears away with her fingers.

"You're little cabbage, hell! I am not a vegetable, I'm a woman! A woman who's very angry with you and your heroics!"

"A rose with thorns, perhaps, is it not?"

Burton looked up and down the corridor. No one in sight.

"Why did you jump on it?" he said. "What did you expect to accomplish?"

"I was going to ride it to its lair, where I might find its master, the Snark, awaiting it. And then I would surprise him and take him prisoner or kill him if I had to. But I forgot, in the heat of combat, that the thing would only make a hole large enough for it to pass through."

"You were lucky that your brains, such as they are, weren't dashed out," Burton said. He shared some of Aphra's anger; he was very fond of the Frenchman. "It was magnificent, but it was not good soldiership."

"Ah, you are just jealous because you did not think of doing it."

Burton laughed and said, "Perhaps you're right."

He indicated the areas where the paint had been burned off.

"The Snark now sees and hears us."

"Odsblood!" Aphra said. "He just showed us how weak and helpless we are. We can't even hide from him!"

"But we did force him to act," Burton said. "He had to find out what we were doing here. He did not disdain us enough to ignore us."

"And so I have worked like a helot with spraying paint, sweated like a slave for nothing," de Marbot said.

"You did get an unusual ride out of it."

De Marbot's teeth shone.

"Yes. It was worth it!"

Burton was not sure. They had not done well. Moreover, the machine probably had cameras that had shown the Snark the open door to Loga's secret room.

"What do we do now?" Aphra said. "Slink back to our apartments like bad little puppies who've been whipped?"

Burton did not answer because of a shout from the right. A flying chair was suspended near the intersection of the corridor, and the voice had come from the opened curtain in an enclosure on the chair. It had been fitted with a frame over which transparent plastic had been arranged. The man in the chair was sitting with his legs drawn up in front of him on the seat.

"Who's that?" de Marbot said.

"Frigate," Aphra said, having recognized his voice.

The chair shot forward and settled on the floor, and Frigate pulled the enclosure, a sort of tiny cabin, from the chair. He got out, looked around, and said, "What happened?"

Burton explained. Then the American had to tell de Marbot and Behn why he was here and what the purpose of the enclosure was.

"Dick arranged with me to come here eight hours after you three had left. The contraption—the enclosure—is to prevent my body heat being detected by the Computer."

De Marbot looked reproachfully at Burton.

"You said that you'd enlisted just us."

"I don't tell the truth if it's useful not to do so," Burton said. "I thought that it would be best if I had two follow us but didn't tell you. I didn't want you and Aphra to be saying anything to each other about this."

"Two?" de Marbot said. "Where is the other?"

"Nur is supposed to come down the corridors on the other side," Burton said, pointing in the direction in which the machine had gone.

"Why?" de Marbot said. Then, "You think that perhaps Nur might have tracked the machine to its lair?"

"We won't know until later."

Burton turned to Frigate.

"I assume, since you've reported nothing, you saw nothing."

"Right."

"The machine could have gone in any direction in this maze. We'll wait until Nur gets here."

"If the Snark didn't catch him," Frigate said.

"You're so optimistic," Aphra said.

"I just like to consider every possibility," Frigate said somewhat heatedly. "It's not my fault that negative possibilities always outnumber the positive."

"They don't. You just see the dark chances easier than you see the bright ones."

Burton looked at his wristwatch. Five minutes had passed since the machine had broken through. He would wait a total of thirty. If Nur did not show by then, they would go back to their apartments. There they might have to wait for a while until Turpin, Alice, and Li Po returned from searching for them. If, that is, they had indeed gone out to look for them. Logic might tell them to stay together in one apartment for defense.

A voice startled them. It was Nur's, speaking from just outside the nearest brick wall.

"Don't shoot. It's I. Nur. I have good news."

"Come in," Burton said.

The little man entered. He stripped off some plastic material from his face and removed his gloves and jacket.

"Hot."

Burton stepped outside the doorway. Nur's chair, equipped with an enclosure like Frigate's, was parked by the wall. Burton went inside. Nur was smiling, as well he might.

"I caught the Snark outside her secret room. I came speeding out of the dark part of the corridor and yelled at her to surrender. She refused; she started to take her beamer from her holster. So I shot her."

"Her?" Burton said.

"Yes. We knew that the unknown could be of either sex, but we spoke of her as him so much that we'd fallen into the habit of thinking that she must be a he. The rest of you did, anyway. I did not."

Nur said it would be best if he took them to the scene of the discovery and then explained what had happened. They followed him in their chairs through the breach in the wall, went down one corridor, turned, and stopped a hundred feet from the corner. The unknown lay on her back, eyes and mouth open, a thin cauterized wound on her throat showing where Nur's beam had pierced it from front to back. She was short and slim and clothed in scarlet shirt, sky-blue slacks, and yellow sandals. A beamer lay near one open hand on the floor.

"She's Mongolian," Nur said. That he would point out the obvious showed that he was not as calm as he seemed. "I don't know if she's Chinese, Japanese, or of some other Mongolian nationality. Li Po might be able to tell us. But it's irrelevant."

There was a large circular opening in the wall, the doorwheel having rolled within the wall recess. Beyond would be her apartment, where she had hidden while keeping herself well informed of the movements of the eight. Wall-screens showed all the rooms in their apartments. The beds of Alice, Tom Turpin, and Li Po were empty; another screen displayed them at a table, playing cards in Turpin's apartment. If they were alarmed, they did not show it. Apparently, they had decided that their colleagues had disappeared because Burton was carrying out one of his secret plans, or they had stayed together for safety. As it turned out, they had elected to hole up for both reasons.

Burton would, however, have to endure their reproaches when he returned to the apartment. He could bear them easily because he came with victory in his pocket.

The night before, Peter Frigate and Nur el-Musafir had gone to their bedrooms. They had hoped that the Snark would be sleeping and that the Computer would awaken the Snark only if it detected someone leaving the suite to enter the corridor. The only detectors on, they hoped, would be the heat devices. They were praying that no video screen would be on the corridor wall facing the suite door.

The two ordered from their converters a pair of suits and helmets for them and enclosures for the chairs. This could have been reported to the Snark, but they were gambling that the Computer—if it had recorded these actions—would not submit them to the Snark until the Snark awoke.

Clad in the heat-retaining outfits, carrying the enclosures, Frigate and Nur had left the suite. And the wall sensors had not been activated by them. The unknown, not having made provisions for such deceptions, had slept on. Unlike the Computer, she could have imagined these, but she had not done so.

"We were very lucky," Burton said. "Events turned out to favor us, and they could just as easily not have done so. In fact, the probabilities that we would succeed were not very high."

"You think that we were too lucky," Nur said. Burton waited for him to elaborate, but Nur said, "The first thing I thought of when I killed her . . . I only meant to wound her . . . was that she would have arranged for an automatic and immediate resurrection."

They followed the Moor into the room. At one corner was a converter, and a few feet near it, sprawled facedown, was another body of the woman. The auxiliary computer console had been destroyed by beamer fire.

"I came into this room as soon as I'd killed her," Nur said. "Her body had just formed, and she was running to get a beamer on a table. I told her to stop. She ignored me, and so I shot her. I immediately rayed the computer and so prevented a third resurrection. Unfortunately, the ray also destroyed her body-recording."

He led Burton to the ruin and pointed at a section that had been cut off. Inside was a blackish, half-melted, cranberry-sized object that had held everything needed to duplicate the body down to the submolecular level.

"I would be devastated with remorse and grief if I thought I had forever eliminated her chance of being resurrected again. But I'm sure that she must have another recording in the Computer file. I doubt that we can reach it, though. She would have inhibited the Computer from enabling us to find it."

"We'll see," Burton said. "You're probably right, though."

"Who the hell was she?" Frigate said. "What was she doing here? Loga said that all the Ethicals and their Agents were dead. If he was right, then she wasn't one of them. But what else could she be?"

"One of Loga's enemies, otherwise she wouldn't have eliminated him," Nur said. "But if she wasn't an Ethical or Agent, what reason would she have to do away with him? If she just wanted complete power, why didn't she kill us?"

Aphra said, slowly, "Perhaps Monat the Operator was more far-seeing than Loga expected. Perhaps Monat made arrangements for an Agent, this woman, to be resurrected if certain events happened. Certain events in general, I mean. Monat could not have anticipated all events in particular."

Burton requested the Computer to identify the dead woman. It replied that the data was unavailable, and it would not or could not say why.

Burton asked it if the dead woman's body-recording was in its files.

The Computer said that it was unavailable.

"One more mystery," said Frigate, and he groaned.

Burton asked the Computer for the location of the machine that had broken through the barricade walls. As he had expected, he was told that that information was also unavailable.

"I've seen all the robots the tower contains," Burton said. "I had the Computer show them on a screen. That machine was not among them."

The woman might have had it made for her by the Computer just to break down the walls.

Nur and Frigate dragged the body from the corridor and laid it down by the body near the cabinet. Stretched out, faceup, they looked like identical twins.

"Shall we have them disintegrated in the converter?" Nur said.

"One of them," Burton said. "I want the Computer to examine the other."

"So you can see if she has a black ball in her brain?"

Burton grimaced. Nur always seemed to be able to read his mind.

"Yes."

The two dumped one body into a cabinet and ordered the Computer to get rid of it. White light filled the cabinet, and, when they looked through the window in the door, the cabinet was empty. There were not even ashes in it.

The other corpse was placed on a table above which was a huge dome-shaped device. Though there was no display of energy, the interior of the body was shown on a screen in a series of images. Burton had the Computer run the images back to the one he wanted. There *was* a tiny black sphere on the forebrain. This had been surgically implanted and, acting at a subvocalized codeword, would release a poison into the bearer's body, killing it instantly.

"So . . . she was an Agent."

"But we still don't know when she came here or what her ultimate intentions were," Frigate said.

"For the moment," Burton said, "we don't have to. It's enough that we've gotten rid of the Snark. Now we're on our own, free."

They were, however, free only in some senses. Burton asked the Computer if the overrides installed by the woman were now removed. It replied that they were not.

"When would they be released?"

The Computer did not know.

"We're stymied," Frigate said.

"Not forever," Burton replied. He was not as confident as he sounded.

On that perhaps forever-lost Earth, so far in distance and time, in A.D. 1880 in the city of London, England, appeared a privately printed book. It was titled *The Kasîdah of Hâjî Abdû El-Yezdî*, A Lay of the Higher Law. Translated and annotated by His Friend and Pupil F. B. The initials stood for Frank Baker, a nom de plume of Captain Richard Francis Burton. "Frank" was from his middle name; "Baker" was his mother's maiden surname. Not until after his death would his true name be appended to a reprint.

The poem, set in distichs imitating the classical Arab form, was supposed to be the work of a Persian Sufi, Haji Abdu of the city of Yezdi in Persia. Haji was a title borne by any Moslem who had made a pilgrimage to Mecca. Burton himself, having made the pilgrimage, disguised as a Moslem, could call himself a Haji. In this poem, Burton poured out his wisdom, pessimism, vast knowledge, and agnosticism, the Burtonian World-View and World-Pain. As Frank Baker, he had annotated the poem by "Abdu" and written an afterword that expressed a somewhat cynical and laughing view of himself. The laughter was, however, sad.

The preface summed up his philosophy, formed after fifty-nine years of wandering over the only planet he would ever know—or so he thought at the time.

TO THE READER

The Translator has ventured to entitle a "Lay of the Higher Law" the following composition, which aims at being in advance of its time; and he has not feared the danger of collision with such unpleasant forms as the "Higher Culture!"

The principles which justify the name are as follows: The Author asserts that Happiness and Misery are equally divided and distributed in the world.

(Frigate's comment on this statement was that it could be valid. But if Burton meant that *individuals* got an equal share of happiness and misery, he was wrong. Some people staggered along under a great burden of misery and had little happiness to lighten their load. Others had far more than their share of happiness. Anyway, Burton had not defined what he meant by happiness and misery. Though, of course, he didn't have to do that for misery. Everybody knew what that was. Happiness, however, what was that? A mere freedom from pain and trouble? Or a positive quality? Was contentment happiness? Or did you have to be joyous to be happy?)

He makes Self-cultivation, with due regard to others, the sole and sufficient object of human life.

(What about your children? Alice had said. You have to cultivate them more than you do yourself so that they'll be better, happier, and more adjusted than yourself. Every generation should be an improvement on the previous. I'll admit, however, that it seldoms happens. Perhaps you're right in that you can't properly cultivate your children if you have not properly cultivated yourself. But you didn't have any children, did you?)

(Self-cultivation is a major and vital principle, Nur had said. We Sufis stress it, keeping in mind that it demands self-discipline, compassion, and intelligence. But most people carry it to the extreme and make self-cultivation self-centeredness. This is not surprising. Mankind always does things to excess. Most people do, that is.)

He suggests that the affections, the sympathies, and the "divine gift of Pity" are man's highest enjoyments.

(A pinch of pity adds savor to the soup of life, Nur said. Too much spoils it. Pity may lead to sentimentality and maudlinism.)

(Pity breeds a sense of superiority, Frigate had said. It also leads to self-pity. Not that I'm decrying that. There's an exquisite joy in self-pity, if it's indulged in now and then, here and there, and you end up laughing at yourself.)

(You forgot to include sex, Aphra Behn had said. Though I suppose that sex is part of the affections and sympathies.)

(Creating something, a painting, a poem, music, a book, a statue, a piece of furniture, childbirth, raising a child properly, these are man's—and woman's—highest enjoyments, Frigate had added. Though there's much to be said for creating pristine sparkling bullshit, too.)

He advocates suspension of judgment, with a proper suspicion of "Facts, the idlest of superstitions."

(But there comes a time when you must judge, Nur had said. First, though, you must be sure that you are qualified to judge. Who knows that?)

(One person's facts are another's superstition, Frigate had said. What does that mean, by the way?)

(You can believe only in what you see, Li Po had said. And even then you can't be sure. Perhaps you can really believe only in what you have not seen, what you've imagined. Dragons and fairies exist because I believe in them. A rock is a fact, and so is my imagination.)

Finally, although destructive to appearance, he is essentially reconstructive.

(Man is the only animal who thinks of the should-be rather than the what-is, Nur had said. Which is why man is the only animal who consciously changes the environment to suit himself. And usually spoils it because of his stupidity and excess. There are exceptions to this rule, of course.)

(A fine statement, Alice had said. But Dick Burton has always been self-destructive. When, if ever, will he stop destroying himself?)

For other details concerning the Poem and the Poet, the curious reader is referred to the end of the volume.

Vienna, Nov., 1880   F. B.

(Has it occurred to you, Nur had said, that you are nearing the end of that book you call Richard Francis Burton? It's been published in two volumes, Earth-Burton and Riverworld-Burton. This tower may be The End.)

(It's always been an excellent philosophy to live as if you're going to die in the next hour, Frigate had said. Everybody agrees on that, but the only people who live it are those who know they're going to die soon. And not even then.)

(That's why I like to go to bed whenever possible, Aphra had said. Marcelin, are you in the mood?)

(Even the most ardent soldier needs to go to a rest camp now and then, de Marbot said. At the moment, I am an old, weary and saddlesore veteran.)

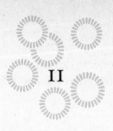

II

Burton also felt like a weary, saddlesore veteran. He had been riding himself—and others—too hard for too long. Now that he had crossed the last of hundreds of obstacles that had had to be dealt with at once, he needed rest and recreation. The problems to be solved, those presented by the Computer, could be tackled later.

Yet, he thought, as he looked into a mirror, *I do not look as if I had lived for sixty-nine years on Earth and sixty-seven years here. My face is not that of a 136-year-old man. It is the face I had when I was a youth of twenty-five.* Minus the long Satan-black drooping moustache, a hairy crescent moon. The Ethicals had arranged that the resurrected males lack facial hair, an arrangement that Burton had always resented. It was true that men did not have to shave, but what about the feelings—the rights—of those who desired moustaches and beards?

Now that I am in the tower, he thought, *why not change those despotic arrangements? Surely there must be a way to start the hair growing again on my face.*

On Earth, he had been afflicted—perhaps afflicted was too strong a word—marked with a slight strabismus. He had a "wandering eye." In more senses than one. This small fault had been corrected by the Computer when he had been raised from the dead in the Rivervalley.

So, loss of beard weighed against correction of focus. But now, why could he not have both?

He made a note to look into that question.

"Brow of a god, jaw of a devil" some impressionable biographer had written of him. An accurate description, however. And one that described the two personae within him, the one who lusted for success and the one who lusted for defeat.

If, that is, the books written about him were correct in their judgments.

Some of them were on the table now. He had requested a few of the titles suggested by Frigate, and the Computer had printed and bound them for him and deposited their reproductions in a converter. The best, so Frigate said, was *The Devil Drives,* written by an American woman, Fawn M. Brodie, first published in 1967.

"I gave up my intention to write a biography of you when that came out," Frigate had said. "But its excellence and wide inclusiveness did not keep others from writing biographies of you after hers. They lacked good judgment. However, you may not like *The Devil Drives.* Brodie couldn't keep from analyzing you in Freudian terms. On the other hand, perhaps you can tell me if she was right or not. But then, you'd be the last person to know, wouldn't you?"

Burton had not read the text yet, but he had looked at the reproductions of photographs. There was one of him at the age of fifty-one, painted by the famous artist Sir Frederick Leighton, and displayed in the National Portrait Gallery in London. He did look fierce, Elizabethan, buccaneerish. Leighton had posed him at such an angle as to catch the high forehead, the swelling supraorbital ridges, the thick eyebrows, the driven hungry expression of his eyes, the thrusting chin, the high cheekbones. The scar left from a Somali spear was prominent; Leighton had insisted on showing that, and Burton had not objected. A scar, if honorably gotten, was a form of medal, and he, who should have been covered with real medals, had been slighted.

"Partly your own fault," Frigate had said. "I can understand and sympathize with that. I, too, was, am, self-defeating."

"My family motto was 'Honour, not Honours.'"

Opposite the Leighton portrait was a photograph of his wife, Isabel, made in 1869, when she was thirty-eight. She looked buxom, regal, and handsome. Like a kindly but domineering mother, he thought. A few pages back was a portrait of her done by the French artist Louis Desanges in 1861, when she had married

Burton. She looked young, loving, and optimistic. Beneath her was the Desanges painting of Burton done at the same time. She was thirty; he, forty. His moustache dropped almost to his shoulder bones, and he certainly looked dark and fierce. And how thick his lips were. Which had suggested to certain biographers, and others, an overly sensual nature. How thin and prim and pursed were Isabel's lips. A flaw in an otherwise perfectly beautiful face. Thin lips. Thick lips. Love, tenderness, and cheerfulness versus fierceness, ambitiousness, and pessimism. Isabel, blond; he, dark.

He turned the pages to a photograph of him at sixty-nine in 1890 and another of himself and Isabel in the same year, same place, Trieste. It had been taken by Doctor Baker, his personal physician, under a tree in the backyard. Burton sat on a chair, not visible in the photograph, one hand on the knob of his iron cane, the other draped over his right wrist. The fingers looked skeletal: Death's own hand. He wore a tall gray plug hat, a stiff white collar, and a gray morning coat. The eyes in the gaunt face looked like those of a dying prisoner. Which, in a sense, he was. Little of the fierceness evident in the earlier pictures was there.

By his side, looking down at him, one white hand held up, a finger extended as if she were chiding him, was Lady Isabel. Fat, fat, fat. While he shriveled, she expanded. Yet, according to Frigate, though she knew that he was dying, she bore in herself the seeds of death, a cancer. She had not said a word to him about it; she had not wanted to upset him.

In her black dress and hood, she looked like a nun, a nurse nun. Kindly but firm. No nonsense.

He contrasted the youthful face in the mirror with that in the photograph. Those old old eyes. Sunken, despairing, lost. Those of a prisoner who had no hope of bail or pardon. Moons in eclipse.

He remembered how at Trieste in September, the last month of his life, he had purchased caged birds in the market, taken them home, and set them free. And how, one day, he had stopped before a monkey in a cage. "What crime did you commit in some other world, Jocko, that you are now caged and tormented and going through your purgatory?" And, shaking his head, walking away, he had muttered, "I wonder what he did? I wonder what he did?"

This world, the Riverworld, was a purgatory, if what the Ethicals said was true. Purgatory was the hardest of the three afterworlds, heaven, purgatory, and hell. In heaven you were free and ecstatic and knew that the future would always be good. In hell, though you suffered, you knew for once and all what your future would be. You did not have to strive for freedom; you knew that you would never attain it. But in purgatory you knew that you were going either to hell or to heaven, and it was up to you where you went. With the joys and freedom of heaven as a carrot, you strove like hell in purgatory. You knew the theory of how to get a ticket to heaven. But the practice . . . ah, the practice . . . that eluded you. You snatched it away from yourself.

Earth had bristled with carrots of many kinds: physical, mental, spiritual, economic, political. Of these, one of the greatest, if not the greatest, was sex.

Frigate had once written a story in which God had made all animals, hence humans, unisex. Every species lacked males; only females existed. Women impregnated themselves by eating fruit from sperm trees. Cross-fertilization was a very intricate procedure in the story, the women shedding genes with their excretion and the trees picking these up through their roots. Thus, males were unnecessary and not included in the parallel world Frigate had imagined.

Every three years, women were afflicted with arboreal frenzy and compulsively devoured the fruit until they became pregnant. In the meantime, women fell in love with one another, lived amicably or passionately or angrily with one another, were jealous, committed adultery, and, of course, often practiced erotic deviations. One of which, not uncommon, was falling in love with a certain tree and eating fruit out of season.

The main plot of the story was about the insane jealousy of a woman who, thinking that she had been cuckolded by her lover's tree, chopped it down. Grief-stricken, the lover went into a nunnery.

A subplot of the story concerned a science-fiction writer who had imagined another world in which there were no sperm trees.

Instead, woman had mates who were their counterparts physically except that they had no mammaries and were equipped with a rodlike organ that shot seeds into the uteruses of their lovers.

This method, according to the science-fiction writer in Frigate's story, was a much better method and also eliminated the competition for trees. The mates with the rods were much like the trees in that their vegetable nature made them subservient to the females. But, unlike the trees, they were useful for something besides reproduction. They did the housework and field-work and took care of the babies while women played bridge or attended political meetings.

In the end, however, the rod-creatures, being more human than vegetable and more muscular than the females, rebelled and made the women their servants.

Burton, hearing Frigate's story, had suggested that a better idea would have been to make the humans of one sex, the male, and have them impregnate the trees. The males would also get most of their food from the fruit of the trees. However, being human, the males would want power, and they would war among themselves for the trees. The victors would be rewarded with vast arboreal harems. The defeated would either be killed or driven into the woods to satisfy themselves with an inferior species of vegetation, a bush which could be screwed but which could not bear children.

"A good idea," Frigate had said, "but who would take care of the infants? Trees can't. Besides, the victorious male, the owner of the harem, or grove, would be so busy guarding his trees from other males that he would neglect the infants. Most of them would die. And if he were overcome by another male, his infants would be left to die or perhaps be killed by the conqueror. The victor would not want to raise the other man's children.

"There doesn't seem to be any perfect means for reproduction and caretaking of the infant, does there?" Frigate had said. "Perhaps God knew what He was doing when He made us male and female."

"Perhaps He was limited in His choices and took the best one. Perhaps perfection is not possible in this universe. Or, if it is, perfection rules out progress. The amoeba is perfect, but it can't evolve into something different. Or, if it does, it ceases to be an amoeba and must give up perfection for certain advantages, balanced or unbalanced with certain disadvantages."

And so the splitting of *Homo sapiens* into two species in the real world and the vagaries of Fate brought together Lieutenant General Joseph Netterville Burton and Martha Baker, the prig and hypochondriac father and the child-spoiling and seductive but moralistic mother. They had gotten married after a short courtship, possibly because the retired officer on half-pay had been induced by Martha's fortune to marry her. He had once had money, but he could not hang onto it. Though he despised gamblers, he did not think that speculation in the market was un-Christian.

On a night circa June 19, 1820, the lieutenant general had launched millions of spermatozoa into the heiress' womb, and one wriggler had beaten the others to the egg waiting in its lair. The chance combination of genes had resulted in Richard Francis Burton, eldest of three siblings, born March 19, 1821, in Torquay, Devonshire, England. Richard's mother had been lucky in not being infected by puerperal fever, which killed so many women giving birth in those days. Richard was also lucky in that he caught only one of the childhood diseases that put so many in the graveyard then. Measles laid him low, but he survived unharmed.

His mother's father was so delighted when his daughter bore a red-headed and blue-eyed son that he considered changing his will and giving the bulk of his estate to Richard instead of Martha's half-brother. Mrs. Burton fought against this, an act for which Richard never really forgave his mother. Finally, the grandfather decided that he would ignore his daughter's arguments and arrange for his beloved grandson to inherit. Unfortunately, Mr. Baker died of a heart attack as he started to get into the carriage that was to take him to his solicitor. The son got the money, was cheated out of it by a sharpster, and died in poverty. A short time later, Richard's red hair turned to jet black and his blue eyes to a deep brown. This was the first of his many disguises, though not, in this case, the first deliberately assumed.

It was his mother's infatuation with her brother that had caused the first of Burton's many misfortunes. Or so Burton had always thought. If he had been independently wealthy, he, a thoroughly undisciplined and argumentative man, would not have had to endure military life so long in order to support himself. He would not have been deprived of the money needed to make his African explorations thoroughly successful.

And his father's decision to go to the Continent, where life was cheaper and where he might find a cure for his more-or-less imaginary ills, had cut off the father's connections with old school friends who might have advanced his son's career. It also made Burton a wanderer, rootless, one who never felt at home in England. Though it was true, as Frigate pointed out, that he had never felt at home anywhere.

He could not abide to stay in one place more than a week. After that, his restlessness drove him on. Or, if circumstances forced him to stay, he suffered.

Which meant that he was indeed suffering here.

"You could move from one apartment to another," Nur had said to him. "I doubt that that would satisfy you. This is a small world, and you can take only small trips. Anyway, why move? You can change your apartment so that it looks like another world. And when you're tired of that, change it again. You may travel from Africa to America without taking a step."

"You were a Pisces," Frigate had said. "The fish. Ruled by Neptune and Jupiter and associated with the twelfth house. The principle of Neptune is idealism and that of Jupiter is expansion. Pisces harmonizes. Pisces' positive qualities make you intuitive, sympathetic, and artistic. Its negative qualities tend to make you a martyr, indecisive, and melancholy. The characteristics and activities of the twelfth house are the unconscious mind, institutions, banks, prisons, universities, libraries, hospitals, hidden enemies, intuition, inspiration, solitary pursuits, dream and sleep patterns, and your pets are large."

"Sheer jobbernowlry, darkest superstition," Burton had said.

"Yes. But you have always been a fish out of water. Idealistic, though cynical. Expansive, certainly. You've tried to be everything. You have tried to harmonize many fields, synthesize them. You are intuitive, sympathetic, and artistic. Certainly, you've made a martyr of yourself. You have often been indecisive. And melancholy! Read your own books.

"As for the unconscious or subconscious, you were more than an explorer of unknown lands. You also explored the darkest Africas of the human mind. You had many hidden enemies, though you also had many open enemies. You did depend on intuitions hunches, quite often. You loved the solitary pursuits: scholarship and writing. As for institutions, you did not like to work in them but you studied and analyzed them. As for dream and sleep patterns, you were fascinated by them, and you became a skilled hypnotist.

"Large pets. That seems not to be true. Yours were mostly bull terriers and gamecocks and monkeys. But you did love horses."

"I could take any one of the other zodiacal signs or all of them," Burton had said, sneering, "and I could show you how each and all would apply most appropriately to me. Or to you. Or any of us."

"Probably," Frigate had said. "But it's fun to dabble in astrology, if only to demonstrate that it doesn't work. However . . ."

Nur and Frigate were convinced that the universe was one cosmic spiderweb, and a fly landing on one strand sent shivers through the entire web. Someone sneezing on a planet of Mizrab somehow might cause a Chinese peasant to stub his toe on a rock.

"Environment is as important as genes, but the environment is much vaster than most people think."

"Everything is," Burton had replied.

He was thinking of this when the wall before him began glowing. He straightened up and leaned back. This was going to be a much larger screen than usual. When it ceased growing it was ten feet across.

"Well?" he said as the expected face, one of the seven, did not appear. Instead, the light dimmed until it was a blackness on the gray of the wall. Faint noises came from it.

He told the Computer to amplify them and leaned forward. The sounds were as faint as before. He repeated his command; the Computer failed to comply.

Suddenly, light made a ragged hole in the center of the screen, and the sounds loudened, though they were still unintelligible. The hole expanded, and he was looking at something white and streaked with blood. Something wet with other than blood.

"Here comes the little devil," someone said.

Burton shot from the chair.

"Good God!"

He was seeing through someone's eyes. The white thing was a sheet; the water, that which burst before birth; the red streaks, blood. The voice was unfamiliar. But the scream that drowned it out was, he did not know how he knew but he knew, his mother's.

Suddenly, the screen showed him more, though it was a dim vision. Around him was a room containing giants. The screen was blanked out as something passed across it. And then the room rotated, and he glimpsed giant arms, bare from the elbows down, rolled shirt sleeves above. A big bed was turning also, and in it was his mother, sweaty, her hair dank. His mother was young. A giant hand was pulling a sheet over the bare stomach and legs and the bloody hairy home from which he had been pulled.

Now he was upside down. A sharp slap. A thin wailing. His first blow.

"Lusty little devil, isn't he?" a man's voice said.

Burton was witnessing his own birth.

12

Burton could see and hear what was happening to him, to the newborn, rather, but he could not feel its, his, reactions. He felt no pain, except emphatically, when his cord was clipped. Indeed, he did not see the operation, but, when he was picked up, he glimpsed the umbilicus on a towel. Nor did he know that he was being cleaned off until a towel pressed down on his, the baby's eyes. Then he was wrapped in a blanket and placed in his mother's arms. Of this he saw only the nurse approaching with the blanket, her stiff white pinafore, the upper part of his mother, and then her face from underneath.

Presently, his father entered. How young that dark sallow Roman face was! And his father was smiling. This usually happened only when Mr. Burton had made a profit in the stock market, and that was not often.

He shuddered when he saw the doctor's hands. They were being wiped on a towel, not given a thorough scrubbing. Doubtless, the doctor had not bothered to wash his hands before delivering him. It was strange, though, unusual, anyway, that the doctor had personally delivered him. If he remembered correctly, most doctors at that time instructed the nurses or midwives but did not touch the woman in labor. Some did not even see the mother's lower parts, which were hidden by a sheet, but heard the details of the delivery from the midwife and then gave their instructions.

A huge hand, his father's, came down and lifted something from him. The blanket.

"A fine son you've given me, my dear," his father said.

"He's beautiful, beautiful," a croaking voice said. His mother's.

"Now, now," a deep voice said. The doctor's face hove into

view. "We mustn't tire Mrs. Burton. Besides, the little devil seems to be hungry."

At this point, he must have fallen asleep. His next view was of an enormous breast, a swollen, pale red nipple, and his little hands reaching out. Then he saw with one eye a field of pink flesh and the underpart of his wetnurse's face. Mrs. Burton, being a genteel lady, would not have nursed the baby herself.

"I wonder who she was?" Burton muttered. "Some Irish-woman?"

He had a vague memory of his mother having mentioned the nurse's name once. A Mrs. Riley? Kiley?

He was shocked but not so much that he could not think clearly. The Computer had read his memory from his body-recording, reeling it up as a fisherman did a trout. After storing it in a separate file, the Computer was feeding it back to him via the wall-screen. The showing of the whole of it, if done in the same time as that in which the events had occurred, would take a lifetime. However, no one's memory held everything that the person had seen, heard, tasted, felt, and thought. Memory was selective and there were great gaps when the person was sleeping, except when he was dreaming, of course. Thus, it did not take as much time as might have been expected to display all that was in the subject's memory bank.

The film, it was a film of sorts, could be speeded up or slowed down or run backward. The Computer might be doing this now. On the other hand, he could have fallen asleep shortly after birth.

Burton, now watching his diapers being changed by another servant, a maid, wondered why this memory display had been commanded. And by whom?

Before he could question the Computer, several small screens whitened wall areas. Frigate's, Turpin's, and de Marbot's faces appeared. They looked shocked.

"Yes," he said before they could begin talking, "I'm being vis-ited by the past, too. From bloody birth onward."

"It's terrible," Alice said. "And wonderful, too. Awesome. I feel like crying."

Frigate said, "I'll call the others and see if they're going through the same thing." His screen dimmed to gray.

Tom Turpin was weeping.

"I'm telling you, seeing my own momma and poppa and that old shack . . . I don't think I can take it."

Burton glanced at the big screen. There he was again, being lifted toward that titanic breast. He could hear his infant's cry of hunger. The scene faded and was replaced by a view of a blue canopy, and the room rocking. No, a great hand was rocking his cradle.

The screens of the others came on. Seven faces with various emotions looked at him.

Li Po, grinning, said, "It is something indescribable, except for a poet, of course, to see yourself suckled by your mother. But . . . who ordered this?"

"Wait a moment," Burton said, "and I'll ask the Computer."

"I have done that," Nur said. "It says that the who and the why are unavailable. But it did not refuse to tell me the when. The order was given two days ago to start the memory-display this morning."

"Then it must have been given by the woman you killed," Burton said.

"She's the most likely candidate."

"I'm completely at sea about why she ordered this memory-display," Burton said.

"Obviously," Nur said, "it was done to accelerate our ethical advancement. If we're forced to know our past, how we behaved, how others behaved, we'll see our weaknesses, faults, and vices in all their details. Like it or not, we'll have what we were, exactly what we were, rubbed into our noses. Ground into our souls. By watching that inescapable drama and comedy, we might be so strongly affected that we'll take steps to eliminate our undesirable character traits. And then become better human beings."

"Or it might drive us mad," Frigate said.

"More likely it will drive us to ingenious methods to shut it out," Burton said. "Nur, did you ask the Computer to stop the display?"

"Yes. The Computer did not reply. Obviously, the woman's command is another override."

"Just a minute," Burton said.

He walked out of the room into the corridor. The screen had slid along the wall of the big room until he left the room. Now it appeared on the corridor wall opposite him. He cursed and spun on his heels and walked back into the room. The screen accompanied him.

He told the others what had happened. "Apparently, we can't get rid of it. It's like the albatross around the ancient mariner's neck."

Burton shut his eyes. He heard himself screaming. Opening his eyes, he saw the canopy above him and then heard, faintly, the maid's voice. "Saints presarve us! What is it now?"

"I think," he said slowly, "that if we're going to shut this out, we'll have to paint our walls. We can't use the Computer in our apartments, though I suppose we can use the auxiliary computers. And we'll have to wear ear plugs if we want to sleep. There's no way of getting away from this outside the apartments."

"We'll go crazy!" Frigate said.

Nur said, "Surely, the woman must have realized that. Perhaps we'll get relief during certain hours of the day. And at night, too."

Burton asked de Marbot and Behn about the locations of their screens.

"One is on one wall and the other on the wall opposite it," the Frenchman said. "We can take turns, my little diamond and I, watching each other's so charming infancies."

"How the devil can I get any research done with that going on?" Burton muttered.

He said so-long to the others after agreeing to meet them at the swimming pool. The Computer did not refuse to make him a pair of earphones that blocked off the sounds. The only way he could escape the sight on the wall was to stare at the display screen of the auxiliary computer. And he found that he could not concentrate on his work. He was too curious. He could not resist looking at scenes that he did not remember. Yet, after a minute, he got bored. Not much happened to a baby outside of routine, and seeing his parents when they were young quickly lost its interest. They did not talk of anything except him when they were together, and his mother only spoke baby talk. Which he, of course, had been too undeveloped to understand, though he must have responded to her face and the tones of her voice. Now he became sick of them. Not that she was with him much. The people he mostly saw were the wetnurse and the two maids who took turns cleaning him or carrying him around.

At 11:00 A.M. he went to the swimming pool. The screen followed him along the walls. The pasts of the others accompanied them, too. The screens were at first on one of the long walls, then they were on all the walls.

"Familiarity, I hope, will breed deafness and blindness," Aphra said as she came up out of the water next to Burton.

"It'll never be familiar, even though it now has mostly to do with the family," he said. "What it will breed will be shame, grief, and anger. And humiliation. Do you want to see yourself when you were mean, childish, degraded?"

"Oh, I was never mean. And I was never degraded, though others tried to degrade me."

He did not think that she was as unperturbed as she seemed to be. No one could be.

It was difficult to swim and talk and have fun. He could not keep from glancing at the screens.

Frigate bobbed up from the surface of the pool beside Burton.

"Look at that," he said. "I can see myself now."

His mother, a slim woman with Indian-black hair, dark brown eyes, and high cheekbones, was holding her baby up to a mirror. The infant Peter was nude and grinning, his mouth so wide that he looked froglike.

"It's a jolt to see yourself at that age. And I can expect many thousands of mirror images, from the puling baby to the old man of sixty-five. Jesus H. Christ!"

That evening, Frigate asked the Computer when the life-recordings started. It replied that they started from the moment of conception. The Computer could not answer Frigate's question about why the display had not started then. But Frigate and some of the others decided that that was because the nine months in the womb were mostly darkness and silence. They could learn little from it and could easily ignore it.

However, when Frigate asked the Computer to run off his

gestation period and show only those moments when sound did penetrate to the embryo, he was astounded. Many times, though the sounds were muffled, he could clearly hear those close to his mother, and his mother's voice. There were other sounds, too, car motors, locomotive whistles and escaping steam, firecrackers, excretory noises, crashings of fallen glasses or dishes, loud laughter, and, embarrassingly, his parents making love. After two hours of this, Frigate ordered the Computer to stop the recording.

"I suppose that the woman who started this did not do it out of malice," he said. "Its purpose must be to show us, whether or not we want to see it, our weaknesses, vanities, pettinesses, meannesses, selfishnesses, stupid thinking, prejudices, you name it, everything undesirable in us. With, I suppose, an end in mind, a goal. That we should be able to change ourselves for the better. Ethical advancement."

"That's probably true," Nur said. "But . . . why the secrecy on her part? Why did she kill Loga?"

"That's something we'll have to find out," Burton said. "If we can."

The woman who had ordered the merciless recordings had had some compassion, however. At 8:00 P.M. the screens' displays faded out, and they did not reappear until 8:00 A.M. There would be some respite.

Burton left early that evening for his apartment. However, a sufferer from insomnia all his life, he was unable to sleep. After two hours of tossing and turning, his mind filled with scenes from the past-displays, he rose, dressed, and left the apartment. For three hours, he rode his chair through many corridors and into many rooms and up and down many shafts. His wanderings were aimless until he decided to organize his explorations. Why not get a diagram from the Computer and start from the top and work every level thoroughly down to the bottom? He had no goal in mind, no thought that he'd find something new. He was restless, he wanted to keep moving, and, perhaps, he might come across something novel or useful or both.

On the way up to the hangar, his starting point, he changed his mind again. The twelve vast rooms that had been the private worlds of the Council of Twelve beckoned him. They, at least, would offer a variety, something different from the monotonous sameness of corridor and rooms. His tour lasted four hours. When finished with all of them, he knew that he would tell the others that they, too, should explore these fascinating worlds.

Burton visited the hangar again and found it, as far as he could see, unchanged. He counted the craft to make sure that none were missing. That did not mean that the woman Agent had not used one since his last visit.

He returned to his apartment at four in the morning and slept from 4:30 to 7:30. After showering, he decided to go for breakfast at Li Po's. First, he called him to make sure that the Chinese would be his host for today. The handsome, somewhat Mephistophelian face was smiling.

"Yes, I am eager to have you as my guest. I have a surprise for you."

He turned his head and said something in Chinese.

Another face appeared by his. Burton was startled. It was a stranger's, a beautiful Chinese woman's.

13

Some men and women seem to be steam locomotives chug-chugging steadily on their tracks, slowing down uphill but working steadily and running freely downhill. Others are like internal combustion automobiles that take different roads but now and then run out of gas and wait to be refueled.

Li Po seemed to be a rocket with inexhaustible fuel. He was always exploding, propelled here and there, noisy, sometimes obnoxious, but always letting you know that he was not to be ignored. His face, expressions, and gesticulations reminded Burton of the final stanza in Coleridge's *Kubla Khan*:

> *And all should cry, Beware! Beware!*
> *His flashing eyes, his floating hair!*
> *Weave a circle round him thrice,*
> *And close your eyes with holy dread,*
> *For he on honey-dew hath fed,*
> *And drunk the milk of Paradise.*

Li Po, also known as Li T'ai-Po and Tai-Peng, had been born in A.D. 701 in the oasis town of Yarkand. At the time he was born, the vast desert territory did not belong to any Chinese kingdom. Yarkand was on the trade route between Persia and China, and Li Po's great-great-grandfather had come there from China. According to family tradition, he had been banned for some political reason. He brought his wife and children with him, and his oldest son married a Turkic-speaking woman, a Uigur. Their eldest son had married a Chinese woman; the second son of this marriage had taken for wife an Afghani-Uigur woman.

The family had become well-to-do, and, five years after Li Po was born, he went with his parents to the southwest Chinese province of Szechwan. They settled in a city that harbored many foreigners, Zoroastrian Persians, Hindus, Jews, Nestorian Christians, and Muslims from Persia, Afghanistan, and the Mesopotamian area. Li Po knew the languages of all of these and was later to add Korean and some Japanese to his stock.

He was almost an inch over six feet, a height attributed by the Chinese to his foreign blood. At an early age, he began composing poetry and drinking wine. Though he had a great reputation as a drunkard later in life, he was not condemned for this. Heavy drinking was endemic among the upper classes; liquor was regarded as an aid to opening the gate to divine inspiration. The speed with which he could compose poetry while drunk dazzled his contemporaries. Strangely, much was great enough to make many rank him as China's foremost poet.

In his twenties, he began the roving that so many Chinese poets, statesmen, and artists were famous for. For a while, he became a knight-errant, a wanderer who tried to right wrongs by his sword. During this time, he killed several warriors in duels and was widely known as a demon with the blade. Once, he was jailed for killing a man in a tavern brawl but escaped before a sentence could be passed.

Yet, he was very studious and had learned, among other things, the physics and chemistry of his time.

In many respects, he was not only the Byron of his age but also the Burton. Like the latter, he roamed everywhere, became a scholar and a fine swordsman, was politically naive, was very angry at all types of suffering, was versed in many tongues, and was not very discreet or polite.

Unlike most Chinese males, he had empathy for the slavelike bondage and sufferings of the Chinese women. This, however, did not keep him from exploiting them. Even discounting his boasting, he was extraordinarily virile. "Three women at one time are not enough!"

After his knight-errantry days, he lived for a time with a hermit named Tung Yen-tsu on Mount Min in Shu Land. Here he furthered his knowledge and love of Taoist philosophy and became a sort of St. Francis. He and Tung tamed and raised wild birds and taught them to come at the sound of their voices to be fed from their hands.

Chinese "hermits," however, were not like Western anchorites. They were usually men who had retired from public life but lived with their families and retinues of servants and often entertained friends and travelers.

When twenty-five, Li Po left Shu Land to travel through the eastern and northern provinces. He stayed longest at Anlu in Hubei because he had fallen in love with a woman named Hu. She became his first wife and bore him several children before she died.

Once, he traveled with a friend to a famous lake, but the friend died there. Li Po buried the body near the lake, but, since his friend wanted to be buried in his ancestral lot, Li Po dug him up, wrapped him, and carried the corpse on his back for a hundred miles to Wuchang in Hubei.

"I had no money to buy a horse. I had given it all away to the poor."

Li Po's reputation as a poet caused the T'ang emperor, Hsüan Tsung, to summon him to his court in A.D. 742, although the arrogant poet had refused to take the examinations for the civil service. Li Po became disgusted with the laziness and lechery of Hsüan, with the corruption of the court officials, and with the consequent impoverishment and great suffering of the people. Once, commanded to appear before the king to recite his poems, Li Po showed up drunk at the palace and insisted that the chief eunuch, a very powerful official, take off his boots for him. This insured that he would have no friends in court and that the emperor's spies would watch him closely.

It also insured that Li Po would have to travel many places to look for patrons. He did not mind that, since he loved to wander.

His second wife died, and he and his third wife got a divorce by mutual agreement after a very short marriage. His fourth wife would outlive him.

In A.D. 757, the emperor's sixteenth son, the prince of Lin, collected an army and fleet, supposedly to fight the rebel An Lushan. Li Po, not knowing that Lin intended to revolt against his father, joined him.

"I was fifty-seven years old then but very strong and agile for my age. I thought that it was not too late to gain glory for myself as a warrior, and the emperor might change his mind about me and raise me to some high post. At least, he might give me a pension."

Unfortunately, Lin's treason was exposed by an older brother, and his forces were slaughtered. Li Po was sentenced to death—guilty by association—but the emperor decided that Li Po was too great a poet to kill. He was banished, but he was pardoned when he was sixty. On his way home to his fourth wife, he got drunk in a boat and tried to grab his reflection in the water. He fell overboard, caught pneumonia, and died shortly thereafter.

"Were you really convinced at that moment that you could seize your image in the river?" Frigate had said.

"Yes. Had I had one more cup of wine, I could have done it. No one else could, but I would have managed it."

"And what would you have done with it?" Nur had said dryly.

"I would have made it emperor! One Li Po is unconquerable by any fifty men! Two Li Pos would have conquered all of China!"

He had laughed so loudly and long then that the others were convinced that he knew that his boasting was ridiculous. Still, they could not quite be sure.

"The world's greatest wino," Frigate had said.

Li Po had awakened from death on the bank of The River. There he had started his wanderings again, but, as he said, he was used to such a life. On Earth, he had been up and down all of China's great rivers and many of the lesser.

One night, he was aroused in his hut by a masked and hooded man. That stranger was the one who had also wakened Burton and many others to enlist them in his cause. Of the many re-cruited by the renegade Ethical, Loga, Li Po had been one of the very few to get to the tower.

"And what have you learned during your sojourn here?" Nur had said. "How has it changed you for better or worse, if it has?"

"Unlike you, my Muslim if heretical friend, I did not believe in a hereafter. I did agree with The Sage that the spirit-land was none of our business. I thought that when I died, I would become rotten flesh and then dust and that would be that. Awakening by The River was a great shock, the worst in my life. Where were the gods who had raised me from the dead, the gods in whom I had not believed? There were no gods or demons here, only human beings like myself who, though in another world, knew no more about the why and wherefore of it than they had of Earth's. Poor wretches! Poor ignoramuses stumbling in the dark. Where were those who had lit us up once again so that we'd be little flames looking for the mother flame?"

"Where are the snows of yesteryear?" Frigate said. "Easy to answer. They melted and became clouds and became snow again, today's."

At the end of wandering on Earth and the Riverworld, Li Po had reached the tower. He seemed not to have changed, which, Nur said, was regrettable. The Riverworld was designed to make people change. The tall, lean, handsome, devil-faced man with the green eyes and his black hair coiled in a topknot only laughed at that.

"Perfection can change only for the worse."

He had redecorated his suite so that it looked like the palace of the Glorious Emperor. From the Computer's files he had had reproduced many famous Chinese paintings and was painting some of his own works. These were not duplicates of his Terrestrial creations but scenes from the Riverworld.

"I have everything the emperor had and much more. Except, of course, millions of subjects and many wives and concubines. In fact, I have not one wife and so am poorer and more miserable than the lowliest peasant. Not for long, though."

There was one woman whom the historians knew nothing of, though Li Po had written two hundred poems about her. These, however, were among his nine thousand lost works.

In Eastern Lu, a part of twentieth-century Shantung in north China, Li Po had built a house attached to a tavern owned by his fourth wife's family. And in the tavern was a slave girl who served the patrons; her name was Hsing Shih. In English, Star Spoon.

"The most beautiful woman I have ever seen. You will pardon me, Alice, Aphra, when I say that. You two are indeed surpassingly beautiful, but you will surely agree with me, since you're fair-minded for your sex, that you just possibly may not be the most beautiful.

"Star Spoon was quiet and soft-spoken and had elegant manners quite out of place in that tavern and unappreciated by the customers. She was no peasant girl. Her mother had been a concubine of the Glorious Monarch, and Star Spoon was supposed to be his daughter. That paternity, however, was questioned when Star Spoon's mother was caught in adultery with a palace guard. The mother and the lover were beheaded, and Star Spoon, then nine years old, was sold to a wealthy merchant. He took her to his bed when she was ten. After he tired of her, his six sons took their turns with her as they became juveniles. When the merchant lost his fortune and died shortly thereafter, Star Spoon was sold to my father-in-law, the tavern owner. She became his concubine, and she was treated well, relatively speaking anyway, though she had to work in the tavern. After I married his daughter, I came to know Star Spoon well. I fell passionately in love with her. Of course, I do everything passionately. She had a child by me, but he died a few days after birth from a fever. Though I am afraid of nothing, I did not want to cause trouble under my roof. My wife was very jealous and prone to violence. I had a scar on my shoulder from her knife to prove it. So neither Star Spoon nor I ever told anyone who the father was."

If it was only intimate companionship that Li Po wanted, he would have chosen a man. But he needed a female, and his thoughts turned to Hsing Shih. He would find his old comrades later for masculine warmth and uproariousness and mental stimulation.

The first question in locating Star Spoon was: Was she available in the Computer's files?

These began in 97,000 B.C when the predecessors of the Ethicals had landed on Earth. (Loga had said that they started in about 100,000 B.C, but he was speaking loosely, rounding off the figure.) The Computer listed 97,000 B.C as Year One in its chronology. Thus, since Star Spoon had been born in A.D. 721, by Western reckoning, her birth year was 97,724 by computer reckoning.

Li Po had ordered that the search start in that year and in the area where she had been born. Since the Glorious Monarch's palace was a very important place in China, it was probable that Ethical agents had photographed it and its tenants.

The recordings were far from complete, however. It was possible that there were very few films made at this place during the T'ang dynasty. Li Po had, however, reconstructed Star Spoon's features with the aid of the Computer and his memory, which, like Burton's and Nur's, gripped like an eagle's talon.

The Computer had then extrapolated the woman's face backward, as it were, shaping her features as they would have been in childhood.

With this as a model, the Computer had scanned its files for this area and period. And it had located her, not just once but three times. Li Po had been very lucky—so far.

Her *wathan* was now identified from the films, which photographed more than her body. Using this as reference, the Computer scanned the eighteen billion plus *wathans* in the great central well of the tower. If Star Spoon was alive in The Valley, her *wathan* would not be in the well, and Li Po was out of luck. But the Computer found it. Fifteen minutes later, it delivered Star Spoon via the e-m converter to Li Po's apartment.

She was shocked and confused. She had been killed in those horrible days when the east bank of grailstones had failed to provide food for the east bank's inhabitants. She, with hordes of others, had crossed The River in boats to fight for the food supplied to the west bank dwellers. She had not known then that resurrection of the dead had ceased, and so she had expected to awake somewhere along The River.

Instead, here she was in a strange place, one obviously not in The Valley. And who was this fellow countryman grinning like a demon at her?

"Truly, she thought I was a devil at first," Li Po was to say. "She was half-mistaken." He added, "She did not even recognize me until I spoke. Then everything flooded in on her, and she wept for a long time."

It had taken most of the night for him to explain to her just what had happened to him and to her. Then he had allowed her to sleep, though he lusted to get her into bed with him.

"I am not one to force myself upon a woman. She must be willing."

Everyone came to his suite to meet the newcomer. She was

indeed beautiful and delicate, about five feet tall, slim-boned and slim-fleshed but well rounded and long-legged. Her eyes were huge and dark brown, and she was dressed in the same kind of clothes she had worn on Earth. She was not as shy as Li Po had portrayed her. The Riverworld had changed her in that respect. Her voice was, however, low and husky as she spoke to them in Esperanto. She was fluent in a dozen or more languages, but English was not one of them.

Burton was enraged, but, for once, he controlled himself. Star Spoon was a deed done. Reproaching the Chinese for breaking the agreement not to resurrect anybody as yet would upset the woman and only cause Li Po to argue with him or, worse, challenge him to a duel. Burton had lost whatever authority he had. Now that the situation was changed, the danger over, he could no longer be captain of this group of strong individualists. They would pretty much do what they wished.

Burton managed to smile, but his voice betrayed him. He growled, "How many more are you planning to raise?"

"Not many. I am no maniac."

Burton snorted.

"The Six Idlers of the Bamboo Grove, my immortal companions. You'd like them. Women for them and perhaps a few more for me. My honorable parents, my sisters and brothers and an aunt whom I greatly loved. My children. Of course, I have to *find* them first."

Frigate groaned and said, "An invasion. The Yellow Peril all over again."

"What?" Li Po said.

"Nothing. I'm sure that we'll all be happy and pleased."

"I look forward to meeting those you will bring back," Li Po said.

Frigate grinned and clapped Li Po on the shoulder. He was very fond of the poet, though, like the others, he was sometimes irritated by him.

14

Peter Jairus Frigate was born in 1918 in North Terre Haute, Indiana, near the banks of the Wabash River. Though he called himself a rationalist, he believed, or claimed to believe, that each Earthly area had its unique psychic properties. Thus, Vigo County soil had absorbed the peculiar qualities of the Indians who had lived there and of the pioneers who had driven them away and settled there. His own psyche, soaked with the effluvia of Amerindianness and Hoosierness, would never get rid of these no matter how much they evaporated in other climes and times.

"In a sense, I contain redskins and frontiersmen."

His voice reminded people of that of the Montana movie actor, Gary Cooper, but now and then the Hoosier twang appeared in it. He sometimes pronounced "wash" as "warsh," and a "bucket" was sometimes a "pail." "Illinois" more often than not was "Ellinois."

In his childhood, he had been subjected to Christian Science, that melange of Hindu and Buddhist philosophy transmuted into Western religion by the woolly-minded and neurotic Mary Baker Eddy. His parents had originally been Methodist Episcopalian and Baptist, but a "miracle" had occurred when his father's aunt was sent home from a hospital to die of incurable cancer. A friend had talked her into reading *The Key to the Scriptures* and, while she was doing this, the aunt's cancer had remissed. Most of the Frigate family in Terre Haute had become devout disciples of Eddy and of Jesus Christ as Scientist.

The child Peter Frigate had somehow confused the figure of Jesus with those of scientists he read about at the age of seven, Doctors Frankenstein and Doolittle and Van Helsing. Two of these were involved with dead people come to life, and Doolittle, who fused with St. Francis later on, was involved with talking animals. The precocious and highly imaginative youngster visualized the bearded and robed Christ as working in a laboratory when he was not roaming the countryside and preaching.

"Shall we operate now, Judas? I think that that leg goes there, but I don't have the least idea where that eye came from or where it goes."

This conversation would take place when Jesus was trying to raise Lazarus. The problem was complicated by the other bodies that had been put in Lazarus' tomb, before his interment. After lying three days in a hole in a cliff in this hot climate, Lazarus was pretty much decayed and fallen apart, hence the confusion. Hence, also, the gas masks that Jesus and his assistants, Judas and Peter, wore over their surgical masks.

Near them were giant retorts with bubbling liquids and a static generator shooting twisting electrical currents from node to node and other impressive-looking Hollywoodish laboratory equipment. These came, not from the Frankenstein motion picture, which did not appear until 1931, but from a silent movie serial Frigate saw when he was six.

Judas, the treasurer of Dr. Christ's organization, which depended entirely upon voluntary contributions, was nervous about the expense. "This operation will wipe us out," he said hoarsely to the great scientist.

"Yes, but think of the publicity. When the millionaire, Joseph of Arimathea, hears of this, he'll kick in with plenty of shekels. Besides, it's deductible on his income tax."

In later years, when thinking of this scene, Frigate was sure that he had not known about such things as publicity and income tax deductions. He must be reconstructing his childhood imagination. But imagination works backward as well as forward, better in fact.

Perhaps it was this version of Christ as scientist that veered young Frigate toward the reading of science fiction. Though reading heavily in Swift, Twain, Doyle, London, Dumas, Baum, and Homer, he also read the Bible, and an edition of John Bunyan illustrated by Doré. Somewhere, deep in the boiling muddy depths of his unconscious, his religious impulses were mixed with his worship of science as savior of mankind. The early science-fiction magazines and books he read were based on the premise that rationality, logic, and science would get *Homo sapiens* out of the mess it had made during the past hundred thousand years. He had not learned then that, though he lived in a high-technology civilization, the Old Stone Age, the Middle Stone Age, the New Stone Age, the Bronze Age, the Iron Age, and the Dark Ages were in every newborn infant. Baggage that went with every person throughout his or her life. Few there were who would rid themselves of this impedimenta, and no one would ever shuck all of it.

Well, Nur might be an exception.

"There are certain things about those ages that are desirable," Nur had said. "I have not rid myself of them, I am sure."

When Frigate was eleven, his parents slid into religious apathy. They stopped going, for a while, to the First Church of Christ Scientist on Hamilton Boulevard in Peoria. But though they did not want their eldest son to stop attending church, they did not want to transport him every morning to the Christ Scientist Church. So they enrolled him in the Sunday school of the Arcadia Avenue Presbyterian Church, which was within walking distance.

It was here that he ran head-on and at full theological speed into predestination. He had not as yet recovered from the concussion of soul and philosophical trauma resulting from the collision.

"The whole world became for me a convalescent ward after that," Frigate had once told Burton. "Of course, I'm exaggerating somewhat."

Until then, Frigate had been convinced that you were rewarded with Heaven if you lived a life full of good deeds and thoughts and of unshaken doubt in the existence of God and the validity of the Bible.

"The Presbyterians maintained that it did not make any difference whether you thought you were full of grace and were an exemplary Christian. God had decreed thousands of years before you were born, before the making of the universe, in fact, that *this* unborn person would be saved and *that* unborn person would be damned. Their belief was like Twain's theory of predeterminism. From the moment that the first primal atom bumped into the second created atom, a chain of motion was set up the directions of which were fixed by whether the primal atom collided with the second at this angle or that angle and the velocity it was traveling at when it bumped the other. If the angle and velocity had been different, everything that happened from then on would have been different. Your course through life was set. Nothing you did could change it. Everything you did was predetermined. To use twentieth-century computerese, preprogrammed."

The catch was that you could not then say to yourself, "What the hell?" and live a dissolute godless life. You had to behave as if you were a complete Christian. What was worse, you had to *be* one. You had to truly believe; you could not be a hypocrite.

But you would not know until after you'd died whether God had chosen you to fly up to Paradise or to fall into the eternal flames of Hell.

"Actually, if the Presbyterians were right, you could be a wicked person all your life. But if God had marked you as one of the saved, you would repent at the last moment and rise up to eternal bliss. Who, however, was going to take the chance that that would happen?

"I should have told my parents about my spiritual agonies over this. They would have straightened me out by telling me that there was no such thing as predestination and a literal Hell. At least, they would have tried to ease my mind. But I said nothing to them—which gives you an idea of my communicativeness—and I suffered. They, of course, had no idea what I was being taught there in that church within walking distance. A short walk to Despair, Doubt, and Hell."

"Did you really suffer that much?" Burton had said.

"Not all the time. Just now and then, here and there. After all, I was an active healthy boy. And I observed that, if the adults in the church really believed in predestination, they did not behave as if they did. They certainly weren't obsessed with doubts and griefs about their strange doctrine. They paid it lip service in church and forgot about it as soon as they walked out. Maybe sooner.

"Also, reading about Twain's life, I saw that he did not believe in his godless and strictly mechanical universe. He acted as if he had free will even though he talked a lot about its absence from human beings."

At the age of twelve, Frigate became an atheist.

"Rather, I should say, a devout believer in science as our savior. Science as used by rational people. However, I had forgotten that Swift had said, implied, anyway, that most people were Yahoos."

He had hastened to amend and modify his statement. Most people were only Yahooish; only a minority were genuine, dyed-in-the-wool Yahoos. Too big a minority, though.

"Science could only be our savior in a limited sense and then only if not abused. But everything is abused and misused. I did not really learn that I was until thirty-five, though. Midway in my life, like Dante, I was just outside the Gates of Hell."

"It took him a long time to realize that people are irrational most of the time and usually more than that," Nur had said. "What an astounding revelation!"

"Not only the Paleolithic Age but also the bipedal ape lives in us," Burton had said. "I'm not sure, though, that that is not an insult to the apes."

Frigate had maintained for many years that there was no such thing as a soul. But it came to him that if God had not given *Homo sapiens* a soul, then it must make its own soul. He wrote a story based on the idea of artificial souls that insured people the immortality that God, if there was one, had neglected to create.

As far as he knew, no one had ever thought of this, and it made a very good premise for a science-fiction novel. It also made him conscious that, somewhere in him, he still believed that only humanity could save itself. There was no savior to come from Heaven or another planet and redeem humankind.

"I was wrong, yet right," Frigate had said. "Our salvation was the synthetic soul, but it was invented by an extra-Terrestrial species."

"That soul, the *wathan,* is not our salvation," Nur had said. "It is only a means to an end. Salvation must still come from ourselves."

Science and the religious impulse had combined to make the Riverworld and the *wathan,* but these could carry you only so far. At that point, science faded away like a sunset and metaphysics took over.

In the meantime, you had to live one second after the other, move with the flow of time. Like it or not, you had to sleep and eat and excrete and, as Burton said, cultivate your self with due regard to others. You might ask questions, but if you did not get answers just now, you could hope that you would someday.

Frigate was introduced to Star Spoon and talked with her for a while, though he had some difficulty understanding her. She spoke Esperanto, but since she had lived in an area occupied mainly by eighth-century A.D. Chinese and Italic Sabines of the fifth century B.C., her Esperanto had many unfamiliar loan words. After a while, he excused himself and went to his apartment. Like Burton, he was troubled because Li Po had not consulted his companions about Star Spoon. The group did need new members; eight was not enough to give the variety and freshness needed. They were close because of the hardships suffered while struggling to reach their goal, but this very intimacy had made them a family, and like most families, they got on one another's nerves at times and quarreled about trivialities. Nur excepted.

Frigate thought it was both right and necessary to raise others. But these should be carefully considered before being admitted. They did not need troublemakers.

Li Po had opened the floodgates. The rest of the group would want to raise their own dead, and there was, as yet, no limit on the numbers that could be brought in or any qualifications for them.

Burton felt as Frigate and, doubtless, most of the group did. Yet he was helpless, so far, to control these individualists. He was brave, strong, and dashing, but he was not a good leader except in situations that called for immediate and violent action. He just was not a peacetime administrator.

Nur el-Musafir should be the one whom the group should follow and obey now, but he had not volunteered for the office and probably would not. Of them all, he was the most foresighted. He knew that no one could control the inevitable movement to anarchy.

15

Burton saw how shocked Star Spoon was when a screen displayed her birth. He had expected that she would be, but he was surprised that she showed so much emotion about it. Like most Westerners, he regarded the Chinese as a sternly self-controlled nation, the "inscrutable Oriental." Li Po was uninhibited, close to manic, but then he was the exception that tested the rule. In an aside to Li Po, Burton spoke of this. The Chinese laughed loudly and said, "It may be that the Chinese of your time were inexpressive—when around strangers or in threatening situations. But Star Spoon and I are of what you call the seventh century. Do you think that we are the same as the Chinese of your time, any more than Englishmen of the seventh century were like those of your time?"

"I am sufficiently rebuked and chastened," Burton said.

Nur said, "She may be disturbed not so much by what she sees now as by what she knows she is going to see."

It was impossible to be at ease when their pasts were being shown. Burton proposed that they choose an empty apartment for their communal meals from now on. They would paint its walls so that the screens could not be seen. They agreed that that was an excellent idea, after which Burton returned to his apartment. He ordered two androids, protein robots, from the Computer, gave the specifications, then waited exactly thirteen seconds for them to appear in the converters. It had amused him to give one the face of Colonel Henry Corsellis, late of the Native Eighteenth Bombay Infantry, and the other the face of Sir James Outram, late hero of the Indian Mutiny and Her Majesty's Resident at Aden. Corsellis had become Burton's enemy when, during officer's mess, Burton had been improvising poems rhyming with his fellows' names. He had ignored Corsellis' because he knew how hot-tempered and sensitive his commander was. But, when the colonel had demanded that Burton made a couplet based on his name, Burton had recited:

> *Here lieth the body of Colonel Corsellis;*
> *The rest of the fellow, I fancy, in hell is.*

As expected, the colonel had become angry, and they had quarreled. From then on, Corsellis did Burton every disservice that he could.

"Which I should have anticipated. Perhaps I did."

Burton had come into disfavor with Outram, then a general in the Indian army, when Sir Charles Napier, whom Burton greatly admired, got into a long and bitter feud with Outram. Burton had defended Napier with articles and letters for the *Karachee Advertiser*, a private publication devoted to Napier's defense. Outram had resented these and marked Burton down for attack if he ever had an opportunity. Years later, when Burton, then a captain in the Indian army, had requested permission to explore Somalia in Africa, Outram had refused his request. Though overriden by his superiors, Outram had then limited Burton's plans for exploration.

Now the androids, whom he called Corsellis and Outram, stood before him. The former was in the uniform of a colonel; the latter, in civilian clothes. Their faces were expressionless; they would smile only at request and then only if they had been programmed to do so.

"You two arseholes will, as required, paint the rooms with the materials you'll find in that converter there," he said, pointing.

The androids did not follow his gesture, so he said, "Look over there. Where my finger is pointing. That cabinet is the converter I mean. The paint's in sprayers. You know how to use those. The ladders are also in there. You know how to put the sections together and how to use them."

Burton had thought of programming them to kiss his ass

before they started the job, but he had rejected the childish and essentially meaningless act. If he resurrected the real Outram and Corsellis and got them to kiss his ass, that would be different. But they would refuse, of course. Besides, he could not just bring them to life for a while, even if he would have liked them to do menial labor for him. They were human beings, and he could not have them disintegrated when he was through with them.

Nevertheless, he did get some satisfaction, even chuckled, when he saw the two walk to the converter. If only he could arrange it so that the real men, the models, could at least see his androids. They would be outraged, furiously indignant.

He sighed. That form of revenge was petty, and he knew it. If Nur could see this, he would say, "It is beneath you. You have become no better than they."

"I should turn the other cheek?" Burton muttered, continuing aloud the imaginary conversation. "I am not a Christian. Moreover, I never met a Christian who turned the other cheek when slapped."

He would have to keep the identity of the simulacra to himself and that deprived him of the pleasure he had in this. Alice could get away with giving her androids the faces of Gladstone and Disraeli because she had no animus toward them. It was, to her, merely amusing to be waited on by two prime ministers.

He left his apartment for a while, though he was not sure that he should leave the androids unattended. If they had a problem that a sentient painter could have solved, they would either ignore it and go on or stop and wait for orders. He, however, was angered by the events on the past-display screen, not yet covered over. Its sequence was not in proper chronology; it had jumped to when he was three years old and being whipped savagely by his tutor. "All I did was tell him that he had a breath like a sick dog's," Burton said. "And that he farted overmuch. That's all."

Burton could not read at that age, but the tutor had started to teach him to speak Latin. At the age of ten, Burton would know far more Latin than his tutor and speak it fluently.

"But that was in spite of him, not because of him. I had a natal love for languages that no brutal pedant could scourge from me. Unfortunately, most boys hated the subject as much as they hated their teachers' rods. In their minds, one was the other."

The screen displaying his past appeared on the wall beside the door after it had been shut. Burton sat down in the flying chair parked by the door and turned it so that his back was to the wall. Immediately, the screen appeared on the wall opposite him. Burton put soundproof devices over his ears and a long eyeshade on his head. While he kept his eyes lowered, he could not see the screen. Apparently, the Computer had not had orders to shift the screen to the floor. Thus, Burton could read the book he held close to his chest without seeing or hearing the display.

The book was the Roman emperor Claudius' grammar of the Etruscan language, located and reproduced for Burton by the Computer. It had been lost sometime during the Dark Ages of Earth, but an Ethical agent had photographed a copy of it shortly after Claudius had finished it. While Earth linguists were bemoaning its loss, it had been sitting in the records of the Ethicals for a thousand years.

Despite his absorption in the book, he could not keep from glancing at the screen. Now he, as the child, had been swung around to face the red angry features of McClanahan, the tutor. Though Burton could not hear the man, he could read the writhing lips. And he suddenly remembered other occasions when McClanahan had hurled invective and accusations at him, and the prophecy that he would go to Hell when he died—if not sooner.

Burton could not see his own lips, but he was screaming, "I'll meet you there!" His view shifted. He was facing the other way, and the tutor was thrashing him again. He would not be crying or yelling; he kept his lips stubbornly locked so that the tutor would not have the satisfaction of knowing how much he was hurting him. That only made McClanahan angrier, and he increased the severity of his strokes. But he was afraid to whip him as much as he would have liked to. Though Burton's father approved of instilling love of learning and obedience with the rod, he would not have stood for a whipping near to death. The tutor knew that the child would not scream until he was almost dead, and perhaps not then.

Burton turned his head away and focused his intentness into a sword, the tip of which raked across the words of the grammar. He finished two pages, then closed his eyes and projected the pages, as if they had been a film, on the screen of his mind. After which, he opened his eyes to check his accuracy. He smiled. His memory had been one hundred percent perfect.

Book-learning a language was a step toward mastering it. But he should resurrect an Etruscan and imbibe the living speech. However—there was always a however—what would he do with the Etruscan after he had finished with her?

It was then that he thought of the possibility of reading the recordings of the dead in the files. Why not have the Computer unreel their memories? Perhaps the dead could speak.

Using a codeword, he asked the Computer to form a screen on the floor. It did so, and Burton put his question to it. The Computer replied that the memories of the recordings could be extracted and displayed. However, some recordings were not available because of overrides.

He looked at his wristwatch. Time for the androids to have finished their job.

By then the display of his past had leaped to Naples, where the family was staying for a while during its never-ending wandering through southern Europe. Once more, he was being whipped by a tutor, this time by DuPré, an Oxford graduate.

As Frigate had said, their lives were movies, but, before being shown the main feature, they were seeing "previews."

It would be embarrassing when the Computer got to the events of the day before this particular incident. He and an Italian playmate had masturbated before each other.

It was also going to be embarrassing when the innumerable excretions were shown, and the sexual scenes would be downright intolerable. These were why Burton had decided that the idea for painting an apartment where all might meet was not enough. His own apartment was to be painted, and, if the others had any sense, they would follow his example.

He entered the doorway, and the screen was hidden beneath the paint. The androids, sweating, were just finishing up his bedroom. He had not told them to paint every room, since there were several into which he would not go. That is, unless he wished to see his past, and he knew that there would be many times when he would not be able to resist the temptation. He could, however, now view it only when he wished to.

He swore and snapped his fingers.

Perhaps not.

He went to the console of the auxiliary computer, which had not been painted over. Activating it, he stared at the screen. He smiled. The Computer was not displaying the loathed pictures there. Apparently it had been ordered only to use the walls for the memory projections.

The Outram android reported that they were through. Burton told them to store the ladders and the unused cans in a bedroom and to put the used cans in a converter. He disintegrated the cans, then ordered the androids into the converter. They walked into the huge cabinet; he secured the door; energy flashed; not even a speck of ash was left.

It had to be his imagination that made him think that their eyes looked pleading. They had neither self-consciousness nor instinct for self-preservation.

The walls, floor, and ceilings were an appalling egg-white, but he would paint murals over these.

Frigate called him via the console screen.

"I've been exploring the little worlds on that second level down from the top," he said. "I found out that the Computer doesn't show the past there. I don't know why, but I think that the Ethicals had some limitations there that the Snark couldn't override. Anyway, besides that, there are other reasons why we should move into them. They give the illusion of the great outdoors; I felt much freer than I do in my apartment. I'm going to suggest that we move into them, and that anyone who wishes to do so remodel them. I'm going to do it whether or not anyone else does, but it would be nice if everybody did it. We'd be close together and could use the central area for social meetings or whatever."

They met in the central area of the "pie-in-the-sky" level that evening to talk about Frigate's proposal.

"You'll have to see those places for yourselves," Frigate said. "They're fabulous."

The American reminded them that the circular section was divided into segments of thirty degrees each. The points of these twelve segments ended in the huge circular central area.

"It occurred to me that, from a bird's-eye view, the circle looks like a zodiac chart. It's divided into twelve parts, twelve houses, Aquarius, Aries, Taurus, Gemini, and so forth—if you want to look at it that way. I was thinking that maybe each of us could pick the area that corresponds to his or her birth date."

"Why?" de Marbot said.

"It's a conceit of mine. However, since the birth date could determine the particular area in which to live, it'll avoid argument if we use the zodiacal method. Of course, there's no reason for disagreement, since they'll all look alike once the original paraphernalia is cleared out. It's just an idea."

The others said that it seemed as good a way of choosing the areas as any.

"But you don't believe in that astrological crap, do you?" Turpin said.

"No. Not really. However, I do know something about it. Now, Po, you were born, according to the Western calendar, on April 19, A.D. 701. That makes you Aries the Ram, the first house, the principle of which is energy. You certainly are energetic."

"And much more!" the Chinese said.

"Yes. The first house also pioneers, and you were a pioneer. Your positive qualities are outgoing, original, and dynamic."

"Very true! I must learn more about this Occidental astrology."

"Your negative qualities," Frigate said, smiling, "are that you're foolhardy, have low self-sufficiency, and are deceitful."

"What? I? Perhaps I might be foolhardy, though I would prefer to call it absolutely courageous. But how could you say that I have low self-sufficiency, you who know me so well?"

"I'm just telling you what astrology says about your sign.

Anyway, negative qualities are to be overcome, and evidently you conquered yours, if you ever had them."

"One might say that he overcompensated in his conquest," Burton said drily.

"The house of Aries is OK with you?" Frigate said.

"Why not! It is the *first*!"

Frigate spoke to Alice. "You were born May 4, 1852. That makes you Taurus the Bull. Ruled by Venus, the emotions."

"Hah!" Burton said. Alice glared at him.

"Taurus builds. Your positive qualities make you loyal, dependable, and patient. But you have to battle against excessive pride, self-indulgence, and greediness."

"Not to my knowledge," Alice said quietly.

"The second house OK with you?"

"Of course."

Frigate spoke to Thomas Million Turpin, who was smoking a panatela and holding a glass of bourbon.

"You were born on May 21, 1873, under the sign of Gemini, the Twins. You're ruled by Mercury, and you're strong on communication. You're versatile, genial, and creative."

"Keep talking, man!"

"But your negative qualities . . . uh . . . you're two-faced, superficial, and unstable."

"That's a damn lie! I never been two-faced, I always been straightforward. Where'd you get that shit?"

"Nobody said that you were," Frigate said. "What that indicates is that you have had to overcome those tendencies."

"I ain't two-faced. I'm just discreet and polite. No use hurting someone's feelings if you don't have to. It don't pay."

"The third house agreeable with you?"

"One's good as another and maybe better."

"We don't have anybody born under Cancer," Frigate said. "Not yet, anyway. The fifth house is Leo the Lion, representing vitality and ruled by the sun. Leo dramatizes. That's you, Marcelin. Born August 18, 1782."

"So far, excellent," de Marbot said. "I am all those."

"A Leo is regal . . ."

"True!"

". . . entertaining . . ."

"Doubly true!"

". . . and commanding."

"Triply true."

"The bad qualities, alas, are that Leo is pompous, domineering, and conceited."

The Frenchman reddened and scowled; the others burst out laughing.

"He got you there!" Turpin said.

"Leo, the fifth house, OK?" Frigate said.

"If it is understood that we are merely amusing ourselves with this parlor game of astrology and that, though I may be a leader, I am not domineering, and though I have much to boast about but do not, I am not conceited, and that never, never am I pompous!"

"Nobody'll argue with you," Frigate said ambiguously. "Now we come to the sixth house, Virgo, the virgin. Ruled also by Mercury, the communicator. Virgo analyzes. That's you, Aphra, born September 22, 1640. Virgo is practical, analytical, intellectual."

"I've never been any of those," Aphra said.

"Virgo is also critical, hypochondriacal, and prim."

She laughed uproariously.

"I, with my reputation and my bawdy dramas?"

"The sixth house OK?"

"Why not?"

"Why not?" de Marbot said. "I ask, why not? We have been living together, my little cabbage, and I am delighted and content. Now . . . *sacrebleu* . . . we will no longer share a bed and a roof. Have you not thought of that? If not, why not? Are you tired of me?"

She patted him on the arm. "Not at all, my bantam cock, not at all. But . . . well . . . we are always with each other, never out of each other's sight. It's possible, only possible, I say, after all, we're human, that such close and continuous intimacy may pall after a while. Besides . . . I like the idea of having my own world. We can build our own, each to our own desire, and still be with each other whenever we wish. I will stay one night in your world. You, the next night, in mine. We can pretend that we are a king and a queen making state visits to each other's monarchy."

"I do not know about that," he said.

Aphra shrugged. "Well, if it doesn't work out, we can live together as before. Surely, Marcelin, you are not afraid of this venture?"

"I? Afraid? Never! Very well, Peter, I will take up residence in the fifth house and Aphra in the sixth. After all, we will be next-door neighbors."

"With a thick wall between you. Walls make good neighbors."

"But poor lovers," Burton said.

"You are too cynical, my friend," de Marbot said.

"Libra and Scorpio, the seventh and eighth houses, will have to be empty for the time being," Frigate said. "The ninth is Sagittarius, the archer, ruled by Jupiter, the dominant mode being expansion. Sagittarius philosophizes. Which is appropriate, since you, Nur, are Sagittarius. You are, according to the ancient science, jovial, prophetic, and logical."

"And more," Nur said.

"You have the negative qualities of bluntness, fanaticism, and intolerance."

"Had. I conquered those in my late youth."

"We must skip Capricorn. Aquarius, my sign," Frigate said, "is the eleventh house. Aquarius the Waterbearer is ruled by Saturn, which symbolizes lessons, and by Uranus, which stands for opportunities. Aquarius humanizes. Aquarius is diplomatic, altruistic, and inventive. Unfortunately, on the negative side, he is selfish, eccentric, and impulsive."

"Do you plead guilty?" Burton said.

"More or less. Now, Dick, we come to you, Pisces, since you were born March 19, 1821. Pisces the Fish. Harmonizes, haw! haw! Ruled by Neptune or idealism and Jupiter or expansion. No argument there. Positive qualities: intuitive, sympathetic, artistic."

"You've told me, more than once, that I was a self-made martyr," Burton said.

"And so," Nur said, "carrying our baggage of good and bad qualities, we go to our new homes. If we could only leave the suitcases containing the bad at the door."

16

Moving into the "pie-in-the-sky" chambers demanded much preparation. The tenants had to tour their little worlds and decide whether they should keep the present decor or "environment" or make their own. Except for Nur, who was intrigued by the chamber of dark mirrors, each finally had his or her place stripped. While the hordes of androids and robots were doing this, the tenants decided on what kind of private world they wanted. After that, they had to instruct the Computer down to the minutest details about their specifications.

Nur changed his mind. He would remain in his suite though he would visit the mirror-world now and then to meditate.

Burton surprised everybody by his unaccountable reluctance to change homes. He had always been a wanderer who grew restless if he stayed in one place more than a week. Yet he now refused to move until he had made his world exactly as he wished. Halfway through the building of his first world, he stopped the work and had it stripped again. After a long time, he started on a second design but abandoned that after two weeks.

"Perhaps he's so unwilling to go there," Nur said, "because it will be his last home. Where else can he go after he moves into that?"

The afternoon that the six were to move, all eight held a big going-away party in the central area. It was not entirely a joyous occasion because de Marbot and Behn quarreled just before they were to take occupancy. The Frenchman was burned up at Aphra's refusal to live with him in his world, and, after drinking more wine than he was accustomed to, he accused her of not loving him.

"I am entitled to my own world, the world I made," she said loftily.

"A woman's place is by the man she loves. She should go where he goes."

"We've been through this too many times," she said. "I'm weary of it."

"You should be under my roof. It is my right. How can I trust you?"

"I don't have to be in your sight every minute. If you can't trust me, if you think I'll hop into another man's bed the moment I go around the corner . . . Is it just me or don't you trust any woman? You were often absent for many months from your wife when you were a soldier. Did you trust her? You must have, you didn't—"

"My wife was above suspicion!" de Marbot shouted.

"Hail, Caesar!" Aphra said scornfully. "The real Caesar's wife, my precious little piece of shit, put horns on him. So, if your wife was as good as Caesar's wife . . ."

Aphra walked away from him while he yelled at her, and she went through the doorway to the sixth house.

Weeping, she let the door close behind her. She felt as if she were also closing off her lover forever, though she had had enough experience to know that her emotions, not her reason, were speaking. How many men had she parted from and never expected to see again? It seemed like a hundred, but, actually, it must be only twenty. And she could not remember the names of some. She would, though, when the dogging screen of her past showed up again. Here, at least, she could get away from it.

She went up the steps, the door opening for her at the top, and she stepped into her world. There was another flying chair there; she got into it and soared to an altitude of a hundred feet and headed inward. Below her was South American low-altitude tropical jungle, with winding narrow rivers gleaming in the light of the false moon. The cries of night birds rang and clanged below her; a bat shot by near her and dipped toward the dark tops of the trees a few feet below her. The moon was full because she had arranged for one every night, and its light was twice as powerful as that of Earth's. And the stars, also those of equatorial South America, were three times as bright as the real ones. In this luminous night, she saw a shape slip across a glade. A jaguar. And she heard the bellowings of alligators.

The wind cooled her and fluttered her robe as she headed toward the big lake in the middle of the jungle. Its waters sparkled around the floating palace in its center. She had reconstructed this from her memory of an apparition she had seen while voyaging from Antwerp to London. It had appeared suddenly ahead of the ship as if placed there by magic and had startled and frightened everybody aboard. This magical building was square, four stories high, made of marble of various colors, and surrounded by rows of fluted and twisting pillars with climbing vines and flowers and streamers waving in the breeze. Each pillar was carved with hundreds of little Cupids who seemed to be climbing them with the aid of their fluttering wings.

The palace had been seen by everybody aboard the ship. Where had it come from? If it was a mirage, what building did it reflect? There was nowhere in England or the Continent such a rococo fantastic palace.

That unexplainable vision had haunted her the rest of her life on Earth and still did on the Riverworld. She had asked the Computer to explain it to her, but its searches had turned up only the reference to it in the biography of her by John Gildon. This posthumous work had both intrigued and disgusted her because of its inaccuracies and lies. She had then asked for all available literature concerning her and had read Montague Summers', Bernbaum's, and Sackville-West's accounts. These authors had been mainly occupied in trying to sift the truth from the romance and speculations and had usually failed. They could not be blamed. The official records and documents about her were scarce, and getting the historical facts about her from her novels, plays, and poems was hopeless.

Aphra knew, or had been told, that she was the daughter of a barber, James Johnson of Canterbury. Her mother had died a few days after Aphra's birth, and she and her sister and brother had been adopted by relatives, John and Amy Amis. Neither she nor the Amises, of course, had any prescience that the little girl

would some day be the first Englishwoman to support herself
wholly by writing. Nor that one of her poems would be included
in anthologies for centuries afterward and one novel would survive as a minor classic.

Her successful intrusion into the hitherto all-male literary
field had shocked and affronted many. The deepest shock was
felt by the male writers and critics. Their biased and vindictive
remarks and politicking made her furious, and she responded in
kind, and justly so. She suffered all the hardships, the sling-
stones and fiery crosses, of the pioneer, but she blazed the path
for a host of women who earned their living by the pen.

As a child, she had been nervous and imaginative and often
ill. Nevertheless, she survived the six-thousand-mile rough and
dangerous voyage to Surinam, an English possession in north
South America on the Atlantic Ocean. Her adopted father, John
Amis, was not so lucky. He died en route, a victim of a "fever."
He had been appointed lieutenant general of Surinam through
the influence of a relative, Lord Willoughby of Parham. Despite the loss of her father, she enjoyed her life, and she took
full advantage of the exotic land. Here she met a black slave who
had been stolen from his tribe in West Africa and brought to
Surinam. His stories of his homeland and his exalted position
there, whether true or not, were the source of that romantic
novel she was to write years later, *Oroonoko, or, The Royal Slave.*

"Those were the happiest years of my life. There 'twas always
spring, always April, May, and June. The trees bore at once all
degrees of leaves and fruits. There were groves of oranges, lem-
ons, citrons, figs, nutmegs, and noble aromatics continually ex-
uding fragrances. Gaily colored macaws, parrots, and canaries
flashed above the water lilies in the lagoons and trenches. The
twa-twa bird had a cry like a silver gong. The kiskadee called
'*Qu'est-ce que dit? Qu'est-ce que dit?*' I became versed in the
strange language of the blacks, half-African, half-English, and
heard of Gran Gado, the Grand God, his wife Maria, and his son
Jesi Kist. Indians came down from the mountains carrying bags
full of gold dust.

"It was not all lovely and paradisical, of course, I fell sick with
malaria once and almost died."

In 1658, at the age of eighteen, she returned to London. At nineteen she was married to a much older man, a wealthy Dutch merchant, Jans Behn. Though she had no money, her good looks and wit and learning had inspired love in Mr. Behn. Through his connections, he introduced his wife into the court of Charles II.

"And is it true," Frigate had said, "that you were the king's mistress?"

"His Majesty did ask me to bed with him," she had said, "but at that time I was married. I had the conception then, which I later abandoned, that adultery was sinful. Moreover, I loved my husband, no Dutch lump he, and I knew that he would be terribly hurt if I betrayed him."

By 1665, her husband had lost his immense fortune because of the sinking by storms or capture by pirates of the ships bearing his merchandise. He died from a heart attack in early 1666, leaving his widow with only fifty pounds. By the time she had gotten employment, she had only forty pounds left. Through friends at the court, she became an espionage agent and went to Antwerp. She was told that any information she could get on the Dutch fleet would be welcome. But her main assignment was to spy on renegade Englishmen living in Holland. There were many there who had fled England and were conspiring to overthrow the present monarchy.

"A female James Bond," Frigate had said.

"What?"

"Never mind."

"I was especially charged to make friends with an exile, William Scott, and endeavor to get him to return to England. He wouldn't do so until he got a full pardon, but toward that end he agreed to collaborate with me. By then, I was broke. I sent a letter to James Halsall, the king's cupbearer, my immediate superior. I asked him for funds to continue my spying. I got no answer, so I wrote a second missive, telling him how expensive Antwerp was and that I had only been able to feed myself and keep a roof over my head by pawning a ring. Again, no reply. Once more I wrote to Halsall and, at the same time, to Thomas Killigrew, a friend who was also in the secret service. I stated that I needed fifty

pounds to pay debts. I also sent news of the number and disposition of the Dutch ships, of the Dutch army, and of my progress
with Scott. After receiving no replies, I wrote in utter despair to
the secretary of state, Lord Arlington. I told him all that I had
done, how impoverished I was, and that soon I'd be in a Dutch
debtor's prison. But he did not answer."

"Did you then think about going over to the Dutch?" Burton
had asked.

"I? Never!"

"Even then, the British government was mistreating and ne-
glecting its soldiers and spies," Burton had said.

"I wrote again to Lord Arlington and begged him to send one
hundred pounds to pay off my debts and return to England.
Again, silence. So, there I was, not a penny of pay for my services, not a single word from my chiefs. What was I doing there
but making a piteous fool of myself, a poverty-stricken dunce?
Finally, I succeeded in getting a loan of one hundred and fifty
pounds from a friend in England, Edward Butler, and I sailed
back home in January, year of Our Lord 1667."

Weary, sick, and heavily in debt, Aphra crossed the Channel
from Antwerp to London. Here she saw the ruins of the city laid
low by the Great Fire. Yet the terrible blaze had not been without
its good. It had consumed the hundreds of thousands of rats and
millions of lice that had spread the Great Plague. Aphra, however, had little time to think about either the fire or the plague.
Mr. Butler pressed her for repayment, and Lord Arlington and
the king kept on ignoring her just requests for her back pay. The
inevitable came; she was thrown into debtors' prison.

"Where," Aphra had said, "if you had no money to buy food,
you starved to death. That is, if the diseases running through the
prisons like wild redskins on a raid did not strike you down first.
The plagues were democratic, however. They killed you, high or
low, poor or with money in your purse, young or old."

All the City prisons had been burned down or made useless by
the Great Fire. Newgate was hastily repaired, but Aphra was sent
to Caronne House in South Lambeth. The filth and overcrowding
had been bad enough before the fire. They were ten times worse

now because of the lack of prisons and the great numbers of citizens whose houses and property had been destroyed. Unable to pay their debts, they, too, went to jail.

"I lived through it, though there were times when I wished that I would die. The stench of unwashed bodies and clothes, the stink from the sick suffering from the bloody flux, the noisome odor of the open sewers, the wailing of frightened and sick children, the stealing, the screaming of the mad and the furious, the coughing and retching, the fights, the brutality, the utter lack of privacy . . . if you would piss or shit you must do it in a cell with a dozen others watching or laughing at you . . . if my mother had not borrowed money to send me food, half of which was confiscated by the guards for their own benefit . . . I would have wasted away until I was too weak to resist the diseases floating in the sickening air of that hellhole. Whatever sins I had sinned, before I was in jail or after, I paid for them. 'Twas a purgatory without flames, flames that we would have welcomed to keep us warm."

Two of the guards offered to give her a meal a day with meat, vegetables, and wine if she would have intercourse with them both at the same time.

"If my mother had not sent me enough to keep me from completely starving, I suppose I would have consented to their demands sooner or later, probably sooner. My empty belly was sucking wind, and I told myself, though I did not really believe it, that the guards were preferable to starvation. However, one of the guards, in addition to being unusually filthy, one-eyed, humpbacked, and rotten-toothed, had the French disease. I don't know . . ."

"Syphilis or gonorrhea?" Frigate had said.

"Both, I think. What did it matter? Anyway, thanks to my mother, not God, I escaped them. And, eventually, Killigrew did pay me enough to discharge my debts and to live on for a while. A very short while."

She had paused, then said, smiling, and she looked beautiful when smiling, "I lied when I said that I wanted to die when in prison. Oh, perhaps I did briefly consider the benefits of suicide. No, I have always believed passionately that life is worthwhile, and I was not one who hoisted the white flag at the first discouragement. Nor did I ever acknowledge defeat. Not until the last breath came, and then not then. Death had not defeated me any more than life had. It just retired me.

"There I was, just out of prison, thin and wan, my debts paid except for what I owed my mother and not a penny to pay her unless I went without food and lodging and cosmetics and clothes and books."

She was nearing thirty in a time when a woman of thirty looked—usually—much older than the woman of thirty of the late 1900s. Most had lost many teeth, and their breaths stank of rotten teeth. A woman without a husband, father, brother, uncle, or cousin to protect her was considered fair prey. If wronged, she could resort to a law that was far on the side of the wealthy and privileged. The judges, the lawyers, the bailiffs, the jurors, were open to bribery—very few exceptions—and were easily impressed by the rich and the titled. Women writers were not unknown, but these were not professionals. They were the daughters of country vicars who wrote in their spare time or noblewomen who wanted to get a "name" for themselves. No woman in England had tried to get her livelihood from her pen.

Aphra knew that she could write flowingly, wittily, and charmingly, and she had imagination. She was well-read, and she thought that she could do as well as any man in creating novels, poems, and plays. But she would start with a handicap in the literary race because she was a woman.

However, somewhat compensating for the handicap, she looked better than most women her age. She had all her teeth, possibly because she had spent the first part of her life in Surinam and the minerals in the foods there helped preserve them. Possibly heredity was partly her dental savior. She was, though short, long-legged, though the skirts of her time kept most from observing that. She had full buoyant breasts, which the dress of her time did not conceal. She had beautiful yellow hair and large blue eyes with thick black brows that set off a face that was very attractive despite her long nose and somewhat short lower jaw. She had great charm, and she had a will with the momentum of a carriage and six horses galloping downhill.

Moreover, she had determined that she would remain single. As she had once written: "Marriage is as certain a bane to love as lending is to friendship; I'll neither ask nor give a vow."

She also wrote:

According to the strict rules of honor,
Beauty should still be the reward of love,
Not the vile merchandize of fortune,
Or the cheap drug of a church-ceremony.
She's only infamous, who to her bed
For interest takes some nauseous clown she hates;
And though a jointure or vow in public
Be her price, that makes her but the dearer whore. . . .
Take back your gold, and give me current love,
The treasure of your heart, not of your purse.

Despite which, she gave her heart to the wrong man, a barrister named John Hoyle, who ill-used her, took her love and money, gave her back mostly unfaithfulness and contempt, and came close to but did not quite succeed in breaking her heart. (Hoyle was murdered in a tavern brawl in 1692, after she had died. Frigate had told her of this.) "Hoyle was said by someone, I forget by whom, to be 'an atheist, a sodomite professed, a corrupter of youth, and a blasphemer of Christ.'"

"Socrates was also accused of all of that but the last," Aphra had said. "I did not mind that he was that and much more. It was . . . he did not love me as I loved him . . . loved me not all except in the beginning."

"What would you do now if you met him?" Frigate had said.

"I don't know. I don't hate him. Yet . . . perhaps I would kick him in the balls and then kiss him. Who knows? I hope I never see him again."

Aphra became famous, or infamous, and she was dubbed *Astraea* after the star maiden of ancient Greek mythology, daughter of Zeus and Themis, or perhaps of Astraeus the Titan and Eos. Astraea, during the golden age, distributed blessings. But when the iron age began, she left earth in disgust, and the gods placed her among the stars as the constellation Virgo.

Great literary figures and their hangers-on and young play-wrights and poets flocked to her court. Some of them were lucky enough to be her lovers.

"However, many men, as I've said, resented my success, and many critics condemned my plays because they were written by a woman. Damn their rum-soaked brains and wine-bleared eyes and poxrunny pricks, they said my plays were bawdy and ob-scene. So they were, but if a man wrote such, the carpers would not've opened their mouths. Why should bawdiness and ob-scenity be strictly a man's preserve? Are women angels or Eves?"

Nevertheless, she made a fortune, which somehow boiled away under the pressure of her high living and generosity, and she had many lovers, though, as she said, not much true love from them. When she was forty-six, she suffered from the vio-lent and painful attacks of arthritis which were to kill her.

"Though I think that the effects of the pox were as fatal, though more insidious."

Though her writing hand hurt her and there were times when the pen slipped from her feeble grasp, she wrote furiously, and the novel that was to assure her a respectable place in En-glish literature, *Oroonoko,* was published before she died. The six-teenth of April, 1689, her battle against prejudice, jealousy, gossip, and the hatred of the puritanical and hypocritical was over.

William of Orange, the Dutch prince who had become mon-arch of England, did not like Mrs. Behn. Yet, somehow, though she was regarded as a wicked and scandalous woman, she was buried in Westminster Abbey.

"How did that happen? I was interred among the greatest of the great? I?"

"No one in my time knew why," Frigate said.

"Nor in mine," Burton said. "We will have to resurrect one of your contemporaries to determine that."

"Byron was refused a grave in Westminster Abbey," Frigate said. "He was thought to be too blasphemous and wicked to be given that honor. Yet you made it."

"And I," Burton said, "I was also refused. I had deserved it more than many who rested there, but Nigger Dick would not be allowed within the hallowed walls."

Aphra had many miserable and frightening times on the River-world, but life was almost always worthwhile. No fun being dead. So, here she was in the tower and she had just parted with another lover. She might live with de Marbot again, though it did not seem likely just now. Never mind. She did not intend to be alone for long.

17

W hile waiting for his little world to be built, Peter Jairus
Frigate was not idle. He decided that he did not wish to
cut off the "memory movie" entirely. He was too curious about
his past; he had many questions about it that he had thought
would never be answered. Though he'd be pained seeing it, he
was going to force himself to endure the pain. Now and then. So
he removed a square of the paint from a wall of a room in his
suite, and he spent an hour each day in that room. The moment
he appeared in it, the past sprung to life as seen through his eyes
and heard through his ears.

Experimenting, he found that the Computer did not insist on
showing him everything according to the program. If he requested a certain time area, then he got it.

Also, the Computer had a clock synchronized with the time
of its subject's memory. If Frigate had known in the past what
date it was because he'd looked at a calendar that day or someone had mentioned the date, the Computer could flash to that
event. Otherwise, it had to estimate the approximate time and
would scan its track for the area of time first, then the particular
date.

There were, as he soon found out, many gaps in the "movie."
He asked for a date at random, October 27, 1923. At that time, he
was playing around and trying to do some spot-checking. That
day was a blank; he had nothing in his memory about it.

The Computer told him why.

There was not enough space in his memory cells to store his
entire life. A mechanism in the mnemonics complex erased
what was to him insignificant, thus making more room for the

meaningful. Often, though, what his conscious considered un-important, his unconscious considered worth storing.

The *wathan* was supposed to have stored the entire life experiences of the individual. Nothing was left unrecorded. This theory could not be validated, since, so far, no *wathan* could be tapped. Its bright many-colored exterior remained invulnerable to probing. Like the Sphinx, it was beautiful and awe-inspiring but silent.

The Computer figured out for him that he had lived 55,188,000 minutes so far. Of this, 22,075,200 minutes were available at that moment. That was the total, but that did not mean that every one of those minutes could be run off in its entirety. There were many fragments of minutes in the storage. If Frigate cared to know just how many fragments and how long each was, he could get the numbers from the Computer. But he did not care to know.

"Sixty percent of the movie of my life went onto the cutting-room floor," he muttered. "Jesus! If I sit down and watch the whole movie from beginning to end, it'll take me 15,330 days of twenty-four-hour periods to see it. Forty-two years of just sitting watching."

How could the human brain, that small gray mass, contain so many memories, so much data, so many millions, maybe billions, of miles of film?

Frigate asked if the Computer could show him the container unit that contained the "movie." Obligingly, the Computer did so, and Frigate saw on the screen a yellow sphere the size of a cranberry. And that was only half-full.

What he most wanted to see—and also did not want to see—was a very early period. He would have been about a year old, living in a house in North Terre Haute, Indiana. His mother's mother was visiting them then, having come from Kansas City, Missouri, to help his mother with her infant. Frigate had the idea that his grandmother had mistreated him when she babysat him. He believed that it was not because she was cruel or sadistic but because she easily lost her temper. He based this speculation on the visions of her he had had during some sessions with a psychoanalyst in Beverly Hills. There, while trying to probe his infantile memories, he had become convinced that his grand-mother had treated him in such a fashion that he had become subdued, submissive and fearful while a baby. Or that she had laid the foundation for these attitudes, which flowered when he became an adolescent.

The psychoanalyst obviously had not put much credence in this, but he had allowed Frigate to make the effort. Probably, the analyst was pondering the significance of his attempt to fix the blame on his grandmother.

Hesitantly, Frigate ran the movie at high speed until he lo-cated the exact area of time in which his grandmother had taken care of him.

It took a week to convince him that he had been wrong. Cer-tainly, there was nothing in his grandmother's behavior to justify even faintly his fantasy. Because it was a fantasy. His grand-mother had not shaken or yelled at or spanked him to keep him from crying or mistreated him in any way. She had complained a lot to herself because of his crying, but Frigate did not under-stand more than a quarter of what she said, because she usually talked to herself in German. He could have asked the Computer to translate for him but did not bother. At that age, he would not have been affected by what was said but by the way it was said. The tone of complaint would not have meant much to him since she did not make it plain to the baby that she was displeased with him. And she did sing German lullabies to him, though she certainly had not held him much.

"Well, hell!" Frigate said to himself. "There goes another the-ory. Probably I'll find out that my character deficiencies were due to genetic disposition far more than to the environment."

He told Nur about his search. The little Moor laughed and said, "It's not the past that counts. It's the present. You cannot charge the past for your present failures and weaknesses. The present is here for you to change what you have been and are."

"Yes, but the memory-movie is a great psychoanalytic tool," Frigate said. "Too bad they didn't have it on Earth. The patient and the doctor could have gone over any areas in doubt and cleared everything up. The patient could have seen what really happened, and he could have separated the truth from fantasy, the unimportant from the really significant."

"Perhaps. But it's not necessary. You know what you are now. At least, you should, unless you're still fooling yourself about yourself, and that's highly possible. One good thing about the movie is that it would destroy your self-image, would demonstrate that you may have been wrong many times when you thought you were right. Or convince you that others were not entirely monsters or egoistic when they dealt with you. Or show you the times when they truly were so.

"However, aside from satisfying your curiosity, and that may be very painful and humiliating, or satisfying your desire to see the faces of those you once loved or hated, the movies are time wasted. It is now that matters, now is the cliff edge on which you stand and must leap from into the future. What you have been and are is not what you must be. You are avoiding taking action on the now by immersing yourself in the past. The past should be only a light to the future. Or a measuring stick of your progress. That and that only."

"You don't watch your movie?" Frigate said.

"No. I'm not interested in it."

"You don't care to see your parents when they were young, your playmates?"

Nur tapped his head. "They're all in there. I can summon them up when I wish."

"If the movie is a waste of time, then why did the unknown fix it so that it would be with us every second of waking time?"

"The unknown did not arrange just that. The unknown fixed it so that we could see the movie if we wished to. She wasn't unaware of the possibility that we'd paint the walls and so block out the movie. Perhaps, by painting, we failed a test."

"And what would the penalty for flunking it be?"

Nur shrugged.

"I'd guess that the penalty would be self-inflicted. It'd be a failure to progress."

"But you said that you didn't need to see your past."

"I don't. But I am not you or the others."

"Isn't that arrogant?"

"One man's arrogance is another's realism."

"You Sufis like to proverb your way through life," Frigate said.

Nur only smiled. This made the American feel as if he had failed to pass a test. For some time, Frigate had suffered from the belief that he had let Nur down—and himself—because he had quit being Nur's disciple. He had lost faith in his own ability ever to attain to Nur's lofty stature as a complete master of himself, free from neurosis and weakness, always logical yet compassionate. He just could not make it. So, rather than not succeed and be humiliated when Nur discharged him, flunked him, as it were, Frigate had resigned as Nur's disciple.

"A Sufi does not fear failure," Nur had said.

"What if I change my mind and ask you to take me as your pupil again?"

"We'll see."

"I've quit a lot of things or been forced to quit," Frigate said. "But I always went back and tried them again."

"Perhaps it's time that you got rid of this start-and-stop habit. You need to form a psychic momentum that won't run out so quickly."

"The great perhaps."

"What does that mean?"

Frigate did not know, and that made him angry.

"You haven't yet learned, after one hundred and thirty-two years, to meld your opposites into a smooth cooperating whole," Nur had said. "You have always had within you a conservative, which isn't always bad by any means, and a liberal, which isn't always good by any means. You have within you a coward and a brave man. You detest and fear violence, yet there is someone violent within you, a person you've tried to repress. You don't know how to make your violence creative, how to control it so that it discharges into the right paths. You—"

"Tell me something I don't know," Frigate had said and had walked away.

He sometimes got the same sort of philosophical drum-beating from Li Po. The Chinese liked to tell him about the process of becoming "round," that is, making one's self into a "whole" man. Balancing his yin and yang, his negative and positive qualities. But Li Po, in Frigate's estimation, was very unbalanced. He admired Li Po's energy and poetical creativeness and compassion and self-confidence and linguistic mastery and courage untainted by fear. On the other hand—people were bimanual in more than one sense—Li Po had an excessive drive to dominate, was too self-absorbed, and utterly failed to see that these qualities often made him tiresome and offensive. He also was a drunk, though unlike any Frigate had ever known.

Frigate believed that Li Po, despite his apparent superiority, had no more chance of Going On than he. Indeed, of the eight, only Nur and perhaps Aphra Behn and Alice were at this moment promising candidates for Going On. Which might or might not be desirable. The theory was that such a state was the end-all and be-all because it could be attained only if you were ethically perfect or near-perfect. The *wathan* of such a person just disappeared from all detectors and thus, so the reasoning went, was absorbed into the Godhead or God or Allah or What-Do-You-Call-It.

The theory also claimed that the *wathan* then became part of the Creator, lost its individuality, and experienced from then on an eternity of ecstasy. Ecstasy undescribable, unknown in the physical state.

"How do I know," Frigate thought, "that the *wathan* doesn't just disappear? Evaporate like an ectoplasmic bubble? Become nothing, *nada*, nil, zero? Is that something to be hotly wished for? How does that differ from just being dead? Not that there aren't some good things to be said about just being dead. Past knowing, past caring, past torment physical and mental, past frustration and defeat, past loneliness. Oh, Death, where is thy sting?"

Death had no sting. On the other hand, death had no zing.

Gain something, lose something. That was the unchangeable law, the unchanged economy of the universe.

"Am I paranoiac? Is all this a big con game? For what purpose? A con man expects to gain something. Who could gain in this situation? What could be gained?"

Sometimes, his turmoiling thoughts swelled his brain, or seemed to do so, until it seemed that his skull, like a balloon under too much pressure, would burst. Maybe because his thoughts were just too much hot air.

"After a hundred and thirty-two years, I ought to know better than to drive myself into such a state. Will I ever graduate from the sophomore class?"

Life's sophomore, the wise-foolish, could not follow Nur's advice to rid himself of such thoughts, to dump them as if they were ballast on a balloon. Instead, he shunted them, put them on a sidetrack of the Great P.J.F. Railroad, and became for a while an engineer of the G.B.R., the Grailstones-on-the-banks-of-the-River express.

He had found out something that the Ethical, Loga, had not mentioned, though doubtless he would have if he'd lived longer. That was that the grailstones lining both banks of The River were more than just electrical discharge devices to supply the grails with energy converted into food and liquor and various goodies for the Valleydwellers. They were also observation equipment, window-peeping and eavesdropping machines. A person in the tower could see and hear the people within detection range of the grailstones.

Having discovered this, Frigate indulged himself until he became dizzied and confused. He scanned The Valley on the right bank at the rate of one grailstone every two seconds, starting with the first one in the polar zone. After a while, realizing that at this rate he'd take about 232 days to get from one end to the other, he began leapfrogging every twenty grailstones and watched from the twenty-first for ten seconds each. The blur of human bodies and River and plain and mountains stopped. Even so, he got light-headed after an hour. He would have to abandon his plan to zoom by all of humanity, to take it all in two sweeps. No, he was wrong there. Eighteen billion plus were not in The Valley; they were retired, for the time being, in the Computer's records and the well of the *wathans*. But the number he must zip by was staggering.

"Always too grandiose, Frigate," he told himself. "You're just not big enough. Your ambition is a lightyear ahead of your ability. Your imagination is the eight-legged steed Sleipnir, but you, as Odin, have fallen off a thousand leagues ago."

It was hard to tell the nationality of the people he saw. Except for those who were nude, and there were plenty of them, they wore the towels as kilts or loincloths and the women used smaller, thinner cloths as brassieres. The race was usually identifiable, though sometimes he could not be sure. Some of the faces were unmistakably Mediterranean, Spanish, Italians, Greeks, Arabs, and so forth. Still, one could be mistaken about that. Language was a key, but there were thousands of tongues he could not label just from listening. Besides, the majority spoke Esperanto or various dialects thereof.

After two hours, he tired of this kind of observation.

"Well, hell! From the collective to the personal."

Seeing no one who caught his fancy near the stone he'd stopped at, he moved the observation points a stone at a time southward, pausing for twenty or so seconds at each one. It was now early afternoon, and the citizens of the right bank had eaten their lunch and were passing the time. Some were standing or sitting around and talking. Some were playing games. Many were swimming or fishing. A number of them would be in their huts and so out of sight. Those within three hundred feet could be seen closeup and easily overheard, however. The stone, like the TV camera, could zoom in and had built-in directional sound amplifiers.

The Computer could also show what the citizens could not see. Frigate's screen displayed in all their many-colored splendor the *wathans* attached to the heads and whirling just above them. He had had enough experience by now to tell at a glance when a *wathan* was shot with "bad" colors or had a "bad" structure, though "bad" did not necessarily mean "evil." Broad bands of black or red could indicate character weaknesses as much as "evil" traits. Their waning and waxing and writhing—the three W's, Frigate thought—reflected mental-emotional tensions and shifts in both the conscious and unconscious minds. In the entire nervous system, in fact. A sick person could have a lot of black in his or her *wathan*. That entity was not interpreted easily; it took a very skilled person or the Computer to read a *wathan* correctly and even then the reading could be in error.

18

At this moment, his eye was caught by a man whose *wathan* was almost entirely black and red with a flicker of purple here and there. He was a Caucasian, about six feet tall, well-built, blonde-haired and blue-eyed, and, if his face had not been so red and distorted, might have been passably good-looking. He was screaming in English at a woman who was much smaller and seemed frightened. She kept backing away, her eyes wide, while the man advanced with waving fists. Though he spoke so rapidly and in such a garbled way that Frigate could not understand him well, Frigate got the idea that the man was accusing the woman of being unfaithful. The people around the two were watching them warily but none was trying to interfere.

Suddenly, the man's *wathan* became wholly black, and he grabbed the woman by her long hair and began hitting her with his right fist. She slumped to her knees and tried to put her hands over her face. Jerking at her hair viciously, he slammed his fist on top of her head, then punched her on the nose and mouth. She quit screaming and sagged, held up only by his grip on her hair. Blood ran from her gaping mouth; teeth fell out in the red pool on the grass.

Men jumped on him and pulled him, raving, away from her. The woman lay unmoving on the ground.

A man came running from a hut, stopped when he got to the woman, knelt down, moaning, and took the woman in his arms. He rocked her for a moment, then let her down gently, rose, and strode back to the hut. The man who had struck the woman was released, and now he was excusing himself for the attack. She was a slut, a whore, a fucking cunt, she was his woman, and no woman of his screwed another man. She deserved what she had gotten. More. As for Tracy, the man who had laid his woman, he, Bill Standish, would kill him in good time.

If you do, one of the men who had grabbed him said, you'll hang. You may hang anyway.

The man who had gone into the hut charged out with a long stone-tipped spear in his hand. Standish saw him and started running for The River. The man who had threatened hanging yelled at Tracy to put the spear down, but Tracy ignored him. He ran by the group and hurled his spear, and its point went into Standish's back near the right shoulder-bone. Standish fell face forward into the shallow water but struggled up and reached back and managed to get hold of the far end of the spear butt. Tracy was on him then and had knocked him down. Some of the men ran to the two and grabbed the screaming Tracy and pulled him away from Standish. By then, Standish, his skin very pale, his mouth hanging open, had wrenched the flint blade from his back. Before the others could stop him, Standish had plunged the stone tip into Tracy's belly.

Frigate felt as if he were going to throw up, but he managed to watch the drama until its end. He had plans for Standish.

One of the men who had run after Standish had a big oak club. He slammed Standish over the head. Standish seemed to melt into his own flesh and slumped into the water. He was dragged out onto the shore, his head lolling. A man examined him. Looking up, he said, "You shouldn't have hit him so hard, Ben. He's dead."

"He had it coming," Ben said. "We would've hung him."

"You don't know that," the man said.

"If ever a man deserved killing, it's Standish," a man said, and most of the group agreed with him.

Frigate had known that the man was dead before anyone else had. He had seen Standish's *wathan* disappear, whisked away by the magician Death.

He turned off the scene and told the Computer to get a fix on Standish's *wathan*. That was not as easy as it should have been because of the recency of Standish's death. In two minutes, seventeen other *wathans* had entered the well after Standish's.

Frigate asked the Computer if Standish had been killed before this. The Computer said that the man had died three times on this world.

Had the Computer scanned and taped any of Standish's memory during these times?

After carefully defining violence to the Computer, Frigate told it to quick-check all periods of violence in Standish's life. "Beginning when he was fifteen years old."

That meant that the Computer would first have to determine when Standish was at that age. It made a run but took a hour to locate the period that gave definite proof. Fortunately, Standish had been given a birthday party in 1965. (Which meant that he was born in 1950, Frigate thought.) Frigate had the birthday party displayed. Standish's mother was a short, very fat slattern; his father was a big pot-bellied man with many broken veins on his face. Both were reeling drunk. So were all the guests, many of whom were Standish's schoolmates. The house was dirty, and the furniture was threadbare and broken. The father was, according to some remarks made by a guest, a carpenter who did not work as much as he could have. Standish puked up beer and pretzels and bologna sandwiches late in the evening, and the party broke up when the parents started screaming insults and obscenities at each other. It looked as if they were going to hit each other when Frigate shut the scene off.

Frigate told the Computer that that was an example of verbal violence. What he wanted was physical violence. Frigate then went to the evening meeting, held in Li Po's apartment. The Computer continued its search, which was for the time being limited to the ten years between 1965 and 1975.

At the party, Frigate found out that others were also conducting searches. Alice, for instance, was trying to locate her three sons, her parents, and her brothers and sisters.

"Do you plan on resurrecting them?" Frigate said.

Her dark eyes seemed troubled.

"Frankly, I don't know. I think I just wish to make sure that they're all right. Happy. Of course, they, some of them, might be dead. Then, of course . . ."

What she meant was that any who were locked away in the records, their *wathans* in the central shaft, could not live again unless she raised them. But she was not certain what effect their presence would have on her, how they would circumscribe her. Or what their reactions to what she now was would be. What would they think if they knew that she had been the mate of that wicked man, Dick Burton?

Also, the reunion of parents with children could be unhappy. The parents were used to ruling their children, were, at least, in Alice's time. But here there were no evident marks of age; the parents looked as young as their children. Moreover, after a separation of so many years and such different experiences, both parents and children had changed considerably. There was, literally, a world between them, a gap that few could cross.

Yet Alice had loved her mother, father, sons, and siblings.

Frigate noticed that she had said nothing of her husband, Reginald Gervis Hargreaves. He was too discreet to mention it.

"You've had no success so far?" Frigate said.

Alice sipped from her cut-quartz goblet of wine and said, "No. I've given their names and birth and death dates to the Computer, all except the death date of my son Caryl. I don't know that, but I'm sure I can find a book or a newspaper in the records that will, and I'm looking for photographs that the Computer can match up with its files. That all takes time, you know. If any or all are dead and in the records, then they'll be found. But if they're living, the chances that they'll be located are less. The Computer can make a grailstone-scan. However, unless my people happen to be in range during the necessarily quick scan, they won't be found. Perhaps not then."

If you can't find any, Frigate thought, *you'll be relieved of the decision whether or not to resurrect them.*

"How about Lewis Carroll, Mr. Dodgson?" he said.

"No."

She did not offer to elaborate, and she would have been offended if he had asked her to do so.

Frigate left the "shindig" and went to his apartment. Instead of going to bed, he ran some more scenes from Standish's past. These so troubled him that he could not get to sleep after he had shut them off. Standish was a low-life, a creep, a brutal, dirty, nasty, and unintelligent man on Earth and the Riverworld. It was not until two days later, though, that Frigate became so horrified that he quit watching Standish for a while.

Standish was out of a job, his usual circumstance, and living with his sister and her daughter in their apartment in a small Midwestern city. The sister was a twenty-year-old who would have been attractive if she had been clean and shown any signs of intelligence. Her daughter was a blonde, blue-eyed, three-year-old who might have been beautiful if she had not been so fat from eating junk food and drinking enormous quantities of Coke. On this particular display, Frigate was watching through Standish's eyes the living room of the shabby apartment. Standish's sister, Maizie, was drinking beer on a broken-down sofa. The infant was playing with a ragged doll but was half-hidden by a chair in the corner. Now and then, Frigate could see the can of beer Standish held. Judging from the conversation, the two adults had been drinking beer since breakfast.

"Where's Linda?" Standish said, looking blearily around.

"There." Maizie waved a hand at the chair.

"Yeah. Come here Linda!" Standish said loudly.

Reluctantly, the little girl, holding her doll, walked out from behind the chair. Standish zipped open his pants and pulled out his erect penis.

"Ever sheen one of those, Linda?" Standish said.

Linda backed away. Standish yelled at her to stay where she was. Maizie got up swaying from her chair. "What in fuck are you doing?"

"I'm going to fuck Linda."

Frigate felt sick, but he watched, his gorge rising, as Maizie argued with her brother but finally said, "Well, what the hell, she's gotta get fucked some day. Might as well be now."

"Yeah, you know it. You was pronged when you was seven years old, wasn't you?"

Maizie didn't reply. Standish said, "Come here, Linda."

When she shook her head, he yelled, "Come here, damn it! You want a spanking like Uncle Bill gave you last night? Come here!"

Frigate could not endure it any longer. He turned the scene off. Shaking, he told the Computer to run forward three days.

And he saw, through Standish's eyes, the jail cell. Standish was with two others and bragging about how he had screwed his sister's kid.

"The little cunt wanted it, so I gave her what she asked for. Anything wrong with that?"

"The poor little girl," Frigate muttered. "God!"

The Computer was locked into Standish's recording. All Frigate had to do was to order the Computer to destroy it. Standish would be forever dead except for his *wathan,* and that would float aimlessly and blindly through the universe.

Biting his lip, quivering, heat seething through him, Frigate got up from the console and walked savagely back and forth, muttering "Damn, damn, damn! Damn him to Hell and back! No, not back!"

Finally, he charged up to the console and shouted, "When I give you this codeword, destroy Standish!"

There was more to do than that, though. He had to identify the man's recording by the Computer's code, affirm three times that he wished it destroyed, and establish the codeword.

"But for the present, Standish is to be *on hold,*" Frigate said.

For no rational reason that he could find, he felt ashamed of himself a few hours later. Who was he to be the judge? Yet . . . anyone who would rape a child . . . deserved oblivion.

The next day, hesitatingly, he told Nur what he had done. The Moor raised his eyebrows and said, "I can understand your anger. I did not see what you saw, but I, too, am sick and angry. The man seems totally unredeemable and has proved himself to be no better here than he was on Earth. But he still has time to become something better. I know that you don't think that he ever will, and you are probably right. The Ethicals, however, gave everybody a certain amount of time to save himself or herself, and Loga managed to extend that time. You must not interfere, no matter what you feel."

"He shouldn't be loosed on people again," Frigate said.

"He shouldn't, perhaps, be loosed on himself, either," Nur said. "But he will. What drives you just now is revenge. That's understandable. But it's not permitted, and there is a reason for that."

"What's the reason?"

"You know what it is," Nur said. "Some of the most unredeemable people, unredeemable by all appearances, anyway, have saved themselves, become genuine human beings. Look at Göring. And I'm sure you'll find others in your searches."

"Standish died when he was thirty-three," Frigate said. "Drunk, drove his car through a stoplight and smashed into another car broadside. I don't know if he killed or hurt the others, but I could find out. I suppose that doesn't matter. What does is that Standish never learned a thing, never repented, never blamed himself, never thought of changing himself. Never will."

"I know you," Nur said. "If you do this, you will suffer from guilt."

"The Ethicals didn't suffer from guilt. They knew that the time would come when people like Standish would have sentenced themselves to oblivion."

"Your righteous indignation and wrath are clouding your mind. You have just uttered the reason why you shouldn't interfere."

"Yes, but . . . the Ethicals only gave us a certain amount of time. Who's to say that, given a little more time than they've allowed, some might not have attained the goal? Maybe one more year, a month, a day, might have made the difference?"

"That was Loga's reasoning, and he interfered with his fellow Ethicals' plan, and events have gone astray. Perhaps we were wrong to have sided with Loga."

"Now you're arguing against yourself."

Nur smiled and said, "I do a lot of that."

"I don't know," Frigate said. "For the time being, Standish is locked up, as it were. He's not hurting anybody. But when . . . if . . . the day comes that the eighteen billion are to be raised in The Valley again, I might dissolve him."

"If anyone should do that, it's the little girl. Ask her if she wants to do it."

"I can't. She died of a liver disease when she was about five."

"Then she was raised on the Gardenworld. She may be one of the Agents locked in the recordings and so unattainable."

Why am I doing this? Frigate asked himself. Other than the

obvious. Do I get a feeling of power by holding that Yahoo's fate in my hands? Do I like that sense of power? No, I never have liked power. I'm too aware of the responsibility that goes with power. Or should go with it. I've always tried to shun responsibility. Within reasonable limits, of course.

19

Others might be uncertain about whom they wanted to resurrect to populate their private worlds, but Thomas Million Turpin was not one of them. He wanted Scott Joplin, Louis
Chauvin, James Scott, Sam Patterson, Otis Saunders, Artie
Mathews, Eubie Blake, Joe Jordan. Lots of others, those whom
he knew and loved in the ragtime days, great musicians all,
though the greatest were Joplin and Chauvin. Tom could play
the piano like an angel, but those two were three circles of
Heaven above him, and he loved them.

The women? Most of those he'd known on Earth were whores,
but some of them were easy to get along with and better to look
at. When he'd been in The Valley, he'd fallen in love with a
woman he'd never fallen out of love with, an ancient-Egyptian
broad named Menti. Maybe she was filed away; if so, he could
bring her back. It'd been thirteen years since he'd seen her, but
she wasn't going to forget him. She was a Caucasian, but she was
darker than he was, and she wasn't prejudiced against blacks.
She was the daughter of a merchant in Memphis. Memphis,
Egypt, not Tennessee. She . . . she'd be the first one he'd have the
Computer look for.

He had even composed a ragtime tune for her, "My Egyptian
Belle," which he'd play for her after she got adjusted to this life.

Smack dab in the center of his world, Turpinville, would be
his New Rosebud Café. It wouldn't be the original, the square
red-brick building at 2220 Market Street in the black red-light
district of St. Louis. It'd be ten stories high, round, its walls of
gold alloy, thick with diamonds and emeralds. The roof would
be topped with a big gold alloy T. T. for Turpin.

The streets around it would be paved with gold bricks, and

parked around it would be Rolls-Royces, Cadillacs, Studebakers, Mercedeses, Stutz Bearcats, Cords.

The little town would have other buildings around it, three stories high, also made of gold alloy and encrusted with jewels. He'd really be dogging it. There'd be a big fountain in front of the Rosebud, which would spout bourbon day and night onto a golden statue of a piano. There'd be other fountains spraying up champagne and gin and liqueurs onto the statues of Joplin and Chauvin and Turpin. The decorations and the furniture in the buildings would make J. P. Morgan turn green with envy. Not that that old pirate would ever see them.

There'd be a thousand pianos in Turpinville, and violins, trumpets, drums, every instrument that might be needed. The servants would be androids, all white-skinned, and they'd address Tom's guests as Massah and Marse regardless of their gender. But Tom would be the only one they'd call Boss.

Outside the forty-building town would be a forest with a river and creeks and several huge marshes and steep hills here and there. A concrete road would wind through the forest so that Tom and his buddies and fancy women could ride in their expensive cars whenever they felt like it. The woods and marshes and streams would be alive with rabbits and wild pigs and foxes and ducks and geese and pheasants and grouse and turkeys and fish and turtles and alligators. Tom loved to hunt; he figured on bagging lots of rabbits and ducks.

"You're planning on having a good time forever?" Nur said.

"Maybe not forever," Tom said. "Just as long as it lasts."

Nur's expression made him uneasy, though he did not know why.

"It'll be a jumping world," he told Nur, and from then on, when he referred to his private universe, he called it "the Jumpin' Planet."

"You've come a long way, baby," he told himself.

"What?" Nur said.

"I've come a long way. I was born in an old run-down shack in Savannah, Georgia, but my father was a big man, big in many ways. He made good money, and we moved into a big fancy house—I don't mean a whorehouse—I mean a beautiful house like the rich white folks lived in. But then the Ku Klux Klan started making trouble, and my pa decided we'd go to Mississippi. There was a street in Savannah named Turpin Hill after my father and his brothers. That shows you what a big man my pa was."

There was even more trouble with the white folks in Mississippi, so they moved on to St. Louis. There they settled down in the black tenderloin district, and "Honest John" Turpin made a fortune with his Silver Dollar Saloon and his livery stable.

"My pa said he'd never done a day's work for another man after the slaves was freed, and he'd never fought with his fists. He was a fighting man, though. He'd grab his man by the wrist, bend them wrist bones together, and butt his head against the man's. Pa had the thickest skull west of the Mississippi, east, too. He always knocked his man out. The man staggered around blind and seeing shooting stars for a week. Nobody fucked around with my pa."

Like so many Negro musicians, Tom taught himself, but, unlike many, he could read music.

"When I was eighteen, me and my brother Charlie went West just to see the country. We was looking for gold, too, lots of it around then, though it wasn't easy getting it out of the ground. We spent a year in Nevada, but that gold just up and hid when we was around.

"I died August 13, 1922. Old Man Death, he had a harder head than Pa's, and I couldn't pay him off. Old Man Death, the only honest man in St. Louis. No bribes, no money under the counter. This is it, I got a job to do, and I always do it. I didn't have no children, but they called me the father of St. Louis ragtime."

"Your wife was more than well-off, and your brother Charlie did all right, too," Frigate said. "He was a constable, the first black elected to public office in Missouri. When he died, I think it was Christmas Day, 1935, he left a hundred and five thousand dollars in a trust fund for his family. Big money in those days."

"Even bigger money for a nigger," Tom said. "Nineteen thirty-five, you say?"

"I'll ask the Computer if it's got a book titled *They All Played*

Ragtime," Frigate said. "You'll like to read it. Lots about you. It'll make you proud."

"I don't need no book for that, but I'll get it."

The day after the Computer told him that his Jumpin' Planet was finished, Tom Turpin entered it. It was ten in the morning; the sky was blue except for a few high-seeming, thin, cotton-white clouds. Tom went down the steps leading into it and found, as he had ordered, his chauffeur and his pink 1920 convertible Mercedes-Benz waiting for him. The android chauffeur was six feet three inches tall, pale-skinned, blue-eyed, and yellow-haired. He also was the ugliest white man Tom had ever seen, because his face had been designed by Tom himself. He wore a typical chauffeur's uniform except it was pink. "To go with the car," Tom had told the others.

He got in the back seat and said, "Home, James." The beauty started up fine, its motor purring, and they began the long winding drive through the tunnel formed by trees with interlocking branches.

"Shouldn't of made the road so narrow," Tom muttered. "But, what the hell, there won't be any oncoming traffic."

After a while the woods thinned out, and they passed along the edge of a lake. Its surface was brilliantly colored with ducks and geese and herons and cranes in the shallows dipping to catch fish. It was also noisy with honks and screeches and weird loon cries.

The road took them away from Turpinville near the edge of the vast chamber. "Wouldn't know it if I didn't know it," Tom said. "Looks like more forest and hills there. I ain't gonna touch the wall. I want to keep the illusion."

From the entrance, a straight path to Turpinville was only two and seven-tenths miles. The road designed by Turpin took up almost ten miles, however, to the town, and he could have taken a branch road and made his trip twenty-two miles. Now and then he glimpsed the roof of his town, and his heart surged with pride. "Mine, all mine."

When they drove from the dark forest into Turpinville, he wished that he had arranged for a big band and a crowd to greet him. The place was so empty, so silent. "A ghost town before its time," he said. "Well, it'll be leaping with sound and people before long."

The car pulled up in front of the Rosebud, and Tom got out. He walked across the town square to the central fountain, took a silver cup from a hook on the fountain, dipped it into the strong-smelling liquid, and drank.

"Man, that's the best! But I need the old crowd, the music, the smoke, the laughs, the . . . friends. No fun drinking by yourself, talking to yourself." '

He went into the Rosebud, took the ornate elevator to the third floor, entered his suite, went into the room where a huge console stood, and began the search.

Three weeks later, he had not just the forty or so people he had intended, but two thousand.

"It's nigger heaven," he told his former companions during one of the rare times he attended their soirees. "It's like a flea circus. Everybody's jumping."

Tom was amused when Frigate winced at "nigger heaven." Frigate was a liberal who found such terms repulsive. Tom would not tolerate these from others, unless they were black, but he had no hesitation using them himself. When Frigate asked him why he did so, Tom replied that it was just his way. He hadn't been able to break his old Earth habit.

"You've lived long enough on the Riverworld to get over that," Nur said.

"It takes away the hurt."

"Whipping yourself is a curious method of salving wounds," Frigate said.

There seemed to be no answer to that. Aphra said, "When are we going to see your world?"

"How about next Friday?" Tom said. "You'll be all right. You'll have a good time. I told my friends about you, and they don't mind you coming." He laughed. "Long as you know your place."

After Turpin had left, Frigate said, "After sixty-seven years here, the old evils of Earth still fester."

"He'll never Go On until that evil no longer exists in him," Nur said. "I mean, its effects."

What had been born on Earth had not necessarily died on the

Riverworld. Yet as Nur said, humankind in general had made ethical and psychic progress.

"To put it in plain English," Burton said, "you mean that many have become better human beings."

"Yes. The Riverworld is a rough reshaper, but change seldom comes without pain."

Nur was silent for a while, then said, "Tom has many good qualities. He's usually cheerful, always courageous, easy to get along with if you don't step on his toes, which is as it should be. But he has never said he regretted his whoremongering. A man who deals in whores is himself a whore, and he is in a violent and dirty business. He has to be rough and ruthless and bloody his hands from time to time. He lacks a certain empathy.'

There was another silence, broken when Frigate said, "Yes?"

"It's not just Tom I'm thinking of. You have sealed yourself up in your little worlds. Can a person grow in a vacuum?"

"Of course we can," Frigate said.

"We'll see," Nur said.

He alone had changed his mind about moving. He had decided to stay in his apartment. "Which is world enough for me."

"And that means trouble," Burton said. "Some among the newly resurrected are going to want those empty worlds for themselves and they'll be shedding blood to get them."

20

Burton, Frigate, and Behn were talking about the standards for resurrecting people in the tower.

"Don't pick any actors, any stage, movie, or TV actors," Frigate said. "They're all swollen egotists, selfish, opportunistic, and untrustworthy. They may be amusing companions for a while, but they're all self-centered."

"All?" Burton said.

"All," Behn said. "I should know. I wrote plays; I had a lot to do with them."

"There might be some exceptions," Frigate said. "However, there are no exceptions among the producers, and they are even more ruthless and cold-blooded than the actors. Don't resurrect producers, especially the Hollywood kind. They're not entirely human."

"I would class them, then, with politicians," Burton said.

"Oh, yes. No politicians or statesmen need apply. Liars, opportunists all."

"All?" Behn said.

"You should know," Burton said.

"I didn't know all of them, so I can't really judge them fairly."

"Take my word for it," Burton said. "No politicians here. What about priests?"

"Men of the cloth, priests, ministers, rabbis, mullahs, witch doctors, bones, whatever; they're all brothers under the uniform. But . . . not all alike. There are some real human beings there, now and then, here and there," Frigate said. "But you have to be suspicious of anyone who thinks well enough of himself to become a spiritual leader. What's his real motive?"

"Popes are out," Burton said. "They're politicians, liars, cold-bloodedly manipulate people, pervert Christianity for the good of the Church. No popes."

"No chief rabbis or chief mullahs or archbishops of Canterbury and their kind," Frigate said. "What applies to the popes applies to them."

"Mother superiors?"

"Out!" Burton said, jerking a thumb at the ceiling.

"Surely, there are exceptions?"

"Not enough to make it worthwhile to spend time on them," Burton said.

"What about used-car salesmen? Used-car saleswomen, too?" Frigate said.

Burton and Behn looked blank.

"A twentieth-century phenomenon," Frigate said. "Forget it. I'll keep an eye out for them and warn you if I have to. I doubt that I'll have to."

"Doctors?"

"No blanket rule can be applied to them. But most are lost souls in this world where there is little need for them and they have no authority. Be careful."

"Lawyers?"

"Some of them are the best people in the world; some, the worst. Be careful. Oh, by the way, I located Buddha," Frigate said. "Siddhartha, the historical Buddha."

"What's that got to do with lawyers?" Burton said.

"Nothing. But Buddha . . . ah . . . he's noted in the records, plenty of film on him, if you want to see the living Buddha, Gautama, just ask the Computer. That is, he was living on Earth. He was never resurrected on the Riverworld. When he died on Earth, he Went On."

"Ah!" Burton said, as if he suddenly understood much that had been hidden before.

"Ah?"

"Yes. I located the file of the historical Jesus Christ several days ago," Burton said.

"Me, too!" Frigate said.

"Then you know that he was resurrected on the River, died several times, the last time twenty years ago. And he, too, has

Gone On now. But, apparently, Buddha was more ethically advanced than Jesus."

"Buddha had a much longer life on Earth than Jesus," Frigate said.

"I am attacking no one, only pointing out a fact."

"I located St. Francis of Assisi," Frigate said. "He was raised on the River, but when he died ten years ago, he Went On."

"How many popes and cardinals, how many high churchmen of any faith have Gone On?" Aphra Behn said.

"None," Frigate said. "None so far as I've determined, I mean. I haven't located all. Rather, the Computer hasn't. I put it on a scan. It's located all but twelve of the popes . . ."

"Including the first one, St. Peter?" Burton said.

"He wasn't the first pope, he was the first bishop of Rome. Technically speaking, that is."

"Ah, then he really was in Rome?"

"Yes, he was executed by the Romans there. But . . . he's still on The River. He's died three times and still has not Gone On."

"So," Burton said, "we could resurrect him and get the truth about Jesus and Christianity. That is, the truth as he knows it, which may not be the objective truth."

"Jesus' records are still on tap," Frigate said. "His *wathan* is gone, but his life is still there to be run off."

"St. Paul?"

"Ah, St. Paul!" Frigate cried, smiling. "First, he was a fanatical Orthodox Judaist, then a fanatical Christian, probably did more to pervert the course of the founder's teachings than anyone, and now he is a fanatical member of the Church of the Second Chance. Rather, I should say, he was. The Church wants zealots but not fanatics, and so it recently kicked him out. He is now interested in the teachings of the Dowists."

"The Dowists?"

"Tell you about them some other time. Paul is alive on The River. I located him and I watched him for a while. Ugly little fellow, but a powerful speaker. He's no longer celibate; he decided that he *is* burning and wants a woman to quench the flame."

Frigate showed them three men he had located because of their undeniable evil and vast prominence in his time. Burton had heard of them while in The Valley but had known little about them until now. Adolf Hitler was born the year before Burton had died, Joseph Dzhugashvili, better known as Stalin, was born eleven years before Burton's death, and Mao Tsetung was born three years after 1890.

"They're locked up in the files now," Frigate said. "I've not had much time to look at their post-Earth lives, but I've seen enough to be sure that they did not change for the better. Their natures are still essentially like Ivan the Terrible's. Whom, by the way, I've also located."

Nur said, "You believe that there is no hope for them, that they will never change for the better?"

"Yes. It looks that way, anyway. They were and are evil, sadistic, and cold-blooded killers, mass butchers, without love. Psychopathic."

"But Loga said that there were no true psychopaths on the Riverworld. He said that true psychopaths were so because of chemical imbalances in their bodies. These imbalances, these deficiencies, were eliminated when the bodies were resurrected."

Frigate shrugged and said, "Yes, I know. So . . . what is their excuse now? They have none; they have chosen their attitudes through their own free will. They and they alone are responsible."

"That may be," Nur said, "but it is not up to you to destroy them, to cut their alloted time short. Who knows? They might, at the very last moment, undergo a radical change of character. See the light, as it were. Remember Göring."

"Göring started suffering remorse and guilt years ago. These . . . creatures . . . Stalin, Hitler, Mao, Ivan the Terrible . . . are still ready . . . eager, in fact . . . to kill anyone who stands in their way. Which way, by the way, is a steady advancement toward power, supreme power, the power to dominate and control others and crush all who oppose them. Or who they think oppose them. They're all genuinely paranoiac, you know. Though they strive to shape reality, and often do, they're not connected with reality. I mean that they don't truly perceive things as they are. They're driven by their lust to shape reality into what they think it is or should be."

"Most people are driven by the same desire."

"There are great evils and little evils."

"Great evildoers and little evildoers, you mean. There is no such thing as abstract evil. Evil always consists of concrete acts and concrete actors."

Burton, who had been listening, became impatient.

"The true philosophy is not in talk, which most philosophers think is philosophy, but in action. Pete, you're doing a lot of talking about what you'd like to do. Why? Because you're afraid to act, and your fear comes from your feeling not self-justified?"

"I keep thinking, *Judge not lest ye be judged.*"

"Do you think for one moment that you won't be judged even if you refrain from judging others?" Burton said scornfully. "Besides, it's impossible for anybody not to judge others. Even saints can't keep from judging, try though they might not to. It's automatic and takes place in both the conscious and unconscious mind. So, I say, judge right and left, fore and aft, up and down, in and out!"

Nur laughed and said, "But don't pass sentence."

"Why not?" Burton said, grinning fiendishly. "Why not?"

"I've located a real judge, I mean a judge in the legal sense," Frigate said. "A man who sat in the circuit court of my hometown, Peoria, during the Prohibition era. I remember reading about him when I was a kid; I also remember what my father and his friends said about him. He was part of the very corrupt municipal system then, he sent many a bootlegger to prison or fined those found with booze in their homes or in speakeasies. Yet he had a cellar full of whiskey and gin he purchased from bootleggers. Some of whom, by the way, he let off because they were his direct suppliers."

"You've been very busy," Nur said.

"I can't resist it," Frigate said.

Burton understood Frigate's fascination, or, at least, thought he could. Evil people did have a certain magnetism that drew everybody, evil or good or gray-shaded, toward them. First, attraction, then repulsion. In fact, paradoxically, it was the repulsion that caused the attraction.

"The curious thing is," Frigate said suddenly, as if he had been thinking about it for a long time but had thrust it back down, "the curious thing is that none of these, Hitler, Stalin, Mao, Tsar Ivan, the Peoria judge, and the baby-rapist I told you about, none of these thinks of himself as evil."

"Göring did, and that was his first step away from his evil," Nur said. "These men . . . Hitler, Stalin, and others . . . what do you intend to do about them?"

"I've put them *On Hold*," Frigate said.

"You haven't made up your mind yet what to do with them?"

"No. But if the Computer starts releasing the eighteen billion people back into The Valley, it won't do it for those men. Look! I've seen what they've done. Seen it through their own eyes, seen it through the eyes of the people they did it to!"

Frigate's eyes were large and wild, and his face was red.

"I don't want them to keep on doing those evil things! Why should they escape justice now! They did it on Earth, but things are different here! There is some reason why they're locked in the files and why we are in a position to judge. And to convict and execute if need be!"

"It's not divine intervention or intention that caused the lockup," Nur said. "It's an accident."

"Is it?" Frigate said.

Nur smiled and shrugged. "Perhaps not. All the more reason for us to act discreetly, reasonably, and carefully."

"Why should we?" Burton roared. "Who cares?"

"Ah," the Moor said, holding up his index finger and looking at its tip as if it held the answer. "Who knows? Have you perhaps had the feeling, now and then, that we are still being watched? I do not mean by the Computer but by someone who is using the Computer."

"And just whom could that be?"

"I don't know. But have you had that feeling?"

"No."

"I have," Frigate said. "But that doesn't mean anything. I've always had the feeling . . . all my life . . . that someone was watching me."

"Who then is watching the watcher? Who then judges the judge?"

"You Sufis . . ." Burton said disgustedly.

"The thing is," Frigate said, "these men, Hitler, Stalin, Mao, Ivan the Terrible, and so on had immense power in their lifetime on Earth. They were exceedingly important historical figures. And now . . ."

"Now you, the insignificant, have them in your power," Nur said.

"I wish I could have had them in my power when they were just beginning their criminal careers," Frigate said.

"Would you have pushed the *Destroy* button then?"

"Jesus! I don't know! I should have! But . . ."

"What if someone could have pushed a button to destroy you?" Nur said.

"My sins were not that great," Frigate said.

"Their size would depend on the attitude of the button pusher," Nur said. "Or in the minds of those injured by your sins."

Burton left then, though he paused a moment to say good-night to Li Po and his woman, Star Spoon, and his cronies. Li Po had located and resurrected seven of the poets and painters who had been his special friends.

As Burton turned toward the door, Star Spoon said, softly, "We must see each other again. Soon."

"Quite," Burton said. "Of course."

"I mean alone," she said, and she walked away before the others noticed that she had spoken to him.

Burton did not believe that she just wished to *talk* to him. Under other circumstances, he would have been delighted. But Li Po was a friend and was very jealous, even if he had had no right to be so possessive. It would not be honorable to meet her alone.

But she is a free agent, he told himself. Li Po gave her life again, but he does not own her. Not unless she thinks he does. If she wishes to see me and will do so openly, Li knowing all about it, ah, well . . .

The very egotistic Chinese would find it hard to believe that she could prefer another man. There would be a scene, much shouting and bombast and perhaps Li Po would challenge him to a duel. That challenge and his acceptance would both be stupid. Li Po had been born in A.D. 701 and he in A.D. 1821, but neither were any longer bound by the codes of those times and, in fact, never had been entirely creatures of their ages. To fight over a woman was ridiculous. Li Po would realize that. Surely. But Li Po would no longer be his friend. And Burton valued his friendship.

On the other hand, Star Spoon was not a robot, and Li Po must have known when he resurrected her that he could not control her. She was no longer a slave girl.

The swaying of her hips was the tolling of a fleshly bell. Ding, dong! Ding, dong! He sighed and tried to think of something besides his rigid and aching flesh. No use. It had been too long.

But, if he came to know her well, not in the Biblical sense, would he even like her? She was probably not worth the trouble she'd cause, and he was sure that she would.

Being an old man in a young man's body causes conflict, he thought. *My hormones rage upstream against my long experience. 'Tis true a stiff prick has no conscience. 'Tis also true it has no brains.*

However, Star Spoon was not the only woman in the world. He had available, theoretically, anyway, about 9.5 billion. Unfortunately, at that moment, Star Spoon was the woman he wanted. He was not "in love" with her, he did not think that he would ever be "in love" again, no one who was 136 years old and was intelligent could be swept away by romantic love. Should not be, anyway.

Of the 8.5 billion plus males locked in the files, perhaps a sixteenth were as old as he. Of these, a sixteenth might be said to be intelligent enough to have slipped the moorings of romantic love. He did not have much company.

At the moment, his only companion was the memory-viewscreen on the wall alongside his flying chair. The Computer had skipped to the age of thirty-nine and selected a very painful scene. He was in London then, getting ready for the secret journey to Mecca. Since there would be many times when his penis would be exposed before his Moslem fellow-travelers, he had to be circumcised. Otherwise, one look at his foreskin would show them that he was an infidel dog, and he would be killed, probably literally torn apart, on the spot. Though the Muslim men usually squatted to urinate, and their robes usually covered their penises, there would be times when he could not escape their view. Thus, he was being circumcised, and his only anesthetic was a half-quart of whiskey.

Burton stopped the chair. The scene stopped with him. Burton, not knowing why he was doing so, told the Computer to project the neural-emotional field.

At once, he felt a searing pain as the doctor's knife rounded the foreskin.

He clamped down on his teeth to keep from screaming, as he had clamped down on his cigar during the actual operation.

At the same time, he felt dizzy and sluggish. The field was enveloping him with his sensations as they had been at that time, and he had been drunk. Not as drunk as he should have been.

"Enough!" he cried. "Remove the NE field."

Immediately, the pain was gone. Or was it? Was there not the ghost or the shadow of one slowly departing?

Burton was no masochist. He had inflicted pain only so that his desire for Star Spoon, for any woman, would go away. It worked. But not for long.

21

A long time ago, Frigate had said to Burton that it had been impossible on Earth to determine the identity of Jack the Ripper. But since the Ripper must be in the Rivervalley, he could be found there. However, the chances for running across him were extremely slight. Even less were the chances that he, if found, would confess. Also, a man who might admit to the murders might be a liar. Actually, the solution to the enigma was much more likely here than on Earth.

Frigate had stated that a long time before he and Burton had gotten to the tower. Now they were in a place where the odds for finding the man known as Jack the Ripper were high. Frigate knew who the candidates were, though it was possible that the true Ripper might not be among them, and it was likely that the Computer could locate all of these in its files.

Frigate had not gotten around to his suggested project because he was too busy with other lines of research, including tracing his genealogy. This tower, he said, was a genealogist's paradise. He did not have to resort to the difficult-to-find and often-lost records: wills, tax and land deeds, probate and orphan court records, censuses, county histories, newspapers, tombstones, military and pension records, and all the other elusive traces of people who might or might not be your ancestors. Here you could set the Computer on the track, starting with yourself, and it could work backward through your parents. You could see on a screen what a parent looked like, where he or she was, see their lives through their own eyes and what they looked like through the eyes of others. Sometimes, he had to wait while the Computer used an ancestor's *wathan* to search through its files for the matching *wathan* and then identified the *wathan* of that person's parents. Where there was doubt about the paternity of a child, the Computer could compare the genetic makeup of the child and the parent in doubt and establish the relationship. If it proved that a certain child could not be the offspring of a certain adult, then the Computer could examine the genes of those suspected of being the true father. The suspects could be easily identified, since the Computer could review the mother's past and determine exactly when and with whom she had had intercourse. After which, the physical recordings of the suspect or suspects would be examined for genetic identity.

Burton found this interesting but was not, for the moment, eager to establish his own lineage. He had always been enthralled by stories of murders, mutilations, and tortures, and he had read the newspaper accounts of the Whitechapel murders. Once he had decided that he would launch Operation Ripper, as he called it, he asked the Computer for a bibliography of all the books in English regarding the Ripper that its files contained. Whatever Ethical agent or agents had been assigned to obtaining the literature concerning the Ripper had been very thorough. Frigate took a few minutes off from his own work to check them and indicated the ones he thought Burton might find most profitable as starting points.

"I would read first a book by Stephen Knight, *Jack the Ripper, the Final Solution,* published in 1976. That impressed me as not only the most thoroughly researched and brilliant and convincing in its reasoning—would have made Sherlock Holmes proud—but also the only book that might have the true answers. However, some critics have pointed out flaws in it. Whether it's wrong or right or only half-right, it's a good one to use as your springboard to dive from into the incarnadined ocean of the mystery."

It was strange to hold in his hands a book that was copied from a work published eighty-seven years *after* his death. He did not marvel long, since marvels were so many that each could be wondered at only briefly. He read the more than 270 pages in three hours. When he put the book down, he could have repeated without many errors long passages, which in total amounted to at least a fourth of the text.

If the book had been issued in his Earthly lifetime, Burton would have been outraged by its preposterousness. Or would he? Would he not on reflection, knowing what he did of the secret maneuverings for power by those on high, knowing of the inhuman and totally unjust deeds done by the government and upper-class individuals in the struggle to keep their power, would he not have considered that the conclusions drawn from the events described in the book were valid?

What Mr. Knight had shown after deep and wide research and illuminated and illuminating deductions was:

In 1888, the masses, the poor people, of England, Scotland, Wales, and Ireland were, or seemed to be, on the edge of revolution. The radicals of the left, the socialists and the anarchists, were loudly voicing the oppressions and sufferings of the working class. The government was not just alarmed, it was scared stiff, and many of the ruling class believed that the monarchy itself was threatened. They were overreacting; their ignorance of the masses made them unaware of the deep conservatism of the people. What these wanted was not a change in the structure of the monarchy but steady work with good pay, food, adequate housing, and some economic security. They wanted to live as human beings should, not as rats.

Queen Victoria, the ruling class thought, would not be overthrown, but she was old and, at that time, unpopular. When she died, her son Edward ("Bertie") would sit on the throne. And he was a lecherous, pigheaded, and totally immoral man whose activities could not be concealed.

There were then many Freemasons in the upper echelons of the British government, including the marquess of Salisbury, the prime minister. Knight claimed that these highly placed Masons were the power behind the throne, and they were afraid that when the monarchy went, they and their secret society would go, too.

Prince Edward's oldest surviving son, the duke of Clarence and Avondale, Albert Victor Christian Edward, "Eddy" to his intimates, would ascend the throne if his father died. He was a pathetic creature (from the Victorian standpoint), liked to mingle under an assumed name with artists and other Bohemians, was bisexual, and had once frequented a male brothel. Even worse, after falling in love with a shopkeeper's assistant, Annie Elizabeth Crook, to whom he had been introduced by the painter Walter Sickert, the duke had married her in a secret ceremony. It was an illegal marriage in several respects, but the most offensive and and dangerous was that Eddy had taken to wife a Roman Catholic. By law, no English monarch could marry a Catholic. Eddy was not the king, but he could easily and soon become the king. A number of people had tried to assassinate the queen; she was old, and Eddy's father, Prince Edward, could die from overindulgence in food and drink, a venereal disease, a bullet from a jealous husband, a revolutionist or a maniac, or from any of the diseases against which there was then no prevention and for which there was no cure except the afflicted's natural resistance.

Adding to the heinousness of Eddy's deeds was the birth in April 1888 of his daughter by Annie Crook. The infant was the great-granddaughter of Queen Victoria and the first cousin of those men who were to reign as Edward VIII and George VI.

This was too much for the queen, who sent an angry note to the prime minister, Lord Salisbury, demanding that he assure that the newspapers and the public not be made aware of the scandal.

Salisbury, in turn, gave the queen's physician, Sir William Gull, a fellow Mason, the responsibility for the coverup. Gull was a brilliant man and a great physician, by Victorian standards, and was also distinguished by a grotesque and perverse sense of humor and an obvious schizophrenia (obvious to a later generation). He could be very kind and compassionate but at other times was cold, cruel, and callous. The latter behavior was, however, only evident when he was dealing with lower-class patients and their families. He was a kind master to his own pets, but he had justified, to his own satisfaction, a vivisectionist who had slowly baked live dogs in an oven until they died during his experiments.

Following Gull's secret orders, transmitted through the police commissioner, also a Mason, special police agents raided the apartments of Walter Sickert, Eddy's old companion, and Annie

Crook. They hustled Eddy off from Sickert's to the palace and Crook to an asylum. Gull certified that Annie was insane, though she was not at that time, and she spent the rest of her life in asylums and workhouses. In 1920, truly mad, she died. Eddy never saw her again.

The police had intended to pick up Mary Kelly, a young Irishwoman who had witnessed the illicit marriage. Probably, Gull would have certified her as insane, too. Whatever he intended for her, he was frustrated. Somehow, she escaped the police net and dived deep into the labyrinth of the East End. Later, she took care for a while of Alice Margaret, Eddy's and Annie's child. Both accompanied Sickert on his long trips to Dieppe. While in France, Mary Jane Kelly changed her name to Marie Jeannette Kelly.

Eventually, Kelly had to hide again in London's vast people warren, the East End. Here she began the slide downward that ended with her becoming one of the many thousands of alcoholic and diseased whores living miserable and hopeless lives. Like her sisters in the profession, she considered herself fortunate if she earned just enough money to buy gin for a few hours' numbness, enough food to stave off outright starvation, and a roof over her head.

Kelly was not without friends, however, the closest of whom were Mary Anne Nichols, Anne Siffey, alias Chapman, and Elizabeth "Long Liz" Stride, all drunks, diseased, malnourished, and doomed to die soon even if "Jack the Ripper" had not existed. When Kelly met these in taverns or in their lousy apartments and the gin bore discretion away on the golden waves of alcohol, she revealed to them the Prince Eddy–Annie Crook liaison and its terrible results. And, during one of these roaring sessions, the idea for blackmailing Prince Eddy was born.

Knight had suggested that the four had tried the extortion scheme because they were forced to do it by a group of dangerous thugs, the Old Nichol Gang.

Whatever the motivation, the idea was very dangerous and stupid. Salisbury had let the search for Kelly drop because he had not heard from her nor had his police spies heard that she was disclosing anything about the affair. As long as she kept her mouth shut, she was no peril to the establishment that Salisbury represented. Now, however, on receiving a message demanding money for silence, Salisbury put the machinery of retribution in motion.

Urged by Salisbury, Gull lost no time in reacting. The prime minister had given him orders to put the lid back on, but Salisbury probably had no glimmering of how Gull intended to do this. Certainly, desperate as he was to silence the blackmailers, he would have been horrified if he had known what Gull intended. It was one thing to imprison a lower-class woman in a series of hospitals and workhouses for life, a regrettable but necessary deed from Salisbury's viewpoint. But to murder and butcher the women was a deed that Salisbury could not have ordered. Once the slayings had started, however, Salisbury could only let them go on and do his best to protect "Jack the Ripper."

John Netley was the coachman who had driven Prince Eddy to the Sickert home and other places where Eddy did what a prince of the realm was not supposed to do. Gull had insured his silence with threats and bribes after Eddy and Alice Crook had been abducted. Knowing Netley's character, Gull now told him, in general terms, what his plans were for the blackmailers. Netley was eager to serve him. And, since Sickert knew the principals in the affair, was well acquainted with the East End, and had accepted money to keep his mouth shut about Eddy and Crook, Sickert was enlisted by Gull. Though reluctant to take part in the murders, he knew that if he did not, he would himself be killed.

The coach, driven by Netley, holding Sickert and Gull, drove into the Whitechapel area. After a number of reconnoiterings, Gull and Sickert lured Mary Anne Nichols into their coach by requesting her services. Flattered that two such elegant gentlemen would even look at her, though doubtless wondering what kinky acts they had in mind, Nichols got into the coach. Gull offered her a glass of wine containing a drug (Knight had suggested he used poisoned grapes), and, when she was unconscious, he cut her throat from left to right, disemboweled her, and stabbed her. Sickert leaned out of the coach and vomited.

Afterward, the coach drove to the dark and momentarily deserted street of Bucks Row, where Netley and Sickert carried the body from the coach and laid it out. They knew the schedule of the patrolman, but, even so, they drove off only a few minutes before he arrived.

Eight days later, the three struck again, Anne Siffey, alias Chapman, was found dead in the backyard of No. 29, Hanbury Street. Her throat had been deeply cut from left to right and back again. Her small intestines and a flap of the abdomen were on her right side near the shoulder, still attached by a cord to the rest of the intestines in the body. Two skin flaps from the lower abdominal region were lying in a pool of blood above the left shoulder.

This time, Gull had the unconscious woman taken from the coach to the backyard, where he performed the ritualistic mutilations in the dim light.

On September 29, Gull killed two whores. The first murder was hastily done because Long Liz Stride refused to get into the coach. Netley and Sickert left the coach, seized her, and held her while Gull cut her throat. But Gull did not have the time to do what he would have liked. He heard loud voices nearby and so did not want to risk being seen carrying her body into the coach. The three left hurriedly.

Later that evening, the second murder was done with plenty of time for execution. Catherine Eddowes was found in Mitre Square (not a part of the Whitechapel area), part of her nose slashed off, the right ear lobe almost cut off, her face and throat worked over with a sharp instrument, her bowels removed, and her left kidney and uterus missing.

Unfortunately, from Gull's viewpoint—and Eddowes'— Sickert had mistaken Eddowes for Marie Kelly. She had not been Kelly's confidante, was totally unaware of the Eddy-Crook events, and died because the painter had thought, in the dim light, that she was Marie Jeannette Kelly. Though he had discovered his error immediately after her throat was cut, Gull insisted on performing the ritual. Why waste his time? Besides, she was just a whore, and if, by any chance, some policeman had an inkling of the plot, she would be a false clue.

In the late evening of November 9, the last and most important target, Kelly, was subjected to the most savage butchering of all. The ritual took two hours. And the Jack the Ripper murders ceased.

Burton had located the recordings of Gull, Netley, Kelly, Crook, Sickert, Salisbury, Prince Eddy, and Stride. For some reason the Computer could not explain, Chapman's and Nichols' were unavailable. The Computer, however, continued looking for them.

Burton viewed the events from the meeting of Eddy with Annie Crook through the slaying of Kelly via the eyes and ears of the recordings. He replayed some of these several times, though he vomited twice, the first time watching Gull working on Eddowes, the second time during Kelly's dissection. He had thought that he had a strong stomach, but he had overestimated its tolerance.

He then had the Computer run some of the episodes from the Riverworld life of each of the participants in the Ripper affair. Annie Elizabeth Crook had been raised on The River with her sanity restored but with most of her memory from 1888 to 1920 missing.

Sir William Gull's schizophrenia seemed to have been eliminated. Twenty years after the first resurrection, he had become converted to a religious sect, the Dowists, by the founder himself, Lorenzo Dow.

John Netley, the coachman, had been deeply affected by the shock of drowning in the Thames and then awakening on the Riverbank. For six months, his behavior could have been described as Christianlike (according to the ideal, not the practice of most Christians). Once the shock had worn off and he was fairly sure that he was not going to be punished for his sins, he reverted to his Earthly self, an opportunistic, lecherous, self-centered, and cold-blooded criminal.

Walter Sickert, the painter, early converted to the Church of the Second Chance and rose to the rank of bishop.

Long Liz Stride and Marie Kelly were resurrected in The Valley within a few feet of each other. For five years, they had been good friends and close neighbors. Neither had continued as a prostitute, though they had taken a series of lovers, and they drank as much as they could get. Then Stride had gotten religion and joined a popular Buddhist sect, the Nichirenites. Kelly had left her, gone upRiver, and, after many adventures, settled down in a peaceful area. Both had died during the terrible times following the grailstone shutdown on the right bank of The River.

The long journeys of all were ended, for the time being, anyway. They were locked up in the physical recordings and the *wathans* that floated whirling in the central well.

22

His investigation of the Ripper affair was completed; the mystery, solved. Now he could take residence in his private world, but, for some unfathomable reason, he was still reluctant to do so. Nevertheless, he could not put off moving long. It irked him to be unconsciously opposing himself; he would not put up with it.

Before going, though, he considered what he had been living through, vicariously, these past two weeks. He was shaken and appalled, especially by the world as seen through the eyes of the whores. He had witnessed many savage and grisly deeds and much injustice and oppression, but none matched the grisliness and inhumanity of the deed that was the East End of London in the 1880s. In this relatively small area were jam-packed eight hundred thousand people, hungry most of the time, eating swill and glad to have it, drunk if they could afford it and often when they could not, dwelling in small, dirty rooms with sweating, peeling walls alive with vermin, cruel to each other, ignorant, superstitious, and, worst condition of all, hopeless.

Burton knew that the lives of the East Enders had been wretched, but not until he had lived in it, even if in a secondhand manner, was he made sick and guilty by the mere existence of that hellhole. Guilty because he now understood that he and all others who had ignored it were responsible.

From one viewpoint, perverted but nevertheless valid, the Ripper had done a deed of mercy when he had put those hungry, gaunt, diseased, and hopeless whores out of their deep misery.

Also, unwittingly, he had forced the England outside of the East End to look at the inferno they had turned their eyes away from. The result had been a great cry for change, and many buildings had been torn down to make way for better housing. But in time the poverty and pain had resumed its former level—it had never subsided much—and the East End was forgotten by those who did not have to live there.

Frigate, when told by Burton of the results of his investigation, was intrigued. He said, "What you should do is track down those absentee landlords who made money from the horribly poor and deliver them to oblivion."

"That's Marxism," Burton said.

"I despised the practice of communism, but it had some great ideals," Frigate said. "I also despised the practice of capitalism, many aspects of it anyway."

"But it had its ideals," Burton said.

He had looked at Frigate and then laughed. "Has any social-political-economic system ever gotten anywhere near its ideals? Haven't they all been corrupted?"

"Of course. So . . . the corrupters should be punished."

Nur el-Musafir had pointed out what they knew but had ignored.

"It does not matter what they . . . we . . . did on Earth. What matters is what we're doing now. If the corrupter and the corrupted have changed for the better, then they should be rewarded as much as those who have always been virtuous. Now, let me define virtue and the virtuous . . ." He smiled.

"No, I think not. You are tired of the sage of the tower, as you sometimes call me. My truths make you uneasy even though you agree with me."

Frigate said, "About this business of wondering whom to resurrect to be our companions. Take Cleopatra, for instance. You and I would like to see her in the flesh and hear her story, find out the truth of what went on then. But she liked to stick sharp pins in her slave-girls' breasts, and she could enjoy their screams and writhings. Shakespeare ignored that when he wrote *Antony and Cleopatra*. So did George Bernard Shaw in his *Caesar and Cleopatra*. From a literary viewpoint, they were right. Could you believe in or care about the genius and greatness of Cleopatra and Caesar or sorrow over their tragedy if you saw their barbaric sadism and callous murderousness? We, however, live in the real world, not that of fiction. So, would you want Cleopatra or Caesar or Antony as your neighbor?"

"Nur would say that depends upon how they are now."

"He's right, of course. He's always right. Nevertheless . . .'"

He spoke to Nur.

"You're an elitist. You believe, and you're probably right, that very few have the inborn ability to become Sufi or its philosophical-ethical equivalent. You maintain that even fewer will Go On. The majority just don't have it in them to attain the ethical level to do that. Too bad, but that's the way it is. Nature is wasteful with bodies, and she is just as wasteful with souls. Nature has arranged that most flies will become food for birds and frogs, and she has also arranged that most souls will not achieve salvation but will, even though they don't die like the flies, fail to reach the level set for them. A few Go On, but most are like the flies who become food."

"The difference," Nur said, "is that flies are brainless and soulless but human beings are sentient and are aware of what they must do. Should be aware, anyway."

Burton said, "Would Nature, God, if you will, be that wasteful, that callous?"

"He gave mankind free will," Nur said. "It is not God's fault that there is such a waste."

"Yes, but you yourself have said that genetic defects, chemical imbalances, accidents to the brain, and social environment can influence a person's behavior."

"Influence, yes. Determine, no. No. I must qualify that. There are certain situations and conditions where a person cannot use his free will. But . . . that is not so here, not in the Riverworld."

"What if the Ethicals had not given us a second chance?"

Nur smiled and held up his palms outward.

"Ah, but He *did* arrange it so that the Ethicals *did* give us another chance."

"Which, according to you, most people are blowing."

"You believe it, too, don't you?"

Burton and Frigate felt uncomfortable. They usually did when they talked with Nur about serious subjects.

That was the last conversation he had in the apartment. As

soon as the screens had faded, Burton went into the corridor. He thought for a moment of canceling the codeword so that someone else could use the rooms. However, he might need a place to run to, a place where no one could find him.

Carrying no possessions except the beamer, wearing only a towel-kilt and sandals, he passed through the doorway. Immediately, a screen appeared on the wall across the corridor. Ignoring the picture—his father approaching him threateningly, for what reason Burton did not remember—Burton started to get into the flying chair parked by the wall. Then he turned away from it to face the length of the hall. A roaring was coming from that direction. His hand started toward his beamer but stopped as he recognized the sound.

Presently, a huge black motorcycle zoomed around the corner of the hall several hundred yards away. Its driver was leaning the vehicle deeply to take the turn at high speed. Then the machine straightened up, and, accompanied by a wall-screen displaying an event in the driver's past, headed toward Burton. The rider, a big black man wearing a visored helmet and a black leather outfit, flashed big white teeth at him.

Burton stood by the chair, refusing to move even though the handlebar of the cycle missed him by only an inch.

"Watch it, motherfucker!" the man shouted, and his laughter dopplered back to Burton.

Burton swore, and he had the Computer form a screen for him so that he could put in a call to Tom Turpin. He had to wait for several minutes before Turpin's grinning face appeared. He was surrounded by his entourage, men and women flashily dressed, talking loudly and laughing shrilly. Tom was wearing an early twentieth-century suit with a bright and clashing checked design and a scarlet derby with a long white feather. A huge cigar was in his mouth. He had gained at least ten pounds since Burton had last seen him.

"How you doing, baby?"

"I'm not having as good a time as you," Burton said sourly. "Tom, I have a complaint, a legitimate one."

"We sure don't want no illegitimate gripes, do we?" Tom said, and he puffed out thick green smoke.

"You people are speeding through the halls on motorcycles and cars and God only knows what else," Burton said. "I've not only almost been hit twice, but the stink of gas and horseshit is most obnoxious. Can't you do something about them? They're dangerous and offensive."

"Hell, no, I can't do anything about it," Tom said, still smiling. "They're my people, yeah, and I'm the king here. But I don't have no police force, you know. Besides, the robots clean up the horsepoppy, and the ventilators clean up the smoke. And you can hear them coming, can't you? Just stand aside. Anyway, it must be boring and lonely down there. Don't they give you a thrill, make you feel like you ain't alone? Tell you, Dick, you been living too long by yourself. It sours your milk. Why don't you get a woman? Hell, get four or five. Maybe you won't be so bitchy then."

"You won't do anything about it?"

"Can't. Won't. Them niggers are really uppity."

He grinned. "There goes the neighborhood, right? Tell you what, Dick. You just shoot them next time they annoy you. Won't nobody be hurt permanently. I'll just resurrect them, and we'll all have a good laugh. Course, next time, they might shoot you. See you, Dick. Have a good day."

The screen faded out.

Burton was seething. There was, however, little he could do about the situation unless he wanted to start a miniwar. Which he did not. Nevertheless . . . He got into his chair and took off for his private world. There he would be disturbed by no one, and, when he populated it, he would make sure that his companions would be not only agreeable but sensitive. Yet he loved an argument, and he found verbally violent quarrels most satisfying.

Going around the corner from which the black rider had come, Burton almost hit the heads of five people. Startled, he moved the controls on the arm so that his chair lifted above them. They had ducked, but if the chair had been a little lower, it would have struck the group.

His heart pounding hard because of the unexpectedness of the encounter, he stopped the chair, revolved it, and set it down on the floor. The two men and three women were strangers, but they did not seem to be dangerous. They were naked and so had no place to hide weapons. Moreover, they were obviously frightened and unsure of themselves. They did not approach him, though they did call out to him in English. British English, one with the accent of a cultured man, one with a Cockney accent, one with a Scotch burr, one with an Irish lilt, and one with a foreign accent, probably Scandinavian.

Burton had taken two steps toward them when he stopped.

"My God!"

He recognized them now. Gull, Netley, Crook, Kelly, and Stride.

23

Burton usually reacted swiftly to any situation and was seldom jellied with astonishment or fear. But seeing these five here was so unexpected and so impossible that he could only stare at them for a few seconds. If they had been unknown to him, he would have been surprised, but that he knew them so well, and thought them locked up in the recordings, locked his brain.

They, of course, were in a far worse state than he. They had no idea of where they were or why they had been raised. At least, judging from their expressions, they had not been told anything. Whoever had resurrected them here must have left them to their own devices. *Probably,* thought Burton, his brain beginning to flicker with a little fire, *probably it's no coincidence that they were placed near me. But who ... who in the name of God? ... could have done this? And why?*

Gull was now on his bare knees, looking upward, his hands together in a praying position, his mouth moving. Netley looked like a cornered animal, snarling, crouching, ready to spring at some unknown danger. The three women were looking at him with wide-open eyes. He could read both fear and hope in their faces, fear that he might be some horrible creature, hope that he might be their savior.

He got out of the chair and, smiling, approached them slowly. When he was five feet from them, he stopped. He raised his hand and said, "There's nothing to worry about. Quite the contrary. If you will please stop babbling and follow me, I'll tell you what's happened to you. And I'll make you comfortable. My name, by the way, is Richard Francis Burton. No need to introduce yourselves. I know who you are."

He went to an open door, possibly that from which they had

just exited. They started toward him just as he heard a faint roaring. Burton recognized the sound of the motorcycle motor. Instead of seating them as he had planned, he stood by the doorway. The others huddled behind him. Presently, the corridor throbbed with noise, and the cycle leaned around the corner, straightened, and shot by them. The black rider waved a gauntleted hand. "How you like that, motherfucker?"

Burton turned and saw that they were puzzled and even more scared. No wonder. None of them had ever seen a motorcycle before, any internal combustion machine, in fact. Neither had he when he died, but he had become familiar with them through his viewing of films and reading of books since he had come to the tower.

"I'll explain that later," he said. He told them to sit down, and they did so, but all tried to speak to him at once.

He said, "I know you have many questions, but please restrain them. We'll get them in a while. First, though, you might like a drink."

No, first, he would get kilts, bras, and blankets from the converter. For a moment, they were too shocked to be concerned about their nudity. Anyway, after their exposure to naked people on the Riverbanks, they would not be overly anxious about it. They were glad to get the clothing and blankets, and they murmured their thanks before putting them on. Though Netley had lost his wild look, he still seemed suspicious of Burton.

"You must need a drink," he said. "What would you like?"

None seemed to have taken an abstainer's vow. Netley, Stride, and Kelly wanted gin straight. Gull ordered Scotch with water; Annie Crook, wine. After Burton had served them, he said, "Your stomachs'll be empty, but I imagine that you're not hungry just now. When you are, you may have anything and as much as you like. Unlike your situation on The River, you don't have to take what the grail delivers."

They downed their liquor so swiftly that Burton gave them another round. They now looked less pale and disturbed and seemed eager to listen to him.

Gull spoke with a rich baritone. "You are not by any chance Sir Richard Burton, the famous African explorer and linguist?"

"At your service."

"By God, I thought so. You look like him, younger of course. I attended several of your lectures at the Anthropological Society."

"I remember," Burton said.

Gull waved the hand that held the cut-quartz goblet, spilling some Scotch. "But . . . all this . . . what . . . ?"

"All in good time."

Gull and Netley would know each other, of course, even though it had been more than forty years since they had seen each other. Burton doubted that the two recognized the three women. Gull had seen Crook for a brief time when he certified her insane, and she was not now in Victorian garments and had cut her dark hair short. (She did resemble somewhat Princess Alexandra, Eddy's mother, which might be why Eddy, who had obvious Oedipal tendencies, had fallen in love with her.) John Netley had seen Annie Elizabeth Crook, Prince Eddy's lover, many times, but if he knew her now he certainly was not acting as if he did. Perhaps he did not want to acknowledge it. If she did not know him, so much the better. On the other hand, why had Crook not recognized him? His moustache was missing, but even so . . . Perhaps the shock and the lack of Victorian clothes and the long time since their last encounter accounted for her lack of memory.

As for Kelly, she had been picked up by Sickert and Gull on a dark street, taken into a dark coach, and given drugged liquor. Stride had also seen Netley and Gull in dim surroundings and that briefly.

Burton did not know if he should first explain about the tower and the method of getting them here or should introduce them. He relished their reaction when they realized in whose company they were. But he was afraid that the resulting furor would put off the explanation for a long time. On the other hand, the explanation was going to take a long time, and during that they might come to recognize each other.

He decided, and he said, "First, you should know each other."

"That's not needed, dearie, for Annie and me!" Kelly said. "We have long been friends. And Liz and I are old friends."

"Even so," Burton said, grinning, "it's only polite, and the men should make your acquaintance."

He paused—oh, how he enjoyed this!—and he said, "Elizabeth Stride, Mary Jane Kelly, and Annie Elizabeth Crook, meet Sir William Gull and John Netley!"

What followed was what he had hoped for. Gull paled, and the edge of his goblet, just touching his lip, failed to dip. He never did get to finish his drink. Netley also paled, and, after a moment of rigidity, he leaped up and backed away, his eyes fixed on the women.

Annie rose quickly from her chair and said, "Now I know you! You!" She pointed a shaking finger at Gull. "You're the crooked doctor that said I was crazy! And you," she moved the finger to spear Netley, "you took my Eddy away when the police came."

"He also tried to kill your daughter twice," Burton said. "And Mrs. Stride and Mrs. Kelly, this man," he indicated Gull, "is the man who killed you. With the help of that man."

"God help me," Gull said, getting down on his knees. "God help me and forgive me as I hope that you will."

"That was a long time ago," Netley said, snarling. "What difference does it make now? You're all alive and well now, right, so what real harm was done?"

"The thing is," Burton said, "Stride and Kelly know that you killed them, but during their many years on The River, they never ran across anyone who spoke about the Jack the Ripper murders. So they—"

"He!" Kelly said, pointing at Gull. "He's Jack the Ripper?"

"There is no such, that is, Jack was not one but three men working together. However, he, Gull, wrote the letters that made the name famous, and he masterminded the entire business. What you, Kelly, don't know is what he did to you after he killed you. You remember, Kelly, how Catherine Eddowes was mutilated? That was nothing compared to the butchery Gull did on you. Shall I describe it?"

Gull rose to his feet and cried. "No! No! Even now, though I've made my peace with God, I can't forget what I did!"

"What about me?" Stride said. "What happened to me?"

"Your throat was cut, that's all. Gull didn't have time to carry out his ritual on you."

"*That's all!*" Stride screeched. "That's all! Isn't that enough!"

Screaming, she ran at Gull with her hands out, fingers curled. He did not run, though he flinched when she sank her fingernails into his face. Netley had stepped forward as if to help Gull, then moved away after a slight hesitation.

Burton pulled the screaming woman away. Gull felt his bleeding cheeks but said nothing.

"I'd like to cut his guts out and hold them up before his dying eyes," Kelly said. She went to Stride, put her arms around her shoulders, and led the sobbing woman away.

"That's enough of drama, retribution, and reproach," Burton said. "What you do after you're on your own is your business, unless it involves those outside this matter. For the time being, you will behave decently and listen carefully to me. You need an education, and though it inconveniences me to instruct you, I must do so. I can't just leave you to find things out for yourself."

First, he had them describe their appearance in the converter. It had taken place in the huge cube in a corner of this very room. They had awakened from death in the converter, and, after a few moments of confusion, had opened the door and gone into this room. They had explored the other rooms, then gone into the corridor. And Burton had come around the corner in his flying chair.

"Then you saw no one else?" he said.

They replied that they had not.

Burton took Gull into the bathroom of the next room and found, as he had expected, a bottle with a liquid to apply to the scratches on his face. This stopped the bleeding and would, within twenty-four hours, heal the wounds.

He asked them if they were hungry. Netley and the women said they were; Gull shook his head. Burton got their orders and transmitted them to the converter. After they were seated and eating from little tables before them, Burton launched into the very long exposition of the Riverworld, of his and others' tribulations in getting to the tower, and what had happened since. By the time he was through, he had drunk two tall goblets of Scotch, and they were deep into their own cups.

"So you see," he said, "just what the situation is. I know you have a thousand questions, and it will take you some time to learn to use the Computer. Meanwhile, I suggest that you settle down for the night—I can get sleeping pills for you if you wish—and I'll see you tomorrow. I'll also introduce you to my eight companions then. Perhaps not personally but via the wall-screens."

Mary Kelly said, slurring, "How do we know that those two bastards won't try to murder us again while we sleep?"

"I would not even dream of doing such a deed!" Gull said. "I have changed; I am not what I was! Believe me, ladies, I deeply regret my crimes, and I have tried—am trying—to live a Christian life. I would not only not harm you, I would defend you against anyone who tried to do so."

"Fine words," Liz Stride said scornfully.

"I mean them, madam, I truly do!"

"I think he's sincere," Burton said. "In any event, I suggest that you three women sleep in an apartment room separate from that of the men. I will give you a codeword that will prevent anyone from coming through your door except myself and you three."

After he had shown them how to get food and drink from their converters and how to call him, he left them. Instead of going on to his world, he returned to his apartment. Since he would have to show them the ropes tomorrow morning, he should be close to them.

On the way back, he considered the question of who had resurrected the five. Whoever it was had a vicious sense of irony. But who could it be? Only Frigate and Nur knew about his investigations of the Ripper, and neither would have brought five here. Who then? Loga and the Mongolian Agent were dead. Was there . . . he did not even like to approach the thought . . . another unknown, another Snark?

Burton had just gotten into bed when a screen appeared on the wall. Star Spoon's distraught face was in it.

Speaking Esperanto rapidly, tears flowing, she asked Burton if she could come to his apartment.

"Why?"

"I am tired of sharing Po with five other women, though he gives very little time to any of us. He's too busy drinking with his cronies or studying. Besides . . . I do not desire his embraces."

Burton did not have to ask her whose embraces she did desire.

"Does Po know you're calling me?"

"Yes. I told him an hour ago. He raved and ranted and then . . ."

"He didn't beat you?"

"No, he does not beat women, I'll say that for him. Not physically, anyway."

"And then?"

"Then? Oh! Yes, he smiled and blessed me and said he hoped I'd be happy with you. He spoiled it, though, by saying that he doubted that I would."

Burton got out of bed and put on a towel-kilt. "I'd like to speak with him."

Her black eyes widened. "Why? Do you think I'm lying?"

"No, of course not. It's just that I don't want him to think I'm afraid to face him. I also want to make sure that he doesn't think I was sneaking around behind his back."

"Oh, he doesn't think that. I told him that you were not in the least aware I desired you."

"That's a lie," Burton said, but he did not reproach her. There were lies and there were lies, and this was in the "white" category. Besides, who was he to rebuke anyone for falsehood?

"I'll speak to him if he's awake," Burton said.

"No, he's awake, but he won't want to be disturbed. He's with a woman. A woman he just resurrected. He said she'll replace me. Poor devil."

"Perhaps," Burton said. "But for the time being she'll be very grateful he rescued her from the dead."

He was not in love with the Chinese woman. However, he did not consider love to be a prerequisite for a good bond between man and woman. He had certainly been in love with Alice, and look at what had happened to them.

"Come on over," Burton said. "I'll tell the Computer to let you in."

Star Spoon quit weeping and snuffling and smiled like the sun at dawn.

"Just as soon as I repair my makeup and get my belongings together. You do want me, don't you?"

"If I didn't, I would say so," Burton said.

He did not get to sleep until five in the morning.

24

Burton called the three women, in their room, and the two men, who had slept in separate rooms. After bidding them good morning, he told them that he had instructed the Computer to teach them how to operate it. He also invited them to the weekly meeting of the eight—more now—that evening.

"After that, you're on your own. I will, however, call you now and then or even drop in on you, if I'm welcome. And you may call me if you have some problem."

They did not like what he said. Apparently, they felt that he should devote all his time to making sure that they were adjusted. But they could do nothing about it.

He and Star Spoon had breakfast, eggs *au beurre noir*, blueberry muffins, and figs with cream. They then flew to his little world, Theleme, named after the mythical state in Rabelais' *Gargantua and Pantagruel*. Its motto was, in the old Frenchman's work, Do What You Will. Burton's motto was: Do What Burton Wills. The world might, however, have been better called Baghdad-in-the-Tower. Burton had had erected in its center a small town and castle that looked like a romanticist's or Hollywood producer's conception of a place out of *The Thousand Nights and One*. A river ran from the west end of the vast chamber, circled the city, and snaked eastward, disappearing in the sands of the desert not far from the entrance. Outside the city roamed several lions and leopards and many gazelles, antelopes, ostriches, and other desert creatures. Hippopotami and crocodiles swam in the river, and the patches of jungle were alive with monkeys, civet cats, and birds.

As of the moment, Theleme was populated only by himself

and Star Spoon. He planned to bring in some suitable people later, though he was in no hurry.

At 8:00 P.M., he and Star Spoon went to the party, though not without incident. The black motorcycle rider, this time with a black woman riding behind him, roared below them. The man waved a hand at them but his greeting was more courteous. "Hey, Burton, what's happening?" A few seconds later, they traveled over a large pig trotting along, its hooves clicking.

"My God," Burton said. "Now what?"

"I don't know," Star Spoon said. "I talked to Aphra this afternoon, and she said she's running into people she never saw before. Most of them are from Tom Turpin's world. At least, she thinks so, since they're black. But she flew by a dozen people that looked like gypsies."

"Gypsies? Who'd resurrect them?"

They entered Nur's apartment, which was noisy with chatter and laughter. Alice was there, dressed in the 1920s flapper's clothes that she liked so much. She smiled slightly at him but made no effort then or later to talk to him. He had expected to surprise everybody by showing up with the Chinese woman. Apparently, however, Li Po had told them about her. If he was jealous, he did not show it. He was realist enough to know that a display of it would not only be useless but also make him lose face. Besides, he was not suffering from lack of company or sex. He had by now resurrected forty men and forty-seven women, all of whom he had known on Earth. Seven of the women were his, one for each day of the week. Tonight, however, he had brought only one.

"They take turns going with me to these meetings," he told Burton.

"Eventually, they're going to tire of this sharing and resurrect men for themselves," Burton said. "What do you plan to do then?"

"Nothing," Li Po said, smiling. "I am not a tyrant. When that happens, I will raise others to replace them. It is just as well that does happen, since, sooner or later, I will tire of them or, difficult as it is to conceive, they may tire of me."

Burton could visualize the people-burgeoning of Li Po's world. When the saturation point was reached, the excess would have to live in the apartments. The same thing was happening in Turpin's world.

"Man, I don't know," Turpin said, shaking his head. "It all started out with the people I brought in, and then it got out of hand. *They* resurrected people, and *those* raised people, and now those're resurrecting like it was going out of style."

Burton told him about the black motorcyclist. Turpin grinned and said, "That's Bill Williams. I don't know who in hell brought him here. I could find out, but what difference would it make? He isn't an American black, you know. He's Russian."

"Russian?"

"Yeah. He's got quite a story to tell. You ought to talk to him sometime."

Burton had observed Gull, Netley, Crook, Stride, and Kelly when he entered. They were standing in two corners, the men in one, the women in another, and they were obviously not meshing with the others. Burton took them around the room to introduce them. It seemed, however, that Frigate had already spread the news about them. This had aroused curiosity about the newcomers, but many were uneasy with Netley and Gull. Anyone would be in the company of the two-thirds of the unholy trinity forming "Jack the Ripper." So affected was Netley by this that he left early. Burton went into the hall off the main room, where he was unobserved, and ordered the Computer to keep track of him.

Noticing the shyness of Stride, Crook, and Kelly, Nur went to them and soon jollied them up. He was at ease with the high and the low, the educated and the uneducated, the rich and the poor, and he adjusted quickly to any company, though he always kept his dignity. After a while, Aphra Behn and Frigate joined them, and Nur drifted off, ending up with Gull. Curious, Burton invited himself into the conversation.

Gull was telling the Moor about the man who had converted him, Lorenzo Dow. Dow had been born in Coventry, Tolland County, Connecticut, in 1777. A highly imaginative and impressionable youngster, he had become devout beyond his years when he had seen an angel. Or claimed to have done so. As a young adult, he became a traveling preacher loosely connected to the Methodist Church. Of all the wandering ministers of the early American frontier, he had been the most traveled and best known. He was famous from Maine to South Carolina and from New York to the wildernesses of the Mississippi River. Wherever there were even a few people, he traveled by boat, by coach, by horse, or on foot, and he preached his eccentric rambling sermons.

When he was raised from the dead on the Riverworld, he had been surprised but not shocked. "I was wrong in some things," he told his converts. "But mainly right."

He was convinced that the angel he had seen as a child was one of those who had made this Riverworld as a stage through which the worthy must pass to get to a better world. He believed, like the Second Chancers, that all must strive to better themselves morally and spiritually. Unlike the Chancers, he did not believe that the ultimate goal was absorption in the Godhead. No, this River was only a sort of purgatory in which God and his angels had given everybody another chance. But those who attained the rich change of spirit demanded here would go on to another world in which they would be physically resurrected again. However, those who failed would die here and become dust forever.

"I have met your angels," Burton said, "and they are only men and women. In fact, except for one, they were born on Earth and died there when they were children. The exception was Monat, an extra-Terrestrial, a nonhuman, who was in charge of this project. Does this tower look as if it had been built by angels?"

"It certainly does," Gull said. "This Loga you speak of, he . . . he must be a fallen angel."

"You're crazy, man," Burton said, and he walked away.

"That man," Star Spoon said, "will resurrect others of his faith, and we won't be able to go into the halls without bumping into them. His kind won't leave you alone."

"We'll be in Theleme. They won't get in there."

"No person or place is inviolable."

Star Spoon fitted into Burton's way of life as a well-made shoe shaped itself around a foot. The analogy was not just literary.

When he took his shoes off, he did not have to pay any attention to them until he was ready to wear them again. The woman seemed content to be ignored when he was busy studying or working the Computer. She often operated it when he was doing the same. She was an excellent companion, a ready and some- times amusing talker, and she did not insist on interrupting him. She was intelligent, knew Chinese poetry, could paint well, and played the Chinese lute beautifully. She was passionate, thor- oughly versed in every aspect of sex, uninhibited, and yet, when Burton did not make love to her for a week because he was en- grossed in his studies, she did not seem to mind.

The only thing that Star Spoon complained about was that she could not bring her parents to this place. She had located her mother, but she was alive in The Valley. Her father could not be found.

"You would not mind if I could bring them here?" she said. "Perhaps, someday, I will be able to get them here. They could have their own apartment, and they would not bother you. I would see them only when you consented."

"Not at all," Burton said. "Bring your sisters and brothers, too. Your aunts and uncles and your cousins."

He could not have stopped her if had wanted to, but he was not going to tell her that. Why spoil her desire to please him? She was a perfect mate for him.

When he spoke of this to Frigate, the American said, "I'm surprised that she didn't learn to be more independent while she was in The Valley. She was raised in the Chinese culture of the eighth century, but she must have lived in many others in The Valley. Usually, The Valley frees women."

"Not always by any means," Burton said. "She's had a rough life, to put it mildly. You know the sad story of her Terrestrial life. She didn't fare any better on The River. She was raped several scores of times in The Valley, but she doesn't seem to have suf- fered any deep trauma because of that."

"She doesn't seem to, but she's very self-controlled."

"Ah, yes, the inscrutable Oriental."

"She's very beautiful."

"Exquisite. And I must confess that I'm flattered that she

wanted me so fiercely. However . . . I still prefer a blond not-too-bright Caucasian who's devoted to me."

"If you find one and resurrect her, watch out for Star Spoon. There's more fire in her than she lets on to."

Several days after the party, Burton and Star Spoon set out to visit Frigate's world in specially built chairs designed by Burton. These were larger than the others and were completely enclosed in a three-inch-thick irradiated plastic hemisphere. Beamers projecting from the shell could be fired fore and aft, above and below.

Star Spoon, seeing them the first time, had murmured, "Whom are you afraid of?"

"I fear nobody," he said, "but I trust very few. There are too many strangers, unknown quantities, prowling the corridors. Also, we still don't have any assurance that an Ethical isn't hidden here."

They rose in their chairs above the minarets and domes made of gold alloy and glittering with gigantic jewels, and they sped over the river and the jungle to the exit. Burton pressed a console button, which transmitted the coded open-sesame via radio. Star Spoon's vehicle lacked this because he had refused to give her access to the codeword. She had hesitatingly asked him why, and he had told her that he did not want to take the chance that she might be seized and the codeword forced from her.

"Who would do that?" she had said softly.

"Perhaps nobody. But it's a possibility."

"What if they should grab you and torture the codeword from you?"

"I've anticipated that."

She did not ask him what the precautions were. Obviously, if she knew, she could be forced to give that information.

The circular area was empty of people, though a few robots were cleaning up the litter. Halting his chair before the entrance to Frigate's world, Burton shouted Frigate's name. In a few seconds, the American's face appeared on a glowing screen. The door opened outward, and they went through in single file. The second door admitted them into a world where the sun was ten degrees past the zenith, the temperature was 85°F, and the air was wet. They shot over a very thick, lush jungle, a river and several joining streams, and some large clearings. The creatures in the streams and basking on the banks were crocodilian, vast and toothy. Now and then they glimpsed a huge reptilian head at the end of a long neck, and, once, an armor-plated saurian lumbered across the clearing. Winged reptiles swooped by them: pterodactlys. These were not from recordings, since the Ethicals had arrived on Earth seventy million years after the last of the dinosaurs had died. But Frigate had had the Computer fashion living replicas of the mighty beasts, and these reigned in the lush growths. In the center of the Brobdingnagian chamber was a rock monolith, two hundred feet high, with slick leaning-out sides impossible for anything to scale. On top was his stronghold, a flat ten acres with an antebellum Southern mansion in the center of an island surrounded by a wide moat in which swam ducks, geese, and swans. Burton and Star Spoon landed on the green lawn before it.

Peter Frigate was sitting on the verandah in a rocking chair listening to Handel's *Water Music*, drinking a mint julep and surrounded by three dogs. He held a Siamese seal point cat on his lap. The dogs, real dogs, not therioids, leaped barking off the verandah and ran to Burton. They bounded about and wiggled their hindquarters and whined as he petted them. One was a huge Rottweiler; one, a German shepherd; one, a Shetland sheepdog. Frigate rose, the cat jumping off his disappearing lap, and greeted them. He wore a white linen vest with embroidered Egyptian hieroglyphics and a knee-length white linen kilt.

"Welcome to Frigateland!" he said, smiling. "Sit down." He pointed to two rocking chairs. "What'll you have to drink?" He clapped his hands once, and two androids appeared from the front doorway. They wore butler's uniforms.

"You wouldn't recognize them," he said. "They look exactly like two U.S. presidents I had no love for. I call them Tricky Dicky and Ronnie. The sneaky-looking one is Dicky." He paused. "The lady of the house will be down in a minute."

Burton raised his eyebrows. "Ah, you finally decided on a housemate."

"Yes. The dogs and cats are splendid companions, don't talk

back to or at you. But I got lonely for conversation and other things."

The servants brought the drinks, Scotch for Burton and wine for Star Spoon. Burton took a fine Havana from his pocket, and Dicky leaped forward, produced a lighter, and held the flame steady for him. Ronnie did the same for Star Spoon's cigarette.

"This is the life," Frigate said. "I fly around and observe my dinosaurs, really enjoy them. I keep the tyrannosaurs from eating all the brontosaurs by giving them meat at a feeding station at the bottom of my monolith. Even so, it's hard maintaining the balance of prey and predator. I'll get tired of this someday. When I do, I'll erase the Jurassic period and replace it with the Cretaceous. I plan to go through all the evolutionary eras in their various stages to the Pleistocene Epoch. When I get there, I'll stop. I've always been very fond of the mammoth and the sabertooth."

25

B urton waved a fly away. "Did you have to be so authentic?"
"There are mosquitoes, too. I have to retreat into my
stately mansion at dusk because of them. I don't want life here to
be an air-conditioned vermin-free paradise. There was a time
when I cursed flies, mosquitoes, and ants and wondered why
God put them on Earth to bedevil us. Now I know. They are a
source of pleasure. When they've been bugging the hell out of
you—no pun intended—and you get away from them, get to
some place where they can't reach you, you find the zero of their
presence to be a plus-one pleasure. I put up with them so I can
enjoy their absence."

Star Spoon looked at him as if she found him strange. Burton,
however, understood him. To know full pleasure you had also to
know unpleasure. The existence of evil could be justified. Without it, how would you know that good was good? Perhaps,
though, that was not necessary. If it were, why had the Ethicals
worked so hard to eliminate evil?

At that moment, a woman came out of the house. She was gorgeous, auburn-haired, green-eyed, pale-skinned, long-legged, full-
breasted, tiny-waisted. Her face was irregular, the nose a trifle
too long, the upper lip a trifle too short, and her eyes perhaps too
deep-sunk. Nevertheless, their integration gave her a beautiful
and not easily forgotten strong face. She was about five feet seven
inches tall and wore a white gown of some shimmering white
stuff, low-cut and slit to the upper thigh on the left side. Her
high-heeled shoes were open and white. She wore no jewelry or
pearls, but a silver band was around her right wrist.

Frigate, smiling, introduced her. "Sophie Lefkowitz. I met her
at a science-fiction convention in 1955. We corresponded and

met occasionally at conventions after that. She died in 1979 of cancer. Her grandparents came over from Russia to Cleveland, Ohio, in 1900, and her father married a woman descended from Sephardic Jews who came to New Amsterdam in 1652. The funny thing is that I once met the original immigrant, Abraham Lopez. We didn't get along; he was a raving bigot. She was a housewife, but she was active in a lot of organizations, including the National Organization for Women. She also made a pile of money writing children's books under the byline of Begonia West."

"Charmed, I'm sure," said Burton, who meant it. "But you warned against resurrecting writers, remember?"

"They're not all rotten."

Sophie was sprightly and intelligent, though too fond of puns. She also seemed very grateful to Frigate for raising her from the dead, and he seemed delighted with her.

"Of course, we're going to resurrect others. We'd get on each other's nerves if we didn't have other companions. That takes a lot of time judging the candidates, though."

"He's looking for perfection, and he isn't going to get it," Sophie said. "The perfect ones have Gone On. I say, pick those who seem reasonably compatible, and if they don't work out, they can always move out."

"The way things are going," Star Spoon said, "the tower is going to bulge with people. Everybody who's resurrected starts resurrecting others."

"It can house over two million people quite comfortably." Sophie said.

"But if everybody who's resurrected brings in four more, it wouldn't take long at an exponential rate for the tower to fill," Burton said.

"Not only that," Frigate said, "but it may get worse. I was talking to Tom Turpin the other day. He said that two couples in his world are trying to have children. They've had the Computer eliminate from their diet the contraceptive chemicals that make them sterile. Tom was angry. He told them that if the women did get pregnant, they'd have to leave Turpinland. But they said they didn't care."

They were silent for a while, aghast at the news. The Ethicals had insured that no children would be born, because there was not enough room on the Riverworld for an expanding population. Moreover, the stage, as it were, had to become empty so that those born on Earth after A.D. 1983 could be resurrected.

"The whole project is going to the dogs," Frigate said.

"To utter hell and damnation," Burton said. "If it's not already there."

Sophie said, smiling, "This doesn't look like Hell to me." She waved a hand to indicate their private world. From nearby came the songs of birds, anachronistic notes, since there were no birds in the Mesozoic, and the chirping of some raccoons, also out of their era. From over the edge of the monolith came the deep gurgling cries of brontosaurs and the express-train rumbling of a tyrannosaur, like the beginning of a snow avalanche. Pteranodons with thirty-foot wingspreads sounded like giant crows with asthma.

"It's only temporary," Burton said.

The androids, Ronnie and Dicky, brought more drinks. Frigate and Burton, perhaps inspired by the presence of the androids, began talking about free will versus determinism, a favorite subject. Frigate insisted that free will played a larger part in human lives than mechanical, chemical, or neural elements. Burton was equally insistent that most people's choices were fixed by their body chemistry and early conditioning.

"But some people do change their characters for the better," Frigate said. "They do it consciously and with effort. Their will manages to overcome their conditioning and even their basic temperament."

"I'll admit that free will sometimes plays a part in some people," Burton said. "However, only a few do use their free will effectively, and they often fail. Even so, most people are, in a sense, robots. The nonrobots, the lucky few, might be able to exercise their free will only because their genes allow them to. Thus, even free will depends upon genetic determinism."

"I may as well tell you now, perhaps I should have told you sooner," Frigate said, "but I've asked the Computer if the Ethicals had done any work on free will and determinism. Not in a philosophical but in a scientific sense. The Computer told me that it had an enormous amount of data because the first Ethicals, the people preceding Monat's, had worked on that subject as had Monat's people and their successors, the Earthchildren raised on the Gardenworld. I didn't have time to review all the data or even a small part of it, and I probably wouldn't have understood it if I did have time. I asked for a summary of the conclusions. The Computer said that the project was still going, but it could give me the results as of now.

"The Ethicals long ago charted all chromosomes, fixed their exact function, and analyzed the interrelationships of the genes. Charted their individual and interacting fields. Which is why, when they resurrected us, our malfunctioning genes had been replaced with healthy ones. We were raised in perfect physical, chemical, and electrical condition. Any faults from then on were psychological. Of course, our psychic and social conditioning were not removed. If we were to get rid of these, it was strictly up to the individual. He or she had to use free will, if he or she had any or wished to use it."

"Why didn't you tell me about this?" Burton said.

"Don't get angry. I just wanted you to express your opinion and then show you the truth."

"You wanted me to go out on a limb so you could cut it off!"

"Why not?" Frigate said, smiling. "You're such an overpowering talker and so opinionated, so dogmatic, so self-righteous, that . . . well, I thought that for once I could make you listen instead of trying to dominate the conversation."

"If it helps you get rid of your resentment," Burton said, also smiling. "There was a time when I would have been very angry at you. But, I, too, have changed."

"Yes, but you'll make me pay for this sometime."

"No, I won't," Burton said. "I'll use my free will to learn this lesson. I'll keep and treasure it."

"We'll see. Anyway . . ."

"The conclusions!"

"I'll try to put them into plain English. We are not complete robots, as Sam Clemens and that writer I told you about, Kurt Vonnegut, claimed we are. They said our behavior and thoughts were entirely determined by what had taken place in the past and by the chemicals in our bodies. Clemens' theory was that everything that happened in the past, everything, determined everything in the present. The speed with which and the angle at which the first atom at the beginning of the universe bumped into the second atom started a chain of events in a particular direction. What we were was the result of that primal collision. If the first atom had bumped into the second at a different velocity and angle, then we would be different. Vonnegut said nothing about that but claimed that we acted and thought the way we did because of what he called 'bad chemicals.'

"Both Clemens and Vonnegut railed against evil, but they ignored the fact that their own philosophies removed blame for evil from evildoers. According to them, a person couldn't help the way he or she acted. So, why should they write so much about evildoers and condemn them when the evildoer was not at all responsible? Could murderers be held responsible, could the rich help themselves if they exploited the poor, could the poor help it if they allowed themselves to be exploited, could the child-beater be blamed for his brutality, the Puritan for his intolerance and narrow and rigid morality, the libertines for their sexual excesses, the judge for his corruption, the Ku Klux Klanner for his racial prejudice, the liberal for his blindness to the openly declared goals and obvious bloody methods of the communists, the fascist and capitalist for using evil means to achieve supposedly good goals, the conservative for his contempt for the common people and his excuses for exploiting them? Could Ivan the Terrible and Gilles de Rais and Stalin and Hitler and Chiang Kaishek and Mao Tse-tung and Menachem Begin and Yasser Arafat and Genghis Khan and Simon Bolivar and the IRA terrorist who drops a bomb into a mailbox and blows legs off babies, could any of these be blamed? Not if you accept Clemens' and Vonnegut's basic philosophy. The murderer and child-abuser and rapist and racist are no more to blame for their actions than those who do good are to be praised. All behave the way they do because of genes or their chemical or psychosocial conditioning. So why did they bother to write about evils when they themselves could not blame the evildoers?

"They did so, according to their own philosophy, because they had been determined to do so. Thus, they get no moral credit."

Burton had been waiting patiently for the results. Now he said, "Those two said, then, that we are just billiard balls waiting to be struck by other balls and so sent into whatever pocket is determined for them?"

"Yes."

"I'm well aware of that philosophy. As you know, I wrote a poem about it. However, even those who don't believe in free will always act as if they had it. It seems to be the nature of the beast. Perhaps our genes determine that. Now, would you mind getting to the point?"

"There is more than one," Frigate said. "First, the Ethical studies prove that mental potential is equal among races. All have the same reserves of geniuses, highly intelligent, intelligent, fairly intelligent, and stupid. In 1983, when I died, there was still a lot of controversy about that. Intelligence tests seemed to show that the average Negro intelligence was a few points below that of the Caucasian. The same tests also indicated that the Mongolian IQ was a few points higher than the Caucasian. A lot of people claimed that these tests were not accurate and that they ignored social conditioning, economic opportunity, bias against race, and so forth. These objectors were right. The Ethical tests prove that all races have an equal mental potential.

"That goes against the grain of your observations on Earth, Dick. You claimed that the Negro was less intelligent than the Caucasian. Oh, you admitted that perhaps the American Negro might be capable of becoming more 'civilized' and brighter than the African Negro. But the implication was that, if this was so, it was because the Yankee black had a lot of white blood, that is, Caucasian genes from racial mixing."

"I said many things on Earth that I now admit were wrong," Burton said heatedly. "After sixty-seven years of intimate, though often forced, socializing with every race and every nationality and tribe you could imagine, and some you couldn't, I have changed my mind about many things. I'm perfectly willing to call Sambo my brother."

"I wouldn't use 'Sambo' myself. It shows a lingering trace of bad thinking."

"You know what I mean."

"Yes. I remember a line in your poem, 'Stone Talk,' where you criticized the American white because he wouldn't call ... ah, Sambo ... his brother. You were in no position to throw stones."

"What I was is not what I am. Rubbing elbows with many people causes you to rub in some of their skin. And vice versa."

"You did a lot of elbow-rubbing on Earth. Very few people traveled as much as you did and came into contact with all classes, rich and poor."

"It wasn't long enough. Not only are conditions different here, I wasn't only just *rubbed* here. I was shaken and knocked about. That does something to the machinery, you know."

"Let's not use mechanistic terms," Frigate said.

"Psychic machinery is perfectly appropriate."

"The psyche is not an engine but a subtle and complex field of waves. Many fields, in fact, a superfield. Like light, it can be described as being both wave and particle, a psychic wavicle, wavicles forming a hypercomplex."

"The results."

"All right. Every person is a semirobot. That is, each is subject to the demands of the biological machine, the body. If you hunger, you eat or try to find food. No one can rise above himself enough to go without food and not starve to death. Injuries to the cerebroneural system, cancer, chemical imbalances, these can cause changes in mentality, make you crazy, make your motives and attitudes change. There's no way the will can suppress the effects of syphilis, poisons, brain damage, and so on. And everyone is born with a set of genes that determine the particular direction his interests take. His tastes, too, I mean in food. Not everybody likes steak or tomatoes or Scotch.

"Also, some are born with chromosomal complexes that make them more emotionally rigid than others. I mean, they can't adapt to new things or changes as well as others. They tend to stick to the old and to the cultural elements that affected them when they were young. Others are more adaptable, less rigid.

But sometimes reason, logic, can affect the will and the person can overcome his rigidity, defossilize himself, as it were.

"Take as an example a person who's been brought up in a fundamental Christian faith. That is, a sect in which he believes that every word of the Bible has to be taken literally. Thus, the world was created in six days, there was a worldwide deluge, a Noah and an ark, God did stop Earth's rotation so that Joshua and his bloodthirsty genocidal Hebrews could have enough daylight to defeat the bloodthirsty Amorites. Eve was seduced by a snake and in turn got Adam to eat the fruit of the tree of knowledge of good and evil. Jesus did walk on water. And so on. Like others in his sect, he ignores the vast accumulation of data establishing the fact of evolution. He reads the Bible but does not see that, though the Bible nowhere states that the Earth is flat, it clearly implies that the Earth is flat. Nor does he take literally Christ's injunction to hate your father and mother. He ignores those. Puts them in a separate compartment of his brain. Or erases them as if they were on a tape.

"But some fundamentalists do come across evidence that they'd like to ignore. Iron strikes flint, and the spark falls on inflammable material. The fire is off to the races, as it were. He reads more of the evidence, perhaps loathes and curses himself for his 'sinful' curiosity. But he learns more and more. Finally, his reason convinces him that he's been wrong. And he becomes a liberal Christian or an atheist or agnostic.

"Something in his genetic defenses made a hole or the hole already existed waiting for water to pour through it.

"In any event, he was able to use his reason only because his genetic makeup permitted him."

"I thought you said that *Homo sapiens* was a semirobot," Burton said. "You're describing one hundred percent robots."

"No. Robots don't have reason. They can use logic, if they've been programmed to do it. But, if presented with new evidence that says that their program is wrong, they can't reject the already installed program. Humans can. *Sometimes.* Nor do robots have to rationalize their reasons for the way they behave. They just do, but humans have to explain why they're doing such and such. They construct a system of logic to excuse their behavior. The system may be founded on wrong premises, but it's usually logical within its own frame of reference. Not always, though.

"What the Ethicals claim, and they can prove it, is that even the most genetically rigid, the most severely conditioned person has the ability to free himself—partially, anyway—from these constraints, these molds. That a few can do this but most don't . . . the Ethicals say that this is a demonstration of free will. The restrained, the strait-jacketed, don't *want* to change. They are happy in their misery."

"They can prove this?"

"Yes. I'll admit I'm not educated enough to validate their findings. I don't understand the higher mathematics or the extremely involved biology. I accept their proofs, however."

"There is no such thing as absolute or final certainty, is there?" Burton said. "Unless you can see clearly, as through a crystal, exactly what evidence they present, you won't ever really know if they have the truth, will you?"

"Put that way, no. Some things have to be accepted on faith."

Burton laughed uproariously.

The American, red-faced, said, "Unless you're competent to do the research yourself, how do you know that what you read in a chemistry or astronomy or biology book is true? How do you know that anything is true unless you duplicate the research? Even then, you may be in error or clinging to the opposite viewpoint because . . ."

"Because you're genetically inclined to it?" Burton said scornfully. "Because you're predetermined to believe in one thing and not in another?"

"An attitude like yours makes a man believe in almost nothing."

"Right," Burton drawled.

"You certainly voiced enough opinions based on the observations of others while you were on Earth. Often very wrong opinions."

"That was on Earth."

They were silent for a while. The women were talking about

their mothers. Frigate could tell, however, that Sophie was listening to them at the same time. She winked at him and made a gesture that he could not interpret.

Frigate picked up the subject again as if it were a football and he was going to make a ninety-yard run. Doggedly, he said, "About 1978, I think it was, I read in a psychology book that one out of ten men seemed to be a born leader. It was implied that this trait was genetically determined. The Ethical study has validated that and moreover pinpointed the genetic complex responsible.

"Also, it said that ten percent of *Homo sapiens* had always inclined to a certain degree toward homosexuality. The ten percent had certain inclinations, that is. Not all of the ten percent were practicing homosexuals, but the tendency was there. This had been the rule since the Ethicals started making duplicate records of humanity. And it was assumed that this had been so since *Homo sapiens* originated.

"The tendency is genetically determined. What interested me about this is that in 1983, a few years before that, too, the militant homosexuals claimed that they had made a free and conscious choice to be homosexuals. In other words, they weren't born homosexuals, they had deliberately chosen to be such because they preferred that sexual way of life.

"They talked as if, when you reached the age of reason, you made up your mind about your path of action. What they ignored or failed to consider, was that, if this were true, then heterosexuals also made their free and conscious decision to be heterosexual. But this just wasn't so. A heterosexual was so because he was born so."

"What about . . . ?" Burton said.

"You were going to say, 'What about those who have homosexual tendencies but behave heterosexually? Or those who are bisexuals? Or those who marry women but have homosexual affairs on the side?' There are varying degrees of homosexuality . . . and heterosexuality . . . of course. And in any society where it was dangerous to be openly homosexual, the homosexual had to hide his or her tendency. In any event, homosexuality or heterosexuality is not a matter of choice. It's inborn.

"That makes no difference. Being homosexual or not is not a matter of morality. It's not a person's decision. It's what you do with your homosexuality or heterosexuality that matters, that is moral. Rape, sadism, violence are evil whether or not you're homosexual."

Sophie spoke up. "I can't help overhearing you two, you're so loud. What's all this about free will and determinism and genes and choice? I was very interested in those subjects when I went to college. Really interested. I got passionate about such things, I used to enjoy getting angry at those who didn't agree with me, the stupid jerks! But when I graduated, no, some time before that, I saw that . . . well . . . thinking you can solve anything by discussing philosophy or those other matters was foolish. There's no end to it, no possible irrefutable conclusions. Fun, maybe, but profitless. Sophomoric. It really is. So I quit talking about it. If somebody wanted to discuss such things, I steered them to some other subject or just walked away, though I wasn't rude about it."

"Sure, that's right!" Frigate said. "You were right! But the point is that the Ethicals have put these subjects beyond the range of discussion or opinion. They've proved these points. We're no longer in the dark!"

"Maybe. I have to agree with Dick about that. *Maybe.* But that doesn't matter. What was it Buddha said? 'Work out your own salvation with diligence.' Whoever Mr. or Mrs. Diligence is. I've been looking for Mr. Dilegence for a long time. I even borrowed Diogenes' lantern to help me. Which, by the way, the old Greek didn't need. He was honest, why should he go out looking for another honest person?

"Anyway, as Dick said, we all act as if we had free will. So who cares if there is such a thing? All I know is that only I, I alone, am responsible for my moral behavior. Heredity, environment, excuses. Excuses, alibis: scorned. Race, nationality, tribe, parents, religion, society: excuses. I decide what I am. And that's that!"

"Was that why you burned your soufflé yesterday?" Frigate said. "You didn't just forget about watching it. You decided to cremate it?"

Frigate and Lefkowitz burst out laughing. Burton said, "You cook?"

"Why, yes," Sophie said. "I like to cook. When it's not required of me, that is. I was making our dinner last night, and I forgot to watch the soufflé. I was reading a book, and . . ."

They started talking about food and that led to other subjects and finally to dinner. Eating together was a custom more ancient than conversation.

26

On Christmas Day, many guests stood before the door of Turpinworld. Burton was not the only one surprised at the number of Gull's companions. There were forty at least, all Dowists whom Gull had known in The Valley. They looked Roman in their long white togas and sandals, but it was unlikely that Romans had ever worn headbands with a big aluminum D.

"D," Gull said. "D for Dow and Deliverance. D for Deus, too."

"Death and Damnation also begin with D," someone muttered.

Gull was not affronted or, at least, did not seem to be so. "True, my friend, whoever you are," he said dignifiedly. "Death and Damnation for those who do not follow the true way."

"Disgusting," the same voice said.

"Drivel," someone else said.

"Dangerously Dubious," a third person said.

"Devastating Dung!"

"We are used to insults and ill-considered rebukes for 'A, double-L,-part people,'" Gull said. "But Grace abounding is always offered to the chief of sinners."

"What the hell does 'A, double-L,-part' mean?" a woman said softly.

"I do not know," Burton said. "It doesn't mean 'All-part,' as you might think. Gull and his followers refuse to define it. They say that when you understand it, then Grace has come to you and you are one of them."

"It was a pejorative often used by Lorenzo Dow to describe his enemies," Frigate said. "It wasn't much of a description, though it certainly sounds ominous, since his enemies never understood it."

De Marbot muttered, "It was a mistake to invite them. You can't carry on a decent conversation with them. They want only to convert you. Tom should have known better."

"Who resurrected Gull?" Sophie said. "No one in her right mind would."

"No one knows," Burton said. "I asked the Computer for the identity of the person who had raised Gull, Netley, Crook, Stride, and Kelly, but it replied that the datum was available to only one person. It didn't say to whom."

A face appeared in the glowing circle on the door.

"Santa Claus!" Frigate cried.

The man wore a big red stocking cap trimmed with white fur, and he had a huge bushy white beard. His skin was rather dark for the conventional St. Nick, however.

Turpin said, "Yeah, I'm Santa Claus. Tom Ho-Ho-Ho! Turpin hisself to be more exact."

"Merry Christmas!" several shouted.

"And a Merry Christmas to you, too!" Turpin said. "We also got plenty of snow, folks, but it ain't what you're used to. At least, I think it ain't. You're such good folks, ho, ho, ho!"

The door swung open, and there was a jam-up as those in front tried to get their flying chairs through at the same time. These were Li Po and his group, most of them loaded three feet below their Plimsoll line with liquor of various kinds. They had never heard of Christmas until Turpin's invitation, but they were eager to learn about it. After some struggling and good-natured cursing, Li Po got them organized, and they entered one at a time. Burton and his companions went next. The Dowists followed them; they had waited politely for the first two groups at Gull's command. Burton noted that they were trading glances of disdain and sorrow with one another. Evidently, they did not care for the boisterous behavior of the Chinese.

Behind the Dowists were Stride, Kelly, and Crook, dressed in elegant if somewhat flashy Victorian gowns and wearing diamond earrings and many rings bearing huge diamonds, emeralds, and sapphires. He was not surprised to see unfamiliar male faces with them. Annie Crook was accompanied by one man; the other woman had a man on each arm.

About twenty feet behind them was Netley, dressed like a race tout, gleaming with jewelry, with a woman clinging to each of his arms.

Behind them was a group of twenty that startled him. So, it was true that gypsies had been resurrected. They were dressed in the exotic clothes familiar to him, since he had associated with them in England and in Europe. He planned to ask them if they knew their benefactor, but he never got around to doing so. By the time he remembered, it was too late.

The party flew in a long straggling line under an early noon sun and over the forest, marshes, roads, and railroad tracks. Turpin had a railroad! They came down on the designated area, Louis Chauvin Street, one end of which had been roped off as a landing place. Little St. Louis or Turpinville was bright with Christmas lights and decorations and noisy with revelers. It seemed to Burton that the two thousand he had heard about some weeks ago had increased to four thousand. The streets were jammed with dancers and paraders dressed in outlandish costumes. It was more like Mardi Gras than Yuletide. Five bands were playing five different types of music, ragtime, dixieland, hot jazz, cool jazz, and spirituals. Scores of dogs ran around barking.

The group pushed their way through the crowds while liquor bottles and cigarettes and cigars of marijuana and hashish were pressed upon them. The odor of booze and grass was almost solid, and everybody was red-eyed.

Turpin, still clad in his Santa Claus suit, stood on the front porch of his huge red-brick headquarters to welcome them.

"The joint is jumping, the jerks are joyous, and jazzing is jake!" Turpin cried. "Give me some skin, brothers and sisters!"

Frigate was the only one who knew what he meant. He held his hand out palm up and Turpin slapped it. "Right on, brother!"

While the others followed his example, Frigate explained to Burton that some late twentieth-century blacks must have been resurrected here. The outlandish greeting came from that era.

"That's what he meant when he said there was plenty of snow for Christmas," Frigate said. He pointed at two black males sitting on the steps and staring blankly straight ahead of them. "They must be on heroin. Snow in the vernacular."

Turpin was revved up, but his high spirits were not of the alcoholic variety. His eyes were clear, and his speech was distinct. Everybody else might be stoned and, hence, vulnerable, but not canny Tom.

They went inside the Rosebud to the vestibule, which was almost as large as Grand Central Station. There was a big crowd there and twenty long bars of polished mahogany or gold behind which white-skinned androids in tuxedoes served drinks. Burton had to step over several unconscious men and women to follow Turpin. He took them into the big elevator and up to the third floor. They went into an office, which Alice said looked like the reception room in Buckingham Palace.

Tom asked them to sit down. He stood in front of a twenty-foot-long desk and ran his brown eyes over them before speaking.

"I'm the boss," he said, "and I run this place like it's a choo-choo train and I'm the engineer. I have to. But I let them have a good time. Most of them are pretty good, they behave like they should, don't go beyond the limits I laid down for them.

"The thing is I know some of them'd like to be the boss, so I keep an eye on 'em like fleas on a dog. The Computer does that for me. Trouble is I didn't pick most of the people here. Anybody I resurrected, I studied their past. But I couldn't tell by that what people the people I picked was going to pick.

"Besides the ones that'd like to sit on my throne, there's two different kinds of people here. Most of them are good-timers, they was whores and pimps and musicians on Earth. But some of them are church people, Holy Rollers, Second Chancers, or New Christians. They raise hell about the hell-raisers and the hell-raisers raise hell about their interfering."

"Why don't you just get rid of all of them and start over?" Star Spoon said.

Burton was surprised. She seldom spoke up unless directly addressed or asked for an opinion. Moreover, it was a strange question, not in keeping with what he knew about her nature.

Turpin lifted his palms.

"How do I do that?"

"There must be ways. The Computer . . ."

"I ain't no mass murderer. I been pretty rough in my time, but

I ain't going to slaughter people just to get some peace and quiet. Besides, keeping them in line gives me something to do."

He grinned and said, "Time to get them out of the streets and into the Rosebud. We going to have a party here, and it ain't easy to herd them in."

He went to the wall behind the desk, said a few words, and a glowing round spot appeared. Then he uttered some codewords.

He turned, grinning even more broadly. "Man, I got the power! I'm Merlin the Magician and the Wizard of Oz rolled up in one and smoking like a ten-dollar Havana. I'm the Great God Turpinus, the black Zeus, mighty Thor the Thunderer, the Old Rainmaker, the Chief Snake Oil Seller, Mr. Bones the Puppeteer."

Within three minutes clouds had cut off the sun, clouds that thickened and blackened. A wind whistled through the bars in the open windows and lifted the togas, kilts, and skirts.

"They'll all be inside quicker'n you can say scat to a cat," he said. "They be bitching about getting wet, but that don't matter."

"There are unconscious people out there," Alice said. "What about them?"

"They got to take their chances. Besides, it'll do them good. Some of them need a bath. Nobody gets pneumonia, anyway."

He gave them some instructions about keeping out of trouble if the drunks gave them a hard time. "They shouldn't. I gave them orders they was to treat you nice even if you is white."

"What about us?" Li Po said. "We aren't white."

"You are to them. Anybody who ain't black is white. It's a matter of fine but not subtle semantic distinction."

Burton was partly amused by the latter statement and partly irritated. The man deliberately shifted back and forth from the English of the well-educated to ghetto lingo as if he wanted to anger his listeners. Or perhaps to play the clown. Or both. Somewhere in him was a self-contempt engendered by the white-ruled system of his time. He might not be conscious of it, but it was there. According to Frigate, the American Negroes of the later twentieth century had overcome this, or tried to, and claimed to be proud to be black. But Turpin was still playing a game for which there was no need.

But, as Nur had said, one should not be proud to be black or white. One should only be proud to be a good human being, and that pride should watch out for stumbles.

Turpin had replied, "Yeah, but you have to go through certain stages to get there, and being proud you're black is one of them."

"A very good point," Nur had said. "However, one shouldn't get stuck in a stage. Climb on to the next one."

They went down to the vestibule, as Turpin called it. Long before they reached it, the loud music and chatter and shrill laughter and the tsunami of alcohol, burning drugs, and tobacco smote them. Everybody was inside, including those who'd passed out. These had been carried in by the androids and were lined along a wall.

"Mingle, folks!" Turpin shouted, and he waved his hand at the crowd. He did not feel he had to introduce his guests; he had shown their faces and names on the computer screens. However, his guests hesitated. It was not easy to just walk up to a group and start talking. The Dowists were repelled and scandalized and obviously were regretting having come here. Turpin, seeing this, gestured to a small group that had been standing at the far end of the bar. The group made its way through the throng to the guests and began conversation. Their host had picked them out to break the ice, and he had done well. Or so it seemed in the beginning. Some of them were Second Chancers or New Christians; these went to the Dowists. Though they differed in some fundamental principles, all three religions were pacifist and theoretically tolerant. They also had a common bond in that they abhorred excessive use of alcohol and any use of tobacco or other drugs.

The man appointed to keep Burton company was six feet three inches tall, broad-shouldered, huge-chested, and massively limbed. He was wearing a white doeskin headband, a white kidskin vest, a white doeskin belt with a broad silver buckle on which was an alto relief wolf's head, tight white doeskin trousers, and white doeskin boots reaching to just below his knees. His face was broad and high-cheekboned, and his nose was large, long, and aquiline. He looked more like Sitting Bull than a Negro, except for his everted lips and kinky hair. When he smiled, he was craggily handsome.

He introduced himself with a conventional handshake, announcing in a rich basso that he was Bill Williams and was pleased to know Captain Sir Richard Francis Burton. Burton was not sure that his use of the title was not a put-on.

"Tom Turpin didn't appoint me to act as your faithful Indian guide and bodyguard," he said, grinning. "I volunteered."

"Oh?" Burton said, raising his eyebrows. "May I ask why?"

"You may. I read about you; you intrigue me. Besides, Turpin has told me much about how you led him and the others across the mountains and into the tower."

"I'm flattered," Burton said. "However, I do have a slight bone to pick with you. Why did you almost run over me with your motorcycle?"

Williams laughed and said, "If I'd tried, I would've made it."

"And the pejorative?"

"I just felt like it. Choppers bring out the meanness in me. I also wanted to test your mettle. I didn't mean anything personally."

"It makes you feel good to upset Whitey?"

"Sometimes. If you're truly objective, you won't blame me."

"Hasn't sixty-seven years on The River changed your attitude any?"

"That's something you never get rid of. I don't let it bother me though. It's like a dull toothache you get used to," Williams said. "Want a drink?"

"White wine. Any kind."

Burton had decided to stay sober.

"Let's get it in one of the rooms upstairs. It'll be quieter there, and we won't have to shout to hear ourselves."

"Very well," Burton said, wondering what Williams was up to.

They got into the elevator with a laughing, shouting, giggling crowd. On the way up there were cries of protest as the riders groped each other. Someone passed gas before they reached the second floor, and there were shouts of amused outrage. When the doors opened, the culprit, the man blamed, anyway, was thrown headlong onto the floor.

"Everybody's feeling good, real good," Williams murmured. "Won't be so later on, though. You armed?"

Burton patted his jacket pocket.

"Beamer."

The rooms they passed were, except for one, packed and loud. Here a dozen men and women were sitting and watching a movie on a wall-screen. Burton, curious, stopped to look in. It was one that Frigate had insisted he see, the actors Laurel and Hardy selling Christmas trees in Los Angeles in July. The viewers were laughing uproariously.

"They're New Christians," Williams said. "Quiet, harmless folks. They couldn't refuse Turpin's invitation, they're so polite. But they don't hold with most of the goings-on here."

They found an empty room far down the hall around the corner. On the way, Burton admired the reproductions of oil paintings. Rembrandt, Rubens, David's "Death of Marat," many by Russians, Kiprensky, Surikov, Ivanov, Repin, Levitan, and others.

"Why so many Slavs?" Burton said.

"There's a reason."

They got their drinks from a converter. Burton sat down and lit up a cigar.

After a silence, Williams said, "I'm not American, you know."

Burton puffed out smoke and said, "You would have fooled me if Turpin had not told me you were Russian."

"I was born Rodion Ivanovitch Kazna in 1949 in the black ghetto of the city of Kiev."

"Amazing," Burton said. "I didn't know that there were Negroes . . . no, I take that back. There were some Russian black slaves. Pushkin was descended from one."

"What very few people knew, and that Russian government took good care to conceal, was that about twelve million blacks were living in segregated areas of Russian cities. They were the descendants of slaves. The common Russian didn't want to mix with them any more than the whites of America did with their blacks, and the government, secretly, or course, approved and enforced that policy. Despite which, there was some interracial screwing, as always. Can't keep the blood pure no matter how you try. A stiff prick has no bias, and all that. One of my great-grandfathers was a white Russian, and a grandfather was an

Uzbek. Turkic-speaking, he never did learn to speak Russian well, a Mongol.

"I was taught Marxist doctrine, however. I became a devout follower of Marx's principles. As he laid them down, not as they were practiced in Russia. I joined the party, but it didn't take me long to find out that I wasn't going to rise very high in it. I'd always have to take the back seat and do the janitoring, as it were.

"I would have tried the army, but blacks were always sent to Siberia to guard the Chinese frontier. The Politburo didn't want any of us stationed on the western front. We'd have caused attention, and investigation would have revealed that we were kept down. That would've looked bad for the Soviets, since they were always pointing out the inequality of blacks in America. So they kept everything under a lid.

"I did very well in school, even though our schools were inferior to the whites'. I had a driving ambition to rise to the top, but that wasn't my only motive. I wanted to learn, to know everything. I read far more than required; I did especially well in languages. That was one of the things that attracted me to you, you know. Your mastery of so many languages.

"The bigshots heard of me mainly because they were looking for blacks they could send as agitators and infiltrators to the States. They asked me to volunteer my services, and I did. Not too eagerly on the surface, of course. I didn't want them to think that I only wanted to go so I could disappear in Harlem. As a matter of fact, I had no intention of betraying them. I knew what they were and how they looked on me, but I was a Russian Marxist and I loathed capitalism.

"One of the things I fully realized, though, was that Marx's dream of the withering of the state when the proletariat had gained control of the world just was not possible. I'd have rather believed in the second coming of Christ; that, at least, could possibly happen, though it's highly improbable. Once a ruling class has the power in its hands, it won't ever let go. Not until revolutionist take the power from them, and then the new rulers try to make sure they keep in power. The natural withering away of the state, no laws or police force or regulations or bureaucracy, everybody governing himself with love and pure kindness of heart and unselfishness, that's a crock of bullshit. Nobody really believed in it, but the party members pretended they did.

"Nobody pushed that dogma too much, though. If you got enthusiastic about it, you'd be marked down as a fool or a counterrevolutionary."

Williams had slipped off a Polish freighter and into the wilds of Harlem. There he worked his F&A (Fomenting and Agitating) among various black and white liberal groups. But three weeks after he landed he got gonorrhea.

"That was my first but by no means last dose. The Fates were against me. No sooner was I cured of that filthy disease than I caught it again. I was in the U.S. of Gonococcia and no way out. After I got over that second case, I decided to try sexual abstinence. That didn't work. I was just too horny. So, I told myself, twice bitten, never again. It's a statistical improbability that I'll get infected again. But I did."

His KGB contact found out about his dose, reported it to his superior, and relayed a message to Williams. Your social diseases are interfering with your security and efficiency. Stay away from women and dirty toilet seats or else!

After that, every time Williams' contact met him, he asked him if he had gonorrhea. Williams, who was avoiding women and so getting a reputation as a homosexual, could truthfully tell the contact that he did not have the clap. Fortunately, the contact did not ask him if he had syphilis. Williams, at that time, was suffering from the onslaught of the dread Spirochaeta pallida.

"I'll swear I don't know where or from whom I got it. I'd been as chaste as Robinson Crusoe—up to the time he met Friday. I don't know. Some people are accident-prone. Could I be one of those rare and unfortunate persons, cursed by the Fates or by Dialectic Materialism, who could be infected by bacteria borne on the breeze, slipping through the keyhole? Was I VD-prone? The lone sexual ranger destined to stumble onto bandits, the Jesse Jameses of Germs? I do know one thing. I sure wasn't getting much spying, fomenting, and agitating done. I was spending too much time in doctors' offices."

When Williams learned that the FBI and perhaps the CIA had been questioning his physicians about him, he reported this to his contact. Order came back within the hour for him to go to Los Angeles and infiltrate the Black Muslims. The contact gave Williams a bus ticket, explaining that the KGB could not afford airline passage for him.

While riding westward, as every young man should, Williams contracted gonorrhea in the back seat of a Greyhound.

"Yeah, you're laughing again, Burton! It does sound funny now. But, believe me, it wasn't so funny to me then."

Williams' story, in its many details, convoluted windings, and lengthy asides, had consumed an hour. Burton was interested in it, but he felt that he had stayed away from the others too long.

Bill Williams managed to become a member of the Black Muslims. But when they found out that he had gonorrhea—contracted in Los Angeles after the Greyhound dose had been cured—they kicked him out. Then, having discovered that he was a spy—they mistakenly thought that he was an FBI agent—they put an assassin on his trail.

His story became, from this point, somewhat confusing. Burton could have used a diagram to keep it clear, what with all the flights, doublings back, shootings, and mishaps Williams had suffered. He had fled to Chicago, then to San Francisco, where he had gotten into a brawl in a gay bar, been beaten up and raped. Afflicted with gonorrhea fore and aft, as he put it, he had gone to a city in Oregon. Not, however, until he had financed his trip by mugging the KGB contact, who had refused to give him any money at all.

Star Spoon appeared in the doorway. She said softly, "I've been looking everywhere for you."

"Come in," Burton said. "You've met Bill Williams, haven't you?"

She bowed and said, "So nice to see you again, Mr. Williams. Dick, you seem to be deep in conversation. My apologies for interrupting you. I'll return to the party, if you don't mind."

Burton asked her where she would be, and she said that Turpin was with a small select group in his suite. He had asked her to find Burton and invite him to the party.

"I'll be along in a while," Burton said.

She bowed again, said good-bye to Williams, and left.

"A beautiful woman," Williams said, and he sighed.

"She knows how to keep a man happy."

"Do you know how to make *her* happy?"

"Of course!" Burton said.

"Don't get hot around the collar, nothing personal. I'd say she's a quiet but deep one. I'm pretty good at character analysis on short order. I've had to be. Matter of survival."

"She's had a very hard life," Burton said. "It's a wonder she's kept her sanity."

"You trying to be subtle and tell me I'm not the only one who's had a rough time?"

"You're overly sensitive, my friend."

Williams took thirty minutes more to finish his story. He had married a deeply religious black woman who, unfortunately, could not say No to her overpassionate minister. Result: Williams caught the clap again. Overcoming the desire to find her and kill her, he had decided to go hunting instead and sublimate his wish for violence by shooting birds and rabbits. While he was in the woods, he was fatally wounded by a shotgun blast from behind a bush. Dying, he wondered which of the many candidates had shot him. An agent of the KGB, the CIA, the Black Muslims, the Albanians, or the Salvation Army? Actually, the SA itself was not after him, but a soldier in its ranks was. While in Los Angeles, he had pretended to be converted to Christianity during a sermon given by a Major Barbarao. Then he had joined the Army, but a corporal, Rachel Goggin, had fallen in love with him and he with her. At that time, he thought that he was clean, free of VD, but after he and Rachel had made love, he discovered that his nemesis had struck again. Moreover, Rachel had caught the disease from him.

Williams had promised to marry her, but his enemies were closing in, and he had left her to save his own life. Corporal Goggin had apparently gone psychotic because of his unexplained desertion and because of her overreaction to infection with a disease that he had become quite accustomed to. He heard, while he was in Portland, that a woman resembling Rachel was asking about him and that she was packing a gun.

"Everybody except Goodwill Industries was after my ass, and I wasn't too sure about them."

"And what have you learned from these, ah, Candidean experiences?"

"You sound like Nur."

"You've talked to him?"

"Sure," Williams said. "I know everybody here. Very well."

"Yes, but what was the lesson?" Burton said.

"That I'd been the plaything of life but I wasn't going to be anymore. I made sure of that on The River, I fought for power and I got it. If I was in a situation where I was the underdog, I became the overdog as soon as possible. I was tired of being kicked around, the one who got shafted. So . . ."

"Nobody's victimizing you here, am I correct?" Burton said. He rose from his chair.

"And nobody's going to."

Williams smiled, his expression a curious blend of amusement and malice.

"Just sit down for a minute. Then you can go. Hasn't something been perplexing you for these past two weeks? Something you just can't account for?"

Burton frowned and said slowly, "I can't recall anything."

His forehead cleared. "Unless . . . yes, I have been wondering . . . but you couldn't have anything to do with it . . . I have been wondering who resurrected Netley, Gull, Crook, Stride, and Kelly."

"You mean those involved in the Jack-the-Ripper case?"

Burton was startled but tried not to show it. "How do you know who they are?"

"Oh, *I* was watching *you* watch their memory files."

Burton reared from the chair, his face red and contorted.

"Damn you, you've been spying on me! Why do you think you have the right . . . ?"

Williams, still smiling, though his eyes were narrowed, rose from his chair.

"Hold it right there! If you think it's OK to spy on others, why shouldn't others spy on you? Don't throw stones in a glass house, my friend."

Burton was speechless for a moment. Then he said, "There's a vast difference. I observed the dead. You're spying on the living, your neighbors!"

"You didn't observe the living from the grailstones along the River?"

"You soiled my privacy!"

"You can't soil the soiled," Williams said. He was still smiling, but his body stance showed that he was ready to repel attack.

"Very well," Burton said. "You still haven't told me why you took it on yourself to raise those pathological murderers."

"They were, but they aren't. The reason I did . . . I'm a collector and a student of religious types. I got interested on Earth, I had much experience with them, you know. The Marxists . . . they're religious, though they'd deny it, the Black Muslims, the Salvation Army, the Buddhists, the Southern Methodists, you know how many of them I became involved with. I am religious, too, though not in a conventional sense. I am the one who raised the New Christians and the Nichirenites and the Second Chancers who live in Turpinville, and I raised Gull the Dowist. I left it to him to resurrect his fellow, which he did. I have plans for bringing others in."

Burton did not know whether or not to believe him. He snorted and strode out of the room. Williams called, "Don't go away mad, Sir Richard!" and he laughed uproariously.

27

On his way to the elevator, Burton looked back down the hall. Williams was going down the steps, apparently to join the crowd of revelers in the vestibule. The man looked up and waved at him through the railing uprights. He was grinning as if he had been enjoying himself hugely. Had Williams been telling him the truth or had he been fantasizing? The Riverworld was a place where men and women should no longer have reason to lie. They had been delivered from the societies and institutions that had forced them, or made them think they were forced, to form protective self and public images. But most of them seemed unaware of that or found it hard to discard old and unnecessary habits.

However, climbing the steps was a good idea. He needed the exercise. He turned the corner, passing by the elevator, and strode down the long hallway toward the stairway. The music and voices that he had faintly heard in the other hall faded away. The only sound was that of his footsteps. But, as he passed the door of the room next to the stairwell, he thought he heard a scream. He stopped. It had not been loud. So faint was it, he might have imagined it. No! There it was again, and it seemed to come through the door.

The rooms were insulated but were not, like the tower walls, absolutely soundproof. He placed his ear against the intricately carved oak door. He could not hear the screams now, but a man was yelling in the room. The words were not clear; the tone was. It was threatening and angry.

He tried the doorknob. It turned, but the door would not budge. He hesitated. For all he knew, the two inside, if there were only two, might not want to be disturbed. If they turned on him because he was interfering in a matter strictly between lovers, he would be embarrassed. On the other hand, he was not easily embarrassed, and he would feel that he had been remiss if he could have prevented a crime.

He knocked hard on the wood three times, then kicked it twice. A woman started to scream, but she was cut off.

"Open up in there!" Burton shouted, and he struck the door again.

A man shouted. It sounded like, "Go away, motherfucker!" but Burton was not sure.

He took his beamer from his jacket and cut a circle around the lock. When he had pushed the knob and the lock through, he stepped to one side. It was well that he had. Three shots boomed, and three bullets pierced the thick wood. The man—he supposed it was a man who was firing—had a heavy handgun, perhaps a .45 automatic. Burton yelled, "Come out unarmed! Your hands on your head! I have a beamer!"

The man snarled a series of curses and said that he would kill whoever tried to come in.

"It's no use! You're trapped!" Burton said. "Come on out, hands to your head!"

"You can—"

The man's voice was cut off by a thud and a clatter. Then Star Spoon's voice, high and trembling, said, "I knocked him out, Dick!"

Burton pushed the door in and sprang in, beamer ready. A large naked black man was lying facedown on the thick Oriental rug, blood on the back of his head. A gold statuette, smeared with blood, lay by his side.

He swore. She was naked, and her face and arms were blue with bruises. One eye was beginning to swell up. Her clothes were scattered in shreds over the room. She ran weeping and sobbing to him, and he held her shaking body close to his. But, seeing the man push himself up from the floor, Burton released her. He picked up the .45 automatic up, reversed it, and slammed the man on the back of his neck. Without a sound, the man crumpled.

"What happened?" Burton said.

She had trouble getting the words out. He took her to a table and poured out a glass of wine. She drank, though most of it ran down her chin and neck. Still crying, she choked out a story, most of which he had guessed. She had been on her way to the stairwell when the man had stepped out of the door ahead of her. Smiling, he asked her name. She had told him and then had tried to get by him, but he had grabbed her arm. He wanted to party, he said. He had never had a Chinese woman before, and she sure was a doll. And so on.

Star Spoon had struggled as he pulled her into the room. The man's whiskey breath sickened her when he kissed her. When she had tried to scream, he clapped his hand over her mouth, slammed the door shut, hurled her so hard she fell on the floor, locked the door, and ripped her clothes from her.

By the time Burton arrived, she had been raped three times.

He made sure that the man was tied up, got a tranquilizer from the converter, and gave it and a glass of water to her. He put her into the shower then held the douche bag while, still trembling and weeping, she washed herself out.

After he had toweled her dry, he ordered some clothes from the converter, helped her get dressed, and put her down on a sofa. He used the computer console to call Turpin. Turpin, hearing the report, scowled and said, "I'll fix that son of a bitch!"

He looked at the man on the floor and said, "That's Crockett Dunaway. A real troublemaker. I've had my eye on him for some time. You wait until I get down there."

A few minutes later, Tom Turpin, followed by other members of the party, entered. Alice, Sophie, and Aphra took Star Spoon in charge at once and carried her into the room next door. Turpin got a hypodermic full of adrenaline and injected it into Dunaway's buttock. After a minute, Dunaway groaned and got to his hands and knees. When he saw the others, his eyes widened. He croaked, "What are you doing here?"

Turpin did not answer. Dunaway got to his feet and staggered to a chair, sat down, bent over and held his head in his hands. "Man, I got a headache killing me!"

"That's not all that's going to kill you," Turpin said harshly.

Dunaway raised his head. His bloodshot, slightly crossed eyes looked at Turpin. "What you talking about? That bitch come on to me, and when I obliged her, she started screaming for help. You can't blame *me* for what that slant-eyed whore done. She must've heard her man coming, and so she pretended like she wasn't having none of me."

"She couldn't have heard me," Burton said. "I wasn't making any sound in the hall. If I hadn't heard her scream, I would've gone right on by the door. You're guilty as hell, man."

"I swear 'fore God I ain't," Dunaway said. "That bitch asked me to give her a good time."

"There's no use arguing about it," Turpin said. "We'll just run off your memory and get the truth."

Dunaway grunted and shot out of the chair. He was headed for the door, but his legs gave way, and he crumpled on the floor.

"Uh, huh!" Turpin said. "I thought so. Dunaway, no one gets away with rape here. You've had it, man!"

Dunaway raised his head. Saliva ran from his open mouth. "No, I swear to God . . . !"

Turpin told his two bodyguards to set Dunaway in a chair before the computer console. "We'll know in a few minutes what's what!"

Dunaway tried to struggle, but the two blows had sapped his strength. He was set down in the chair, and a bodyguard asked the Computer to extract Dunaway's memories of the past hour and display them. Dunaway sat trembling and gibbering while his guilt was shown.

"I'm not only going to kill you," Turpin said, "I'm destroying your body-record. You ain't never going to get a chance to do this to a woman again. You've had it, Dunaway!"

The man's screams were snapped off by the ray from Turpin's beamer. Dunaway fell over in his chair, a narrow hole, cauterized at the edges, on each side of his head.

"Throw him in the converter and incinerate him," Turpin said to the bodyguards.

Nur said, "Are you really going to dissolve his recording?"

"Why not? He won't ever be any different."

"You are not God."

Turpin scowled, and then he laughed. "You're insidious, Nur.

You've been bending my ear so long with all that religious philosophical hoop-de-la you got me confused. OK. So I don't destroy him? And then, when he goes back to The Valley, he's going to rape and beat other women. You want that on your conscience?"

"The Ethicals in their wisdom set it up so that anyone, no matter how vicious, will live until this project is ended. No exceptions. I trust them. They must know what they're doing."

"Yeah?" Turpin said. "If they're so smart, how come they didn't catch on to Loga? Why didn't they make provisions for someone like him? He's wrecked their schedule and their program."

"I am not certain that they didn't make provisions for someone like him," Nur said calmly.

"Mind explaining that?" Turpin said.

"I have no explanation now."

Tom Turpin took his time lighting up a big cigar. Then he said, "OK. I'll go along with you. Up to a point. Just now, nobody's being sent back to The Valley, so Dunaway ain't going to do anybody no harm. But when . . . if . . . the Computer starts sending them back, it ain't going to send Dunaway back until I say so. Which may be never. I don't know just now what I'm going to do when that time comes."

"There are millions of Dunaways waiting to be released like pent-up hyenas," Burton said. "What good is it going to do to judge just one?"

"It's your woman that was raped!" Turpin said.

"But she is not my property, and I won't speak for her," Burton said. "Why . . . since she is the victim, why don't you let her be the judge?"

Alice, having just come from the bedroom, had overheard him. She said, "Well, Dick! So she isn't your property and she can speak for herself! Imagine Richard Burton saying that! You *have* changed!"

"I suppose I have."

"Too bad you didn't do it before, not immediately after, we parted," Alice said. "That doesn't make me feel very good, you know. You live with the Chinese woman for a very little while, and she works all sorts of changes in you."

"She had nothing to do with it."

"Who did then, God? Oh, you're impossible."

Nur said, "How is she?"

"As well as can be expected after . . . that. Aphra, Sophie, and I will take care of her for a few days. If that's all right with you, Dick?"

"Of course," he said, somewhat stiffly. "It is most generous . . . compassionate . . . of you."

Star Spoon had fallen asleep under the influence of a drug recommended by the Computer. Burton and Frigate carried her out on a stretcher through a side entrance and placed her in the back of a huge steam driven Dobler automobile. Turpin drove it over the winding road to the entrance. Here Burton transferred her to his chair, and, with her on his lap, flew the chair the short distance to his world's entrance and the long distance to the Arabian Nights castle in the center. The others followed him. After Star Spoon had been undressed and put in bed by the women, Alice and Sophie came out from her room.

"She should be all right by the time she wakes up," Sophie said. "Physically, that is. Mentally and emotionally . . . ?"

The women would take care of Star Spoon in shifts. As soon as she awoke, Burton would be called. He protested that that was not necessary. He would sit by her bed until she awoke and then do his best to comfort her.

"Let us do something, too," Sophie said.

Burton said that he would go along with them; he understood why they insisted. They empathized deeply with Star Spoon because they, too, had been raped more than once. They also needed to take care of her; that compulsion, if you could call it a compulsion, was part of their natures.

"Born nurses," Burton said to Frigate.

"How lucky can you get?"

The American was not being facetious. He envied people who wanted to use themselves for the benefit of others.

Star Spoon got up in time for breakfast. Though she drank only a little tea and ate part of a piece of toast, she was well enough to take some part in the conversation. She seemed glad to have the three women with her, and they even got her to laugh several times. However, she did not want Burton to hold her, and she responded to his attempts to talk with her with uncompleted sentences or nods or shakes of her head.

After two days, the three women left. Star Spoon immediately quit staring into space for long periods and busied herself with various projects with the Computer.

"She's withdrawing," Burton told Nur and Frigate. "I won't say it's just into herself. She seems to be burying herself with work with the Computer. She'll stop whatever she's doing—she won't talk about that much—and listen while I talk. But I've spent hours, days, trying to get her back to her old self, and I've failed."

"Yet," Frigate said, "she's been raped before."

"This may have been the final trauma. The last and the unendurable wound."

He did not tell them that she had become animated and genuinely interested for a short time when he asked her what she wanted to do to Dunaway. She had replied that she did not want to destroy his recording. He certainly deserved oblivion forever, but she could not bring herself to do that. Dunaway should be punished, if he would learn anything from it. She doubted that very much. Finally, she said that she was going to forget any punishment or any kind of retribution. She wished that she could forget about him, but she just could not.

The dullness came into her face and voice again, and she became silent.

Nur talked to her but reported that he could find no wedge to open her and let in some light. Her soul had become darkened. He hoped that it would not remain so forever.

"But you don't know if she'll . . . stay the same?" Burton said.

Nur shrugged. "No one can know. Except perhaps Star Spoon."

Burton was frustrated and, hence, angry. He could not take his anger out on her, so he vented it on Frigate and Nur. Understanding what was affecting him, they endured his insults for a while. Then Nur said that he would see Burton again when Burton was rational. Frigate seemed to feel that he should absorb more than Nur had, perhaps for old times' sake or perhaps because some part of him enjoyed the tongue-lashing. An hour after Nur had left, Frigate got up from his chair, threw his half-full glass against the wall, said, "I'm getting out of here," and did so.

A few minutes later, Star Spoon entered. She looked at the spilled whiskey and his brooding face. Then, surprisingly, she went to him and kissed him on the lips.

"I'm much improved now," she said. "I think I can be the cheery woman you want me to be, what I want to be. You'll have no reason to worry about me from now on. That is, except . . ."

"I'm very happy," he said. "I think. There's something that is still bothering you?"

"I . . . I am not ready to go to bed with you yet. I would like to, but I can't. I do believe, though, Dick, that the time will come when I can, and I'll be completely willing. Just bear with me. The time will come."

"As I said, I'm very happy. I can wait. Only, this is so sudden. What caused this metamorphosis?"

"I don't know. It just happened."

"Very curious," he said. "Perhaps we'll know someday. Meanwhile, you wouldn't mind if we kissed just a little longer, would you? I promise not to get carried away."

"Of course not."

Life for Burton returned to the routine it had had before Dunaway's violation. Star Spoon was more talkative, even aggressive at times during the parties. Verbally aggressive, in that she was more willing to argue, to present her views. However, she spent as much time with the Computer as she had when she was deeply troubled. Burton did not mind. He had his own projects.

28

All human beings, Nur thought, reported that time seemed to them to have gone much slower when they were infants. Time speeded up a little when they became prejuveniles, got a little faster when they were juveniles, and stepped up the pace even more when they became young adults. When you were in your sixties, what had been a smooth and slow stream, a leisurely flowing and broad river when one was young, became a narrow roaring channel. By the seventies, it was a short waterfall, time hurtling by. By the eighties, it was a deep mountain cataract, water, time itself, shooting by, disappearing over the edge of life, which was near one's feet, a precipice over which time rushed by as if eager to destroy itself. And you, too.

If you were an old man or woman of ninety, looking back, childhood seemed to be a long, long, long, highway reaching to an unimaginable distant horizon. But the last forty years... how short they had been, how swift.

Then you died, and you awoke on a bank of The River and your body was that which you had when you were twenty-five, except that any physical defects you had had then were repaired. It would seem then that, being young again, you would experience time as a slowed-down stream. Childhood would not seem so remote in your memory, nor would it seem to you as long as it had been before you became twenty-five again.

Not so. The young body held a brain young in tissue but old with memory and experience. If you were eighty when you died on Earth and had lived forty years on the Riverworld, and thus were one hundred and twenty years old, in fact, then time was a series of rapids. It hurried you along, hustled and pushed you.

Keep going, keep going, it said. No rest for you. You don't have the time. No rest for me either.

Nur's living body had existed for one hundred and sixty-one years. And so, when he looked back at his childhood, he saw it as an everstretching length. The older he got, the longer childhood seemed to him. If he should live to be a thousand, he would think that childhood had lasted seven hundred years; young adulthood, two hundred; middle age, fifty-nine; time since then; a year.

His companions had mentioned this phenomenon now and then, but they did not dwell on it. Only he, as far as he knew, had pondered about it. It shocked him when Frigate mentioned that they had been here only a few months. Actually, almost seven months had passed. Burton had put off going to his private world for a few weeks. Or so he had said. In reality, he had taken two months.

What made it easier for them—himself, too—to be unaware of the passage of time was that they no longer watched the calendar. They could have told the Computer to display the month and day on the wall every morning, but here, where time meant no more than it had to Homer's lotus eaters, they had neglected to do so. They should have been shaken when Turpin announced that he was celebrating Christmas, but they had had no reference point to measure the passage of time.

It was this failure to notice the passage of time, this super*mañana* attitude, that had caused them to put off something they had been eager to do shortly after getting here. That was the resurrection of those comrades who had died while trying to get to the tower. Joe Miller the titanthrop, Loghu, Kazz the Neanderthal, Tom Mix, Umslopogaas, John Johnston, and many others. These had earned the right to be brought to the tower, and the eight who had made it had intended to do that. They spoke about it now and then, though not often. Somehow, for various reasons, they kept putting it off.

Nur could not excuse himself for having been shot along with them in time's millrace. He, too, had neglected this very important deed. It was true that he had been even busier than they with various research projects, but it would not take the Computer more than half an hour to locate them—if they could be found—and a few minutes to set up arrangements to raise them.

If you lived a million years, would your childhood then seem to have lasted seven hundred and fifty thousand years? And would the last two hundred and fifty years seem only a century? Could the mind play that sort of gigantic trick on itself?

Time, viewed objectively, flowed always at the same speed. A machine watching day-by-day activities of the people in the Rivervalley would see them as having, every day, the same amount of time to do whatever they did. But, inside these people, would not time have speeded up? And would they not be doing less and less with every day? Perhaps not in the outward physical actions such as eating breakfast, taking baths, exercising, and so forth. But what about mental and emotional processes? Would they be slower? Would not the process of changing themselves for the better, the ostensible goal set for them by the Ethicals, be slowed down, too? If this was so, the Ethicals should have given them more than a hundred years to achieve the moral and spiritual near-perfection necessary for Going On.

There was, however, one undeniable realistic reason why one hundred years was the limit for this group of people. The energy needed to fill the grails, to run the tower, and to resurrect the dead, was derived from the heat from this planet's molten nickel-iron core. The available energy was enormous, but so was the consumption of it. The Ethicals might have figured out that a hundred years for this group, people who had lived from 100,000 B.C. through A.D. 1983, and a hundred years for the next group, those who had lived after A.D. 1983, would eat up almost all the tappable energy. With all the heat that the thermionic converters drew, two hundred years' withdrawal would cool off the core to the point where it could no longer supply the requirements.

Loga, the Ethical, had never mentioned this energy limitation. He must have known it, and it must have caused him anguish and guilt. Nur, having thought of this factor, had asked the Computer to give him the computation for the energy needed for the two projects. And the answer had been what Nur had expected. Yes, even the core of this planet, slightly larger than Earth's, would lose its white-hot glow and become red and dim within two centuries.

Loga's parents, siblings, and cousins were still in the Rivervalley. Every one of them had been killed at least once, and none had Gone On. Loga had interfered with the project and gotten rid of his fellow Ethicals and the Ethical Agents so that his family might live longer than the time allotted to them. And, Loga hoped, attain that level where they could Go On.

That did not mean, however, that this project, the first, would not be terminated when the hundred years were up. He could salvage his loved ones by making sure that their body-recordings would not be erased and their *wathans* released to float for as long as the universe lasted or perhaps longer. He could end the first group and start the next group on schedule. The slight deviation in the procedure would be that his family would continue to live in The Valley. They would be part of the next group and thus get an extra century.

If that were so, why had Loga not just arranged that the Computer would not report that certain persons who should have been disposed of were still living? Loga had been able to fix it so that the Computer had operated illegally in far more noticeable matters.

Probably, Loga had not wanted to take the chance that he could get by with the minor matter—major, from his viewpoint. He had to assure his complete control, even if trying to do this made the risks far greater. He knew that a year or two before the end of this project, a spaceship would arrive from the Gardenworld. It would hold a crew of Ethicals and the body-records of the people for the second project. Loga had to insure that the newcomers would not interfere with him. He had set things up so that the newcomers would be seized or killed when they unsuspectingly got off the ship in the hangar.

Unfortunately, somebody had gotten to Loga, killed him, and erased his body-recording.

All evidence pointed to the Mongolian female agent who had been killed by Nur. But Nur had very little evidence to go by. He had no idea how she had gotten into the tower, what her role was or what it had been intended to be, or, even, whether she was still not hiding someplace in the tower.

Nur and his companions were supposed to have worked on this mystery until it was solved. However, everybody except himself seemed to have neglected it. They were too occupied with the power and the pleasures the tower gave them. Undoubtedly, they had intended to try to solve the enigma, but they had no idea of how much time had passed.

Nur wondered if it would do any good to call this neglect to their attention. He had gotten nowhere in his efforts to clear matters up via the Computer. Why would they do any better?

Yet it was Alice Hargreaves who had thought of the way to trick the Computer shortly after they had gotten into the magic labyrinth, the tower that was also the Computer. Not he, Nur, not any of the others. He knew, however, from observing them, that they just did not think that solving the mystery was urgent. In fact, nothing seemed urgent to them now except enjoying the treasures of the Computer. And they were in no hurry to get all of those.

They were wrong in thinking that. Nur could see another crisis speeding toward them. Li Po had launched that when he had resurrected people without much thought about the effects. Turpin had then raised many whom he had known on Earth and some he had first known in The Valley. These, in turn, had raised those they wanted to have with them. And so on. Turpinville was already crowded; Turpin was going to oust any more newcomers. They would not care; they would just move into one of the unoccupied worlds or into an apartment suite. And there they would continue the populating.

Most of the people brought in had never even heard of computers, not even those primitive and limited ones of Earth technology. Here they were introduced to a machine that made them, in a sense, demigods. But, being human, many of them would misuse the power through accident or design. Williams, for instance, had raised those involved in the Ripper murders just as a rather malicious joke. Nur could not see that there was any harm in that except that Netley might abuse his power. The others seemed to be decent people. Gull had become born again, as the curious Christian phraseology put it, and the three women were not vicious or power-hungry. The men that they had resurrected to be their companions might be another matter, however. And many of those brought to Turpinville had not changed much since they had been on Earth. A town full of those who had been on Earth pimps, whores, drug sellers, bullies, and killers held much danger. Especially when they could operate the Computer.

What Nur had tried but failed to impress on his companions was that the Computer was a genie let out of a bottle or an afreet that had been released from the constraints of Solomon's Seal. Or, as Frigate had put it, a Frankenstein's monster with an unlimited credit card. One person using these powers might suddenly find that another was using them against him or her. The full potentialities of the Computer were still unknown. To use it safely, you had to learn everything it could do, and that would take a long, long time.

For instance, Burton, while watching those in the Ripper case, had not considered that he was being watched while watching. If he had foreseen the possibilities, he would have put an inhibit on anyone spying on him. Now that he knew it could be done, he had ordered the Computer to insure his privacy in his operation of it. But it was rather late for that. Five people, one of whom, Netley, might be a danger to everybody else, had been brought in. Moreover, if Williams had thought of it, he could have told the Computer to override Burton's privacy instructions and not tell Burton about it.

Whoever got to the Computer first could override the latecomers.

Only one who learned the list of all that the Computer could do could protect himself. And the others. Even then, he might be too late. Another might have already put in commands giving himself control channels that he had made sure would be denied to others.

Nur intended to go through the list of potentialities, learn them by heart, and then see to it that the Computer would deny

256 / Philip José Farmer

control to anyone who could misuse certain powers. That would, of course, give him the greatest power of anyone in the tower. But he knew that he would not use it for evil purposes.

For the moment, though, he had other things to do. His allotted work hours for the day were over. He must go now and have dinner with the woman he had raised, his wife on Earth, a woman whom he had not seen much there because he had been traveling in his quest for knowledge and the Truth. He owed her much, and now he could repay her.

29

Alice gave her Mad Tea Party on April 1, April Fool's Day.
It was also a farewell party, not for Alice, who was staying, but for the "decor" of her world and the androids in it. Tired
of the Wonderland cum Looking-Glass motif, she intended to
change it. Her guests would have a last look at it, and sometime
later she would have the Computer remove most of it and replace
it with whatever she ordered. As of the moment, she said, she
had several ideas for the redecorating. What she hoped was that
during the party the guests would give her more ideas.

First, though, she had to make up a guest list, and this caused
problems from the beginning. She had intended to invite only
the seven companions and their mates. Li Po said that he wanted
to bring all of his "wives." She responded by saying that she preferred that he bring only one. That could be whichever woman
was his bedmate for April 1. Li Po replied that his other wives
and his friends and their mates would be hurt if they did not
receive invitations, too. After all, she had a place big enough for
the few people he would like to bring (about a hundred, he estimated). The forty sages (now fifty) and their charming women
were all well behaved. They might get a little boisterous, but she
wanted a lively party, didn't she?

Alice could be very stubborn. But she was very fond of Li Po,
even if she did think that he drank too much and was altogether
too lecherous. Also, he was entertaining, and he seemed determined to be accompanied by his friends. In the end, she gave in
and extended a blanket invitation to the Chinese.

Frigate said that he and Sophie would be very happy to attend.
However, Sophie, who was very gregarious, had by now resurrected ten men and ten women, with his permission, of course.

They were very good friends she had known in New York City, Los Angeles, and, believe it or not, please restrain your laughter, Kalamazoo, Michigan.

Puzzled, Alice asked why he thought she would laugh. Frigate sighed and said, "Kalamazoo was, like some other American place-names, Peoria, Podunk, and downtown Burbank, a risible word, a poke in the ribs and a snigger. Like the English Gotham of the later Middle Ages, the German Schildburg, the town of Chelm in Yiddish stories, the Boeotia of the ancient Greeks. Well, Kalamazoo and the other American cities are not quite like the others I mentioned. The difference is . . ."

Alice listened politely, then said, "You intended to ask me if I would invite Sophie's friends, but you wandered off. Yes, they are welcome, since there are only twenty of them."

Frigate thanked her, but she could detect some hesitancy in his voice. Whereas Sophie was gregarious, he was, not antigregarious, but nongregarious. No doubt he had been glad that he and Sophie now had some companions. On the other hand, he was beginning to feel a little crowded and put upon. The world would never have enough elbow room for him.

De Marbot and Behn also wanted to bring the people they had resurrected recently. Alice said that they could come, but when she had cut off their screens, she sighed. Originally, she had planned for around thirty. Now she had one hundred and three. So far.

Burton, at least, was no problem in terms of numbers. He and Star Spoon had not as yet brought anybody else in.

"Oh, yes," she said. "I have a surprise."

"For all of us or just for me?" he said.

"Oh, for everybody, though it may affect you more than the others."

"I know you, Alice," he said, smiling and, as so often, looking like Mephistopheles himself when he did so. "I know your expressions. You have just regretted adding that last phrase. You're ashamed that you did so. What is the surprise, another man?"

"Go to hell," Alice said, and she told the Computer to cut them off. She had changed in many ways. Never, never on Earth, no matter how angered, would she have said that to anyone. Not even her husband.

After pacing back and forth a while to allow herself to settle down, she called Nur. He said, "Greetings, Alice. It's a pleasure to see you. Could I call you back in a moment? I'm talking to Tom Turpin. There's . . ." He hesitated, then said, "Never mind that."

"I'm sorry to interrupt," she said. "But I just . . . that's all right. I'll call back within the half hour."

She bit her lip as she wondered if she should invite William Gull and his fellow Dowists. He had been, after all, physician in ordinary to Queen Victoria and a baronet. Yet she had long ago rid herself of the class distinctions that had governed her on Earth and for quite a while on the Riverworld, so his high connections should not be considered. Also, he had been a murderer-mutilator. Yet he had repented and was a deacon of the Dowist Church. And she, as one who was no longer a believer in Christianity but still tried to act like a Christian, should not permit his renounced past to bother her. He could be an entertaining conversationalist as long as he refrained from proselytizing. Then he became a nuisance and a bore. But she would insist that the Dowist not push their religion if they attended the party.

Finally, she called him. He was pleased to be asked, almost pathetically so.

"I'm also inviting Annie Crook, Elizabeth Stride, and Marie Kelly," she said, "if that makes a difference to you."

"Oh, of course not," he said. "It is your party, and Mrs. Stride and I get along well now, though we have certain disagreements on theology. Mrs. Cook and Mrs. Kelly are rather cool, understandably so, but I hope to bring them around someday. I assure you that I will not spoil this social function by any unseemly behavior."

Alice then called the three women, and they said they would be delighted. Could they bring their "beaus" with them? Though reluctant to have them, Alice smiled and said they would be welcome. So, that made one hundred and fifty-one guests, since Gull would bring his woman and thirty-two others. Stride and

Crook would each bring a man, and Kelly would, as usual, have a man on each arm.

The second time she tried Nur, he was ready to talk to her. He thanked her for the invitation and said that he and Ayesha would be happy to come. He had just had a rather intense conversation with Tom Turpin. Both of them were disturbed because of the two women who had become pregnant. The first birth would occur in four months, the second, two weeks later.

"Tom has told the women many times that the babies will have no *wathans*. Since the Ethicals did not intend to have babies here, they made no provisions for creating *wathans*. I asked the Computer if it had the schematics for making a *wathan* generator, and it said that there was no such thing in its records. That means, as you perhaps remember, that the babies, lacking *wathans*, will hence lack self-consciousness. For all exterior purposes, they will behave just as babies with *wathans* will. But they will not be self-conscious. They'll be biological machines, very superior machines, but still machines."

"Yes, I know," Alice said. "But what can one do?"

"If those women want to bear and raise what will be the equivalent of androids, that would be only their business. *If* that was all there was to it. However, their example may stimulate others to imitate them, to have babies also. Eventually, this tower will be jammed with people, a good part of whom will be soulless. What happens when the overcrowding causes fights for space? War. Suffering. Death. I don't have to fill in the picture for you."

"Yes, but . . ." Alice said.

"Turpin has threatened to kick them out if they bear the children. They don't care. They'll just go to an apartment with their men and live there. But this little trouble will lead to great trouble. Somebody . . . we . . . will have to take drastic action to stop this and make sure that it doesn't happen again."

"You mean . . . kill the babies?"

"I don't like to contemplate that, it pains me greatly, but it will have to be done. The babies, as I said, are really androids, and one should have no more compunction about destroying them than about destroying androids. They look completely human and behave like human beings to a certain extent. But they are not self-conscious; they do not have that which makes *Homo sapiens* human. The babies can't be allowed to grow into children; they should be eliminated now before they know what's happening."

Alice knew that their death would be instantaneous and painless. They would be placed in a converter and reduced to atoms in a microsecond. Nevertheless, the idea horrified her.

No doubt the kind-hearted Nur felt horror, too. But he knew what had to be done, and he would do it. If Turpin could not get the job done, Nur would see to it.

"If we had a *wathan* generator," Nur said. "I would insist . . . I think almost everybody would agree with me . . . that these two infants be the exception. We would see that they had *wathans,* but there would be no more children born. Any woman who used the Computer to make herself fertile would be killed and her body kept in the records until the day . . . if it ever comes . . . that the Computer starts resurrecting people again in The Valley. Any man who knowingly made the woman pregnant would also be slain. However . . ."

"Yes?"

"*Allah!* That won't be necessary. I should have thought of this before. The Computer can be ordered not to make anyone fertile from now on. Why didn't I think of that long ago? Time . . ."

"Time?" Alice said.

Nur waved his hand to dismiss the phrase.

"Then I see no reason to destroy the babies," Alice said. "Surely they won't be any problem."

Nur sighed with relief, though he still looked troubled. Perhaps that was because he had been so slow in arriving at the very obvious solution.

He shook his head. "There's a possibility I must check on at once. What if someone has given a command to the Computer that anybody who wants to become fertile can become so? That would be the prior command and the authoritative one. The only one who could override that would be Loga or the woman whom I killed . . . if I did kill her. Just a moment. I'll check."

Alice could have listened in on him, but she would never have done that unless he gave permission. A minute later, the screen before her glowed, and Nur's face appeared. She knew at once what had happened from his angry expression.

"Someone has done just what I hoped would not be done. He . . . she . . . whoever . . . has made it possible for anyone who wants to become fertile to do so. The Computer would not tell me who gave it the command."

"My God!" Alice said. Then, "Dick told me about that black man, Bill Williams, resurrecting Gull and the others. Do you suppose . . . ?"

"I don't know. We'll probably never find out. It's possible that Wandal Goudal or Sarah Kelpin, one of the women having babies, did it. In any event . . ."

Though not very often at a loss for words, Nur was so now.

"Tom will have to be told," she said. "Surely, he'll do what must be done."

"I'll call him now," Nur said.

She sat down to wait, thinking that she would hear from him in ten or fifteen minutes. However, the screen glowed on the control console in less than six minutes. She was surprised to see, not Nur's, but Tom Turpin's face. It was red under his dark skin, and his face was contorted.

"I'm contacting all of you!" he shouted.

You, she understood, would be the seven companions. But what was he doing in the central area forming the O at the tips of the pie-slice-shaped private worlds? And why were his favorite women, Diamond Lil Schindler, his cronies, Chauvin, Joplin, and other musicians, and their women there?

"OK! I see all of you there! Man, I'm mad! Mad, do you hear?"

Nur's voice, quiet and soothing, came.

"Calm down, Tom. Tell us what happened."

"They threw me out!" he screamed. "Overpowered my guards, grabbed me and my friends, and threw me out! They said I wasn't King Tom no more! I was through! I couldn't ever get back in! So long, good-bye, farewell, adieu, adios, motherfucker!"

"Who's they?" Burton's voice said. "Was Bill Williams the ringleader?"

"No, not him! He moved out two days ago into one of the

empty worlds! It was Jonathan Hawley and Hamilton Biggs did it! They were the ringleaders, I mean!"

Alice had probably been introduced to the two, but she did not remember the names.

"Something like this was to be expected," Nur said. "There's little . . . nothing . . . you can do about it, Tom. Why don't you move into one of the empty worlds? And be very careful the next time you select someone to bring in?"

"I can't even do that!" Tom yelled. He raised his arms and brought them down violently, his hands slapping his thighs. "Can't even do that! Williams is in one of them! The gypsies have taken another! I know 'cause I saw them coming out of it! I can't get into any of the other four! Somebody's locked them with codewords! I don't know who did it, but I think Hawley and Biggs did it! They're holding them for excess population or whatever! Maybe they did it just out of spite!"

"It could be worse. They could have killed you," Nur said.

"Yeah, Pollyanna, it could have been worse!"

Turpin was weeping now. The big black woman, Schindler, put her arms around him. He sobbed on her neck while she smiled, exposing the twinkling gems set into her teeth. On Earth, she had been one of the most important madams of the St. Louis Tenderloin district and one of Turpin's lovers.

Alice waited until he had released himself from Diamond Lil's embrace, and she said, "You and your friends can stay at my place, Tom."

The others, Burton, de Marbot, Aphra, Frigate, and Nur, hastened to extend their invitations.

"No," Turpin said, wiping his eyes with a huge violet handkerchief, "that ain't necessary, but I thank you. We'll just move into apartments."

He raised a fist and began howling, "I'll get you, Hawley, Biggs, you other motherfucking Judases! I'll get you! You'll be sorry, you sons of bitches! Watch out for Tom Turpin, you hear me!"

She could not see the screen that must have appeared on the wall before Trupin. But she could hear the loud laughter and the triumphant words.

"Get lost, you blubbering blubber!"

Tom howled with anger and anguish and began striking the wall. Alice cut off the screen. What next?

What indeed? That was only one of the upsetting events leading up to the party. Which, she would say later to anyone who would hear—there were few of those left—was, she was not exaggerating in the slightest, the worst party she had ever given.

30

The morning of April the first, Burton and Star Spoon breakfasted on the balcony outside their bedroom. The sky was clear, and the breeze was gentle and cool because Burton had ordered it so. Now and then, an elephant trumpeted and a lion roared. The shadow of a roc crossed over the table, the bird with a forty-foot wingspread designed by Burton and fashioned by the Computer. Star Spoon started when it darkened them.

"It won't hurt us, it's programmed not to attack us," Burton said, smiling.

"It could be an ill omen."

He did not argue with her. Li Po and the men and women of the eighth century A.D. whom he had brought in were intelligent and much-experienced, yet they had not rid themselves of their superstitions. Li Po was perhaps the most flexible, but even he reacted now and then to something that he should by now laugh at or not even think of.

He wondered if one had to desuperstition oneself, as it were, before one could Go On. What did the holding of absurd beliefs have to do with gaining compassion and empathy and freedom from hate and prejudice? It had much to do with it if it caused fear and cruelty and irrational behavior. But could one be afraid that bad luck would come if a black cat crossed one's path and still be a "good" person? No, not if one threw a brick at the cat or treated one's friends badly because one was in an ill humor from anxiety.

"You, too, are afraid," Star Spoon said.

"What?" He stared at her.

"You knocked on wood three times. On the table."

"No, I didn't."

"I'm sorry to have to contradict you, Dick. But you did. I would not lie."

"I really did?"

He laughed uproariously.

"Why do you find that funny?"

He explained, and she smiled. That, he thought, was the first time in days that she had lost her blank expression. Well, if he had to pull her out of her soberness by making a fool of himself, he did not mind.

"I did not ask you how you are," he said.

"I am well."

"I hope that you will be happy soon."

"I thank you."

Burton was thinking about proposing to her that the Computer locate in her memory all her experiences of brutality, especially the rapes. The Computer could excise them as a surgeon could a rotting appendix. Though the erasing would eliminate much from her memory, perhaps many years if the time of events were totaled, she would be free of painful thoughts. On the other hand, though the memories would be gone, their emotional impact would still be there. The Computer could not remove that. Star Spoon still might be repulsed by lovemaking but not have the slightest idea why.

The mind had to operate on itself, but it was seldom a skilled surgeon.

Burton silently cursed Dunaway and wished that there was a hell to which the man could be sent.

Star Spoon lifted a forkful of trout to her mouth, chewed while staring out over the gardens below the castle, the jungle river, and the desert beyond. Having swallowed, she said, "I want you to bring in another woman, Dick. One who can take care of your needs. A woman who can laugh and love. I do not mind, I not only do not mind, I would be very pleased."

"No," he said. "No. That is most generous of you—also very Chinese. I admire the culture and wisdom of your people, but I am not Chinese."

"It's not just Chinese. It's good common sense. There's no

reason why I should be—what did you say the other day?—a dog in the . . . ?"

"A dog in the manger. One who owns something he can't use but won't let anybody else use it because he's selfish."

"A dog in the manger. I am not that. Please, Dick, it would make me less unhappy."

"But I wouldn't be happy."

"If it would embarrass you to have another woman here, put her in an apartment and visit her. Or . . . I could leave."

He laughed and said, "Human beings are not androids. I couldn't just raise a woman and imprison her for my own pleasure. In the first place, she might not like me. In the second, even if she did, she would want the company of others. She'd want to be free, not a caged odalisque."

She reached across the table and put her hand on his. "It is too bad."

"What? What we've just been talking about?"

"That and much more. Everything." She waved a hand as if to take in the whole universe. "Bad. All bad."

"No, it's not. Part is bad, part is good. You've just had more than your share of the bad. But you have time, a long, long time, to get your share of the good."

She shook her head. "No. Not for me."

Burton pushed his plate, still half-full, away. An android silently took the plate away.

"I'll stay and talk with you, if you like. I have work to do, but it's not more important than you."

"I, too, have work," she said. He rose, went around the solid gold table to her, and kissed her cheek. He was curious about what she was doing with the Computer, but, when he asked her about it, she always said that it was uninteresting and she would prefer to hear about his studies.

However, when they left the castle in the armored flying chairs, she seemed to be excited about the party. She chattered away about some amusing incidents in her childhood, and she even laughed several times. Burton thought that it was no good for her to be alone so much or just with him. Yet when they had gone to the weekly meetings, she had been subdued and withdrawn.

During flight, Burton spoke over the transmitter to Star Spoon. "I tried earlier this morning to call Turpinville. Which I suppose will have another name by now. I got no answer. Apparently, who-ever's running Turpinville now is not taking calls."

"Why did you call them?"

"I was curious. I wanted to find out if whoever's in charge in-tends to be aggressive. It's possible, you know, that he . . . they . . . won't be content with just ruling Turpinville. He might have some plans for taking over the entire tower."

"What sense would there be in that?"

"What sense was there in ousting Turpin and grabbing the seat of power? I also called Tom to determine his mood. It was black. Or perhaps scarlet is a better description. He is still vow-ing vengeance, but he knows that he has no chance of getting that. All they have to do is stay shut up in their world."

They floated through the doorway into the central area. Bur-ton was surprised by the crowd and the uproar there. Turpin was with Louis Chauvin, Scott Joplin, and other musician-friends who had two days ago been in Little St. Louis. Evidently, these had also been hurled out from the little world without anything except the clothes they were wearing. There were also about a hundred other blacks, some of whom he recognized. And some-thing had also happened to Frigate and Lefkowitz and her friends. They were gesticulating angrily and shouting words unintelli-gible in the great noise. This was added to by the blaring voices from the wall-screens showing each one his or her past.

Li Po and his comrades left their world just then, and their questions swelled the volume of sound.

Burton and Star Spoon eased the chairs onto the floor. He got up and yelled, "What's going on?" but only those very near him could hear.

Frigate had put on an outlandish costume for the party. A huge scarlet bowtie, a lemon-yellow vest with enormous silver buttons, a big sky-blue belt, tight white pants with scarlet seams, and lemon-yellow Wellington boots. His skin color almost matched that of the bowtie.

"We came out of my place," he said, "and found Netley and a dozen others there. They had beamers and guns, and Netley told me that if I didn't give him the codeword, he'd shoot all of us! So I gave it to him! I had to, nothing else I could do! He and his gang went inside and closed the door . . . and . . . and that's that! We're locked out! Dispossessed! My beautiful world taken away from me!"

"Not to mention from me and my friends," Sophie said. She was dressed in ancient Egyptian fashion, à la Cleopatra. A uraeus headband, a naked torso exposing big shapely breasts—what would Alice think of that?—and a long skirt split in front almost to the crotch. She even had a staff with an ankh at its end. Her companions were in costumes of many periods, Asiatic and European.

"I should have been more cautious!" Frigate cried. "I should have checked on the area outside before we went through the door!"

"He's locking the barn after the horse is stolen," Sophie said. "Crying over spilt milk. Pardon the clichés, but crises always bring out clichés. They're not very creative situations, verbally, anyway."

Tom Turpin, dressed in tails and a stovepipe hat, came up to them. "It's Thieves' Week!" he said. "They're doing all right, too."

"What about those?" Burton said, pointing at the weeping and bewildered-looking blacks.

"Them? Those're the good folks, the churchers, Second Chancers, New Christians, Revised Free Will Baptists, and Nichirenites. Boggs and Hawley threw them out a couple of minutes after Pete got his world taken from him."

At that moment, Stride, Crook, Kelly, and their men came out of the elevator shaft. Burton left it to others to explain what had happened. He ordered a screen on the wall and called Alice. Her dark eyes widened when she saw the scene behind him and heard the babel. Burton told her what had happened, and he said, "I'm afraid that this may spoil your party."

"Not at all," she said. "I'm not going to allow anything to do that. I suppose it will take Tom and Peter some time to simmer down, but they can do it, I know. As for those poor people those ruffians kicked out, well, tell them they can come to the party if they wish. It might make them feel better. Of course, it's not as if they can find no home or have to go hungry. Well, anyway, you invite them for me. I'll be waiting."

Burton went to the milling exiles, asked for quiet, got it, and passed on Alice's invitation. All accepted. These had no flying chairs, but they could have them made in the converter in the anteroom to Alice's world.

Frigate had some drinks made for his party by the anteroom converter so they could soften the shock with liquor while en route to their destination. Sophie took one, a tall glass of gin, but she said, "I'm not so sure that we should spend any time having fun now, Pete. We ought to go over the list of Computer potentialities and put in all the prohibitions we can. We have to forestall anything those scumbags might think of."

"Good thinking," Burton said, though he had not been addressed. "However, Alice won't like it if you miss her party. And I am sure that the dispossessors are going to be so happy celebrating that they won't be plotting any more trouble for some time."

"You may be right," Sophie said. "But I think we should all put our heads together tomorrow and try to figure out everything those assholes could do."

"Our heads are usually not worth much the day after a big party," Burton said. "I'll call you and the others tomorrow about ten in the morning for the big powwow."

Nur and his woman entered the anteroom, halted, looked around, and then made their way through the crowd to Burton. Nur introduced Ayesha bint Yusuf, a thin brown woman even shorter than Nur. Though she was not pretty, she looked quite charming when she smiled.

Burton said to Nur, "I'll explain later. We have to get out of this noisy mess."

As he turned to sit down in his chair, he saw Gull and a score of Dowists, all dressed in long flowing white robes, enter. They looked as if they were stunned.

Burton lifted the chair up and shot it through the wide doorway. He climbed until he was two hundred feet high and sped over the massive oak and pine forest, the Tulgey Wood, and the river Issus toward the huge clearing at the foot of the high hill on which Alice's mansion stood. The field was three hundred yards square, perfectly flat, and covered with a bright green grass that never needed mowing. The field held a huge ferris wheel and a roller coaster on one side and a merry-go-round and a small skating rink and many tables on which were placed food and drinks and white open-sided tents and a bandstand on which androids were playing a waltz and small buildings like tiny Roman villas, which he supposed were comfort stations, and a croquet field and badminton nets and equipment and a dance floor of polished wood and many android servants, almost all of them looking like characters from Lewis Carroll's two famous books.

Under a giant oak at the edge of the field was a house with chimneys shaped like a rabbit's ears and with a roof covered with rabbit fur. Before it was a large table set for teatime and many chairs around it. A man-sized March Hare and Mad Hatter and a little girl sat at the table. Though she was dressed as Tenniel had illustrated Alice, she did not have her long blonde hair. Alice had ordered an android that looked as she did when she was ten.

"Alice has certainly done herself proud," he muttered as he steered the chair toward the foot of the hill.

She stood there by a chair that looked like the coronation chair in Westminster Hall. There was another and similar chair by it; a tall yellow-haired man stood by it.

"Her surprise!" he said. "I knew it!"

He was hurt, and he was also angry with himself because he could be hurt. So, he had been lying to himself when he had told himself that he felt nothing for her anymore.

She certainly looked beautiful. She was wearing her favorite, the flapper's garments of the 1920s. She should have been wearing a hat, since this was an afternoon affair, but Terrestrial rules did not hold now. Her bobbed hair shone black and glossy in the sun. The man, judging by Alice's height, was about six feet four inches tall. He wore the uniform of a Scots chief, kilt, tartan, sporran, and all. As Burton descended, he could make out the black and red checks of the Rob Roy clan on the kilt. The man was a descendant of the famous Scots outlaw, which made him a distant relative of Burton's. He was broad-shouldered and well-muscled, and his face was handsome but very strong. He smiled on seeing the turbaned and robed Burton, and, like a sword cutting a rope and releasing a drawbridge, the smile opened Burton's memory. He was Sir Monteith Maglenna, a Scots baronet and laird. Burton had met him in 1872 when Burton spoke in London before the British National Association of Spiritualists. Burton had upset his audience because of his firm declaration that he did not believe in ghosts and would have no use for them if they did exist. The young baronet had talked with him for a while at the party following the lecture. Both had traveled in the American West, and the Scot was, like Burton, an amateur archaeologist. They had spent an interesting halfhour while others, hoping to get a chance to defend spiritualism, fretted by them.

Alice, smiling—was there some malice in it?—introduced Burton and Star Spoon. Burton shook his hand and said, at the same time that Maglenna did, "We've met."

They talked for a few minutes, recalling their old acquaintanceship while the line of people waiting to greet the hostess or be introduced grew longer, and then Burton said, "I say, Alice, how did you know of him?"

"Oh, I met Monty in 1872 when I was twenty years old and he was thirty, at a ball given by the earl of Perth. We danced together quite a few times . . ."

"Did we ever," Monteith said.

". . . and I saw him several times after that. Then he went off to the States, where he came close to dying, an outlaw shot him, quite accidentally, though, and he did not return until 1880. By then, I was married."

"I was unable to keep up our correspondence," Maglenna said. "I did write her about my disability, but my letter never got to her. And so . . ."

Some androids, at a signal from Alice, picked up the chairs in which Burton and Star Spoon had arrived and carried them across the field to the east end. It would have been quicker and more efficient for them to have flown the chairs to the parking area, but Alice had not had the time or had not wished to take the time to program them to operate the chairs.

Burton listened as Alice told Star Spoon in detail how grief-stricken she had been when she had believed that Maglenna had lost interest in her. Partway through her story, he decided that he had heard more than enough of that. He excused himself and wandered around until Star Spoon rejoined him.

"Did you know about Mr. Maglenna?" she said.

"No!" he said savagely. "She never mentioned him in all the many years that she was with me!"

"It's very fortunate that they've finally been reunited. Just think, if it weren't for you, they would have never found each other."

She was smiling as if she were very pleased. Was that because Alice was happy? Or, unhappy creature that she was, did Star Spoon get satisfaction from knowing that he was anything but glad about Maglenna? Some people were so abysmally wretched that their only joy was that others also suffered.

31

They took a ride on the roller coaster, but Star Spoon got sick during the up-and-down-and-arounding and threw up in the seat. The android operating the ride called two others to clean up the mess after Burton had told him to do so.

"You seem even more nervous today," Burton said.

"It's all those strange creatures," she said, waving her hand.

She was not, of course, familiar with the beings with which Carroll had populated the Alice books and which the real Alice had brought to life. They made her uneasy, because she had not been conditioned to them through the books. What made her especially nervous was the Jabberwock, which looked exactly like Tenniel's illustration. Its scaly body was that of an attenuated dragon, and it had leathery dragon wings, but the exceedingly long and relatively thin neck, and the narrow face, which looked like a very evil old man's, and the absurdly long toes of the front paws made it like no other dragon in myth, legend, or fictional literature. It was huge, its head reaching to thirteen feet when it stood upright. The Jabberwock, however, did not venture upon the field but prowled around within a confined area under a gigantic oak, its long tail always lashing.

"It frightens me," Star Spoon said.

"You know that it's been programmed not to hurt anybody."

"Yes, I know. But what if something went wrong in it? Look at those terrible teeth. It has only four, two above and two below, but think what those teeth could do if they bit down on you."

"You need a drink," he said, and he steered her toward a table. The androids serving there were a Fish-Footman, a Frog-Footman, and a White Rabbit. The former two wore the eighteenth-century garments and white powdered wigs Tenniel had portrayed. The

White Rabbit had pink eyes, a stiff white collar, a cravat, a checked coat, and a waistcoat. A gold chain inserted by a stud into a buttonhole in his waistcoat was attached at the other end to a large watch in a pocket of the waistcoat. From time to time, the White Rabbit took the watch out and looked at it.

"Excellent," Burton said, grinning.

"I don't like them," Star Spoon whispered, as if it made any difference if they heard her. "Those huge goggly eyes."

"The better to see you, my dear."

He looked up as a shadow passed over him. It had been cast by the chair of de Marbot, who was leading a flight of thirty or more of his friends. He was dressed in a Hussar's uniform; so were some of his friends. Others wore field marshals' uniforms, though none had ever attained that rank. Most of the ladies were dressed in the style of the 1810s.

A few minutes later, Aphra and a dozen others arrived. Everybody who had been invited was here, Burton thought. He was wrong, though. Shortly after the last of Behn's group had left the host and hostess, a motorcycle roared onto the field. Sitting in the front was Bill Williams and clinging to him was the black woman Burton had seen with him in the corridor. Williams wore a black astrakhan hat, very Russian, but his face was painted like a witch doctor's, his torso was bare except for a necklace of human hand bones, and he wore black leather pants and boots. The woman had come-upped Sophie; she wore nothing except a necklace of huge diamonds and a complex painting of many bright-colored figures, which covered her front and back and her legs.

Burton had not known that Alice had invited Williams. Judging from her expression, she was sorry that she had. However, she smiled as a hostess should and introduced the couple to Maglenna. His eyes were as wide as his grin when he took the woman's hand. Burton wished that he were near enough to hear their conversation.

Frigate strolled up to Burton and pointed at the late-comers. "Quite a sensation, right. The last shall be first."

"Quite," Burton said.

"Sophie doesn't know if she should be delighted or furious."

The White Knight rode by on his sorry white nag. His helmet was off, revealing a face that looked exactly like Carroll's except for the very long drooping white moustache. A scabbard holding a huge straight two-edged sword was attached to a belt, and a big club with a wooden shaft and a knobbed end with spikes was stuck shaft-down in a boot hanging from the saddle. Attached to the back of the armor was a box, upside-down, its lid hanging. This was, in *Through the Looking-Glass,* supposed to have been the White Knight's invention, a container for his sandwiches and clothes. But it was upside-down to keep the rain out of the box, and so its contents had fallen out.

Behind him rode the Red Knight on a roan stallion. It was a sinister figure with its crimson armor, horsehead-shaped helmet, and big spiked club.

A Walrus and a Carpenter in its paper hat and leather apron walked by, conversing. Trailing them on thin spindly legs were forty or so oysters, each with long antennae with eyes on the ends projecting from their shells.

"This must have taken Alice a long time to prepare," Frigate said. "Think of all the details she had to put into the Computer."

"Oh, look," Sophie said, pointing at a tree. "Can you believe it? The Cheshire Cat!"

As they walked toward the tree, the cat, which was the size of a large lynx, began to disappear. The tail vanished, then the hindquarters, then the front quarters, then the neck, then the head. Except for a cat's grin hanging in the air above the branch on which it had sat, it was invisible. They walked underneath it, looking for a mechanism of some sort, but could find none.

"Have to ask Alice how this is done," Burton said. "Probably, though, she won't know. The Computer would've taken the order and done its scientific magic, no explanations needed."

The Gryphon and the Mock Turtle walked by conversing. The Gryphon was a lion-sized creature with the body of a lion and the head and wings of an eagle. The Mock Turtle had the body of a giant tortoise, weighing perhaps six hundred pounds, and the head and back legs of a cow. It crawled slowly but, once, halted, and pushed with its short but immensely powerful front legs, causing it to spring upright. While it teetered on the end of its shell, its bovine legs braced, the hoofs digging into the ground, tears flowing, it sang in a magnificent contralto, "Beautiful soup, so rich and green, Waiting in a hot tureen!"

But when it reached the chorus, beginning with "Beau—ootiful Soo—oop!" it lost its balance and fell heavily on its back, still singing. There was some consternation then until six androids turned it over. After which it resumed crawling and singing.

Star Spoon said, "I think I'll go sit down for a while, Dick. I'm tired, and these animals"—she nodded at the Gryphon—"look so dangerous. I know they're not, but . . ."

"Very well, I'll check on you later," Burton said.

He watched her walk to the west end of the field and sit down in a very comfortable chair. A very fat, bald-headed and old-looking android—it had to be Father William—came to her side. It must have asked her if she wanted anything, because she nodded and her mouth moved.

Burton walked around and looked at the Queen of Hearts and the other androids fashioned to simulate the living pack of cards. From the front, they looked exactly like Tenniel's draw-ings, but they presented a much thicker profile, about three inches wide, he estimated. The Computer could do only so much in making a reality of fantasy. The things had to have space for muscles and organs and blood. Their faces were painted on the oblong bodies, but, though the painted mouths did not move, voices issued from them.

"Marvelous!" Burton said.

Aphra Behn happened to be standing near him. She said, "Yes, aren't they? It's such a childish conceit, however. Not that I disparage Alice for all this. We've struggled so hard to get here, endured so many dangers and tribulations, that we've relaxed and become children again for a while. We have to play, don't you think?"

"The playtime, unfortunately, is over," he said. "What hap-pened to Turpin and Frigate may happen to us."

He went to a table and ordered a glass of Scotch from one of the living chess pieces, a Castle. He also got a fine Havana pana-tela. Cigar in one hand, glass in the other, he strolled over to the croquet field. The field was as in the book, ridges and furrows with bent-over card-androids serving as arches, flamingoes as mallets, and rolled up hedgehogs as balls. Since Alice was not cruel or callous, she must have made arrangements in the neural systems of the birds and animals that would prevent them from being hurt.

Turpin seemed to have forgotten his troubles; he was having a good time at croquet.

An hour passed. Burton had two more Scotches. He took rides on the merry-go-round and again on the roller coaster and watched the orchestra for a while. Most of the musicians were Frog- and Fish-Footmen, but the conductor was Bill the Lizard, a giant saurian smoking a cigar and wearing a flat cap. They had been programmed to play any kind of music from waltzes to dixieland to classical. At the moment, they were blasting out a wild barbaric piece that Burton thought must be the rock-and-roll described by Frigate. After listening for a while, he could understand why Frigate had been tempted to erase all of this type of music from the records.

An ugly Duchess and a Queen of Hearts waddled by him.

"Off with their heads! Off with their heads!"

"Beat him until he sneezes!"

Burton went back to the croquet field, played a game, wandered around, stopping to chat with several people, and then watched the Mad Tea Party for a while. The child-android playing Alice was charming; the large dark eyes had the real Alice's dreaminess. Burton could understand why Mr. Dodgson had fallen in love with the ten-year-old girl.

When the Mad Hatter said, "And ever since that, he won't do a thing I ask! It's always six o'clock now," Burton walked away. It was amusing to watch them go through the whole scene once, but the repetition was boring.

Feeling in need of exercise, he played volleyball for a while. The game was fun and vigorous, and he loved to watch Bill Williams' woman leap into the air to bat a ball back. Then, sweating, he walked to a chair and sat down. A Tweedledee and a Tweedledum asked him what he wanted. He ordered a mint julep. The two grotesquely fat androids went to a table and there had an argument—programmed in, of course—about which one would serve him. While their heated and amusing discussion was going on, he watched the blue caterpillar on a nearby giant mushroom smoking its hookah. In a way, he thought, it was a pity that all these things were to be destroyed. Yet, he could understand why Alice had tired of them.

He watched the dance floor for a while. The orchestra was playing some type of music he did not recognize. Frigate was walking by then, and Burton called him over. "What is that music, and what kind of gyrations are the dancers doing?"

"I don't know the particular piece," Frigate said. "It's from the 1920s, sounds familiar, but I can't quite place it. The dance is called the Black Bottom."

"Why do they call it that?"

"I don't know."

Alice and Monteith seemed to be enjoying the wild motions. At last she had found a partner to share her love of dancing. Burton had never cared for it. In fact, he had only danced several times in his life, and that had been for the edification of a black African tribal chief.

The fat identical-twin schoolboys, Tweedledee and Tweedledum, walked by him. Neither had a drink on a tray. Burton said, "What . . . ?" and at that moment the music stopped in the middle of a bar. He rose and stared at the stand. The musicians had put aside their instruments and were getting down off the bandstand.

"What's going on?" Frigate said.

Alice was staring puzzledly at the departing musicians.

"Not planned for," Burton said. A chill passed over his skin.

The little Frenchman, de Marbot, his blue eyes wide, trotted up to Burton. "Something is wrong," he said.

Burton turned to take in three hundred and sixty degrees of vision. The androids were hastening to the woods, their pace increasing. All except the Mock Turtle, which had fallen on its back and was bawling and kicking its legs. No, not all were heading for the trees. A number were spreading toward the west end of the field, where the hill began. Among them were the Red and White Knights on their chargers, the Lion and the Unicorn, and the Gryphon. They stopped just before coming to the hill and turned around to face the field.

By then the other androids had disappeared into the shadows under the massive oaks.

Burton glanced at de Marbot's scabbard and the hilt of the saber sticking from it.

"I daresay you may have to use your snickersnee, Marcelin," he said. "How many . . . are all your Hussars armed?"

"Why, yes," de Marbot said. "We have twelve sabers among us."

"Tell them to draw them," Burton said. "Listen, Marcelin, I think we're going to be attacked. Somebody, I'm sure, has put in an overriding program in the androids. Alice didn't plan this."

He glanced around. Star Spoon must have had the same idea. She was running for the roller coaster now. He looked at de Marbot.

"You have the most military experience," he said. "You're in command now."

He turned and began yelling. "Everybody over here! Quick! On the double!"

Some of the crowd came running. Others stood still as if frozen: the rest ambled toward them.

Maglenna, pulling on Alice's hand, ran up to Burton. "I say, what's going on?"

"I am not sure." Burton looked at Alice. "You don't have the slightest idea?"

She shook her head. "No. Could the Snark be behind this? What can we do about it?"

"That's up to Marcelin," Burton said. "But I think we should make for the chairs. You and Monteith can sit on somebody's lap. We can't get through them—" he indicated the grim beasts guarding the west edge "—without serious loss."

De Marbot was talking in rapid French to his friends. But he stopped and looked at the south edge of the field. The androids were coming out from the forest with weapons: spears, swords, maces, morning stars, and daggers.

Burton swiveled to take in the north and east sides of the

field. Androids were emerging from the shadows there; all were similarly armed. And those from the east side were hurrying to place themselves between the guests and their flying vehicles.

"Too late," Burton said.

De Marbot was bawling orders out in Esperanto so that all would understand him. They began to form a ragged square with the Hussars on the eastern side. Burton called to him, "I'm going to get some weapons."

"Where?" de Marbot said.

"The musical instruments. Some of them can be used as clubs."

He ran to the bandstand with some men behind him. The androids from the north, those nearest the stand, did not change their pace or utter a sound. If they had run, they could have cut Burton off. But he was able to pick up a saxophone, and the others got guitars, bass fiddles, flutes, French horns, anything that might be wielded as a blunt instrument of warfare.

They ran back to the square, where they were arranged in a ragged fashion by de Marbot. He was quivering with eagerness, his blue eyes bright, his round face split with a smile. "Ah, my darlings!" he cried to his Hussars. "You will show these monsters how the soldiers of Napoleon fought!"

His voice was stilled by a great whistling bellow. All looked at the south side of the field, where the Jabberwock was rearing up on its hind legs, stretching its snaky neck out, its mouth gaping, exposing the four sharp teeth. It did not, however, as Burton had feared it would, charge at once. It dropped to all fours and walked slowly toward them, bellowing.

Burton was on the western side of the square, facing the beasts and the Knights there. At the same time that the Jabberwock had begun advancing, the beasts and the Knights' horses had begun walking slowly toward the humans.

On all sides of the group, the androids walked toward it in formation, silently.

Suddenly, Burton was aware that Star Spoon was not with them. She had climbed up the side of the roller coaster and was perched near the top of a cross-piece.

It was too late to go after her. Calling to her to come down would only attract the attention of the androids to her. Perhaps they would not notice her. In any event, she was on her own. No. If he could get to a chair, he could fly to her and take her away.

32

They outnumber us three to one," Burton said loudly to anyone who would hear. "The big beasts and the Knights make the odds even worse. But try to grab their spears and clubs away from them. If any of them fall, pick up their weapons."

De Marbot repeated the advice for the whole group. A black woman, one of the Second Chancers, shrilled, "Oh, Lord, what can we do? We can't shed blood! We're pacifists, peaceful in your sight, Lord!"

"Damn it, woman!" Burton shouted. "Those things aren't human! They're machines! It's no sin to fight for your life against them!"

"That's right!" a black man shouted. "It's no sin! Fight, brothers and sisters! Do battle for the Lord without sin! Tear them apart!"

One group, Burton thought it was the Revised Free Will Baptists, began singing a spiritual. They had not gotten more than a few words out when de Marbot roared for silence.

"If you sing, you can't hear my orders!"

With the Frenchman leading, the square began trotting toward the chairs. Burton, in the rear, kept glancing backward. The Knights and the beasts had not stepped up their pace. Apparently, they were set to close in on the group at a predetermined rate.

The Jabberwock was near the end of the line of androids, coming in from the south side of the field. The monster was the most dangerous attacker, and it should be opposed by at least six sabermen. Burton swore. If only he had a sword instead of a saxophone in his grip.

The group, the women inside, the men forming a shell around them, trotted toward the ranks of creatures standing before the chairs. There were about two hundred or more there, the thickest concentration of bodies. Whoever had planned this had guessed correctly that the humans would try to get to their vehicles. To attempt the hill so they could get inside the house, they had to attack the big beasts and the Knights, and the aspect of these was so fearsome that the humans would prefer to go the other way.

Suddenly, the people ahead of him screamed. He jumped up so he could get a better look at what was frightening them. He saw that chairs were flying up without riders, and he groaned. Androids hidden behind the defensive lines were sending the chairs up. Even if the humans did fight through, they would have no aerial escape; they would have to keep on going into the forest. And they would be hunted down.

De Marbot understood this at once. He cried out a command to halt. The people, however, kept on moving ahead, pushing and shoving, until de Marbot's sabermen succeeded in stopping them. Instantly, the Frenchmen raced around the group to the back, which had now become the front.

"We must get through them to the hill and to the house!" de Marbot shouted. "Dick, you take your men to the left flank! The honor of defending us against the Jabberwock is yours!"

Burton hustled his group as ordered. The androids continued to advance slowly and voicelessly. By now, they were within sixty feet of the humans.

De Marbot raised his saber and yelled, "Charge!"

He and his sabermen leaped ahead of the others, who took more time than they should have in attaining any speed. They were undisciplined and scared, and thus some ran faster than others, jostling those ahead, and some, as was inevitable, fell down, and some tripped over these. Burton only had time to glance at the screaming milling crowd and at the Frenchmen closing with the Red and White Knights, the Lion, the Unicorn, a Walrus, the Gryphon, and a Humpty Dumpty. Then the open mouth of the Jabberwock, its four teeth flashing, saliva running from its lower lip, roaring, was shooting at him. Burton threw the saxophone with all his force into its mouth, and the thing closed its jaws automatically on it. Its nose struck Burton on the chest, knocked him backward, and rammed the air from his lungs. He rolled away while trying to regain his wind, and several women fell on top of him.

The saxophone, spat out, landed near his outstretched right hand. He grabbed it. One of the struggling black women on top of him shrieked, and she was lifted up in the Jabberwock's mouth. The teeth closed through her body; she became limp and silent. With a toss of the head, the monster threw her body away and whipped the snaky neck and head outward and down and seized another screaming woman.

Though he had not yet gotten all of his breath back, Burton heaved the one woman on top of him away, rolled, and ran by the Jabberwock's giant right front foot. A Tweedledee and a Tweedledum walked steadily toward him, holding long spears, their huge fat faces expressionless. Yelling, Burton ran at them, his saxophone held high.

They were programmed to do only certain things, though these were many. One thing they had not been commanded to do was to avoid the area of the Jabberwock's lashing tail, something any human would have consciously done. As a result, the two identicals were knocked flat by the enormous scaly tail. No, not just knocked down. The tail had broken some of their bones. They were crumpled on the grass and groaning.

He glanced back and up. The Jabberwock was not aware of his presence; it was engrossed in killing another woman. Burton ran to the rear flank and waited for the tail to lash to his left. As he did so, he glimpsed the head and shoulders of Williams running toward the chair-parking area. Androids were clumsily stabbing at him with spears and hacking at him with swords, but he was zigzagging desperately. Then Burton could give him no more attention; he leaped forward, landed, stooped, and grabbed a spear the fallen Tweedledee or Tweedledum had dropped. He straightened up, whirled, and leaped back into the protection of the monster's flank. He lifted the spear with both hands and drove it into the heaving side. It sank halfway into the body; blood spurted out and around the shaft. Bellowing deafeningly, the thing reared up on its back legs; the woman in its mouth dropped out.

Burton had turned and run away. The end of the tail came within an inch of hitting him. A green pig charged him, its curling tusks wet and yellow. Burton leaped up and came down on its back but slipped and fell on the grass, bracing against the impact with his hands. One of the card people, a trey of hearts, lay facedown near him, its spindly legs kicking. Burton scrambled up, seized the spear it had been carrying, and thrust upward into the belly of the Mad Hatter, who had just missed him with the edge of a saber. The Hatter reeled backward, its hands by its sides, instead of reacting instinctively, as a human would, by grabbing the shaft. Its face, however, was twisted with agony.

Burton let loose of the spear and picked up the saber it had dropped. Now he did not feel so naked and helpless; now he had a weapon he could use as few could. Immediately a Frog-Footman, a giant owl, and an ugly Duchess attacked him. The bird's weight, sharp beak, and beating wings made it the most formidable. He slashed half a wing off, cut through the shaft of the Frog-Footman's spear, severed the head of the owl with a back-slash, parried the ugly Duchess' spear, and ran her through the belly.

The whole field was a melee now, individuals and clusters battling one another. Many of the humans had grabbed weapons. Though outnumbered, they had one advantage. The androids were neither skilled weapon wielders nor capable of improvised action. They could only thrust straight ahead of them with the spears or hack down with the swords, and their ability to parry was nil. As a result, those humans who were armed were outfighting their opponents, and more and more humans were grabbing weapons. On the other hand, being inferior in number, they could not guard their flanks and sides as well as they would have liked.

The big beasts and the Knights had to be dealt with first. Then, just possibly—it was a fighting chance—the humans could mop up on the lesser creatures.

Burton was free of any immediate attackers for a moment. He looked around swiftly, trying to gauge how the battle was going.

He could not find Alice, but Star Spoon was still high up on the roller coaster. She should come down and help them, but he did not blame her for fearing to do so. The field rang with hoarse cries, screams, yells, groans, and roars. The White Knight and the Red Knight were still on their horses, their arms rising and falling as they brought down their spiked clubs on the heads of the humans. The White Knight had not put his helmet on; his gentle face was as placid as if he were discussing the weather.

The Unicorn was dead, its horn stuck through the chest of a Hussar. The man's saber had not yet been picked up by one of his fellows. The Lion, roaring, was rearing up, a paw ripping off a woman's breasts and sending her whirling. Its sides and mane, however, were dripping with blood, not all of it its enemies'. Even as Burton watched, a Hussar brought the edge of his saber down with both hands just back of the mane, and the beast fell.

A black woman was riding the back of a Walrus, holding on with one hand and stabbing repeatedly with a dagger. Then the Walrus stood up and fell backward, crushing her. But it was too wounded to do anything but bellow and wave its flippers.

The Jabberwock had three spears in it now but was still ravaging. It bit a man in two as Burton watched.

A pink flamingo leaped at Burton, its wings fluttering, its toes out to grab him. He lopped its head off, whirled, parried a sword thrust by a White Rabbit, stepped in, grabbing the gloved hand of the Rabbit, and jerked it off balance. Before it could regain it, its neck was cut half-through by the saber.

Burton turned to defend himself against a tove, a creature the size of a dog and looking like a combination of badger, lizard, and corkscrew. Its three-foot-long nose handicapped it, because it had to rear up to get the nose out of the way before it could bite. Burton severed the nose and ran at three living cards, a deuce of hearts, a four of diamonds, and a jack of clubs. They were side by side and holding spears, but he was going to attack the one on his left and dispose of him before the others could get behind him. His feet slipped on blood on the grass, and he slid feet first into the legs of the one in the middle. The four of diamonds fell forward, but his wide flat body acted as a plane, and he flew over Burton. The others turned slowly and clumsily.

Burton rolled away, holding the saber above him, got to his feet, and cut the two down.

Now the March Hare approached, the shaft of a morning star in his hand. This was a medieval weapon consisting of a two-foot-long wooden stick to which was attached a length of chain to which was attached a large spiked steel ball. Handled properly, it could crush armor. Burton had to retreat before it, meanwhile glancing around to make sure that no one was about to jump on him from behind or on his sides. Then he stepped forward as the spikes just missed him and severed the hand holding the wooden shaft. The March Hare screamed, as it was programmed to do if hurt, but it did not run away as a human might have. It stood there until the loss of blood from the stump caused it to crumple.

Burton saw another Walrus, the last one, go down before a flurry of cuts from three men. Then the White Knight was on these and felled two before Burton had to turn away to defend himself against a Carpenter and a chicken-sized gnat. After putting them away, he attacked a Red Queen from behind, sliced off her crowned head, and whirled just in time to defend himself against the Cheshire Cat. This lynx-sized creature's enormous head was blood-smeared; evidently, it had done considerable carnage. Yowling, it sprang at him, its dripping paws out, but he brought the saber against its skull, between the eyes. He was bowled over, but when he got up he saw that the feline was permanently out of action.

Something hit him from behind. Stunned, his sight dimmed, not knowing who he was or where, he fell to his knees. He was easy prey now for whoever had hit him, but a man he did not recognize rushed by him. He heard the thud of weapon on weapon as he fell to all fours and shook his head. Then a hand was helping him up. His senses came back slowly, the back of his head hurting abominably. The man who had rescued him was Monteith Maglenna. He was holding a bloody two-edged sword. His clothes were torn and cut, and blood was welling from a dozen wounds.

"Close call, that," he said hoarsely.

Burton looked at Bill the Lizard and at the reddened flat cap and the club on the ground beside his body.

"Thanks," he said. "I'll be all right."

"Good," Maglenna said. "Have to get that bloody Jabberwock out of the way. Come help when you feel up to it."

The big blonde man ran off, his sword held high with both hands as if he were holding an ancestral claymore. By now, the Jabberwock was showing signs of internal bleeding from the spear thrusts and other wounds. The blood flowing from its mouth could not all be that from its victims. It was crouching on all fours, its tail still lashing but not as vigorously as before. Its head turned this way and that as it bellowed at the pestiferous men and women surrounding it. These were not, however, coming close to it; they were leaping in and out, slashing at it but not daring to come within reach of the still-dangerous head. Behind those keeping it distracted was a line of people fighting off the androids, guarding the backs of the Jabberwock attackers. They, at least, had some organization.

He turned around, fighting dizziness and nausea. The White Knight and his horse were down, but the Red Knight, aided by some cards, Father William, some Eaglets, two White Rabbits, some toves, and a Carpenter, was bashing heads right and left. Its horse slipped several times on blood but recovered and stumbled once over a pile of bodies. He groaned, heartsick. So many human bodies. And there were many androids still standing. Some were not fighting but were killing the wounded humans. They must have had orders to finish off all those they downed before going on to do more battle.

He caught sight of Alice. She was holding a rapier, and her clothes were crimsoned. She had broken free of the melee and could have fled to her house. Perhaps she had thought of that, since she looked several times longingly up the hill. But she turned away, ran down the slope, and thrust her rapier through a Carpenter's back.

Star Spoon was climbing down from the roller coaster. Whether she was doing so to join the fray or to run for safety he had no time to find out.

He turned away and walked up to the back of a Dodo that was beheading wounded humans. Under its wings, it had short arms at the ends of which were human hands, just as in Tenniel's illustration. The shortness of its arms made its sword strokes ineffective, forcing it to hack again and again before it could get its victims' necks completely cut through. Burton snickersneed its head off just as it was about to deliver a final stroke to a Chinese man.

Burton wondered where Li Po was. No sooner asked than answered. There was the tall Chinese on a big table, fighting off a trio of cards with his rapier. They kept thrusting their spears at him from three sides, but he danced around, leaping to avoid thrusts, kicking with one foot against the shafts, and flicking the rapier point at them. Then Frigate, covered with blood, ran up holding a strange weapon. For a moment, Burton did not know what it was. When it was brought up and down against one of the cards, Burton recognized it. It was the Caterpillar's hookah. In short order, Frigate had smashed down two of the cards, and Li Po had run the other through twice.

Burton turned again to help those fighting the Jabberwock. Maglenna was running straight at it, his sword held high.

With his vorpal blade, Burton thought.

A dozen men and women were still harassing the monster; a dozen were protecting the attackers' backs. While Maglenna was running, the rear guard was cut down to six, and some androids immediately launched themselves at the other humans after dispatching the wounded. These caught four of the Jabberwock attackers from behind, and the rest of the humans were caught between the great beast and the other androids. Maglenna ignored all of them. He leaped from a body just as the Jabberwock dipped its head to close its jaws around the head of a man. Burton could hear the Scot's war cry from across the field. Maglenna was going to sever that thick neck, no doubt about it. Unfortunately, the corpse he used as a launching platform turned a little under his foot, and the tip of his blade only nicked the scaly neck. He fell flat on his face, his blade flying from his hand at the impact. He was up quickly, looking for his weapon, but the Jabberwock opened its mouth and dropped the lifeless body on top of Maglenna. He pushed it aside and stood up. The gigantic jaws seized his head and shoulders, and his writhing body was lifted up. It came down minus head and shoulders, which were spit out a moment later.

He could hear Alice's scream through all the noise; he knew it from long experience. Turning, he saw her standing horrified, the back of her hand over her mouth, her eyes huge dark holes.

He also saw the Red Knight on his galloping horse, charging toward him, the spike-knobbed club held high. The crimson armor and the horse-head-shaped helmet were a terrible sight. The beat of the horse's hooves was like the roll of a drum just before the gallows trapdoor was dropped.

Burton shifted the saber to his left hand, stopped, picked up a spear, and braced himself for the throw. His target was not the Red Knight but its charger. When the armored thing was thirty feet away, he cast the spear, and its sharp broad head plunged into the horse's shoulder. It fell forward, turning over. Its rider flew through the air and landed with a crash of steel upon the grass. Burton took the saber in his right hand and ran to the horse, which was starting to get up, and he slashed its jugular. It, too, had been programmed to kill; it had bitten and kicked while its rider was swinging its club; it had to be made harmless first.

The Knight lay prone and motionless. Burton turned the heavy body over and undid the helmet fastenings. He had to make sure that the thing was dead, not just unconscious. Seeing the face, he recoiled with shock. It was his face.

"One of Alice's jokes," he said.

He rose, looked at the dead features, and thought of how strange it was to see himself as a corpse. He gazed over the field between him and the foot of the hill. There were bodies everywhere, some in heaps. The only one standing in that direction was Alice, who was just pulling her rapier from a Humpty Dumpty. Her tears were washing the blood from her face.

Then he saw Star Spoon running down the hill with a beamer in each hand. She had fled, but only to get weapons from the house that would assure their victory, though she might be the only one left alive.

He turned. There were ten androids on their feet, not counting the Jabberwock. Three humans were still fighting, Li Po, a black man, and a white woman, one of Aphra Behn's friends. The woman went down under a rain of swordstrokes as he watched.

The Jabberwock, breathing in short unsteady gasps, waddled toward the cluster of battlers. It turned when it got near, and its tail whipped out, catching three androids and the black man. Li Po rapiered the White Queen in front of him and ran for the parking area. There were still three chairs there.

Frigate came from somewhere and also headed toward the chairs. The remaining androids hacked at the fallen black man before pursuing the two men.

The Jabberwock swung its head from left to right, saw Burton, and lumbered toward him.

The field was comparatively quiet now, but, suddenly, Burton heard a motor turning over. That was followed by a series of explosions, and Bill Williams, bloody but grinning, rode his cycle from behind the little house with the chimneys like rabbit's ears and the fur-covered roof. Burton did not know what he had been doing there or how he had gotten his cycle there. Perhaps he had pushed it there during the fray, intending to get away at an opportune moment. Perhaps, and this was more likely, he was just waiting for a chance to use it. Or he might have gotten the machine hidden and then fainted from his wounds. Recovering, he had followed his original plan. Whatever had happened, and Burton was never to know, the fellow was now doing what only he could have thought of.

As the monster advanced toward Burton, not turning its head to find the source of the new noise, Williams speeded up the machine. Dodging around the bodies, sometimes driving over an outstretched arm or leg, Williams sped straight at the side of the Jabberwock, and he smashed his motorcycle into its ribs.

So great was the impact, the Jabberwock was moved a few inches to one side. Williams flew headlong over its back and slammed into the ground. The monster raised its head as high as the neck could reach, gave a great bawling cry, and died.

Burton ran to Williams and turned him over. He was dead, his face smashed and his neck broken.

Though doomed, the androids advanced toward Burton as programmed. They never reached him. Frigate's and Li Po's chairs smashed into them and knocked them down again and again until they could no longer get up. Then the two men got out of the chairs and finished their work.

Burton heard a gasp behind him. Turning, he saw that Star Spoon had slipped and fallen on her face. She had let the beamers loose to soften the fall with her hands. He walked up to her and picked her up. Sobbing, she went into his arms.

Except for the weeping of Alice, Star Spoon, and Frigate, the field was silent. Only he, those three, and Li Po had survived. No. The Blue Caterpillar was sitting on the giant mushroom, and the rocking-horse-fly, a creature too fragile to have been programmed to kill, was alive. They did not, however, count.

He felt more weary, more emptied, than he had ever felt in his long life. He was in shock, numb, the world around him seeming alien and drifting way.

"Who could have done this horrible thing?" Alice wailed.

Who, indeed?

At that moment, William Gull groaned and sat up from the dead.

33

Though covered with blood, the Englishman was uninjured except for a bump on the back of his head.

"I was knocked out, and some of those killed fell on top of me. The androids did not see me."

He gingerly touched his head and grimaced.

"You were very fortunate," Burton said dully. "I think you were the only one who went down who escaped beheading."

Why did Gull have the good luck? Why couldn't Nur or de Marbot or Behn have been spared?

No, that did not matter, he told himself. They can be resurrected.

And then he knew that the murderer would have insured that they would stay dead. Why bother to kill them if they could be brought back? It made no sense.

He would have to find out about that. Just now, they must recover from their exhaustion and shock. Then the dead must be converted into ashes; the horrible mess cleaned up.

"Let's go to the house," he said. "There's nothing to be gained by staying here."

First, though, he must take precautions to guard himself and the others. He picked up the two beamers and said, "Star Spoon, were there any androids in the house when you got these?"

"I didn't see any," she said. Her voice was as empty of expression as her face.

"We'll have to do everything for ourselves," he said. "We can't trust the androids."

He stopped walking. The beamers seemed rather light. He opened the bottom of the beamer butts and looked into the receptacles for the powerpacks. He swore. They were empty.

He showed them to Star Spoon and said, "These would have been useless."

"I'm sorry," she said. "I was too excited to notice."

She shuddered. "It's a good thing I didn't have to use them."

"Yes. But whoever did this is very clever. Only . . ."

They were trudging up the hill, every step forward seeming to be in a thick and heavy substance, as if they were walking at the bottom of a treacle well.

"What?" she said.

"Why didn't the killer have the androids take the beamers from the house and kill us with them? It would have been very easy. We wouldn't have had a chance."

Li Po had been listening in. He said, "Perhaps the killer likes the sight of blood. Or it may be that he wanted us to suffer or to think that we might survive. As it turned out . . ."

"He won't stop," Burton said.

"He failed," the Chinese said. "All we have to do is raise our friends, and he will be . . ."

His mouth fell open. "Ah! What if he has inhibited their resurrection?"

"Exactly," Burton said. "Well, we'll soon find out.'

Frigate caught up with them. He looked behind, and Burton turned to see what he was staring at. Gull was far behind them, moving slowly up the slope.

"I could be overly suspicious," the American said, "but don't you think it's funny that he wasn't killed after he fell? I have no evidence for my suspicions, but, after all, he *was* Jack the Ripper. Maybe he played it safe, programmed the androids to spare him. He might even have fixed it so that one would knock him out or tap him lightly on the head if it looked as if we'd win. I hate to say these things, but we can't take any chances now."

"I've thought of the same thing," Burton said. "However, his story could be true."

They walked the rest of the way in silence. The sky was still blue, and the sun was about where it would be at six o'clock. He thought of what the Mad Hatter had said. "It's always six o'clock here."

The birds were singing again in the woods, and an angry

squirrel was scolding something, probably one of Alice's cats. The wild animals must have been frightened into silence by the uproar, but now that that had ceased, they had resumed normal life. All the noise and the babel meant nothing to them after they had passed. Those innocent creatures lived only in the present; the past was forgotten.

He envied them their innocence and unawareness of time.

They paused to catch their breaths in the large and beautiful garden of flowers at the top of the hill. Burton scanned the sky, wondering if the chairs were pressing against the blue wall somewhere out there. They would keep doing that until their power supply weakened, and then they would settle down slowly into the trees.

They entered the huge empty house—he hoped it was empty—and they searched every room, their weapons ready. Satisfied that no one, human or android, was hiding in ambush, they showered. After putting on new clean clothes, simple robes, they met in the large library. By then the antishock pills given by the Computer were doing their work. They were still very tired and dispirited, however. The drinks did not seem to help much. Nor was anybody hungry.

"Well, there's no use putting it off," Burton said, and he seated himself in front of the computer console. Though he dreaded to ask the question, he did so. And what he did not want to hear was what the Computer, through the computer, told him.

The dead, Nur, Turpin, Sophie, de Marbot, Aphra, all the slain, could not be raised. Someone had inhibited the raising, and the Computer would not say who that person was.

"Oh, my God!" Alice said, and she moaned. "I had Monty for six days, and now he's gone forever!"

"I wouldn't say forever," Burton said. "We'll find a way to cancel the overrides. Someday."

"We should warn the others," Alice said.

"The others?" Burton said. "Oh, you mean those in Turpinville. And Netley and his people and the gypsies."

"Tell the gypsies," Frigate said. "Never mind those who threw Tom and me out of our places. They don't deserve to be warned. What they do deserve . . . well . . ."

"I understand your feelings," Burton said, "but, in a way, they're our allies. The Snark or whoever the killer is won't be attacking just us."

"How do you know that?" Frigate said.

"I don't know that, but we must warn them."

He tried Turpinville first. Though the screen was activated, there was no reply, and they could see only a dim diffuse dark amber light.

Burton was about to try Netley when Li Po said, "Wait! I thought I saw something!"

"What is it?" Burton said, squinting his eyes—as if *that* would help.

"Something dark. Moving," Li Po said.

The others crowded around the console. They, too, squinted.

"I don't see anything," Burton said.

"You don't have my eagle eyes," Li Po said. He pointed. "There! Can't you see it? It's dark, and it's moving, though very slowly. Wait."

Presently, Burton could see a dark vague bulk. It swelled almost imperceptibly, taking a near-unendurable time to float nearer. Minutes passed, and then the outlines became more distinct. Alice gasped and said, "It's a man!"

Burton asked the Computer to make the area brighter if it could. The fluid—it had to be a fluid since the man was floating in it—was illuminated a little. More minutes passed, and then they could see the face of a black man, eyes staring and mouth open.

"I don't know what's happened," Burton said, "but something horrible has. The screen for receiving messages from outside Turpin's world is in the room next to Turpin's office. Obviously, it's filled with water or some kind of liquid."

"That can't be!" Star Spoon said.

"Oh, yes, it can. The Computer can do almost anything."

"Try Netley's," Frigate said.

Burton did so. This time, the screen showed them a clearer fluid. They could not see very far into it, but they could distinguish a shadowy bulk that looked like a sofa. Near it was a small dark object too fuzzy to be identified. But it was floating. It could be a plastic bottle of some sort, partly full, perhaps, and buoyed by the air in it.

"Definitely another flood," Burton said.

"Ask the Computer if it knows what happened," Frigate said.

Burton glared at him. "Don't be a stupid ass. Whoever did this would command the Computer not to tell us anything."

"You don't know. Maybe the Snark doesn't care. Maybe he'd like us to know. Anyway, if he thought that we'd all be dead, no one around to question it, why conceal anything?"

"Anything is possible. Sorry about the remark."

Burton asked the Computer if it had made recordings of the recent events in Turpinville and Frigate's world. It replied that it had. Burton then ordered it to run off the pictures of Turpinville, starting from the moment that the liquid had poured into that world.

They had thought that the only video-audio transmissions inside the worlds were made through the computer sets inside the private worlds, these being connected through cables to the floors of the worlds. But the Snark, the unknown, had found a way to break this communication and video-audio barrier. Selected areas of the world's wall had been made into screens, and Burton and his companions saw the deluge as a flying bird would see it. They watched as the waters of the fountains and the river and the marshes and lake were replaced by the amber liquid. Which, the Computer told them in answer to Burton's question, was bourbon.

"Bourbon?" Burton said, and he asked the Computer to repeat the statement.

It was bourbon.

The inlets for the various water sources had poured in the liquor under great pressure. The fountains had soared up until they almost touched the top of the Brobdingnagian chamber, and the river and lakes and marshes had spewed forth the swift raging floor of whiskey.

"No doubt, it was the best bourbon," Burton muttered.

The citizens of Turpinville had been panicked, but, after a few minutes, they had taken every means of transportation to the exit. They had fought each other for the hundred available flying chairs, hitting, knifing, and shooting. Those left behind had fought for the automobiles, motorcycles, and horses and buggies. They had jammed into the railroad train and climbed on top of the cars. Those in the chairs had gotten swiftly to the exit, only to find that they could not open the door. The people on foot and in the ground vehicles were drowned before they reached the exit.

If they had not panicked, they could have made flying chairs in the e-m converters and flown to the exit. Where they would have discovered that their efforts were in vain.

Though the liquor poured out swiftly, it had an enormous volume to fill, and the surface of the fluid body was only one-fourth of the way up the walls. The people in the chairs had taken them to the ceiling, but they had been overcome by the fumes or died from lack of oxygen. Some of them might still be alive; they would not last long. Though the flood had ceased to rise, it did not have to do so to complete its work.

"What a way to die!" Burton said.

He looked at the pale set faces. "I suppose we might as well try Netley's world."

The same thing had happened there, except that the liquor was gin. The best, of course.

Burton anticipated that those who had died in both worlds would be denied resurrection by the Computer, and he was right.

The gypsies had been traveling in a corridor leading to the well of the *wathans*—perhaps they meant to sightsee it—when a big wheeled robot had come upon them and pierced them with beamer rays. Ten minutes later, robots had cleaned up the blood and carried the bodies off to be turned to ashes in converters.

"That leaves six of us alive," Burton said. "Seven if the Snark is counted. But . . ."

"But what?" Alice said after a long silence.

He did not reply. He was thinking that the killer could have done away with them much more easily if he—or she—had flooded Alice's world. Why the different means? Was it for grisly amusement, using the exotic androids against them, the charming creatures of two fantasy books for children suddenly turned into bloodthirsty monsters?

It seemed more probable that the killer had made an exception in Alice's world because he or she had been one of the guests. And that guest had perhaps wished to see that his or her enemies, people he or she must have hated deeply, would be slain most bloodily.

And that guest had made arrangements by programming the androids to spare him or her.

He knew Alice, Peter Frigate, and Li Po too well to suspect them. That left only two. William Gull, who claimed to be a changed and deeply religious man, but had once murdered five women. And Star Spoon, who, however, had no motive—as far as he knew.

Yet Gull had not been in the tower long enough to learn how to operate the Computer with the skill, no, the ingenuity, that the killer needed.

Star Spoon had been studying the Computer long and hard, but would she have been able in such a relatively short time to gain knowledge that those who had been using the Computer much longer than she did not have?

It could be that there was a second Snark.

If so, then the six were at his mercy.

Still, it was possible that one of the six had probed deeply into the Computer's potentialities and learned how to carry out the slaughters.

Why would any of them wish to do so?

He got up from the console chair and said, "We have to run off the memories of everyone for the past six weeks."

"I'm too tired for that just now," Frigate said. Alice, Gull, and Star Spoon also protested that they were exhausted.

"Let's do it tomorrow after we get rested," Alice said.

"Anyway, it's a waste of time," Star Spoon said. "You know that anyone who has done all that," she waved her hand, "will have set up false memories."

"Yes, I know. But we have to do it."

They sat around for an hour, their brief and dull sentences floating between long gloomy silences. Frigate finally said that he thought that he could get some food down. The others agreed to try it, and they ate more than they had expected to. They also drank much and became more animated, even if not carefree. Burton spoke then of something that had occupied his thoughts ever since he had entered the house.

"Our enemy closed the exit on the Turpinites and Netleyites. He should be able to do the same for this place. Since he failed to kill all of us with the androids, he may use the very successful method of drowning us. It might be best if we left here and moved into a suite."

They talked about that at some length. Finally, Alice, at Burton's suggestion, ordered that the door to the central area be opened. The screen showed them that it was operating.

"But that does not mean that the Snark cannot close it on us when he wishes," Burton said.

"Then let's get out," Frigate said. "The trouble is . . . what's to prevent the Snark from closing the suite door?"

"I don't know," Burton said. "At least, he can't drown us."

They had the e-m converter make chairs for them, and they flew out over the darkened world and under the simulated full moon. Nobody said a word about the bodies on the field. They would not have time to dispose of them; the crows, eagles, and hawks would strip them of their flesh. By the time they returned, if they ever did, they would deal with bones only.

After another nightcap, they went to separate bedrooms in the suite, except for Burton and Star Spoon. She crawled into bed at once, said, "Good night, Dick," and was asleep. He followed her a few minutes later, and, against his expectation, passed into sleep at once. He awoke four hours later, his lifelong insomnia clutching him like the Old Man of the Sea. The woman was on her side, facing away from him, and snoring softly. He got out of bed, put on a robe, went to the main room and got a big cup of coffee. After that had removed some of his weariness, he set to work at the computer console. Five hours later, he had put into the Computer every injunction and override he could think of to protect all in his suite. He was sure, however, that there were others. He would ask his companions to add to the list.

"I should have done that long long ago," he told himself.

He decided that he would not wait until his fellow tenants got up for breakfast. As tired as they were, they might sleep until

noon. He began scanning the corridors because, at that moment, he could think of nothing else to do. He started from the
top of the tower with the hangar, worked the first level and then
the second. That was quick because a glance showed that the
circular area was empty, and there was no life except animal in
the little worlds.

The scan moved into Level 60 and raced up and down the
corridors and into the rooms along them. It came to a corridor
the inner wall of which formed a side of the *wathan* well. Here,
he knew, was where an observer could see the surface of the
mass of *wathans.*

He cried out, "Stop!"

He stared at the curving transparent wall of the shaft.

The beautiful, bright, many-colored, swelling, shrinking, and
whirling entities called *wathans* were gone. The well was empty
and dark.

34

Peter Frigate was the first to enter the room. He stopped, and he looked at Burton, at the beamer on the table, and at the half-opened door to the corridor. "What's going on?"

Li Po came in just as Burton opened his mouth to answer Frigate. Burton said, "Have some coffee first, Pete."

"How are you, Dick?" the Chinese said.

"I've been up most of the night. Working."

Li Po also glanced at the weapon and the door. He raised his eyebrows but did not comment. Frigate, after pouring out coffee from a pot on the table said, "You look awful. The dark circles around your eyes . . . you look like a debauched raccoon. What've you been doing?"

"I feel more than awful," Burton said slowly. "I feel . . . how would you feel if you knew that the end of the world was near? Or perhaps I should say that the world has ended—for all practical purposes."

Frigate drank the whole cup of very hot coffee without flinching. He said, "The end of the world happens every second."

Burton did not know what he meant and did not think it worthwhile to find out. In any event, Frigate's words were just a means for putting off the bad news.

Li Po took a sip of coffee and said, "What do you mean?"

"Perhaps I should wait until everybody's here. I don't like to repeat."

"Sure you don't," Frigate said. "Let's hear it."

Burton told them that the *wathan* enclosure was empty.

Li Po and Frigate paled but said nothing.

"I checked the body-records then," Burton said. "I had to force myself to do it because I didn't want to know what had been done to them, although, of course, I already knew. But it needed doing, and so I did it."

"And they . . . they . . ." Frigate said, choking.

"They had all been erased. All thirty-five billion six hundred and forty-six million plus. No exceptions. All. And no *wathans* have come in since I made the discovery."

Li Po sat down. "I've had too many shocks lately."

After a long time, Frigate said, "So . . . when we die, we die for the last time."

"Quite."

After another long silence—only a supercatastrophe could have kept Li Po's mouth shut so long, Burton thought—Frigate poured brandy into a half-full cup of coffee and downed all of the steaming liquid. Li Po looked as if he would like to do the same, half-rose, shook his head, and sank back into the chair. This was the first time Burton had ever seen him reject a drink.

The brandy had restored some of the American's color. He drank more, straight this time, and said, "The Snark has over-ridden that automatic function . . . I mean, no bodies will be recorded from now on?"

"Right."

"But if we can survive until the Gardenworlders get here, we can be recorded again. Otherwise, we, too, will lose our chance for immortality forever."

"Of course," Burton said. "But when they get here, our time will be up anyway. If we're not ready to Go On, our records will be erased. And if we're not, we'll be erased."

He got up and poured himself more coffee, looked at the brandy bottle, and decided against it. "I immediately asked the Computer about that. I was shocked, of course, and I cursed myself, railed against the fates, if you must know, because as soon as we got here from Alice's, I commanded the Computer to refuse to erase any body-records. I was forestalling that. But I was too late. I did not know that then because the Computer, the idiot, did not tell me that my command was too late. It should have, but the Snark had told it not to display that data unless it was asked for it."

"We've all been just drifting along, doing things too late,"

Frigate said in a dull tone. "Sometimes . . . I wonder if the Snark has had the Computer broadcast some sort of neural suppressant field, something dampening our intelligence?"

"I doubt it. We've just been playing with our toys . . . like children. However"—Burton lifted a napkin and revealed a yellow ball the size of a cranberry—"I've been busy while you were sleeping. This is the sphere that records a body. I had the Computer duplicate one for me. It's empty now, but I wanted to see one. And holding it in my hand enabled me to postulate something . . . a theory, but the only explanation I could come up with that was reasonable. That is, how could the Snark get into Alice's world, into Turpin's and yours . . . Netley's . . . and there arrange for operations that just could not be done from outside those worlds?"

Alice entered a minute later. Burton had to repeat his story and to wait for her to recover enough before he could continue.

"First, though, I don't think that the Snark did it. I mean I don't think that there's an Ethical hiding in the tower. Nur eliminated her, though we cannot, of course, ever be sure. But the murders in the little worlds were done by one of us. By one of the survivors."

Li Po shot up from his chair, and, quivering, said, "Gull! Or Star Spoon! But why?"

Burton nodded. "Gull may have reverted, but he would have to have gone mad to do that. Star Spoon? She would have to be insane. If either is, he or she has concealed it well. First, let me tell the rest of my theory."

"First . . . pardon the interruption," Frigate said, "we have to consider that it may be neither Gull nor Star Spoon. What if somebody we haven't even seen is the killer? After all, Williams raised Gull and the others involved in the Ripper killings. And there are the gypsies. We don't know who raised them, but I suspect Williams did it just as a joke or just to bug us. Or maybe somebody else did. Anyway, what if someone raised a person who was destructively insane, to put it mildly, and that person is our second Snark?"

"I asked the Computer to scan the tower for other people. It reported that it could find none. I asked for a rundown of all those who'd been raised, and the number corresponds exactly with my calculations. Still, the Computer could be reporting only what it's been told to report."

Frigate threw his hands up. "Nothing's certain!"

"It never has been. However, I think that we don't have to consider a third party or parties."

He held up the yellow sphere. "Here is how I think he . . . or she . . . did it."

The killer had ordered a number of his body-recordings made in an e-m converter.

"Nobody had inhibited this action until I told the Computer not to allow that, but I was too late. The deed was done."

The Snark, Snark the Second, as it were, had been given an opportunity to enter the worlds of Turpin, Frigate, and Alice. Perhaps all the worlds and some apartment suites, too.

"There the Snark put the recording-spheres in converters that were out of the way, seldom if ever used. And the Snark also concealed them in other places for easy access and probably carried them around in his clothing."

The Snark then killed himself in the privacy of an unused apartment. By prearrangement with the Computer, the Snark was resurrected in a converter inside a world.

"The converter in which the Snark died would then disintegrate the body. The Snark did not want anybody finding it, though that possibility was remote."

Once inside Alice's world, Snark II did what had to be done. The androids were verbally programmed when they were out of sight of Alice and Maglenna or perhaps they were programmed before Maglenna showed. Since the Snark had to be furtive about the process, it undoubtedly took weeks to complete it.

The flooding of the two worlds, though, was ordered from the outside.

"The Ethicals thought that they were one hundred per cent safe when they were in their private worlds. Of course, they were not nearly as security-conscious as we since they believed the tower to be an impregnable fortress. They knew that one of them was a traitor, but they still could not conceive that he would actually personally endanger them.

"But an ingenious person could flood the little worlds by ordering the liquid supply to pour into it until it was completely filled or its inhabitants had been drowned."

"That may be true," Alice said, "but how could the Snark shut the doors to the worlds? And how could he see what was going on in the worlds when the flooding began? The Computer had commands to open the door only to authorized codewords, and it would not transmit pictures or any communications except as ordered by the tenants. No one could override those."

"But they could be bypassed by various means. The Snark made cameras in the worlds he had gotten into via the recording-spheres, flew the cameras to the ceilings, probably at night, and attached them there. You see, the Computer had orders not to transmit wave frequencies through the circuits of the walls except through certain channels, but the Computer interpreted those orders literally. It did have orders to transmit the frequencies through the wall circuits to the converters and the computer auxiliary and communication devices. It did not distinguish between those computers installed and authorized by the Ethicals and any installed later. It would assume that the additions were authorized."

"But the doors?" Alice said.

"The Snark sealed the exterior of the door with a substance that hardened and so resisted the operating mechanisms of the doors, which open outward."

That meant that the Snark had sealed the doors while Alice's party was going on. The Snark had killed himself or herself, had been resurrected in an apartment, and then had flown in a chair to the central area and applied the substance to the exit doors of two of the worlds. Then the Snark had ordered the liquid supply to convert to bourbon and gin and started the deluging. After which, the Snark had committed suicide, been resurrected in an apartment, and returned to Alice's place as a guest. There the Snark had waited until the androids had started their predetermined attack. During the battle, the Snark had made sure that he was not harmed by the androids. His or her plans had not been completely successfully, but the Snark was not dismayed. There would be other opportunities.

Li Po said, "Ah! Only those at the party could be suspects! So . . . Gull or Star Spoon!"

"Not necessarily," Frigate said. "The Snark could be someone else, if that someone had had an opportunity to get into the worlds. It would have to be one of those raised, someone we know or ought to know. It could be many people. After all, we haven't seen all the bodies in Turpin's or Netley's . . . my . . . world. We should find out if anyone is missing from there."

"First, we put Gull and Star Spoon through the grinder," Burton said.

If one of them was so infernally clever, he thought, wouldn't he or she have anticipated that one of the others might be Sherlock Holmes enough to narrow the suspects to two?

If that was so, the Snark would know that his or her identity would soon be revealed.

Li Po, as if he had been reading Burton's thoughts said, "That accounts for the beamer on the table? You'll be ready for the Snark?"

"Yes. If one of them walks through the doorway with a weapon in hand, I won't be caught surprised."

"It seems to me," Alice said, "that they . . . one of them . . . could kill himself . . . or herself . . . and be resurrected elsewhere. What's to keep the Snark from coming through there?" She pointed at the open door to the corridor.

"Ah, that," Burton said. "Well, you see, I copied the killer's modus operandi. Very early this morning, I sealed Gull's and Star Spoon's doors."

Burton did not have to tell them what would happen. The guilty one would be unable to get out, and it would not be long before he or she knew why. The only escape was the route the Snark had often taken. Commit suicide and be resurrected elsewhere.

"What if the Snark pretends innocence and asks us to let him out?" Frigate said.

"We won't let either out. Sooner or later, the Snark will leave."

The immediate excitement had lifted them from the shock of finding out that the *wathans* were gone and the records erased. They were not concentrating on the numbing realization that they would be dead forever the next time they died. Or that those still alive in The Valley would not be raised again after they had died. Or that all that they had suffered to get here had been in vain.

No, he thought. It was not in vain, not wasted time. We have lived far longer than we thought we would when we died on Earth. Our youthful bodies were restored, and we fought and loved with the full vigor of youth and perfect health. We lived fiercely, we were active, and we worked hard for a goal. It has been worthwhile. And if we can live until the Gardenworlders come, we . . . no. This phase of the project will be over, and we must die to make room for the resurrected in the next.

He would worry about that when the time came. Just now, the only thing to consider was the Snark.

"There's the screen," Frigate said. Burton got up and walked to the console in the corner. Gull looked out from the display. Seeing Burton, he said, "Good morning. I don't know what the matter is, but the door won't open for me."

"That's strange," Burton said. "Have you asked the Computer why?"

"Of course, but it says that it does not know."

"We'll see what we can do about it," Burton said. "Meanwhile, you don't have to starve. Get yourself breakfast, and we'll investigate."

When the screen had become blank, Burton asked that the screen in his bedroom be activated. It showed the room at once— Burton had not been sure that it would not have been cut off— and he saw that the bed was unoccupied. Star Spoon was not in sight, but she could be in the bathroom. He verified that his voice could be transmitted, and he called her loudly. Though he repeated her name several times, he was not answered.

"She's gone."

Frigate said, "Where's her body?"

"I don't know," Burton said. "We'll have to find out."

They went down the bedroom hall, all armed with beamers. Burton and Li Po used them to burn the sealing agent off. Since the smoke had an acrid odor, which made them cough, they had to slow down the burning to give the air-conditioning time to suck the smoke away. When the last of the glossy violet substance was gone, Burton gave the codeword, and the door swung open. Cautiously, he entered first, the beamer ready. The bedroom and bathroom were empty.

"She must have killed herself by stepping into the converter cabinet and having it incinerate her," Frigate said.

"That would make her disappearance more mysterious," Burton said. "I wonder where she could be."

Alice said, "You don't seem surprised, Dick."

"No. I didn't think that Gull had had time to learn how to operate the Computer well enough to do all the Snark has done."

"For God's sake!" Frigate said. "Why would she *do* that? What did she have against us? She must hate us! Everybody! Why?"

"I think," Li Po said, "that she has always been very sad behind that merry face she put on. She has had a bad life, many bad times, anyway, so many that she thinks of her life as all bad, too horrible to endure any longer. She has suffered so much, been raped and abused so much, and the attack by Dunaway was just too much. I think—I could be wrong, though I doubt it—that she decided that we would all be better off dead. *She'd* be better off dead. *Everybody* would be. She told me more than once that she was sorry that we had been resurrected, that it was horrible that no one could take refuge even in death. Did she ever say anything like that to you, Dick?"

"Several times."

"There has to be more than that to it," Frigate said. "If she wanted to be dead forever, all she had to do was erase her own recordings."

"She's not sane," Burton said. "She may have it in her mind that she's doing everybody a favor by making sure that they don't have to suffer as she did. Also, I suppose, she wishes to insure that those who made others suffer could no longer do that."

He was appalled, more shaken by her deeds than by anything he had ever experienced. But he did not hate her. Though she had committed the greatest sin in the world, the irrevocable and unforgivable sin, he could not hate that demented sufferer. He pitied her. Grieved for her, in fact. But he would have to kill her. No one would be safe until she was dead, and he would be doing her the greatest kindness by putting her out of her wretchedness.

He was sure that she planned to end herself eventually but not until after everyone left in the tower was dead. She would, he supposed, have liked to dispose of all in The Valley, too, but that she could not do. She would have to be satisfied knowing that they would finally pass away.

35

N onsense!"

"What?" Alice said.

"We don't have the slightest idea of what's really going on in that twisted mind. It doesn't matter if we do or don't. What does is that she must be stopped."

A loud pinging began. Burton started, though he had been expecting the noise, and he went to the console. The screen was displaying a diagram of a tower level section and a tiny but bright orange light was moving along one of the corridors. In the corner of the screen was: LEVEL 4, CORRIDOR 10.

The others had crowded behind him. Frigate said, "What now?"

"She must have just left the room in which she was resurrected," Burton said. "The room would have been painted, of course, so that her past-display would not be visible to her, and I suppose that the Computer shows it only when it can be seen by the subject. What I did, I told the Computer to show me where her past-display is. Star Spoon has undoubtedly commanded the Computer not to reveal her presence by allowing us to scan the halls near where she is. But one thing she cannot do is to prevent the past-display from accompanying her as soon as she leaves her room."

"She's intelligent," Li Po said. "She'll soon realize that you may be tracking her through the display. What we can do, she can do. She'll ask the Computer to show her our displays."

"Yes," Burton said, "but the thing about the Computer is that whoever gets ahead of the other with his command can forestall the other. I told it not to show her where ours are."

"She'll know that when the Computer doesn't show them to her," Li Po said. "That'll make her very cautious."

"She would be anyway," Burton said. "Pete, go burn off Gull's sealant. Tell him what's happened, give him a beamer. We need everyone we can get."

Frigate looked reluctant to leave, but he did so at once.

"We can't stay in this place," Burton said. "She can't seal up the door as long as it's open, but she could set up something—a robot machine that would automatically beam us the moment we stuck our heads through the doorway, for instance—so we won't stay here."

The orange light had stopped at a shaft, VC-A3-2.

"That leads up our corridor," Burton said. "We haven't much time."

He got up from the console chair and went through the doorway leading to the bedroom corridor. Frigate had just finished melting off the sealant and was waiting for the smoke to clear away. The door to Gull's room had swung open. Burton shouted, "Tell him to hold his breath and get right out here!"

The others went to their bedrooms and got their weapons and extra powerpacks. Burton watched the screen while the others were busy. When they were all in the main room, he told them what they must do. Gull was confused and did not know all that had happened, since Frigate had only had time to give him a few facts. Nevertheless, he nodded when Burton rapid-fired instructions at him, and he ran off.

All left the apartment then, and Burton had the Computer close the door. The apartment was halfway on the corridor between two lift shafts. Star Spoon was by the fourth-floor entrance to the shaft to their right as they left their place. They sped down the corridor toward the shaft, Alice dropping behind them to enter an apartment on the right side. She would station herself in the darkened area by the door, which would be left half-open. From there she could cover the shaft entrance, about four hundred and fifty feet away.

The four men separated when they came to the cross-corridor. The lift shaft was in the center of the cross-corridor, and there were deep bays at each corner to permit traffic of big machines. The shaft could be entered from four sides. Li Po and Gull went to the right down the cross-corridor and took positions behind partly closed doors about a hundred feet from the shaft. Burton continued down the corridor and entered a room that was about a hundred feet from the shaft. Frigate was to go to the left at the intersection and take a station behind a door about two hundred feet from the shaft.

When Star Spoon left the shaft at this level, she would be the target of cross-fire from five beamers.

Burton's room was dark except for the glow of the computer console screen. He watched the orange light, waiting for it to move into the shaft and ascend toward the third level.

"She's certainly taking her time," he muttered. What was she doing? Trying to imagine all the possible traps? Or had she lost her nerve?

Very early that morning, Burton had taken one hundred pounds of plastic explosive from the e-m converter. Using his flying chair to elevate himself to the tops of seven lift shafts and along the sides, working furiously, he had pressed the explosive around the entrances of the nearest shafts. He had not applied the plastic to the bottom of the entrances because Star Spoon would probably see it before exiting. By the time she had left the shaft, even if she saw the plastic on the sides, she would be too late to escape. Proximity fuses would set off the explosive.

These might be useless, since she might take a distant shaft. But if she passed close to a mined opening, she still might set off one.

He looked down the corridor and through the opening of the shaft. Then he glanced back at the screen. Ah! The orange light was ascending the lines indicating the shaft near which they waited.

He crouched by the door. A few seconds later, a transparent vehicle, in the center of which Star Spoon sat, rose into full view. It halted, suspended in the shaft, allowing him to see it in all its details. It was much like the armored chair that he had fashioned except that there were more heavy beamers than in his.

He could only see her back until she turned her head to give him a half-profile. She was expressionless.

The armor would resist for a while the ray of a beamer on full-power. Only if the ray could be kept on one spot could it penetrate the armor. And Star Spoon would keep her vehicle moving.

What was discouraging was that, if she was killed, she would be resurrected elsewhere in the tower. Any victory by her enemies was only a half-victory for them and a temporary setback for her. Yet they had to keep fighting and hope that they would catch her before she could kill herself or be killed. Or that her record-spheres would be found out and, eventually, she would be in the same situation they were. The next death would be the final death.

Burton had expected her to appear in an armored vehicle, and he hoped that its armor would absorb just enough of the explosive shock to knock her out. That was why he had lined each entrance with only 3.57 pounds of the explosive. As it was, he was not sure that he did not have more than he needed for his purpose.

He said, "Go on! Go on! What're you waiting for?"

The moment the vehicle moved from the center of the shaft toward the opening, he would step back, and, pressing his fingertips into his ears, would stand by the wall out of the way of the direct shock waves. So would the others.

At last, Star Spoon made up her mind. She had looked down the corridor straight ahead and seen that all the doors to the apartment suites were open but one. She would know that the door was Burton's, and she would, he hoped, believe that all five were holed up in it. Her survey of the corridor at right angles to the one straight ahead had shown her that all the doors on both sides were open. That was as it was almost everywhere in the tower.

Satisfied that she was headed toward the exit, Burton backed away a few feet from the door. Then he lost consciousness; he never heard the explosion.

When he came to, his smitten senses not yet fully recovered, he was coughing on the burning fumes pouring around him. He sat up, his back against the wall, and tried to get up but failed. His strength had gone for a walk and his wits had scattered like picnickers before the sudden appearance of a bear. When he did manage to get up, he staggered across the room, the air of which was getting somewhat clearer as the air-conditioning sucked the smoke away. The screen still glowed, showing the orange ball down the corridor around the corner. He dimly realized that this was where Li Po and Gull were stationed.

At least, he knew who he was and where he and the others were. His movements were slow, though.

"Got to get out there, get her," he said. His lips had moved with the thoughts, but he could not hear his own voice anymore than he could hear the voices of himself and Isabel, his Earthly wife, from the past-display on the wall near the door.

By the time he had reached the door, he could think clearly enough to know that something had gone wrong. The explosion had been far more violent than it should have been. Could he have miscalculated so much, or had something unforeseen happened?

He looked around the side of the doorway, realized then that he had dropped the beamer, went back to retrieve it, and returned to the doorway. The smoke was a thin veil now. He could see the far-strewn pieces of the vehicle on the floor. The sphere had been made of some shatterable material. The explosive lining the opening nearest Burton had gone off. Probably, a piece of the machine shot through this opening had activated the fuse. The additional explosion had doubled the effect of the shock waves, but even that was not near enough to account for the violence that had knocked him out.

The vehicle must have contained a large amount of explosives, and this had gone off when Burton's trap had erupted. Or perhaps it was a coincidence that the explosives in the vehicle had gone off just as the vehicle cleared the entrance shaft.

The thing operating the vehicle had been an android, the exact duplicate of Star Spoon, who had sent it ahead as a sacrifice.

Burton's head still hurt. His thoughts had been climbing a steep hill, struggling to get to the top, where they could re-form and become a potent force. Most of them had gotten up the hill, but they were not yet organized enough. Why had the past-display accompanied the false woman and not the real one?

Slowly, it came to him that she must have sent the android out first. And the idiot Computer, identifying her as the real Star Spoon, had sent the past-display along by her side. Then the real woman had emerged from her hiding place ... she must have muffled her features in a hood or masked them ... and she had come up an unmined shaft.

There she was, coming around the corner of the intersection from the corridor where Li Po and Gull were stationed. She was, as he had expected, inside a spherical armored flying machine, the duplicate of the android's. If she had been masked, she was not how. Unlike the android, her face was expressive, set in a demon's smile except for the lips, which moved as she talked to herself.

The machine came to the middle of the corridor just past the walls of the shaft—he could see through its openings—and it stopped, then made a quarter-turn so that she faced down the corridor. What had happened to Li Po and Gull? Were they still groggy from the explosion? Or had they foolishly attacked her as she passed them? He had no way of knowing; he would have been deaf to any cries.

The machine, moving six feet above the floor, came to the one closed door. It stopped and turned. A barrel slid out from the box beneath the seat, went through a hole in the sphere, and shot out a violet liquid. His mental processes were still sluggish; he should have recognized the fluid at once as the sealant. She was entombing the people that she believed were in the suite. Or, if she was not sure they were in there, she had to carry out this operation anyway.

He saw Alice's dark head stick out from the half-open door. She ducked back after a very quick look. Star Spoon, intent on moving the vehicle along the sides of the door of Burton's suite, had not seen her.

He could distinguish a glowing patch on the wall beside Star Spoon. That had to be the display of her memory. The Computer, after the android had disappeared in the explosion, had switched the display to accompany the real woman. Now that she was closing in for the kill, she did not care if they knew where she was. Perhaps she wanted them to know so that they would venture out to attack her.

Li Po, a beamer in his hand, stepped out into Burton's sight. Seeing the woman, he stepped back. He was fortunate that Star Spoon had not noticed him or his past-display, which would have appeared on the wall of the bay opposite him.

A small TV set was mounted on her left. She would be in communication with the Computer and would be using it to find out if the five were loose, and, if they were, to track them down.

By now, the violet liquid had hardened over the door and the wall area around it. He expected her to turn the machine down, but she did not. Instead, she started to repeat the sealing process. Evidently, she wanted the door to be doubly unmovable.

He had a minute, perhaps two minutes, before she began searching. He strode to the e-m converter and gave instructions to the Computer. He was not worried that Star Spoon would be listening in or be able to learn anything of his activities or location at this moment. He had long ago told the Computer that it was not to reveal anything about himself or his companions to her. She could scan all the rooms in the tower, and she would not be shown this room. However, the refusal of the Computer to scan would give her negative knowledge. If he was not in the rooms scanned, then he must be in one of the other rooms.

He opened the converter, stooped, and picked up with one hand a gray doughy mass, 3.75 pounds of the plastic explosive. After carrying this to the doorway and putting it on the floor, he went back to the converter. He shut its door; two seconds later, he opened it. The proximity fuse lay on its floor. Going back to the doorway, he inserted the long, thin metal rod protruding from the small metal box into the center of the mass.

He set the fuse by voice and looked around the door again. He said, "Oh, my God!" Star Spoon had somehow determined that Alice was in her room, perhaps with a heat-and-sound detector. Alice had done the only thing she could do, closed the door with a codeword. And Star Spoon was sealing it.

Burton jumped out from behind the door, aimed the beamer, and saw the ray, a bright scarlet rod with a diameter of one-fourth of an inch, leap from the bulb at the end of his weapon to the side of the transparent sphere. If the ray could have pierced the shield, it would have gone through Star Spoon's head near her left ear. Instead, the armor glowed at the point, and she saw it at once. She moved a control on the board by her right hand. The vehicle, rotating, moved away from the door, stopped, and shot toward Burton.

36

He turned and ran close to the wall, hoping that the second door would block him from her view. If he could avoid being hit, if she came by the door just as the explosive went off, if he could get inside the next door before it did . . . He wanted to look behind him to calculate the velocity of her vehicle. She might have accelerated to the point where she would pass the trap before it exploded. But he could not afford to glance behind because it would slow him, and there was nothing he could do about it anyway.

He grabbed the edge of the door and swung himself around it so vigorously that he banged his left shoulder on the doorway and was spun halfway around. Two scarlet rays shot past the door. Probably, other rays had hit the door. *No matter,* he thought. *I'm in.* Another shock wave knocked him down, but this one had far less impact than the first.

He got up, praying, and, clinging to the edges of the door, looked around it. Since there was not much smoke, he could clearly see the vehicle against the wall opposite the doorway where the charge had been placed. The explosion had thrust it across the corridor and slammed it against the wall. Star Spoon was unconscious. Burton watched as the car resumed its original speed, grating against the metal wall, and collided with the wall at the next intersection. There it stuck.

Li Po and Frigate, beamers ready, ran around the corners and up to Burton. "I boobytrapped her," he said. "But we have to get her out before she comes to."

"Where's Alice and Gull?" Frigate said.

"No time for that," Burton said. "Pete, have the hypodermic syringe ready. Po, you come with me."

Frigate removed the syringe from the case attached to his belt. While Burton held his beamer ray steady on one point of the armor, the Chinese ran to the nearest room to order from the converter a ladder and two stepladders to use to climb up to the car. Burton wanted to take her alive, but he hoped that, if she showed signs of rousing, the hole would have been burned through the shell so that he could put a hole through her body.

However, Li Po returned quickly, and they burned off the hatch locks while she lay unmoving. Burton crawled in, took the syringe from Frigate, blew the drug into her arm, and used the controls to ease the vehicle to the floor. They carried her into the nearest room, placed her on a bed, stripped her, searched her clothes, and then put her in the converter so that the Computer could probe her neural system. It reported that her brain was too complex to be an android's.

"I'd say we have her," Burton said. "Only . . . what if she's anticipated this possibility and ordered the Computer to make a false report? She'll be alive somewhere in this labyrinth."

"I don't believe that she would consider that possibility," Li Po said. "She must have believed that she was invulnerable in her armored vehicle. You have to take some things on faith."

"No, I don't."

Though he thought that Li Po was right, he intended to search the tower thoroughly. Not until then would he be at ease about her.

Leaving Frigate to watch the woman, Burton and Li Po burned off the sealant over Alice's door. Though not hysterical, she needed a long drink to quiet her nerves. She had thought that she might be imprisoned in the room forever or at least for a time that would have seemed forever.

On the way back to the room where Star Spoon was, they saw Gull's body lying faceup on the floor of the corridor. Li Po explained that Gull had been caught by a ray from the vehicle as Star Spoon was pursuing Burton.

"He must have left the room just as I dived into mine," Li Po said. "I don't know why he did it. He told me just before we took our stations that he could not use his beamer. It was all right to kill the androids because they were not human beings, but he could not fight Star Spoon."

"He should have said so at once and stayed with Alice," Burton said.

"I think that he probably went out into the corridor to plead with Star Spoon," Li Po said. "He was as crazy as she."

After conferring, they decided that it would be cruel to lock Star Spoon up in a room with the hope of curing her insanity. Questioning the Computer, they learned that the cryogenic techniques of the Ethicals far surpassed those of Earth. She could be frozen instantaneously without tissue damage, and so she was. Star Spoon would wait in her casket until the Gardenworlders arrived.

After a day of rest, they began the search. The first room they went to was the one she had left when she set out to finish them off. The Computer would not directly give them the location, but it immediately yielded the records of the passage of the orange light on the diagrams. Entrance to the room on the one hundred and sixteenth level—the Ethicals counted the stories from the top instead of the bottom—was easy. Star Spoon had not closed the door, because she had thought that only she would be alive when her mission was accomplished.

They went cautiously into a very large room with halls running off it in two directions. There were five rooms off each hall, all but one with closed doors, which would not open at Burton's request. Though he could not get into them, he could see into them by simply asking the Computer for screen vision. And he wished that he had not been so curious.

The only one of the all-male prisoners, one in each room, whom he recognized was Dunaway, the man who had raped Star Spoon in Turpinville. The others were three Chinese, two Caucasians, an Amerindian, two Negroes, and a Neanderthal. Li Po knew one of the Chinese.

"He is Wang Chih Mao, a minor official of the emperor. I met him once. Star Spoon later told me about him. He is the man who raped her when she was ten years old."

Four of them were gibbering insane. Two seemed to be close to going crazy. Dunaway was one of the two who had retreated into catatonia. The ninth was hiding under the bed and would not come out when Burton called him via the screen.

Burton watched the past-displays on the ceilings, floors, and walls of all the rooms. Over and over again, as seen through Star Spoon's eyes, the rapings were shown on large screens, in living color, and at high volume. The men could escape these only by sleep, which would not have come easily, by madness, or by death. Suicide was almost impossible. They were naked and so could not make nooses from their clothes. Their converters gave them only bread, boneless meat, and vegetables. Except for the beds, which consisted only of frame and mattress, there was no furniture. The bathrooms had a seatless toilet and a faucet for cold water above a small bowl. No soap, no towels, and no toilet paper.

Alice shuddered. "She got her revenge. Horrible!"

"Poetic justice," Frigate said. "Gotten with the aid of science."

"There's nothing we can do for them," Burton said, "unless we can shut off the converter power and let them starve to death."

Questioned, the Computer said that it could not do that without Star Spoon's authorization.

Finding nothing revealing in the main room or Star Spoon's bedroom, they began working the areas that the Computer refused to scan for them. Though they came across twelve such, they could not get into the rooms that they knew were behind locked doors or blank walls. At the end of three weeks they quit. There was still another place to investigate, the vast deep underground preresurrection chamber in which Burton had awakened so many years ago. But they could not get into this.

"Neither could Star Spoon," Burton said.

Now that the immediate major problem was out of the way, they had to consider their future. They could not get out of the tower, and they could bring in no lovers or companions. They were three men and one woman who would have only each other.

The years ahead of them, Burton thought, were not just bleak. The future was a psychic Siberia, an emotional Ice Age. It was true that the four of them had known one another intimately for many years and had gone through many hardships together and had worked as an excellent team—none better—for their goal. They were getting along now without suffering the abrasions that usually wore people out with one another's too-close and too-often contact, but, eventually, they would grow sick of one another.

They must have more than a community of four. They would need lovers and good friends and the occasional new person to meet.

"Man does not live by bread alone," a wise man had once said. He could also have said that no one lives, truly lives, without others to talk to, many others.

By the time that the Gardenworlders came, the four would be twisted, cranky, eccentric. Strange. Odd hermits. Stir-crazy.

There was also the problem of sexual release. Alice would not take all three as lovers, or even one. Alice firmly believed that to be a lover, you had to be in love.

One evening, the men sat on chairs on a balcony of the castle in Burton's world, where all were living for that month. The artificial sun was ten degrees above the artificial west horizon, and they were having their drinks while they waited for Alice to join them. Li Po had said that the longer time went on, the less repulsive was the idea of making beautiful female androids programmed to be bedpartners.

"You'd know that they were not truly human, that they'd be submorons," Frigate said. "You couldn't talk to them as you would to a real woman. You'd know that their passion was simulated, mechanical, and unconscious. OK, so you'd get sexual relief. But that's not enough."

"True," Li Po said, "but they'd be better than nothing."

"Would they?" Burton said.

Alice came onto the balcony then. The men dropped the subject, not because Alice would have been embarrassed by its nature but because she would have felt bad that she could do nothing to help them. They talked about what they had achieved during their studies that day, Burton with his investigations into the dialects that had formed the Urmother of the Semitic languages, Li Po in his studies of English and French, so that he could read their poetry, Frigate in his study of every motion picture that had been made (or at least preserved by the Ethicals), and Alice with her newfound passion of painting with oils.

At dinner, served by androids, they talked about the yet-to-be-solved mystery of Loga's murder and the identity of the woman whom Nur had killed.

Burton pushed his chair away from the table, pulled a cigar

from his shirtpocket, lit it, and said, "I'd devote most of my time to sleuthing those enigmas if I thought it would do any good. I'm convinced, however, that the Computer won't—can't—permit us to even get a foot in the door, as it were. We will never know until the Gardenworlders come and perhaps not then."

"You won't have to wait that long."

Alice screamed. Burton gasped, shoved his chair back, and rose to face the man who had spoken.

Loga, smiling, stood in the entrance to the dining room.

37

Loga had lost his fat-turkey look. His clothes, a sky-blue kilt, open yellow robe with blue dragons, and blue sandals, showed a stocky and powerfully muscled body without an ounce of excess weight.

He was unarmed.

Loga held his hand up. "Please. If you'll quiet down, I'll explain all. First, though, my apologies for startling you."

Burton had recovered enough from his shock to say, "You always did like the dramatic."

"True."

Li Po said, "How did you get in here?"

"I'll tell you all in due time. However, I had no trouble over-riding the codeword. After all, I control the tower."

He went to the sideboard by the door and poured himself a goblet of cognac. Alice, a hand on her breast, sat down. The men exchanged glances the meaning of which they understood from long intimacy. *If he makes the slightest move that seems danger-ous to us, we'll all jump him at the same time.*

Loga, however, was very much at ease, almost hail-fellow-well-met. That meant nothing. He was a superb actor. *On the other hand,* Burton thought, *why should he have anything bad in mind for us?*

"Am I right in assuming that your melting . . . your death . . . was a trick, a simulation by the Computer?" Burton said. "And that you've been watching us since you disappeared?"

Loga faced them, his thick legs braced as if he were on the foredeck of a sailing ship. He smiled and said, "Yes. I know that that was one of the possibilities you considered."

"So you were spying on us, eavesdropping!" Burton said angrily.

"Everywhere except in those rooms you painted. That was a clever idea, but then I've always known that you were intelligent and imaginative. That, of course, is one of the reasons why I chose you as my Agents. It's not true, though, that you completely blocked my monitoring. When you used the auxiliary computers, I tapped in on those."

He sipped on the cognac while regarding them over the rim. When he moved the goblet away, he said, "It's good to have someone to talk to. Not just anyone; you are special. I feel very close to you. Though I imagine that, at this moment, you're rather furious with me. I don't blame you, but I'm sure that after you've heard my story, you'll forgive me."

"I don't think so," Alice said, her dark eyes narrowed, her lips stretched back. "I don't know what sort of game you've been playing, but you're responsible for dooming—" She stopped as if something had just occurred to her. Her cheeks became even more red.

"I repeat, I'm sorry to have had to put you through an emotional mincer. But you survived, and you would have survived even if you hadn't, in a manner of speaking.

"What I had to do was to insure that you would be capable of operating the tower and could be trusted not to be corrupted by the great power in your hands. I believed that you could pass the test, but my thinking, my wishing, didn't make it so. I had to give you the *practice* of power. It's not what a person says but what he does that reveals his true character.

"You did fail in some things. You should have resurrected your comrades who died during the expedition to the tower. I'm sure that, if events hadn't stopped you, you would have done so soon. I was disappointed, however, because I wanted to put them through the test too."

"Most of them would have done what we did," Burton said.

"I know, but I wanted them to prove themselves in the field."

"They proved themselves along the way," Burton said. "Just as we did."

"To a point," Loga said. "But the ultimate test was how they would behave in the tower. Turpin, for instance, was not selective enough in resurrecting his friends. Nor were you, Li Po. You erred grievously in resurrecting Star Spoon."

Li Po shrugged. "How was I to know?"

"Have you learned your lesson?"

"I am even quicker at learning than I am to take offense," the Chinese said. "If I could do it over again, I would make sure that the Computer would give those we brought in no powers that could be used against me."

"Very good. But would you also make sure that you had no powers that you could use against others? They're a danger to you as well as to the others. Your powers might be seized by others despite all your precautions."

"Somebody has to be in charge," Li Po said. "Somebody has to possess the powers, somebody who can be trusted with them."

"The point is," Burton said, "are we to be trusted now?"

"What if you resurrected somebody who seemed to be trust-worthy but proved not to be? That person might take away your powers and use them for purposes that you would reject because they would be bad."

He sipped again and then began pacing back and forth as he talked.

"You're thinking that my disappearing was criminal because it resulted in the erasure of the body-recordings and, so, the loss of immortality for almost all of the resurrected. That is not so, and I'm disappointed that you could believe that I would permit such a horrible thing. What really happened is—"

"You had the Computer make a duplicate of itself or a duplicate already existed," Burton said. "The duplicate has the records. Or there is only one Computer, but it gave us false reports."

Loga stopped pacing and looked at Burton with amazement, then burst out laughing.

"When did you think of that?"

"A minute ago."

"I did have a backup Computer made before I disappeared."

"Then it was no test for us when we first entered the tower and prevented the Computer from dying? Göring's sacrifice was in vain?"

"No, that was for real. It frightened me so much that I at once had the backup made. Actually, the backup has become the primary since I let you use the first one as your toy."

"It seems to me," Frigate said, "that it would have been standard engineering procedure to install the backup from the very beginning of this project."

"We thought that the Computer could not malfunction, not to any dangerous extent, anyway. We thought that it was invulnerable."

"Yes, and the *Titanic* was declared unsinkable."

"What about the Mongolian woman whom Nur killed?" Alice said.

"Ah, her! She was part of the plot to confuse and mystify you. Someone had to be held responsible for my death, and she was placed so that you would think that she was responsible. You would then have to try to find out who and what she was, but there was no way that you could do that."

"She was an android?" Frigate said.

"Of course."

"Some of us thought that Nur killed her rather too easily," Frigate said.

Burton blew out smoke, hoping that he looked more cool than he felt. He said, "I thank you for the explanation. I won't thank you for the stress, the anxiety, and the bloodshed. But, as you say, we had to learn the hard way, and no doubt your intentions were good. However, as you yourself said, it's not what one thinks, what one's intentions are, but one's actions that reveal the true character. Be that as it may, I have a question, perhaps the most important of all!"

He paused, then said, "Do we stay in the tower? Or must we go back to The Valley?"

Loga grinned and said, "What would you like to do?"

"I can't speak for the others, but I would prefer to stay here."

The others said they would also like to remain.

"Why?" Loga said.

"For two reasons," Burton said. "One, life is much more enjoyable for me here—despite the events you caused. It affords me an opportunity to study, to gain knowledge, which I would have given my soul on Earth to have, if I'd thought I had a soul and if someone had made me an offer. It's also much more luxurious, about as close to Heaven, a physical Heaven, as one could imagine. Two, I think that I am worthy of being here. I have come as close to Going On as I ever will. Sending me back to The Valley would only impoverish and frustrate me and would not raise my ethical level one bit. In fact, it might lower it."

Loga asked the others if they had similar or different reasons. Their answers were much like Burton's.

"First, before I tell you what you so evidently are desperate to know, I'll tell you something else. Burton, when you said that you were as close to Going On as you would ever be, you unconsciously spoke the truth. Your saying that makes me curious. Is there more behind that remark than appears on the surface? Have you some inklings, some suspicions, that . . . ?"

He smiled and took another sip of the cognac. Burton felt that Loga expected him to expand on his statement. If he did, he was going to be disappointed. Burton had no idea what Loga was hinting at.

"You'll have to continue," Burton said. "You were saying . . . ?"

"Very well. You've been told by me and by the Church of Second Chance that, when you've attained a certain high level of character and morality, become compassionate and empathetic and free of psychosis and neurosis to a certain degree, then you'll be ready to Go On. When you die, you won't be resurrected on the Riverworld again. Your *wathan* will disappear; it can no longer be caught or detected by our instruments. You have been told that your *wathan,* or soul, if you prefer that term, goes to God or is absorbed in the Godhead. That, of course, is an explanation that covers ignorance. It was the only explanation that seemed to fit. But . . ."

He sipped again. His gaze moved over them as if he were anticipating their reaction to his next words. He looked delighted.

"The sad truth is—though I don't really know if it's so sad— the sad truth is that no *wathan*s ever disappear, ever Go On! Not as long as the bodies they've partnered continue to be resurrected!"

Burton was not as surprised as he should have been. Once,

long ago, he had considered that possibility but had rejected it. Alice was shocked; she looked as if she could never again believe anybody. Li Po smiled and stroked his moustache. Frigate's face was impassive.

Burton thought about the Computer report that such people as Buddha and Jesus Christ had Gone On. Obviously, they had not. The Computer had given false data. Why? Because Loga had ordered it to do so to further the deception.

Burton sighed, and he said, "What is the truth? You will tell the truth this time, won't you? You'll pardon me if I'm skeptical. You've lied so many times."

Alice's voice trembled as she said, "The *wathans*? You told us that they were artificial. If it had not been for that ancient race that made them, we'd all be soulless. Is that true, God's own truth?"

"Who knows what God's truth is?" Loga said. "God's truth is that What Is Is. But yes, it is a fact that those ancients did make *wathans,* and we who have inherited their work have made sure that every human being conceived on Earth had a *wathan.* What is not true is that the *wathans* go to God or are absorbed into the Godhead. Perhaps they will be someday. I don't know; no one does.

"The truth is that you can be immortal, relatively so, anyway. You won't last beyond the death of the universe and probably not nearly as long as the universe does. But you have the potentiality for living a million years, two, perhaps three or more. As long as you can find a Terrestrial-type planet with a hot core and have resurrection machinery available.

"Unfortunately, not all can be permitted to possess immortality. Too many would make immortality miserable or hellish for the rest, and they would try to control others through their control of the resurrection machinery. Even so, everybody, without exception, is given a hundred years after his Earthly death to prove that he or she can live peacefully and in harmony with himself and others, within the tolerable limits of human imperfections. Those who can do this will be immortal after the two projects are completed."

"Then," Burton said slowly, "the standards, the ethical goals, are not so extremely high, so demanding, as we have been led to believe?"

"They are high, though not impossibly high for forty percent of the resurrectees."

"The other sixty percent?" Alice said.

"Their body-records will be destroyed."

"That seems hard."

"It is. But it's absolutely necessary."

"And then?" Frigate said. He looked anxious.

"The survivors will be carried, as body-records in the form of the yellow sphere, to Earth."

"Earth?" Burton said. He had never been told so, but he had had the feeling that Earth had been destroyed.

"Yes. Most of life on Earth was killed by radiation in the hydrogen and neutron bomb war. But the Gardenworlders have cleaned it up—it took them one hundred and sixty years—and have been restocking it with plant and animal life. Earth will be ready for you, but you won't be the kind of people who will abuse it and slowly kill it by pollution. And—"

"Then we won't be permitted to have children?" Alice said.

"Not on Earth. It won't have room, though there will be plenty of living room, I think you call it elbow space, for you. However, there are millions of planets without sentient life in this universe, and you can go there if you want children."

"Earth!" Burton said dreamily. His homesickness was so keen that his chest ached. Earth. It would not be the Earth he had left, but surely its topography had not changed. And that it would not be the Earth that had existed when he had died was, he had to admit, for the good.

"This is quite a shock," Alice said. "I was a devout member·of the Anglican Church and then, when I came here, I lost my faith and became an agnostic until recently, when I was seriously considering joining the Church of the Second Chance. Now . . ."

"Loga," Burton said, "since you are finally telling the truth, tell me this. Why did you turn renegade and pervert the course of events that your fellow Ethicals had decided upon? Is your story that you could not bear that your family, your loved ones, might not Go On, the truth? Go On in the sense you've just explained, not the old sense? Did you cause all this blood struggle, this overthrow of your comrades, just to give your parents and siblings and cousins more time?"

"I swear to you by all that was, is, or might be holy that that is the truth."

"Well, then," Burton said, "I don't understand how you, who were raised on the Gardenworld from the age of four, could have passed the test. If the Ethical standards have any meaning, any value, how did you escape being eliminated? How could you have become a criminal? A criminal with a conscience, but still a criminal. Or were you truly ethical, and then, somehow, you became crazy? And if you can become crazy, what's to prevent others who've also passed from going insane?"

38

L oga paled, turned, set the goblet on a table, and turned again. He was smiling, and his eyes moved from left to right and back again as if he were looking for something beyond the group.

"I'm not crazy!"

"Consider all that you've done for the sake of a score or so of people," Burton said.

"I am not crazy! What I did, I did for love."

"Love has its insanities," Burton said. He leaned back in his chair, blew cigar smoke out, smiled, and said, "It doesn't, for the moment, matter if you are insane or not. You still haven't answered us. Must we go back to The Valley or may we stay here?"

"I had thought you could stay," Loga said. "I had judged that you had attained the level where you could be trusted and where we could all enjoy each other's company in love. You could bring in others. I intend to bring in my family and show them what they must do if they would be immortal. Some of them . . ."

"You're doubtful about some of them, then?" Burton said.

Frigate leaned over the table and, staring hard at Loga, said, "We were told that passing the test, Going On, was an automatic event. It involved no judging by human beings. Now . . . who judges?"

Burton was annoyed by the question, though he had wondered about it. The important question was the one he had just put. The others could be answered later.

"That will be done by the Computer. After that, the people in this project, the Valleydwellers, will eat food that will cause them to fall asleep and die. Their *wathans* will then be scanned by the Computer. As you know, the *wathan* displays through its colors and their relative breadths the ethical development of the individual. Those that meet the standards will be reunited on Earth with their bodies. Those that do not will be released and go to wherever they go."

"Judging by a machine?" Frigate said.

"It is infallible."

"Unless it's tampered with," Burton said.

"That is not very likely."

"Not until you made it likely," Burton said.

Loga glared at him. "I won't be here."

"Where will you be?"

"I will have gone on one of the ships in the hangar to an uninhabited planet."

"You could have done that at any time after you got rid of your fellow Ethicals and their Agents," Frigate said. "Why didn't you just pick up your family and take them with you?"

Loga looked at Frigate as if he just could not believe that anybody would say that.

"No, I couldn't do that."

"Why not?" Burton said. "It seems the logical action to take."

"They wouldn't be ready. They wouldn't have passed the test; the Computer would reject them. They'd be doomed."

"You don't make sense," Frigate said. "What do you care about that? You'd be safe on some planet where they wouldn't find you for a thousand years, maybe never, and you'd have your family."

Loga frowned, and sweat oozed on his forehead.

"You don't understand. They shouldn't be living then. They would not have Gone On. I couldn't take them until they had attained the level that makes immortality bearable for them."

The others looked at each other. Unspoken: he is crazy.

Burton sighed and leaned forward, reached under the table, and withdrew from its shelf a beamer that had been there since the day the castle was built. His finger moved the dial on its side to stun-power. He brought the weapon out swiftly and pressed the sliding tongue that acted as the trigger. The very pale red line struck Loga in the chest, and the Ethical fell backward.

"I had to do it," Burton said. "He is hopelessly psychotic and he would have sent us back to The Valley. God knows what he would have done then."

At Burton's orders, Frigate ran to get from a converter a hypodermic syringe containing the needed amount of *somnium*. Burton stood guard, waiting to stun Loga again if he showed signs of consciousness. The man was immensely powerful; a bolt that would knock most men out might make him only semiconscious.

Burton paced for a few minutes while he thought of how he could solve the problem of Loga. He had to be kept alive. The moment he was dead, he would undoubtedly be resurrected in a hidden chamber. That would mean *finit* for the four tenants because Loga had prime control of the Computer. If he were put in a cryogenics cylinder, he would be dead as far as the *wathan* was concerned, and he would be resurrected in a secret room in the tower. Should he be awake but imprisoned, he could kill himself no matter what security arrangements his captors took. Even if the tiny black ball in his brain, the ball that could release a deadly poison with one mentally projected codeword, were surgically removed, Loga could swallow his tongue and choke to death. The tongue could be cut out, but Burton was not tough enough to do that no matter how desperate he was.

It was possible to keep Loga drugged. Burton, however, doubted that the Ethical could survive thirty-three years in that state. It was useless to ask the Computer to display Loga's memory so that Burton could locate Loga's hidden-body recordings. The Computer would have orders from Loga not to reveal these.

Burton stopped, and he smiled. There was a way out.

Working out the plan took two days, since he had to be very careful. One mistake, and Loga might win out after all.

He ordered the Computer to make a modified android that looked exactly like Loga and had a voice exactly like his. Inside the skin, the android matched Loga except for the brain structure, which was much simpler than Loga's. If the android had been a one hundred percent duplicate, it would, in many respects, have been the Ethical and would have behaved as he would. The only difference, and it was a great difference, was that the android would have lacked self-consciousness.

Burton verbally programmed it in the speech of the Ethicals and then had it transmit his orders to the Computer. The Computer matched the voiceprints, electric skin field, face and body shape, skin, hair, and eye color, ear shape, and the chemical composition of the odors of perspiration with Loga's prints. It also scanned the finger, palm, and foot prints.

Unfortunately, despite everything else, the Computer refused to obey the android unless the proper codeword was given.

"That's very frustrating," Burton told the others. "One word or perhaps a phrase is all that's blocking it. It might as well be a million words."

No one said anything; all looked gloomy. Even Li Po was silent for once.

After two minutes, Alice, who had been frowning and biting her lip, said, "I know that none of you believe in feminine intuition. I don't either, not as it's usually defined. I think it's a form of logic that doesn't follow the rules of logic, Aristotelian or symbolic. I don't think that feminine intuition, call it that or something else, is confined to women. Oh, what am I talking about?"

"Yes, what are you talking about?" Burton said.

"It's such a silly idea, so wild. I'd be making an utter ass of myself!"

"Anything will be appreciated," Burton said. "I promise not to laugh."

"None of us will," Frigate said. "Anyway, what's the difference if we do?"

"It's just that there's no rhyme or reason to it," she said. "Well, perhaps there is some reason to it. Loga is such a trickster, and he does like to play games, rather childish, I think, but there it is."

"There is what?" Burton said.

"It's such an improbability. The odds against it are fantastically high. But . . . I don't know. It couldn't hurt to try. It wouldn't take much time."

"For God's sake, what?" Burton said.

"Well, do you remember what Loga cried out just before he cracked? Seemed to crack, I mean."

" '*I tsab u*,'" Burton said. "Ethical for 'Who are you?'"

"Yes. Could Loga have been giving us a clue, the real codephrase? He would have been very amused doing that because there was no chance that we would ever use it. We just simply could not ever find out that it was the open-sesame, the most important identification. Yet he couldn't resist saying it. We'd think that he was addressing the person who had killed him, a person we now know didn't exist. And at the same time . . ."

"He'd have to be crazy to play with us like that," Burton said. "Well?"

"It's nuts, but it'd only take a minute," Frigate said. "What do we have to lose? Besides, Alice may be rather quiet, but she does have a keen insight into individual psychology."

"Thank you," Alice said. "I wasn't very good at reading people's characters when I came to the Riverworld, but I had to develop that talent to survive."

They went into the room where the android was sleeping. Burton awoke it gently and gave it a cup of coffee. Then he slowly and carefully told the android what it must do. Once more, it stood in front of the screen on the wall, and it said, *"I tsab u."*

The screen flashed the characters of the Ethical alphabet.

"That means 'ready,' " Burton said.

The android then told the Computer that it was transferring prime control to Burton. But the Computer refused to do that.

"Now what?" Frigate muttered.

Burton called the android to him and told him to go into the corridor with him. Though he did not know if that precaution was necessary, he could not afford to take chances. Having instructed the android what to say, he watched from the doorway as it relayed his commands. And the Computer obeyed.

They cheered and hugged each other, and Li Po did a little dance.

The android had ordered that all persons in the records, except for certain ones, whose names and record numbers it gave, be resurrected in The Valley. Henceforth, the process of resurrection would continue until the project was closed down.

The android also said that it wanted its, that is, Loga's, security measures canceled. Immediately, the Computer replied that it had done so. And it displayed diagrams showing where Loga had hidden his body-records.

"Very good," Burton said, smiling. "If we have to deal with the Computer through the android, so be it. I can endure that."

It took them an hour to collect the thirty-nine records cached in rooms at different levels.

"I'd be completely confident now that Loga can't be resurrected without our knowledge," Burton said, 'if he wasn't so canny. What if he hid some records without telling the Computer where they were?"

"In that case," Frigate said, "he couldn't be resurrected because the Computer would not be connected to it and so could not carry out the operation."

"He might have put the record in a converter unconnected to the Computer except for the power source. An auxiliary computer could have performed the process."

"Then we'll tell the Computer to notify us of any power demands that are unusual. Loga's orders to the Computer to suppress the indications resulting from his use of the power have been nulled."

"We'll have to risk it. We can't just not act because of the very slight chance that Loga might get loose."

The others agreed with Burton that they could start repopulating the tower. They would do this, though, after the three private worlds had been cleaned up. They unanimously supported his suggestion that the Valleydwellers be told the truth, in fact, the whole story from the beginning.

"The Ethicals thought it necessary to spread half-truths through the Church of the Second Chance because of their belief in the strength of the religious impulse. But I believe that the whole truth, palatable or not, should be given. We'll resurrect some people in the tower, let them live here for a while, then transport them to The Valley in the aircraft. We'll give them photographs and powerpack-operated film projectors. That should convince the skeptics. The truth will spread very slowly because of the enormous population and the length of The Valley, but it will get to all eventually. Of course, some will refuse to believe. That'll be their misfortune."

Loga was placed in the cryogenics chamber.

Li Po resurrected his companions; Alice, Monteith Maglenna, and several others, including her sisters, Edith and Rhoda; Frigate, Sophie Lefkowitz and twenty others; Burton, Loghu the blonde ancient-Tokharian, Cyrano de Bergerac, Joe Miller the titanthrop, Kazz the Neanderthal, Tom Turpin, Jean Marcelin, Baron de Marbot, and many others whom Loga had recruited in his war against the Ethicals.

Six months passed, and Burton invited all the tenants, now numbering over two hundred, to his castle for a dinner party. After the tables had been cleared, he ordered an android to strike a huge bronze gong that hung behind his chair. He rose, raised a glass of wine, and said, "Citizens of the tower, your attention. I propose a toast. To us."

They drank, and he said, "Another toast. To all those who hold dual citizenship, that of Earth and that of Riverworld."

He put the glass down.

"We all seem to be well situated and happy, and I pray that we will be so until the Gardenworlders arrive. And perhaps after that. When that time comes, though, we will, whether or not we like it, return to the restored Earth or go into oblivion. I hope, and I believe, that we here will be qualified to go to Earth where we should enjoy life until the Earth's core cools and we must move on to a young planet. That should be quite a few million years in the future, however, and who knows what will happen in that inconceivably long time?"

He stopped, sipped wine, put the goblet down, and stared around at them.

"As I understand it, Earth's core will be tapped for the use of e-m converters. But this power will be used only to raise those who die there, and with the type of people on Earth then, there should not be much need for resurrection power. There will be no grails or converters to furnish food. Food will be grown on the soil. Earth, if events work out as the Ethicals plan, will be a nice quiet place. Peace and harmony will reign, though I have doubts that the lion will lie down with the lamb. Not if it's hungry. Lions do not and never will find grass nourishing.

"And, of course, even those who have Gone On will not be perfect. No human being, with perhaps a few exceptions, and these might be unendurable models for the rest of us, is perfect or will be."

Many of his audience were looking at him as if they wondered what he was preparing to spring on them.

"Some of you, I'm sure, anticipate life on Earth with great pleasure. You know you'll always have intellectual adventures because the opportunities for study and for artistic creation will be equal to what the tower provides. And you're happy with the idea that life will be serene, well-ordered, and secure. You luxuriate in that prospect."

He stopped, and he frowned.

"However, there is an alternative to the Earth I've described. I have investigated the spaceships in the hangar, and I have discovered that they do not require highly trained crews to navigate and operate them. They are complex in themselves, but an intelligent child of twelve, after some study, may get into one and have the ship carry him to whatever destination he wishes. Provided, of course, that the ship has enough fuel."

Frigate smiled up at him and held up a thumb and a finger to form an O.

"What if we reject the return to the near-Utopian Earth?" Burton said. "What if we prefer another kind of life or are not sure that, even if we would love Earth as I've depicted here, we will be chosen to be among her citizens?

"Nothing can stop us from boarding a spaceship, all those in the hangar if we wish, choosing one of the virgin planets catalogued in the ship's navigation system, and then going there.

"What would we do there, our motley group of near-immortals of many races, nations, languages, and times? We wouldn't have the rich, easy life we have here, or the more restricted but still easy life on the Earth-to-be. Though we can carry with us the science and technology of the Ethicals in records, we could use very little of it for centuries. It would take a long time before our population increased to the point where we would have enough hands to do all the dirty and hard labor needed to get the raw materials for processing.

"These planets have been seeded with *wathan* generators and catchers just as was done on ancient Earth. We can have children because they will be born with *wathans* and will be self-conscious and free-willed. But—" he looked around him again "—if any of us or our children die, we will be dead for a long time. Perhaps forever. Should the Ethicals be able to track us down, we who went on the ship from the tower will be judged then and there, at once. We may have passed and so be allowed to live. Or we may not. In any event, if we should die early, we will have to stay dead for a long time, because the Ethicals may not get to our planet for many thousands of years. And if, during that time, our descendants do build resurrection machinery, how do we know they'll decide to raise us? We can't foresee the political or religious or economic situation of that time. Our descendants may think it best we not be raised.

"That is by no means the worst thing that can happen. In the beginning, after we've landed and built homes with our own hands and tilled and planted and reaped and brought forth the first generation, we'll be a fairly harmonious society. But as the centuries, the millennia, go by, our common language, Esperanto, will become dialects, then language families as unintelligible to one another as French and Albanian. Though there will be much miscegenation, some groups will keep their racial characteristics, and our brave new world will have differing races.

"Different languages and different races. Just as on old Earth. But it will have variety.

"And, try though we will to bring up our children with love, in time, as generation succeeds generation, or perhaps in a very short time, we will have the same kind of people that we had on old Earth.

"Ladies and gentlemen, after we have labored long and mightily, survived many hardships and dangers, and perhaps established a just and equitable society for all, we will nevertheless see the inevitable degeneration of our society. As on Earth, there will be multitudes of the strong and the weak, the rich and the poor, the pushers and the pushed, the brave and the cowardly, the dull and the bright, the open and the shut, the givers and the takers, the compassionate and the indifferent or cruel, the sensitive and the callous, the tender and the brutal, the victimizers and the victims, the sane, the half-sane, and the mad.

"There will be hate but love, despair but joy, defeat but triumph, misery but happiness, hopelessness but hope."

He looked briefly at them, seeing all their faces as one. They knew the spirit if not the exact form of what he was going to say.

"But . . . we will have immense variety, the richness and the full spectrum that a secure life cannot give.

"And we will have adventure.

"We will be rejecting the promised Heaven of Earth. But we will be taking some of Heaven with us, and, I'm sure, more than a bit of Hell. Can Heaven exist in a vacuum? Without Hell, how do you know that you are in Heaven?

"I ask you, my friends, and even those who are perhaps not very fond of me, which shall it be? The new Earth? Or the unknown?"

His audience was silent. Then Frigate called out, "Is all this rhetorical? Where are *you* going, Dick?"

"You know where," Burton said.

He waved his hand to indicate the stars.

"Who's going with me?"

AFTERWORD

While of course an author would like to believe that his every word remains engraved forever on the hearts of his readers, it may be that some of the events of the previous four Riverworld novels have grown dim in some memories. Here is a brief look at the adventures that have led up to Gods of Riverworld:

Richard Francis Burton, the famous (or infamous) English explorer, linguist, author, poet, swordsman, and anthropologist, dies in A.D. 1890 at the age of sixty-nine. Contrary to his expectations, he awakes from death. He is in a vast chamber containing billions of bodies floating in the air. All those he sees are human except for one near him. This body is humanoid but definitely not that of a member of *Homo sapiens*. Before Burton can escape from the chamber, he is rendered unconscious by two men who appear in some kind of aerial craft.

When Burton again awakes, he is lying naked on the bank of a wide river in a narrow valley surrounded by high, unscalable mountains. His body is like the one he had when he was twenty-five, minus its scars. He is only one of an estimated thirty-five billion who have been resurrected under an unfamiliar sky on the banks of a River ten million miles long.

The resurrection is not, as events will show, caused by supernatural means. It has been effected by scientific devices invented by beings unknown during the early part of the first book, *To Your Scattered Bodies Go*. The people responsible for this, the

Ethicals, planted recording machines on Earth long before the first humans evolved from the apes. (Or so Burton and others are told during the course of the series.) These machines have recorded every human being from the time of his or her conception continuously to the moment of death. And, as is discovered in the fourth volume, *The Magic Labyrinth*, the souls (called *wathan*s by Ethicals) are artificial. There is no such thing as a natural soul; these have been provided by the Ethicals.

In the early days on the Riverworld, its inhabitants believe that everybody from approximately 2,000,000 B.C. to A.D. 2008 has been resurrected. It soon becomes apparent that children who had died on Earth at or under the age of five, the mentally retarded, and the extreme psychopaths have not been raised on the Riverworld. These, Burton finds out from a renegade Ethical, have been resurrected on a planet called the Gardenworld. And it is revealed in a later volume that only those from approximately 99,000 B.C. to A.D. 1983 have been placed on the Riverworld. After this current Ethical project is over, those who died after A.D. 1983 will be raised.

The Ethicals are the heirs of several preceding cultures, some nonhuman, which had assumed the task of recording and resurrecting the sentient species of many worlds throughout the universe. If they did not do so, all sentients who died would be forever dead.

Some Ethicals, disguised as Terrestrials, have spread throughout the Riverworld the religious concept of Going On. A Valley-dweller cannot Go On unless he or she attains a certain high ethical standard—in other words, a certain state of being "good." At the end of a hundred years this project will be phased out, and those who have not arrived at a certain ethical development will die forever. The *wathan*s of those who have reached this stage will be absorbed by the Godhead.

This concept is planted by the Ethicals and transmitted through various religions—for instance, the Church of the Second Chance. The missionaries of the Church also teach their disciples to speak Esperanto. A language that everybody can understand is necessary because of the mixture of peoples from many times and places.

Burton and some others are early on visited by an Ethical who won't reveal his identity. Burton and others call him X or The Mysterious Stranger. X (revealed as Loga, a member of the Ethical Council of Twelve, in *The Magic Labyrinth*) is thwarting the plans of his fellows. He gives various reasons for this, but the true reason for his becoming a renegade is told in the fourth volume, *The Magic Labyrinth*. X is recruiting some of the resurrectees to help him in his plot. Among these are Burton, Sam Clemens, Cyrano de Bergerac, a gigantic titanthrop called Joe Miller, and other exceptional men and women.

The River, they find out, starts from a small sea at the north pole of this planet, winds back and forth down one hemisphere, circles the south pole, and winds back and forth on the other hemisphere, finally plunging back to its source, the north pole sea. A vast tower built by the Ethicals rears up from the bedrock at the bottom of this sea. It is the headquarters of the Ethicals and contains the circuitry and the huge protein brain of the Computer. It also houses in a central well those *wathan*s held while the dead are stored in the physical recordings. When a person is resurrected, the *wathan* immediately reattaches itself to the raised body. This entity, the *wathan*, contains all the memories that the body also has, duplicates them, as it were, and also provides self-consciousness for the mind of the body. Without the *wathan*, the physical part of the individual would lack self-consciousness and the means to keep its identity.

The first volume, *To Your Scattered Bodies Go*, is mainly concerned with showing the setup of the Riverworld and Burton's efforts to escape the Ethicals. These have found out that he was awakened in the resurrection chamber by their unidentified renegade colleague. Burton commits suicide 777 times while fleeing the Ethicals, but is finally caught. He is questioned in the tower by the Council of Twelve, one of whom is the renegade. His memory is taped so that the Council may see the renegade through his eyes. But the renegade has secretly rearranged various circuits in the Computer, and he has also arranged it so that the Council believes that Burton's memory of his questioning has been erased. He returns to The Valley with a complete memory.

In the second volume, *The Fabulous Riverboat*, Samuel Clemens, the American writer, dreams of building a great paddle-wheeled riverboat on which to travel up The River to its source. From there he will go on foot to the seagirt tower. He can't start fulfilling this dream for a long time because the planet is poor in iron and other heavy metals. X arranges to divert a large iron-nickel meteorite into The Valley, and Clemens uses this for the needed metal. His boat is stolen by his partner, King John of England, brother to Richard the Lion-Hearted. Sam vows to build another boat, catch up with John, and get vengeance.

In the third volume, *The Dark Design,* Clemens finishes his second boat after many hardships and attempts by others to steal this one, too. After he leaves, another group at the base builds a dirigible and flies it to the tower. Only one of the crew can get inside the tower, and he does not come back out. On the way back, one of the crew is discovered to be X, but he escapes, and the airship is blown up by a bomb he planted.

In the fourth volume, *The Magic Labyrinth,* the two heavily armed riverboats meet. Both are sunk in the battle, and their captains die along with most of their crews. Burton and some of X's recruits survive. They go up The River as far as they can in a small boat, then climb the massive and rugged mountain range ringing the north polar sea. Burton is convinced that one of the party is X. After the party gets into the tower through an entrance secretly installed by X, Burton does find out who X is.

However, in the long absence of all its Ethical and Agent tenants (slain by X), the unattended tower mechanisms need some maintenance. Not getting it, a valve that admits seawater is stuck, and the protein brain of the Computer is threatened. If it dies before the valve can be repaired, the entire project will be doomed, and all the body-recordings will perish.

Hermann Göring, ex-Nazi and late *Reichsmarschall* of the Third Reich, is one of the party. He has repented his evil deeds on Earth and has converted to the Church of the Second Chance. He sacrifices his life trying to get to the malfunctioning valve to repair it. He fails, and it seems that the Computer will perish and with it all hope of immortality for the thirty-five billion people.

However, Alice Liddell Hargreaves, one of the party, ingeniously figures out a way to circumvent the Computer's suicidal obedience to certain inhibitions, and the project is saved.

Now the Valleydwellers will be given the extra time that Loga, the renegade Ethical, claims they need in order for all to attain the level where they may Go On. The project will be resumed as originally planned with this exception. Loga's fellow Ethicals and their Agents will not be resurrected because they would interfere with his plans.

The book at hand, *Gods of the Riverworld,* starts a few weeks after the ending of the fourth, *The Magic Labyrinth.*